CIARA GERAGHTY

Finding Mr Flood

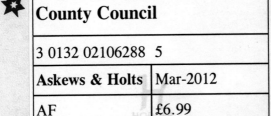

First published in Great Britain in 2011 by Hodder & Stoughton
An Hachette UK company

This paperback edition published 2011

1

A CIP catalogue record for this title is available from the British Library

B format paperback ISBN 978 0 340 99809 0
A format paperback ISBN 978 0 340 99590 7

Typeset in Plantin Light by Hewer Text UK Ltd, Edinburgh
Printed and bound by CPI Group (UK) Ltd, Croydon, CR0 4YY

Hodder & Stoughton policy is to use papers that are natural, renewable
and recyclable products and made from wood grown in sustainable forests.
The logging and manufacturing processes are expected to conform
to the environmental regulations of the country of origin.

Hodder & Stoughton Ltd
338 Euston Road
London NW1 3BH

www.hodder.co.uk

For my grandmother, Emer Trainor

Who never let the facts get in the way of a good story

PROLOGUE

Dara Flood always said that the most interesting thing about her happened before she was born.

It was a Tuesday. Mr Flood drove down the road in his beaten-up old Ford at six o'clock, the way he always did. He parked the van, rolled down the window and leaned out, a cigarette dangling precariously from the corner of his mouth. He winked at her mother, who stood at the front door waiting for him, the way she always did.

'It's well you're looking, Mrs Flood,' he said. His usual greeting.

She smiled, the palms of her hands pressed against the enormous swell of her belly.

'The cot was delivered today,' she told him. 'It's in a box in the hall.'

He got out of the van and rubbed the dust of the day off his trousers. 'Grand,' he said. 'I'm just going up the road to get a pack of fags.'

She nodded and began her slow walk back inside. She remembers turning, just before she reached the front door. She doesn't know why she did that. And there he was. Halfway up the road. Just standing there. Looking back at her. He raised his arm in a sort of a wave and his mouth moved, although she couldn't make out what he was saying. She waved back, even though this was not part of their usual routine. He turned then and she stood for a while, pretending to worry at a bit of dirt on the front room window but really, watching him. The broad line of his shoulders and the pitch black of his hair, tossing with that cocky gait he had. She watched him until he disappeared around the curve of the road.

She stepped into the house and squeezed herself past the bulky box, into the tiny kitchen where two chops spat under the grill.

She turned them, poked at the potatoes with a fork and opened a tin of peas. She checked on Angel, still asleep in her pram, and smiled when she felt Dara kick, low down in her belly.

Then Mrs Flood sat down and waited for Mr Flood to come home.

But he never did.

And she never saw him again.

PART ONE

I

The phone rang at two o'clock in the morning.

Dara Flood was sleepwalking at the time. She never went far, mostly down the stairs, then a slow lap of the ground floor that didn't take long and back upstairs, careful to avoid the second step from the top that creaked on contact. She knew she did this because Angel – her sister – sometimes followed her, just to make sure she didn't trip over the loose piece of carpet in the hallway or wake up in the middle of a dream about dying and then keel over with the shock of it. Mrs Flood had heard of that happening to somebody. Or maybe she read about it in one of those magazines she liked with those kinds of stories. The '*I gave birth to TWINS on my 67th birthday!*' kind of thing. According to Angel, Dara always checked the front door and the back door, pulling at their handles, making sure they were locked. She also checked the windows in the front room and the back room. If the top window was open even a crack – as it sometimes was on rare hot nights – Dara closed it and moved along to the next window. She never woke up. 'Thank God,' said Mrs Flood, blessing herself.

Dara was lifting her foot over the second step from the top when the phone rang. She froze, her foot suspended over the offending step, and woke with such a start that, had she not been gripping the banister – or had she been dreaming about death instead of Kimberley, the latest addition at the dog pound where she worked – she would surely have met a troublesome end at the bottom of the stairs. Instead, she brought her foot down with force on that notorious step, and the noise of it, coupled with the shrill insistence of the phone, was enough to chase away the torpor of sleep and jolt her into an adequate state of alertness. She turned and ran down the stairs.

Mrs Flood heard the telephone from her bedroom. She woke with the start of a person who hadn't realised they were asleep. The remote was still in her hand, the telly tuned to the Shopping Channel. Now they were selling a round-cut, blue topaz solitaire pendant for €15. Worth €80, according to the presenter, tapping the stone with her French manicure. Sterling silver, she said, her voice a breathy whisper, as if she didn't want anyone else to know. With her wide smile and her small teeth, she reminded Mrs Flood of a crocodile. She swung her legs off the bed. They still ached. Saturday was the busiest day for her mobile hairdressing company, Bobs Away. She ignored the pain and ran for the door of her room.

But it was Angel who got to the phone first. She was in the kitchen when Dara passed by with her arms outstretched, like a proper sleepwalker that you'd see in a cartoon. Angel had smiled at her sister, careful not to make any noise and wake her. Of course she didn't believe Mrs Flood's theory about waking a sleepwalker, with the supporting anecdotal evidence. But there was no point tempting fate, was there? Angel was the type of person who went to bed late and got up early. If life was a dishcloth – and let's face it, sometimes it was: a threadbare, smelly one – Angel was determined to wring it out. Make the best of it. Every day. Until it was bone dry. Tonight, she'd been to the theatre and then a late supper with Joe, her firefighting and generally all-round-fabulous boyfriend. She was setting the alarm on her mobile phone to go off at 7 a.m. the following morning – climbing Lugnaquilla in Wicklow – when she heard the phone ring in the hall. She didn't allow herself to hope or even to think. She just dropped her mobile and ran.

'Hello?' It came out like a question and she held her breath, waiting for the answer. Dara and her mother ran down the short length of the hall and skidded to a halt behind her.

Nobody spoke. Angel stood there, clutching the receiver, nodding her head. Up and down, up and down. Dara tried to catch her eye but the hallway was dark, the only light offered by a narrow sliver of moon glancing through the mottled glass pane of the front door. Besides, Angel's eyes were squeezed shut. Dara looked at her mother, who did not look back. She concentrated instead on Angel. Dara could tell by the way her lips were moving that she was saying a prayer.

When Angel finally spoke, it was in a high, breathless voice, as if she'd run a long way. 'Yes, I will. Thank you. I'll be in as soon as I can. Thank you. Thank you so much,' she said. She replaced the receiver before turning around to face her sister and her mother. They knew what she was going to say before she said it but they waited anyway. Beside her, Dara could hear her mother holding her breath. Just for a moment, Dara thought about taking her mother's hand and squeezing it. Tight enough to leave red lines across her fingers when she finally let it go. But she didn't do that. Instead, she concentrated on Angel and waited.

Angel stood and looked at them. The pearly light of the moon pooled and shimmered against the sallow skin of her face, giving her a ghostly appearance. Dara shivered.

'They've got one,' Angel finally said, throwing the words up, releasing them like confetti on the wind.

'Oh Jesus,' said Mrs Flood and she sank on to the bottom step of the stairs and buried her head in her hands. 'Oh thank you, Jesus, thank you, thank you.' She rocked her heavy body back and forth as she said the words and for a moment she seemed unaware of her daughters, standing in the hall in front of her. It was Angel who knelt beside her, then held her hands, pulling them gently from her mother's face.

'It's all right, Mam,' she whispered, and Mrs Flood glanced up and spread her arms wide and pulled Angel against the soft swell of her chest and rocked her, just as she had done when Angel was a baby. Dara stood beside them and tried to think of something to say. A feeling widened inside her, pushing itself against the narrow cavity of her chest until she felt she might burst with it.

Happiness.

That's what it was.

Dara was shocked at how physical it was, this feeling. The force of it. Strong. Almost painful. When she spoke, she expected her voice to strain against the size of it. But it sounded as it always did. Hoarse. Gravelly. Worried.

'We should go,' she said.

When Mrs Flood looked at Dara, her expression was one of puzzlement, as if she was trying to place her youngest daughter. As if, in fact, she had forgotten Dara was there at all. She released Angel and stood up. She looked down at herself. 'I'm already dressed,' she said, surprised and pleased.

'I'm going to grab my hospital bag', said Angel, taking the stairs two at a time.

Dara was the only one who wasn't dressed. She wore pyjamas. Men's ones. Only because they were warmer than their female counterparts. Also, she preferred the colours. She dragged her duffel out of the cloakroom under the stairs, clamped a hat on her head and tucked the bottoms of her pyjamas into her Doc Martens. 'I'm ready,' she said.

That Mrs Flood did not comment on Dara's appearance was a measure of the moment. When you spend five years waiting for something to happen, and then it does, acerbic comments about the unsuitability or otherwise of attire are brushed away. There is no space for them, in among the happiness.

Mrs Flood ran into the kitchen to get her glasses, as Angel leaped down the stairs. She skidded to a halt beside Dara, her hands covering her mouth.

'We got the call,' she whispered, the words muffled against her fingers. 'I knew we'd get the call.'

Dara smiled and nodded, even though she had known no such thing. She looked at Angel. Her big sister. Although there was barely twelve months between them. Twelve months and a world of difference. Angel's real name was Angela, but everyone called her Angel. Even now, at twenty-eight, there was something ethereal about Angel, with her fine blond hair and her impossibly blue eyes, wide with the attributes that Angel treasured. Things like faith. And hope. Dara found these things difficult to come by.

'Come on, we'd better go,' she said, removing from the corner of Angel's mouth a strand of the fine blond hair that she tended to chew when she was nervous or excited.

'Could you ring Joe?' Angel's voice was a whisper. 'I promised I'd ring him when I got the call. He wants to be there. At the hospital, I mean. But I . . .' She trailed off, and Dara could nearly feel the anticipation in the air between them, bristling like electricity.

'I'll ring him,' she said, running upstairs to grab her mobile.

End-stage renal failure. It sounded so final when you said it like that. But that was what Angel had. That was what the professionals called it. Dara had read everything there was to read on the subject, and that was the expression used in all the literature, usually in capitals and bold lettering, often with a picture of an exhausted-looking kidney slumped against the words.

Her fingers shook as she punched Joe's number into the phone. She couldn't find his name in her contacts, even though it was there. She knew it though, as it was a jumbled combination of Angel's date of birth and her lucky number – six. That was the way she remembered numbers. In patterns. Still, she had to dial it three times before she got it right and she cursed herself and the way she crumbled under pressure.

'Dara? What's wrong?'

'Joe? It's Dara.' She cursed herself for telling people things they already knew, another symptom of her crumbling under pressure. 'Don't worry. Nothing's wrong.'

'Is Angel OK?' Joe said the words quickly and Dara heard him holding his breath when he got to the end of the question.

She hurried to tell him. 'She's fine. We got the call. Just now. From the hospital, I mean.'

'They've got a kidney?'

'They've got a kidney.' Dara had to sit down when she said that. After five years of waiting, five years of dreaming and hoping and praying to a God she didn't really believe in, five years of disappointment every time the phone rang, it now seemed to Dara an impossible thing to be saying out loud. For a moment she wondered if she was having one of those daydreams she sometimes had when she ate too much cheese, where the world is golden and bright and everything works out better than you supposed. But there was Mrs Flood, running down the stairs, clutching the bag she called her 'hair bag' in one hand ('because you just never know, do you?') and punching the air with her fist with the other in a way that was, at the very least, out of character. It must be true.

'We're on our way to the hospital now,' Dara told Joe.

'I'll meet you there in twenty minutes,' he said and hung up.

Dara grabbed Angel's car keys, her bag and coat, her sister and mother and herded them out the front door.

'You can't drive, Dara,' Mrs Flood said, looking fearfully at the keys in Dara's hand. 'We want to get to the hospital in one piece.'

'I'll drive' said Angel quickly, stepping between them, even now. 'You're still on your provisional and—'

'You can't drive yourself to the hospital,' Dara told her.

'But we need to go as quickly as possible and . . .' Angel tapered off, and Dara knew that she was torn between not wishing to be unkind and desperately needing to get to Beaumont as soon as she could. Since Dara had started learning, she had acquired the tedious habit of driving like a little old lady: slow and anxious. Also, her parking technique needed work, given that her spatial awareness was not what it should be, resulting in a tendency to graze the wing mirrors against inanimate objects, such as walls and other people's cars.

'I'll drive like the clappers,' she promised, sending up a silent prayer to St Jude, the patron saint of hopeless causes, to save her family – and other road users – from harm.

Mrs Flood said nothing. Her pursed lips said it all. She reached for the font of holy water at the front door, below the little statue of Our Lady. She dipped her index finger into the water and blessed herself, leaving droplets of water like puddles in the deep furrows of her forehead. She wet her finger again in the font and pushed it against her daughters' foreheads.

'Bless yourselves, girls,' she said, as she always did.

From their house on the Raheny Road, it was only a ten-minute drive to the hospital and Dara surprised herself by getting there in just under eight. Mrs Flood held Angel's hand all the way. Dara gripped the steering wheel, her knuckles straining white against her skin. There was one hairy moment when she approached an amber light at the junction of Tonlegee road.

'Go for it,' yelled Angel from the back seat. Mrs Flood said nothing. Just clamped one hand over her eyes, while the other hand tightened around Angel's arm. Dara pressed hard on the accelerator and roared through the junction, possibly even closing her eyes as she did so, although she couldn't be certain of this. It seemed a desperately reckless thing to do in the circumstances, but with Angel's encouragement from the back seat, she felt like she could make it and she gunned it and almost smiled when she cleared the junction with her family intact.

Looking back, Dara found that she couldn't remember much about the journey. She thinks she skidded to a halt at the main entrance to the hospital. She remembers a man in a dressing gown with an oxygen tank looking up from his cigarette as Angel and her mother raced out of the car. She drove to the car park, where she stopped too far away from the ticket machine and had to get out of the car and walk across the divide between the car and the machine to press the button. The car behind her beeped and she dropped the ticket under the car and had to get on all fours to reach it. She remembers that.

As for the hospital bit, it was impossible not to remember every single detail, however hard she tried not to.

The usual lights: impossibly bright and hot. Ideal for growing tomatoes, Dara often thought.

The nurses. The night-shifters. Different from the daytimers in a way that was hard to put your finger on. But with the same brisk uniforms and slow smiles and gentle hands. Dara decided she could never be a nurse. She cried any time one of *her* customers had to be put down. And lots of people couldn't understand how the passing of mangy strays and unwanted dogs could move you to tears. 'You must be used to it by now,' they told Dara in cheerful voices, and she nodded without saying anything.

Angel submitted to the usual tests and the usual waiting in her usual uncomplaining way. Joe sat beside her, holding her hand. Attracting the usual looks from passing women and even a couple of men, full of longing and the kind of wishing that never gets anyone anywhere. Joe was the type of man that people *coveted*, especially when he was in his 'firefighter's costume', as Mrs Flood called it.

It was Dara who saw Dr Templeton first. She saw him through the narrow slits in the venetian blinds and she knew immediately. It was the walk that gave him away: not the sprightly gait of someone bearing good news, but with a heaviness of step that betrayed the bad. Dara looked behind her, into the room where they waited. First at her sister, with her impossibly blue eyes, wide with the things she held dear. Things like faith. And hope. Sitting on the edge of the bed with her long legs dangling, as if nothing terrible was going to happen. And at her mother. Mrs Flood. She sat in an armchair, knitting with the resigned air of someone who was very good at waiting. In fact, she was much better at waiting than she was at knitting. She could only knit scarves and she used only two stitches (plain and purl), because they were the only ones she knew. But she liked to do it. She said it relaxed her. For as long as Dara and her sister could remember, Mrs Flood had knitted them scarves every Christmas and they were always a motley crew of colours and at least two metres long.

For one ridiculous moment, Dara thought about pulling the blinds shut, slamming the door and bracing her body against it so Dr Templeton couldn't get in. But then what possible explanation could she offer Angel and Mrs Flood and Joe? And was she strong enough to withstand the might of Dr Templeton – a solidly made man – and his team, as they stormed the door?

But of course Dara didn't do anything like that. In fact, she didn't move at all and in no time at all, Dr Templeton – despite the heaviness of his step – was inside the room, clearing his throat and not quite catching their eyes as he opened his mouth to speak.

It seemed to Dara that he said a lot of things and that it took him a long time to say all of those things. But really, he only had one thing to say. That Angel was not a match for the kidney. Or the kidney was not a match for Angel. Dara couldn't remember exactly how he phrased it. Even after he'd said it – this one thing that he came to say – he didn't stop talking. He was the same that time he told Dara that her kidney was not a match. And when he told Mrs Flood. Full of the same explanations then as he was now. It was Mrs Flood who made him stop eventually. She stood up. 'Thank you, Dr Templeton,' she said, wrapping the beginnings of a scarf around her fingers and pushing the sharp ends of the knitting needles into a huge ball of hairy wool. It made Dara's neck itch, just looking at it.

Angel stood up too. She let go of Joe's hand. She moved towards the door.

'I'll come home with you,' said Joe, already at the door beside her. He reached out a hand to touch her, but Angel stepped away. She said nothing. Instead, she shook her head, not looking at any of them, and walked out the door and down the corridor. Joe turned to face Mrs Flood and Dara. His face was a question but they had no answers to give him. Not today.

The drive home felt a lot longer than the one to the hospital. Much longer. Dara did her best. She chatted about anything at all that came into her head. Even though her driving instructor had strictly forbidden her to speak at all when she was behind the wheel. This was on account of Dara's tendency to look at the person she was speaking to, instead of at the road or in the rearview mirror or at the speedometer. Now, she concentrated on driving and chatting at the same time. About anything at all. Ridiculous things. Things like Kimberley and the way Tintin called her 'Pick 'n' Mix' because she wasn't one breed or another but a hotchpotch of several, which lent her an air of haughty indifference, belying the nature of her that was marshmallow-soft.

When Dara ran out of things to say, she was grateful to Mrs

Flood, who took up the reins of the conversation, speaking at length about *poor Mrs Butcher*. She always called Mrs Butcher *poor Mrs Butcher*, even though the woman was, it seemed to Dara, quite well-off, living in a lovely home with one husband, three children, two dogs and a guinea pig. Dara thought the title might have something to do with Mrs Butcher's hair, which tended towards frizzy.

This frenzy of conversation dribbled away like a burst ball somewhere around the Tonlegee road. It was only then that Dara and Mrs Flood heard it. The sound of Angel crying. It was a hard-to-hear cry. A barely-there cry. An under-your-breath kind of cry. That made it worse. That, and the fact that Angel *never* cried. Not *ever*. Not when she was a baby, according to Mrs Flood. Not when she found out she'd been born with only one kidney. Not when she'd been told about the end-stage renal failure. Not when she started on dialysis. Not when Dr Templeton told her that neither Dara's nor her mother's kidneys were a match for her, because of their blood types, which were common, unlike Angel's, which was a frustratingly rare one.

Because Angel believed in things. Things like guardian angels. And Fate and Destiny. And things happening for a reason. She was an optimist. A glass-half-full kind of a person.

Except she wasn't any more. She cried like a person whose glass is not even half-empty. It's just empty. A glass with nothing in it at all.

Mrs Flood wrapped her arms around her eldest daughter and told her to, 'Hush now, hush now, alanna, everything will be all right.' In her voice were equal measures of pain and love. Dara heard them both, as if they were two voices. She gripped the wheel in both hands and twisted the rearview mirror so Angel's reflection disappeared from view. She concentrated on driving.

Neither Mrs Flood's words, filled with equal measures of pain and love, nor Dara's careful concentration on the road made any difference.

Angel cried all the way home.

2

Angel hadn't always been sick. In fact, whenever Dara thought about it – which she often did – she had to concede that it was her and not Angel who, during their formative years, had succumbed to the usual childhood coughs and colds, infections and upsets.

Mrs Flood attributed this to the fact that her first daughter had been born in the caul, perfectly encapsulated in the protective bubble of her amniotic sac. There was a moment, just before the midwife punctured the membrane and reached inside to pick the baby up. A vivid moment, when Mrs Flood saw Angel for the first time, lying between her legs, perfectly visible through the clear pane of the sac. She remembers Angel's eyes, the trusting blue of them, full – even then – of the things that Angel held dear. Things like faith. And hope. The midwife told Mrs Flood not to worry, as she set about releasing Angel from the bubble. But Mrs Flood wasn't worried. She felt – for maybe the first and last time in her life – a kind of peace that was close to perfect. A feeling that nothing could go wrong. That everything was just the way it should be. She remembers how the noise of the delivery suite fell away as she and Angel looked at each other, as if they shared a delicious secret that nobody else knew and – just for a moment – Mrs Flood felt that anything was possible. She insists that, even when the nurse fished Angel out of the sac and cut the umbilical cord as if it were a string of sausages, Angel did not cry.

Later, people told Mrs Flood that being born in a caul is rare. Fewer than one in a thousand babies are born in this way. Some people believed that it was a symbol of good fortune. Mrs Flood never doubted it.

Dara had heard her own birth story many times and it wasn't nearly as pretty. Born by emergency C-section after a hefty twenty-six-hour labour that involved awful things like forceps and ventouse and bright lights and panic-riddled voices and green surgical gowns and one plaintive cry from Mrs Flood – near the end – for a husband who had walked up the road thirteen days before for a packet of cigarettes and never returned.

The birth was followed by a worrying period in an incubator – Dara was jaundiced, underweight and anxious. She refused to suckle. She squirmed in Mrs Flood's arms, as if she were afraid her mother might drop her. It took a week for Mrs Flood to realise that her daughter's eyes were navy blue, just like her father's. A week for Dara Flood to stop squeezing those navy blue eyes shut when she cried, which was all she did, that first week, in between brief bouts of fitful sleep. After that first week, when Dara opened her careful navy blue eyes and took the weight of the world in, Mrs Flood steeled herself against the stark similarity between this baby and her recently departed husband. She vowed never to think on this similarity – or on her vanishing act of a husband – again. It was a promise she would not be able to keep.

At the six-week check-up, Mrs Flood admitted to feeling a little . . . detached from the baby. There seemed to be some kind of distance between her and Dara that she wasn't able to cross. The nurse reached for Dara, crying in her carry-cot, and laid her in the crook of her arm. Dara stopped crying. Then she fell asleep.

'She never does that for me,' Mrs Flood said.

'She will. You just need to spend a little more time with her, maybe.'

'Don't I spend every day and night with her?' Mrs Flood said, exasperated.

'No, I mean, maybe just hold her a bit more. Just sit with her and hold her. Some babies are more anxious than others. They need more attention.'

'I don't have time to pander to her any more than I already do. I have Angel to worry about as well.' She nodded to Angel and the nurse looked at her, sitting on the floor, quiet as a mouse, reading a book. Without realising it, they both smiled, the nurse and Mrs Flood. Like they couldn't help it. That was what happened to people when they looked at Angel. Mrs Flood sighed and looked at Dara. 'I know this is going to sound a bit, well, odd, I suppose, but . . .'

'Go on,' the nurse told her, in a voice that suggested she'd heard it all before.

'I don't think she likes me. Dara, I mean.'

'Of course she likes you. You're her mother. You just need time to get used to each other.'

'No.' Mrs Flood was adamant. 'It's not that. It's something else.'

'What do you mean?'

'I didn't feel like this with Angel.'

The nurse reached for the telephone.

At first, the doctor called Mrs Flood's depression 'the baby blues'. He told her this was normal. Advised her to wait it out. She would feel differently soon. When she didn't, he prescribed a course of antidepressants.

'How long will I need to take these for?' she asked the doctor.

'As long as it takes,' the doctor told her, with the cheery manner of someone who was certain that his children liked him.

Twenty-seven years later, Mrs Flood was still taking them.

3

The house on the Raheny road looked the same as it always did, but everything was different now.

Angel was different.

In a way, it felt to Dara that Angel was already gone. There was a stranger where Angel used to be. A stranger who didn't speak. Who didn't eat. Who didn't go out. A stranger in her sister's room. Through the locked door, Dara could hear the muffled sounds of cries against a pillow.

'But nothing's changed,' Dara told her through the door. 'We're still waiting, aren't we? Waiting for the call. Just like we were before.'

To this, there was no response.

Dara left plates of Angel's favourite food outside the door. A plate of flapjacks, chewy ones, just the way she liked them. A dish of fruit, peeled and cored and chopped up into bite-size chunks. Careful measures of juice and water. A bowl of steak and kidney pie: ironically, her favourite dinner. A slice of the carrot cake Dara had made earlier. Carrot cake was at the frontline of comfort food, in Dara's opinion. Maybe because of its name. Maybe people felt better about eating a cake called after a vegetable.

Later, Dara removed the dishes and cups and glasses and bowls and even the carrot cake, everything untouched.

'Joe's on the phone for you,' she called through the door. This was the third time he had rung. 'He says he's coming over,' she told her.

No answer.

Mrs Flood had also taken to her bed, complaining of a migraine. Dara moved into her mother's room, setting tablets and a glass of water on the bedside locker. The room was an exercise in a lopsided sort of symmetry. One enormous double bed divided it down the middle, the left side where Mrs Flood slept, the right side pristine with the bedclothes pulled taut, as if Mr Flood had never slept there. A bedside locker on either side, the left one cluttered with books and magazines and curlers and dryers and straighteners, the right one empty, apart from a thick coating of dust and a set of cuff links, tarnished now with the years. Two wardrobes on opposite sides of the room, one so full the doors hadn't closed properly in years. The other contained one suit – the one Mr Flood had called his funeral suit – one pair of trousers, three shirts, a pair of runners with no laces, two ailing boots and one green jumper with a hole in the elbow. When Dara moved towards it to press the door shut, the empty hangers bumped softly against each other in an eerie sort of melody.

Dara poked her head around the door an hour later. Mrs Flood's eyes were closed, but Dara did not think she was asleep. Her mother still wore her Bobs Away uniform. Her hair – her best advertisement, she often said – lay neglected on top of her head, devoid of its usual billboard shine and bounce. Dara could hardly bear to look at it.

When Angel didn't come out of her room the following day, fear wound its long, bony fingers around Dara's heart and squeezed tight.

She recognised the fear from before.

Twice before.

Once when she had first found out about Angel's end-stage renal failure.

The other time – the first time – was years before, when Dara was in primary school. Sixth class. Twelve years old, scrawny and small, all angles and bones. Worried navy eyes. Dyslexic, although nobody knew that yet. Everyone just assumed she wasn't all that bright, the way she read so slowly with her finger moving under each word as she navigated a sentence in a book. Her large, loopy writing, the phonetic way she spelled words that she should have known. One teacher told Mrs Flood that Dara was 'practically illiterate'. That was in third class. Dara wasn't sure what illiterate meant when Mrs Flood accused her of it that evening, but the way her mother said it, it didn't sound like a good thing to be. In fact, her dyslexia went unnoticed for years. Until she got a new maths teacher in sixth year in secondary school. Mr Horan. Mr Horn, some of the girls called him, sniggering in that high-pitched way that schoolgirls have. Mr Horan had dark, close-cut hair, sallow skin, big brown eyes, a wide silver ring on his little finger with curious markings engraved on it that spoke of some mysterious tribe somewhere in a mountainous region far, far away, and a tattoo just above his right wrist that he never tried to conceal, despite the principal's attitude towards all manner of body art. There was endless speculation about what the tattoo said – lines of tiny writing – and even though Dara knew (on account of all the time Mr Horan spent squatting at her desk, explaining things), she never told them. She felt that he was entitled to his privacy, such as it was, as one of only two male teachers in the vast tide of females, ebbing and flowing within the confines of the all-girls' school.

Mr Horan clocked the dyslexia straight away.

'You're just dyslexic,' he told her cheerfully, smiling in that way he had that nearly made Dara smile back.

'Can you fix it?' Dara asked, not entirely sure what being dyslexic involved.

'We can work around it,' he told her with a smile and a wink.

But that all happened when Dara Flood was eighteen.

When Damien Butler arrived into Dara's sixth class in primary school, nobody knew about Dara's dyslexia. Everyone – Mrs Flood, Dara's teachers and especially Dara herself – had settled on the explanation that Dara was a little *slow*.

'Big D', everyone called him. The term was used reverentially by most, and with studied informality by the handpicked few who were allowed to call Big D their friend.

Dara kept out of his way. Kept to herself as she had done most of the way through her schooling, not being as able as Angel to withstand the naked curiosity of her peers as to the whereabouts of Mr Flood. Of course, she wished she could be more like her sister, who laughed at the questions and told people to 'mind their beeswax', while still managing to be the most popular kid of every class she was ever in. But that was like the puppy she wished for every Christmas. There was no point to it.

Dara's clothes were Angel's hand-me-downs and never fit her. How could they, when Angel was tall and sturdy and Dara so small and skinny? Also the pale colours – so pretty on Angel, with her blond hair and sallow skin – seemed out of place on Dara, with her pale face and dark hair.

Big D didn't have to separate Dara from the herd. She was already alone and perfect for him in every way.

It happened every day on her way home from school. Dara walked home alone since Angel had graduated to the secondary school on the other side of Raheny. Big D would lie in wait for her. Up a tree, behind a car, down a lane.

At first, the bullying was only verbal. The usual crass remarks about Mr Flood and the speculation as to why he left.

'You know why your daddy left, doncha? Cos he saw your ugly face comin' outta yer ma's hole.'

'Whatcha get your daddy for Father's Day? Directions to your house?'

Once he spat in her face. She didn't wipe it, letting it slide instead down the length of her face until it hung from her jaw in a wet slippery itch.

She tried everything.

She stood at the top of the line, the first kid out of the traps when the bell rang for the end of school. She streaked through the gates, not even stopping when her lunchbox slipped from her sweaty grip, landing with an empty bang in the gutter running alongside the pavement.

Big D caught up with her.

Mostly he took things. Her lunch. Her pencil case. The itchy woolly hats her mother made for her. The few coins Mrs Flood left for her on the kitchen table on a Friday morning.

It didn't take long for Big D to realise that Dara Flood was not going to tell. He began to hurt her. Tight pinches that left fingertips of bruises along the skin of her arms that she hid under her school jumper. Careful shoves in the yard, with his posse drawn in a ring around them so that no one else could see. Dara waited til she got home before she picked the tiny stones out of the cuts on her knees.

Every morning, she walked to school, forcing one leg in front of the other. She was often late. Her schoolwork, never exemplary, worsened. She fell asleep in class. A note was sent home. Her mother called to the school. Angry words in the kitchen. Dara promised to try harder.

It was Angel who worked it out.

'How did you get that cut on your leg?'

'I fell in the yard.'

'Again?'

'Yes.'

'That's a new bruise on your arm.'

'I banged it against the wall.'

'Dara?'

'I did, I wasn't looking where I was going.'

Dara knew that this would never happen to her big sister. She would not allow it. That was why she didn't tell her. She was ashamed. Of herself. Her weakness. She kept going.

On Friday, she ran home from school, Big D a streak of navy behind her. In fairness, Dara could run very fast, although not for very long. If there had been a hundred-metre sprint team at the school instead of a cross-country team, things might have been different for Dara Flood. She had just passed the line of shops when Big D caught up with her. He pulled her by the hood down the lane between the butcher's and the vegetable shop. The hood came away from the back of Dara's coat and he threw it on the ground, using it as a mat to wipe his feet on. Despite the months that had passed, Dara still struggled against him, and even though she cut such a slight little figure against the fleshy heaviness of Big D, she sometimes managed to slip out of his grasp, being wiry if not very strong. He pushed her against the pebbledash of the wall. This was one of the worst places to get caught. The hard pebbles bit into her head like glass.

'Let her go.' The voice took Dara as much by surprise as it did Big D, who stepped back, releasing his hands from their grip around Dara's neck.

'Angel,' said Dara, not moving.

'Are you all right?' Angel glanced at her sister as she moved with purpose up the lane, towards Big D. Dara nodded and looked at Damien. He seemed smaller now. Fat rather than muscly. There was a gathering of spots – red and wet – on his forehead that she hadn't noticed before.

Angel kept walking until she reached him. He stayed where he was, holding his ground. After all, Angel was only a girl. Not quite as tall as him. With her blond hair and her wide baby-blue eyes, she did not present much of a threat. This is what Big D must have thought, as he stood there, swaggering. He was wrong.

Angel gripped the lapels of his jacket with both hands curled into fists. She hooked her foot around the back of his leg and pushed. He went down slow and heavy, like a sack of potatoes. She swung her leg back and kicked him. Hard. In the ribs. There was no need to do it again, because Big D began to cry. His cry was high and furious, like a baby with wind. He made fists of his hands and clamped them against his eyes, but the tears leaked through anyway. Angel squatted beside him. She didn't have to pin him down. He made no move to get up.

'If. You. Ever. Hurt. Dara. Again. I. Will. Kill. You. Do? You? Understand?' The words were delivered in a slow staccato, so quiet they were nearly a whisper. When Damien did not answer, Angel pushed her knee against his neck and pressed down. Hard. He screamed then, a long, thin squeal, like a stuck pig.

'Do? You? Understand?' she asked again, leaning towards his face.

He nodded his head quickly. Angel released him, wiping her hands on her school coat with a look of disgust she made sure he could see. She picked up Dara's hood, her school bag, her hat and her scarf. She nodded to Dara, who began to walk, back up the lane, towards home.

'Aren't you supposed to be at school?' Dara asked.

'I mitched off,' Angel told her. Dara looked at her sister. There was nothing Angel couldn't do. This is what Dara thought at that moment. She smiled at her and slipped her hand into Angel's. Angel squeezed it tight before she let go.

'Why didn't you say something?' Angel asked when they got home. Mrs Flood was at work.

'I didn't want to worry you. I thought he'd stop.'

Angel shook her head as she picked bits of pebbledash out of Dara's hair.

'Promise me you'll tell me? If it happens again?'

But it never happened again. It had lasted three months, two weeks and four days. For those three months, two weeks and four days, Dara had felt it. The fear. It twisted inside her like snakes. It made food taste like nothing. It blotted out the light and made the nights darker. Longer. It left her mouth dry and her heart hammering inside her chest, hard enough to hurt.

Dara felt that same fear now. But this time, she didn't have Angel standing square in her corner. This time, Dara was on her own.

Even though Angel was still here, it felt like she was already gone, and there was nothing Dara could do but look at the space where Angel used to be and wish that things were different.

4

Dara remembered when Angel got sick. Because it was Angel's first experience of illness. She was twenty-three. Recently qualified, about to start her second year at the local primary school and deliriously dripping with love for Joe, her fabulous firefighting boyfriend.

Dara was twenty-two. She could remember the detail of that year. Every single day. Because she'd been happy. Right up until Angel got sick. That was what made it stand out. That was the year she got George. Her cocker spaniel. The dog Mrs Flood said she couldn't keep. The one none of the families visiting the pound wanted, probably because of the three legs he had, as opposed to the traditional four.

It was Angel who lobbied Mrs Flood and persuaded her to take George in. And even though she stated her intention to have nothing whatsoever to do with *that dog*, it was Mrs Flood who carried George home after the accident, two years later. Mrs Flood who decided that George should be buried under the pear tree in the back garden where he had loved to snooze in the shade of a Sunday afternoon. Mrs Flood who had wept as Dara threw the first shovel of muck over his cold body.

That was the year she was offered the full-time job at the pound. It paid less money than the job she already had – as a secretary in the school where Angel worked – and would delay her plan to save enough money to move out from under Mrs Flood's feet. Rent an apartment, maybe. Or even a little house with a garden. Somewhere not too far, so she could visit the house on the Raheny road. But far enough to accommodate the distance that Dara felt between her and her mother. A distance that she had never quite been able to bridge.

That was the year she discovered confidence and what life could be like if you had some.

The year she'd met Tintin and Anya.

They planned to move in together: Dara, Tintin and Anya. Then Angel got sick and everything changed. So Tintin and Anya moved in together and told Dara that when she was ready, they'd get a place with three bedrooms instead of two. Two years later, when their lease was up, they asked her again. And again, a year after that.

'I can't,' Dara always said.

'Why not?'

'You know why.'

'You can still visit your mother and sister. Every day if you like. It's not like we're moving to outer fecking Mongolia or . . . or . . .' Tintin struggled to find some place equally obscure, 'or . . . Leitrim,' he finally came up with.

'They need me. Angel's not well, and Mam worries if she doesn't know where I am. I need to be there when the phone call comes through. You *know* that.'

'You'll only be in Bayside, for the love of God.'

Dara shook her head. Angel had put off moving in with Joe. 'Just till I get my new kidney,' she told him, as if it would happen any day. That's how she'd been back then.

So Dara put off moving in with Tintin and Anya. Angel had always been there for her. Now she could, in her own small way, do the same for her sister.

It began with something as trite as a sore throat.

'I've got a sore throat,' Angel told Dara and Mrs Flood, with some fascination. 'Look, it even hurts to swallow,' she said, wincing as she demonstrated. Dara reached into her bag for the lozenges she carried on her person, being no stranger to sore throats herself. Mrs Flood recommended her mother's old remedy – gargling with salt and slightly cooled boiled water. The next day Angel had a temperature. A high one.

'Look, my hands and legs are shaking,' she commented, holding her limbs up for inspection. 'And I'm actually clammy. Feel my forehead. I've got a *fever*. A proper one.'

Even though she was twenty-three, Mrs Flood insisted on bringing her to the doctor's surgery. 'Just because it's your first time,' she told her lucky charm of a daughter.

'Streptococcal throat,' the doctor told them cheerfully, scribbling a prescription that neither of them could make out.

The novelty of being sick wore off after a week. Angel's temperature continued to spike and in spite of nearing the end of the course of antibiotics, she felt no better. A second dose of antibiotics was prescribed.

'My back hurts,' Angel told Dara, who sat on her sister's bed and kneaded her back with both hands, like dough.

'Don't go too far,' Dara shouted from the front door as Joe took Angel for a walk to St Anne's Park. Her first outing. Two weeks later.

'Don't worry about me, Dara,' Angel said, turning and blowing her sister a kiss. In spite of the sickly pallor of her skin and the narrowness of her frame from the recent weight she had lost, Dara remembered thinking how beautiful her big sister was at that moment, with her blond hair falling around her face and her smile as warm as freshly-baked bread.

An hour later, a phone call from a frantic Joe from Beaumont Hospital.

'She just collapsed!' he shouted down the phone. 'At the pond. She nearly went in. They're doing tests. I don't know any more. I'm so sorry.'

Even then, Mrs Flood knew there would be some reasonable explanation. It seemed impossible that any ill could penetrate the caul that Angel had been born in.

It was only a matter of time – what with all the tests Angel was subjected to – that her missing kidney was discovered.

'Well,' said Mrs Flood, collecting herself after she was told this bit of news, 'you only need one kidney. Am I right?' She looked at the doctor's face and waited for him to nod and smile at her. He did not.

'That's true,' he admitted. 'You *do* only need one kidney.'

But the bacteria from the streptococcal infection had somehow found its way into the one kidney that Angel needed.

'So you just need to put her on some more antibiotics, right? Stronger ones, obviously. To make the infection go away? Yes?' Mrs Flood's voice rose and rose, until it seemed to Dara that she was shouting.

In fairness to the staff at the hospital, they did everything they could before they reached their conclusion. But nothing they did was good enough.

And so, in spite of Angel's good-luck caul, in spite of the fact that she'd never been sick before, in spite of the novenas Mrs Flood intoned and the bargains Dara made to a God she didn't believe in, in spite of all Angel's positive thinking and her faith and her hope, she was diagnosed as having renal failure and preparations were made to put her on a dialysis machine. That was five years ago.

A lot had changed since then, Dara often thought.

Five years ago, Dara had jumped up every time Angel's dialysis machine beeped or stuttered and run for the nurse. Five years ago, she had been a non-smoker. A proper non-smoker. Someone who had never smoked. Someone who thought she never would.

Five years ago, people couldn't believe it when Mrs Flood told them that she had two grown-up daughters. She had been slim back then, with a youthful disposition. Dara could almost trace the five years across her mother's body. It was in the lines of her face and the thickening of her waist and the slope of her shoulders that seemed to bow under the weight of her worry.

For Angel, those five years were like an extensive trip to a foreign land, where she had learned the language and sampled the food and navigated her way around the unreliable public transport system. It wasn't a place she had wanted to go, but now she was there, she was determined to make the best of it. That was Angel's way. Until now.

5

It wasn't as if Stanley Flinter had a *bad* life. It was just, well, certain assumptions had been made. About how his life would be. Way back. He had it all sewn up at a very early age. That's what stymied him. His assumptions.

Stanley had assumed – like all the men in his family for generations – that he would be an upstanding member of the Garda Siochána by now, married to Cora, with two children – a boy and a girl – and weekly visits to his parents' house for Sunday lunch, where stories of high-speed car chases and shady drug barons and the IRA – both the real *and* the pretend – would be exchanged, exaggerated and embellished.

But things hadn't worked out that way.

Instead, Stanley Flinter got the *wrong* life. In fact – and this sounded a bit melodramatic, so Stanley never voiced it aloud – it was his eldest brother Cormac who got Stanley's life. Or at least the life that Stanley had *assumed* would be his. It was Cormac who joined the Garda Siochána at the age of twenty-one, having surpassed himself in the medical exam and the written exam and the interview. It was Cormac who lived with Cora in their semi-detached home in the suburbs with their beautiful baby daughter, also named Cora.

Stanley, on the other hand, received a letter from the Garda Siochána, formal in expression and apologetic in tone. He didn't have to read to the end of it before he knew. He supposed that he'd always known but had allowed himself to hope, being an optimistic type of a person back then. But there it was. In black and white. At five foot five, he was short – although this, they claimed, played no hand, act, or part in their decision. No, it was the hearing problem (being born partially deaf in one ear, for no particular reason that anyone could discern), that rendered him unsuitable for The Force.

Stanley drove to his parents' house to celebrate Cormac's recent promotion to Detective. He sat in his ancient Ford Transit van that used to be a police van. Cormac had got it for him on the cheap and Stanley knew that he should be grateful. It was perfect for his line of work. Just perfect. Apart from the gaping hole in the middle of the dashboard where the police radio used to be. It was like a cruel joke, that gap. A constant reminder, no matter how much stuff Stanley crammed into it. Beside him, on the passenger seat, sat a huge dog with his head stuck out the window and the seat belt struggling against his massive torso. 'He's a lurcher,' Sissy had told him. Sissy was Stanley's friend-since-junior-infants, housemate and all-round know-it-all. 'That's a *type* of dog, not a breed,' she said, keeping a healthy distance between herself and the dog. Chief Inspector Jacques Clouseau, his name was. Clouseau for short. Bequeathed to Stanley recently by a client of his. A little old lady called June Robinson, a tiny thing, sweet as marzipan. A huge Peter Sellers fan.

Everyone assumed that Sissy and Stanley were lovers, but this wasn't the case. They were just great friends who happened to live together. It was true that Sissy had once made a lunge at him after too many homemade Mojitos one night on his couch. He had disentangled himself from her with the care and the gentleness that she loved about him.

'I'm a mess, Sissy. You've said it yourself a million times,' he reminded her.

'I know,' she said, hanging her head that had grown too heavy for her neck. 'But it would be so *handy*, wouldn't it?'

He shook his head. 'It would never work.'

'Give me three good reasons why not.' She held up four fingers and waited.

'I'm poor,' he told her.

'Only because you've poured all your money into that business of yours and you keep letting people pay you in sterling silver photo frames instead of cold, hard cash.'

'I'm too short. Much shorter than you. We'd look weird.'

'But you're a ride. A short ride. Everyone says it.'

'Everyone?'

'Well, my sister says it.'

'But she thinks everyone is a ride. Even Gérard Depardieu.'

'That's true.' Sissy slumped against the couch and sighed a long, ragged sigh that stank of mint. 'You're right. It would be a disaster.'

'Well, I wouldn't go so far as to call it a *disaster*.'

'I'd try to change you,' Sissy told him.

'Which bit?'

'All the bits,' she said, waving her hand in his direction. 'I'm a desperate control freak, so I am. You'd be *exhausted*.'

The dining-room table in Stanley's family home had been there as long as Stanley could remember. A great slab of dark wood, so thick and so sturdy you could put a wok on it straight off the hob and it wouldn't leave a mark. Not that his mother would ever use a wok, mind. She had no truck with exotic food, as she called it. Wooden benches ran down either side, like the benches you get at picnic tables. The brothers sat where they always sat. Along one bench, in age order. The girlfriends sat on the opposite bench, whether they liked it or not. That was just the way things were at the Flinter family home.

Stanley smiled and listened and nodded in all the right places. He ate the food his mother put in front of him – Beef Wellington, *because it's Cormac's favourite*, she said, patting her eldest son's arm with an indulgent smile – joined in a heated debate on the appalling behaviour of some referee during a recent Manchester United match (even though he had no interest whatsoever in football), and laughed in his good-natured way along with everyone else when he produced the banoffee pie his mother had asked him to bake for the occasion. Stanley was the only one who liked to bake.

'There's nothing wrong with a man baking,' their mother often said, licking her fingers and using them to try to press Stanley's fringe into a sitting position. She'd been doing this ever since he was a child, even though it had no tangible effect on the fringe – hindered by a cowlick – which stood to attention like it was in the front row of a Garda band parade.

In spite of the spate of good-natured slagging that followed the production of the banoffee pie, Stanley noticed that everyone ate it. All of them: Cormac, Declan, Lorcan, Neal and Adrian. That was the five of them. In age order. Six, if you included Stanley. He was the youngest. The 'gap baby', Adrian informed him. 'Love child' was the term preferred by Lorcan, who would wrap his arms around Stanley's waist and simulate some enthusiastic dry-humping. Lorcan was, by his own admission, immature and a sex addict. Not that he had a lot of sex. He talked about it more than anything else. He was a thirty-four-year-old garda who loved talking about sex.

'I have an announcement to make,' said Cormac, standing up.

'Another one?' This from Neal, who was anxiously waiting for the meal to end so he could make it to his local – the Flying Fish (on the quays and in business since the time when there were actual living fish in the Liffey) – before closing time. After weeks of courting and cajoling, the barmaid, Freda, had finally given him reason to hope last night. 'Tomorrow night could be the night,' was all she'd said, and even though she said that most nights, this time she licked her lips and Neal took it as a positive sign.

Cormac continued as if Neal had not spoken. 'Cora and I are getting married.'

The pause after this piece of news was so tiny, it was barely there. But Stanley felt it, this barely-there pause, like a punch to his solar plexus and for a moment, no, not even a moment, more like a particle of a second, he thought he might throw up or keel over or even black out. But where would they all be then? It was Stanley who kept the Cora and Cormac road-show on the move. Stanley who had urged them all forward, with his quiet acceptance and his stalwart smile. In that tiny flicker of time where Stanley groped for something to hold on to, he remembered everything.

Like the first time he'd seen Cora (in biology class in sixth year). Her very presence seemed to change the colour of the classroom – ordinarily a porridge grey – to something vibrant and almost alive, like orange mixed with purple.

Like how everyone wanted her. She was American, recently moved to Ireland from Boston with her family, she had tanned, smooth skin, blond hair, green eyes, a beautiful mouth, legs like Maurice O'Halloran, the head prefect (they went on and on . . .), and the greatest selection of shoes any of them had ever seen. In fact, Stanley had never seen her in the same pair twice.

Like how Stanley wanted her. It was a physical pain, this longing. Coupled with the sure knowledge that he would never get her, the pain sharpened, like an appendix about to burst.

Like how it was *her* who singled *him* out. 'How come you don't ask me out like all the other guys?' Stanley never told her the reason. He just smiled and shrugged and shoved his hands deep into the stiff pockets of his grey school trousers. Cora mistook his shyness for mysteriousness and pursued him with a single-mindedness that, quite frankly, took Stanley's breath away.

Their first kiss. *She* kissed *him*. She had to bend a little to reach him. 'I knew you'd be a great kisser,' she told him when she straightened.

The first time they had sex was three years later, when she returned to Dublin after her obligatory round-the-world trip after 'graduation', as she called it. Stanley had just finished his Social Science degree in UCD. Mr Flinter Senior said that he knew his boys would be guards. And that was fine. But they had to do something else first. Get a bit of an education.

Cora had called into Stanley's flat, a dark, poky affair with a smell of damp that wrapped itself around everything like a sea mist. It was two months after he got the letter. The one from the Garda Siochána.

For the first time since he received the letter, Stanley forgot all about it. He didn't care any more. About anything. Other than this beautiful creature splayed on his bed, a splash of colour in an otherwise dreary world, where deafness (albeit partial and only in one ear) was enough to scupper your dreams. Stanley closed his eyes and held her close, inhaled her like she was air and watched her as she slept, careful not to wake her, careful to remember everything. Because – despite his assumptions – he knew deep down that it would never last. There are certain things that people just know. Inherently. And this was the thing that Stanley knew. And he was right.

Because something *did* happen.

Cormac happened.

Cormac went through girlfriends the way some people go through a packet of Maltesers: carelessly, thoughtlessly, enjoying them but always reaching for the next one. And the next. And then he met Cora. She got pregnant while still dating Stanley (that's what she had called their relationship: 'dating').

'Hit me,' Cormac had ordered him, pointing to his face. 'You can hit me twice, I won't even try to defend myself.' That was Cormac's way of saying he was sorry. And Stanley had to forgive him. For his family's sake. Every one of them was on his side, but there was a baby to consider. The first grandchild. Stanley's first niece. He retreated. What else could he do? To be honest, he never thought it would last.

They moved in together.

Stanley presumed Cormac would stay until the novelty wore off. But when Baby Cora came, he was still there. Stanley gave it three months of night-feeding, nappy-changing and colic before Cormac had his fill of domesticity. But here they were, fifteen months later, announcing their engagement.

It didn't take Stanley long to think all these thoughts and to remember all these memories. Probably because he thought about them so often and remembered everything so clearly. They were like a DVD he kept watching, even though he didn't like it. They fitted perfectly into the barely-there pause that greeted Cormac's piece of news. Then Stanley stood up so quickly, he banged the back of his knees against the sturdy wood of the bench. He saw his mother scan the table anxiously as if she were afraid Stanley might be considering throwing a piece of her good delft at her eldest son's head and was cursing herself for not using her second-best dinner set, which was easily fifteen years old and not wearing well. But Stanley didn't do that. Instead, he lifted his glass and raised it towards Cormac and then at Cora. 'Congratulations,' he said, smiling. Everyone checked to see if the smile reached his eyes – it did, but only just – before jumping to their feet, smiling relieved sort of smiles, raising their glasses and roaring 'CONGRATULATIONS!' at Cormac and Cora. Luckily, baby Cora chose that moment to wake up – and who could blame her, with all the tension, the relief and the roaring – and Cora sighed the way she always did and got up to tend to her daughter, so Stanley didn't have to look at her face while trying to make his smile reach his eyes again. He had done it once but he didn't think he could manage it a second time.

Later, Stanley stacked the dishwasher and took to the worst of the pots at the sink with a Brillo pad. He whistled while he worked, to give the impression that he was delighted with life and not skulking in the kitchen in an effort to avoid his brothers and his parents and his brothers' girlfriends and especially Cora.

'Hello, Stanley.' He knew before moving his fringe out of his eyes who it was. He planted a smile on his face like a fist before turning.

'Cora.' Casual. Unconcerned. He fought to get his tone somewhere in that vicinity.

'It's lovely and quiet in here,' she said, approaching him. 'Compared to the bedlam out there.' She tossed her head in the direction of the dining room, her blond hair falling across her face as she did so. She slid her feet out of her shoes and stood beside him. He remembered them, those feet. Long and thin. He remembered the feel of them in his hands, his fingers pressing into the high arches, kneading and massaging just the way she liked, especially after a hard day's shopping. Even without her heels, she was still two inches taller than him. She rested her hand on his shoulder. 'What would you like me to do?' she asked, licking her lips before arranging her mouth into a very pink pout. Stanley knew she was just being friendly. Cooperative. Helpful. It was just his overactive imagination that made her sound so . . . so . . . *suggestive*. In his head, he slapped himself across the face. He knew he should really punch himself with a closed fist. That's what his brothers would do if they ever resorted to imaginary violence, which was unlikely. But Stanley Flinter abhorred violence of any kind. Even imaginary violence. He moved sideways, so that Cora's hand had no choice but to come away from his upper arm. His own hands were covered with suds, which dripped onto the ceramic tiles. His head moved this way and that, frantically looking for more dishes to wash.

'Eh, no, you're all right, Cora. But thanks all the same. I'm nearly finished here.'

'Here, allow me,' said Cora, reaching for a dish towel and wrapping his hands in it. 'You're dripping all over the floor.'

It was the smell of her that did it. The same scent, even after all this time. Yes, she used different perfumes and body lotions, he felt sure. But that underlying scent was still the same. A ferociously clean smell. You could cut it, it was that sharp. Stanley held his breath and practised smiling.

'What are you up to, Stanley?' Cormac said, appearing in the doorway. He smiled when he said it and Stanley knew for a fact that Cormac would never suspect him of being up to anything.

'I was just . . .'

'Stanley was cleaning up after you lot of dirty dogs,' said Cora. 'It's a pity you wouldn't take a leaf out of his book.'

'You're a good one to talk,' said Cormac, hunting in the cupboard where their mother kept the stash of biscuits. 'Your handbag hasn't been cleared out since 1987.'

'My handbag is none of your business,' said Cora, slapping his hand away from the biscuit tin. 'Stop it, you'll never lose that weight before the wedding at this rate.'

Cormac sighed but moved away from the tin.

'Cora is crying again. She needs her nappy changed.' Cora jerked her head in the direction of the dining room, folding her arms tightly across her chest.

'I changed her last time,' said Cormac with the air of a man who knows the situation is hopeless but has decided to fight anyway.

'And I changed her the five times before that, while you were at work,' Cora said.

They had always argued. Right from day one. 'It's their version of foreplay,' Adrian said. 'Some couples do that.' Because
Adrian had such a low, serious voice, everyone believed him.

'I'm going to say goodbye to your poor, unfortunate mother,' said Cora, flouncing out of the kitchen.

Stanley turned back to the sink and breathed a sigh of relief. A quiet one, so Cormac wouldn't hear him. For a while
there was silence. Just the lapping of water in the sink and the
steady sound of Cormac eating his way through a packet of
Jammie Dodgers, still his favourites.

'How's business?' he asked, punching Stanley's upper arm
with a closed fist. Even though it hurt, Stanley smiled. He
knew that this was the way men like Cormac communicated.
There was no malice in it.

'Oh, you know, grand.'

'I've another case for you,' said Cormac, pushing his finger into his mouth to slide Jammie Dodger mash off his back
teeth.

'No, it's OK, really, Cormac, I've got enough . . .'

'Consider it a favour from your big brother.' Cormac
kept sending him cases 'as a favour'. Mostly fellow police-
men who were convinced their wives were playing away,
as Cormac put it, while they wrote up speeding tickets on
night duty. Because they were his brother's friends, Stanley
felt awkward about charging them full price, but even when
he mentioned the lowest price he could possibly do it for,
they did a double take and expressed disbelief about the
cost of surveillance. It was an expensive business. People
really had no idea.

'That's great. Eh . . . thanks a million, Cormac.'

'No problemo,' said Cormac, smiling at him before tossing the empty packet of biscuits on the counter, scattering
crumbs everywhere. 'I'm going to take the Coras home. Like
a bag of cats they are.'

'Cora's probably tired, with the baby and everything,' Stanley offered.

'She's always bloody tired,' Cormac said, taking a carton of milk out of the fridge, putting it to his lips, draining it and returning the empty carton to the fridge. 'She should try working for a living sometime.' Stanley didn't like to remind Cormac that Cora had worked. As a beauty therapist in one of Dublin's biggest hotels, until she was made redundant a year ago. Cormac had called it brilliant timing, what with the baby and everything. Stanley wasn't so sure if Cora appreciated the job loss as much as Cormac did.

Behind his brother, Stanley could see Cora approaching. He narrowed his eyes at Cormac.

'What?' Cormac was a little sluggish after the guts of a bottle of wine during dinner, two beers beforehand and a generous tumbler of brandy afterwards. Cora stepped into the kitchen.

'I suppose I'll have to drive home,' she said. 'Again.'

'Oh, eh, right then,' Cormac said, nodding his thanks at Stanley.

It took them ages to leave. They kept coming back. To pick up the baby's teddy. Then Cora's handbag. Then the nappy bag. Then the baby bottles, which Stanley had washed and rinsed and set to dry on the draining board. The house felt emptier – and quieter – when they finally left.

Stanley stood on the edge of the pavement and watched them go, waving and smiling like everyone else. What else could he do? The life Stanley Flinter had planned for himself was currently being lived by one Cormac Flinter, and all Stanley could do was stand on the sidelines and watch.

6

'What's going *on* in there?' Miss Pettigrew's normally refined and dulcet tones were shrill with anxiety and, yes, a certain degree of vexation. 'No one's been in to see me for two days. I could be lying in a heap at the bottom of the stairs with only Edward to see to me. I might have broken a hip. Or a nail.'

In spite of everything, Dara couldn't help smiling down the phone. It was Monday. Angel was still in her room. She was due in the hospital for dialysis at three. Mrs Flood had gotten out of bed, although she'd only made it as far as the bath. She'd been in it for hours. 'Oh. My, Lord.' Miss Pettigrew breathed down the phone.

'Is everything alright?' asked Dara.

'It's Edward,' she said in a hushed voice. 'He's managed to beat his own brain training record. I can't talk Dara. I have to amend his star chart.' The line went dead.

Then Dara had rung work and told barefaced lies down the phone. She wasn't very good at lying.

'I'm . . . I'm not very well,' she'd said. She knew she would tell them about Angel's found-and-lost kidney. Just not today. She didn't know where to start.

'What's wrong with you?' Anya was pound manager and was nothing if not direct.

'Eh . . . a headache. And diarrhoea and, eh, vomiting too.'

'Did it come on suddenly?'

'Eh, yes, I think so.'

'What's your temperature?'

'I'm not sure,' said Dara. 'But I feel hot.' This was, in fact, true, as colour crept up Dara's neck and leaked into the normally pale skin of her face.

'Oh my Got!' Anya's voice grew faint with worry.

'What?' Dara found worry infectious.

'It sounds like dengue fever. Those were my *exact* symptoms when I thought I had it. Remember? Last year? I Googled it?

'You did *not* have dengue fever, Anya.' Dara could hear Tintin in the background. Of course, his real name wasn't Tintin. It was Terence O'Neill. He'd acquired the nickname as a teenager, when he first began to drink cold tins of beer in damp fields. Two cold tins. That was all he could drink before he threw up. And even though his tolerance for alcohol had improved with age – he was twenty-seven now – the name Tintin had stuck like mud. Even his own mother called him Tintin.

'I know that, but I had the exact same symptoms. *That's* what I'm saying.' Anya's voice came from far away, as if she had turned away from the receiver.

'Eh, Anya?' Dara called down the phone.

'You had a very light cold,' she heard Tintin say.

'And diarrhoea,' Anya insisted.

'You'd had that dodgy kebab after the pub. I told you not to buy it from that stall but you insisted.'

'And vomiting. Don't forget, I vomited.'

'Anya?' Dara tried again.

'Of course you vomited,' Tintin said. 'Pure Guinness with bits of kebab floating in it. You got a bit on my shoes, remember, and—'

'ANYA!' Dara shouted down the phone.

'Yes?' Anya sounded surprised, as if she had forgotten Dara was there at all.

'So I won't be in today, all right? Maybe tomorrow. I'll ring you.' She hung up before Anya and Tintin could resume their argument.

As soon as she put the phone down, Miss Pettigrew rang back. 'So, as I was saying, I could have broken a hip or a nail.'

'And did you?' Dara asked her.

'Did I what?' the old lady asked.

'Fall down the stairs and break a hip? Or a nail?'

'Are you being facetious?'

'I don't think so,' said Dara, who wasn't entirely sure what being facetious involved.

'Oh, of course you weren't, Dara. I'm sorry. It's just, well, I've been on my own the past two days and—'

'Did Electric Eddie not call in? I texted him and asked him to bring Edward for a walk,' Dara said.

Eddie was an electrician two doors up. Electric Eddie seemed like a lazy name to call him, but that's what everyone called him nonetheless.

'Oh that fella.' Miss Pettigrew's tone was brisk with impatience. 'All he ever wants to do is *fix* things.' It was true that Eddie was a kind man who had repaired many an appliance in both the Floods' and Miss Pettigrew's house. Dara told Miss Pettigrew that he was only being helpful. Miss Pettigrew called it a *fixation*.

'I've baked macaroons,' Dara told her next-door neighbour. In fact, she had baked many, many things. That was what Dara Flood did when she couldn't sleep. She baked.

'I *am* fond of your macaroons,' Miss Pettigrew had to admit, as Dara knew she would.

'I'll bring some in.'

'Now?' There was a childlike hopefulness in the question that made Dara feel shabby. She should have visited yesterday. Even for five minutes. Angel and Mrs Flood would not have noticed her absence.

'I'm on my way,' Dara told her.

'Don't inconvenience yourself,' Miss Pettigrew sniffed down the phone, her tone haughty, now that she knew Dara was coming round. 'Not on my account.'

Dara crept upstairs, careful to avoid the second step from the top that creaked on contact. She pressed her ear against Angel's shut bedroom door. Nothing. From the landing, she could hear the lap of water against the sides of the bath and the drip-drip-drip of the cold tap. It had been doing that for weeks now. She'd have to get Electric Eddie in to have a look at it.

Dara left the house for the first time in two days with a degree of guilty relief.

Miss Pettigrew hadn't left her house for five years. When Dara first began walking Edward – only a pup back then – Miss Pettigrew still ventured out the odd time. To the shops or the vet's or – occasionally – as far as St Anne's Park. She never went into the park of course, just made it as far as the gates and turned back. That was the measure of a very good day, back then.

But for the past five years, as far as Dara could work out, she hadn't been out of the house at all.

Not that you'd know to look at her. She had the sprightly gait of a woman many years her junior. Even though she'd never told Dara what age she was and Dara was much too polite to ask. But she'd lived next door to the Floods for years. Long before Mr Flood walked up the road and never came back. Liver spots stained her long, slender hands, and despite the lotions and potions that she rubbed into the soft skin of her face by day and by night, it was the wrinkles that had the upper hand there, criss-crossing her skin like railway tracks at a busy junction. Her hair was snow-white and she wore it in a bun that sat like a Danish pastry at the nape of her neck. It kept her warm, she said. She refused to wear her glasses, even though she couldn't see a thing without them and she painted her face with the ardent attention of a debutante.

Dara knocked her usual knock on the back door – three

slow knocks followed by two short raps – before she let herself in with the key Miss Pettigrew had given her years before.

The house smelled like it always did: of Edward and 4711, the scent that Miss Pettigrew favoured.

'Hello,' Dara called out. 'It's me.'

'Of course it's you,' said Miss Pettigrew from the front room. 'Who else would it be?' Her voice retained its clipped British accent. As if she'd never left London all those years ago.

'Well, it might be a burglar. Or someone selling cobblelocking,' said Dara, taking off her grey anorak and setting a plate of macaroons on the counter.

She could hear Miss Pettigrew struggling out of the huge armchair where she sat at the front window so she could 'keep an eye on things'.

'Those door-to-door bandits don't bother me any more. Not after the last time.'

She appeared at the kitchen door, much smaller than her voice suggested. Tiny, really. But perfectly formed. Today, her nails – long and always immaculately manicured – were purple. 'Purple is *in*,' she said when Dara admired them.

'What happened the last time?' Dara asked, putting the kettle on and taking milk out of the fridge. She took this opportunity to scan the shelves, as she always did, checking the stocks. Mostly dog food, but she could also see three eggs and a triangle of Brie as well as a tin of tuna, open. 'I'll just put the rest of this into a Tupperware container, OK?' she said, lifting the tuna out. 'It'll keep better.'

'You and your Tupperware,' said Miss Pettigrew, shaking her head. 'One of these days, 1979 is going to give you a call and ask for its Tupperware back, you know.'

Dara scalded the teapot with boiling water before putting the three heaped spoons of leaves in, just the way Miss Pettigrew liked it.

'Dara my dear girl. Is that a *man's* shirt you're wearing?' said Miss Pettigrew.

'Eh . . .' Dara looked down at her shirt. A cotton one. Navy. A good, sensible colour to wear to work. And at weekends. Great for hiding dog hairs and drool stains. That was the criteria by which Dara did most of her shopping. 'No,' she said. 'I don't think so. Why?'

'The buttons are on the wrong side,' said Miss Pettigrew, shaking her head. 'And really, Dara. Navy? Would it kill you to wear some other colour for a change? And you can't even tell if you've got any breasts, it's that shapeless.'

'I *have* got breasts,' Dara said, looking down at herself.

'Not in that . . . that get-up you don't,' said Miss Pettigrew, putting a slice of bread into the toaster.

'Is that all you're having for your lunch?' Dara asked, nodding towards the toaster.

'I had my lunch earlier,' she replied, but Dara knew it was a lie. It was the telltale appearance of two bright pink spots on Miss Pettigrew's cheekbones, the height of which she was very proud.

'I'll poach you an egg to go on top of your toast, OK?' Dara said.

'Only if I can put as much salt as I want on it,' said Miss Pettigrew, her mouth set in a straight line.

'Fine,' sighed Dara. 'But I don't know how you're still alive, with all the salt you eat.

'It's *because* of all the salt I eat that I'm still alive,' said Miss Pettigrew. 'It's a preservative, you know.' Because there was no arguing with Miss Pettigrew, Dara didn't. Instead she poached an egg, buttered the toast, poured tea into Miss Pettigrew's favourite china cup and put everything on a tray. She looked away when Miss Pettigrew picked up the salt cellar and watched the line of traffic outside instead. She knew her neighbour was waiting for the right moment to ask her what was going on. And Dara would tell her. Of course she would. She just needed to work out how to begin.

'Where's Edward?' Dara asked instead.

'Upstairs,' replied Miss Pettigrew. 'He's in a huff. Just because I bathed him this afternoon.'

Edward was bathed much more often than necessary, in Dara's opinion. Granted, he was a white poodle and any stains on his coat were immediately obvious. But there never *were* any stains on Edward's coat. Miss Pettigrew simply didn't permit it.

'I'll get him,' Miss Pettigrew said, putting the tray down on a stool. She'd only eaten half the egg and a quarter of the slice of toast but she'd drained the tea and hadn't refused the bar of Bournville that Dara always brought, so at least that was something.

In the kitchen, Dara returned the egg poacher to the second drawer, where it lived along with the bread knife, the cheese grater and the only photograph Miss Pettigrew kept of herself and Manus MacBride. As far as Dara knew, they had never actually made it as far as the altar. But there had been a promise of an altar. And vows. And a happy-ever-after that turned out to be not so happy after all. Dara wiped the dust from the surface of the framed photograph with her thumb. Miss Pettigrew was beautiful back then. Still tiny, with long blond hair like a halo around her head. Her face tilts towards the sun, giving it a hopeful air. A ghost of a smile haunts her delicate features. Behind her stands Manus MacBride. Her fiancé. The man she left London for. The man with the promises that he turned out to be brilliant at breaking. That he was handsome, there could be no doubt. Devilishly handsome, with dark hair falling across a square forehead and those blue eyes, bright with possibilities. In hindsight, it was easy to imagine him as a man who would break hearts. Well, one heart anyway. Miss Pettigrew's. And the truth was she never got over it. And she never returned to London. Too ashamed, she told Dara once, after two glasses of sweet sherry one Friday evening.

Dara heard her coming down the stairs and replaced the photograph in the drawer, closing it quickly. Miss Pettigrew entered the kitchen, her nose buried in the crook of Edward's neck.

'I know, my darling,' she whispered into the tight perm of his coat. 'But Mummy was only trying to wash you, poppet. Because of the nasty dirt on your paw-paws.' Dara looked at Edward's paws. They were as white as the fleece on Mary's lamb. Dara stretched her arms out. 'Here, give him to me.'

Edward, who loved Dara almost as much as he loved Miss Pettigrew, allowed himself to be passed along. He licked Dara's neck before draping his front paws over her shoulders and moving his wet nose through her short dark hair. That made her laugh. It was a relief to laugh. She laughed louder than she usually would. And for longer.

'So,' said Miss Pettigrew, settling herself once again in her armchair by the window. 'It's bad news, isn't it?' The right moment, it seemed, had arrived. But it didn't feel right. Nothing did. Dara lifted one of Edward's toys off the couch before lowering herself on to it. She opened her mouth to say something but nothing came out. She nodded instead. For a while, Miss Pettigrew said nothing either. Just sat in her chair with her head down, as if she were saying a prayer, with her eyes squeezed shut. When she opened them again, the faded blue of her eyes were bright and Dara knew that if she blinked, a tear might slide down the almost translucent skin of her face in a way that would be unbearable to watch. Dara had never heard Miss Pettigrew cry, but she imagined the sound she might make. A quiet sound. Hollow with a lifetime of loss. Mournful. Like the whimpering of one of her dogs at the pound, recently abandoned. Dara couldn't bear to hear a sound like that. Not today.

She leaned forward and took one of Miss Pettigrew's long, thin hands in her own. She could feel the old lady's bones through the soft skin, delicate as crêpe paper. Dara patted her hand: It was not one that could be squeezed. After a while, Miss Pettigrew collected herself, drawing her hand back, using it to pat the Danish-pastry bun that kept her warm. She didn't look warm. She looked cold. Cold and old. Dara looked away.

'At first I thought it might be good news,' Miss Pettigrew said, after a while. 'When you scorched off in the car in the middle of the night. But then you came back so soon. The three of you. And when you didn't call in yesterday, well . . . I thought . . . I was afraid that . . .' Dara often wondered if Miss Pettigrew ever actually slept, but Miss Pettigrew said that sleep was overrated and anyway, wouldn't there be plenty of time for all that later? When her time came?

'I'm really sorry,' said Dara. 'I should have come in. But Angel, well, she isn't very well at the moment and I didn't like to leave her on her own.'

'Was there a kidney?' Miss Pettigrew asked.

'Yes,' said Dara. 'But it wasn't suitable in the end. We had to come back.'

'You've been through a lot,' Miss Pettigrew said, patting Dara's head as if she were patting her bun.

'I haven't been through anything. It's Angel, she's been waiting for so long and—'

'You've been waiting too. Just as much. You've put your whole life on hold.'

'No, it's not the same, I—'

'Life is short, Dara Flood. You wouldn't believe how short. You can't afford to waste one minute. Not one. Not when you're young.' Miss Pettigrew looked at her hands when she said this. She hated her hands. They were always on show, she said. They gave you away.

'How is Mrs Flood?' she asked then. Dara shrugged and shook her head.

'She's in bed. She's got a migraine.'

'She's lucky she has you to keep things going,' said Miss Pettigrew. Dara nodded but said nothing. She was not sure her mother would consider herself blessed in this regard.

'I just wish there was something I could do,' Dara went on.

'Sure, don't you do so much already?' Miss Pettigrew told her. 'You keep Angel company on your days off, when she's going to her dialysis. You're always cooking and baking for her. Making the few bits of food the poor girl's allowed to eat taste lovely. Well? Aren't you?'

'No, I mean something practical. Something that would help. If I could have been a match for her . . .' Dara's voice dribbled away. She'd been down the road of this conversation before. Even though she knew it was a dead end.

'Macaroons,' Miss Pettigrew suddenly announced, rising from the chair so fast, Dara could hear every single bone in her back crackle like static. She turned to Dara. 'Let us eat macaroons.' As ideas went, Dara had to admit it wasn't a bad one. They ended up eating the lot, with whipped cream and chocolate ice cream and a glass of sherry, which Dara drank even though she wasn't fond of its syrupy sweetness. But Miss Pettigrew didn't like to drink alone in the afternoon – she called that the 'slippery slope' – so Dara drank the sherry with her.

Edward had his sherry from the china dog bowl Dara had bought him. ('Just a tiny bit every day, it does him the world of good,' Miss Pettigrew insisted whenever Dara expressed concerns about his habitual alcoholic intake.) Then he swallowed two macaroons without chewing before he ran to get his lead and his coat, which he placed in front of Dara's feet.

'I'd better bring him for a walk,' Dara said, getting up.

'I wonder is it a bit cold?' Miss Pettigrew's forehead wrinkled in concern and they looked out the window. It was one of those early spring afternoons that holds a tentative promise of summer. Mild and still, with fingers of heat reaching through the window and warming their faces. It was not cold.

'Just a short one. I'll need to get back to the house,' Dara said, attaching the lead to Edward's collar. 'I have to bring Angel to the hospital for her dialysis.' Dara wasn't entirely sure how she was going to get Angel out of her bedroom, but she didn't share these concerns with Miss Pettigrew. She felt that she had had enough for one day.

'You won't overexert him, will you?' Miss Pettigrew fondled the poodle's head.

'Don't worry. We'll be back before you know it,' Dara said, standing up. 'You could come with us if you like?'

'Not today, thank you, Dara dear.' Her usual response. 'Besides, *Countdown* is starting in a minute.' She offered her face to Edward. 'Give Mummy her kissies now, Edward darling,' and the little poodle obliged, stretching his head towards Miss Pettigrew and depositing two licks with his tiny pink tongue on the tip of her nose.

Edward pranced rather than walked, his head held high, his paws pointed like the toes of a prima ballerina. He was popular with the dogs on the street and insisted on stopping each time he encountered one, to sniff at their bottoms or their mouths, depending on which end was handiest.

Dara walked up the road, the same direction her father had walked all those years ago. Some days, when she walked up the road, she thought about Mr Flood. Her father. The man who walked up the road and never came back. She wondered what he had been thinking. Had he planned it in advance? Or was it a spur-of-the-moment decision? Was it the sight of the cot in its bulky box in the hall that did it? Another cot. Another baby. So soon after Angel. Mrs Flood sometimes spoke of that year. The year she got married. The year Angel came. Just one year. That's all she'd had. But she'd been happy. She looked happy when she spoke of it. There were Sunday roasts with gravy and stuffing and apple tarts, and walks in the park afterwards, with Angel in her pram and Mr Flood's hands on the bar, pushing, and Mrs Flood running to get whipped cones from the van outside the park that everyone said were the best ice creams on the north side of Dublin. Picnics on the beach with sandy ham rolls and tea made in tin cups with boiled water from a tiny gas stove. Trips to the zoo, a visit that Christmas – that one Christmas – to the moving crib on Parnell Square. When Mrs Flood tells the stories, the sun is always shining and the day is always warm. Even the day that Christmas – that one Christmas – was warm. 'I never remember a December day as warm,' Mrs Flood says, smiling into the middle distance. 'Either before or since.'

When Dara was younger, she imagined different scenarios. He'd been murdered by a serial killer who cut him up into tiny pieces and buried him in a suitcase in a shallow grave up in the Wicklow mountains. Or he'd had a terminal illness and couldn't face telling Mrs Flood, knowing that she loved him too much to cope with it. Or perhaps he fell down and banged his head off the edge of the pavement and got amnesia. That's why he never came home. Because he couldn't remember where home was ... These were some of the options Dara had considered over the years. She'd only briefly entertained the notion that he'd been abducted by aliens and that was when she was much younger and going through a virulent science-fiction phase. Even then, it had seemed a little far-fetched. Although Tintin's uncle swore he'd been abducted years ago and he *did* have funny green marks on his right shoulder that nobody could explain.

In more recent years, something had settled in Dara Flood. The most obvious explanation.

Mr Flood walked up the road and never come back. He had decided not to come back. A conscious decision had been made. There was no accident, no serial killer, no amnesia, no alien abduction.

There was just a man, who had been happy for a while. When it was only the three of them. Him, Mrs Flood and Angel. There were photographs to prove it. Still in frames, some of them, on the sideboard in the front room. Then Mrs Flood fell pregnant with Dara. That was the way she put it. And the man who had been happy for a while wasn't happy any more. Work was scarce, money was tight. Mrs Flood's lips are always pursed when she gets to this bit. The shape of them makes her voice shrill. But no matter how shrill her voice gets, how tightly she presses her lips against her teeth, the ending never changes. Mr Flood is just a man. Neither happy nor sad. A man who decides to walk up a road and never come back.

But today, Dara didn't think about Mr Flood at all. She thought about Angel. She tried to picture her smiling. But all she could see were Angel's hands over her face as she cried her barely-there cry in the back of the car. She forced herself to think something positive and hold on to that positive thought with both hands. Grip it. Concentrate on it. Like the call from the hospital. That was something positive, wasn't it? But if Dara was honest, she'd never really believed they'd get the call. Five years of waiting can do that to you, can dull your expectations. Especially if your stock is low to begin with. And now she had to persuade her sister that there would be another call. Any day now. From the hospital. Another kidney. One that would be a perfect match this time.

There *would*, Dara told herself, in a fierce kind of whisper that made Edward whimper.

Wouldn't there?

7

The invitation arrived in the post.

A pink envelope sealed with red wax that had melted in the heat of the hallway and now ran down the paper like a wound. In the line provided after the word 'Dear', Cora had written in her flowery handwriting, *Stanley and friend,* with an exclamation mark after the word *friend,* like some kind of a private joke between the two of them.

The engagement party was being held in the Odessa Club on Dame Lane. *We would love you to come and share our happiness,* the invite read. There was an RSVP, but Cora had handwritten at the bottom, *I know you're coming so you don't have to bother RSVPing. C. xxx*

Stanley crumpled the page and threw it towards the bin. It glanced off the edge and landed on the floor beside his feet. He kicked it. Clouseau – who thought this might be the start of some new game – barked loudly and ran to retrieve the ball of paper, returning it to Stanley's feet and headbutting Stanley's knees until he had no choice but to pick the page up once more and throw it. Clouseau barked, ran to retrieve it and dropped it once more at Stanley's feet.

'What kind of presents do people bring to engagement parties?' he asked Sissy.

'A present for the engagement of your ex-girlfriend who is marrying your brother?' mused Sissy. 'It's a tricky one. My advice would be nothing.'

'I can't go with nothing.'

'OK, then. A bottle of whiskey.'

'But Cora hates whiskey.'

'Precisely,' Sissy told him, clicking her tongue with impatience. 'And you should bring someone. Someone fabulous, all legs and hair. I could lend you Kay, she's not too tall, she'd be perfect.'

Kay was one of Sissy's colleagues, as far as Stanley remembered. A fashion journalist, he thought. 'You can't *lend* me someone, like a . . . a book or something. Besides, I thought she was gay?' Stanley said.

'Cora doesn't have to know that, does she?' said Sissy, smacking her big lips in satisfaction.

Stanley shook his head. He wasn't into game-playing. There had been enough of that. It was time to get on with things. Accept this changed landscape of his life, and move on. Wasn't Sissy blue in the face telling him that?

'You could come with me?' Stanley said.

Sissy stopped what she was doing – sitting on the counter and eating Doritos from a party-sized bag – and looked at him. 'You know I'd do anything for you, don't you, Stanley?' she asked him, dropping her face towards his to make sure he could hear her. He nodded. He knew. 'Except this,' Sissy added. 'And it's for your own good, too.'

Stanley sighed. In his experience, things that people did for his own good were never the things that he wanted them to do.

'Fine,' was all he said.

'Don't bother your arse going,' Sissy said, getting back to the Doritos.

'I have to. It'll be awkward if I don't.'

'Don't you ever get tired of doing the right thing?' Sissy asked him. Stanley didn't have to think about the answer to that one. He *did* get tired.

She jumped off the counter and threw the Doritos bag – emptied even of crumbs, much to Clouseau's disappointment – into the bin. Stanley watched it go straight in. 'Now, I'm going to wax my upper lip, clip my toenails and trim my bush, if you'll excuse me.'

Stanley winced. 'I thought we agreed that you'd just call it personal grooming?' he reminded her.

'I know, but I like to be specific, you know that.' Sissy blew him a kiss before taking the stairs two at a time, making the two upturned wine glasses on the draining board shudder.

He rang Adrian to see if he had any ideas about a gift for the engagement party.

'I'm on a stakeout,' Adrian told him in a voice that was stiff with boredom.

'Shouldn't you have your mobile switched off?' said Stanley, lowering his voice automatically.

'I have it on silent.'

'Well, can you talk?' Stanley asked.

'Yeah. Nothing's happening here. I think we got a bum steer.' Stanley heard the rustle of a paper bag and guessed that Adrian was shoring up his boredom with doughnuts. He had a low boredom threshold and a very sweet tooth.

'I was just ringing about the engagement party. Do you have any ideas about—'

'Aw shite, we don't have to go, do we?' Adrian spluttered through a mouthful.

'Well, I— '

'I mean, I'll go to the wedding no bother, but an engagement party as well? That's above and beyond, man.'

'Anyway, the thing is—'

'Declan didn't have an engagement party, did he?'

'Well, no, he didn't but they were going to, remember? Him and Cathy. Only Cathy . . .'

'Oh yeah, it's coming back to me now. She did something to her eyebrows, didn't she?'

'And her fringe. And her eyelashes and, in fact, her, eh . . .'

'"Tache?' Adrian supplied with a snigger.

Cathy was a lovely-looking girl. It was just that she had very thick, very dark hair which was indiscriminate about where it grew. Bending over the gas hob that day to light her cigarette was perhaps the best thing she ever did because, oddly, the hair on her upper lip never grew back. The lashes, eyebrows and fringe made it back just in time for the wedding day, but the engagement party had to be cancelled.

Stanley waited for Adrian to stop laughing. 'Anyway, I wondered if you'd had any thoughts about a gift.'

'A wedding gift?'

'Well, that too. But no, I was thinking about a gift for the engagement party.'

'Aw Jaysus, we don't have to buy a present for that too, do we?'

Stanley sighed and wondered why he had bothered phoning Adrian.

'Oh, hang about,' Adrian whispered down the phone.

'What? Have you had an idea?'

'About what?'

'Eh, about a gift? For the engagement party?'

'Christ, no. But I have to go now, Stanley. The Baddies have arrived, thank fuck.'

Adrian was good at his job on the vice squad, but sometimes Stanley felt that he played it, like the games of Cops 'n' Robbers when they were kids. Stanley worried about this. 'Take care,' he told his brother.

'Listen, whatever you get for them, say it's from both of us and I'll throw a few quid your way, yeah?'

'Yes, but that's the thing, I don't quite know what . . .'

But the line had gone dead.

*   *   *

When he rang Neal, all his brother wanted to know was if he could bring Freda the barmaid.

'I thought you'd given up on her?' Stanley asked.

'Christ, no.' Neal was stung that Stanley would entertain such a notion. 'She's sniffing at the bait. Just about to sink her teeth into the hook and then I'm going to reel her on in,' said Neal, as if he'd already snagged her.

'Nice analogy,' said Stanley.

'Nice what?'

'Oh forget it.'

Lorcan wondered about the availability of women at the party: the kind of women who were open-minded about casual, no-holds-barred, no-questions-asked, no-strings-attached, good old-fashioned sex. Stanley couldn't say for sure.

He didn't ring Declan, in case Cathy answered the phone. She had taken the cancellation of her engagement party badly and he didn't want to bring back painful memories. Besides, Declan was probably the worst of them for presents. Last Christmas he had given their mother a tub of Silcock's Base.

'It's an emollient moisturiser,' he'd explained, smiling.

'What's an emollient moisturiser?' Stanley had asked him.

'If you don't know by now, there's no point in my telling you,' Declan told him snippily, which led Stanley to the conclusion that his brother had no idea what an emollient moisturiser might be either.

'Oh . . . thanks, love,' said Mrs Flinter faintly. She couldn't say anything else. After all, it was she who'd beaten into her boys from an early age that they should appreciate any gifts they ever got, because '*it's the thought that counts, isn't it?*'

★   ★   ★

So that left Cormac. And while his eldest brother would have no hesitation in recommending a gift for himself and Cora, Stanley didn't want him to know that he had given it this much thought.

8

It was the little things that Dara noticed most. The little things that she missed.

Like the dishwasher, and how Angel used to insist on stacking it in a particular way. The cutlery separated in compartments of knives, forks, spoons and *implements*. Implements were anything that didn't fit into a particular category. Things like potato peelers, apple corers, spatulas. Wooden spoons were not allowed. They had to be washed by hand. Angel had a system. An exacting one. The plates stacked in height order: tall ones at the back, saucers in front. The cups with their handles facing out, all the better to lift them when unloading.

Dara remembered this now. This small thing. She remembered it every time she opened the dishwasher door. Because now, there was no method. No system. There were just dishes. Dirty ones. Clean ones. Dirty ones. The cycle went on and on but the order was gone.

With Angel spending so much time in her room, Dara and Mrs Flood found themselves alone together. The relationship between them chafed, like a pair of new shoes that worry at your heels.

Dara did her best to fill the quiet with conversation that soured as it dribbled between them, like milk forgotten on a doorstep.

'I think Angel is a bit brighter today, don't you?'

Mrs Flood shook her head, not looking at Dara.

Dara persisted. 'I mean, she's not back to her old self or anything, but . . .'

'She's *nothing* like her old self,' Mrs Flood spat.

'No, you're right, of course. I just meant . . .' Dara stopped. She didn't know what she just meant. Her mother was right. Angel was nothing like her old self.

Mrs Flood looked at Dara. 'I hate the way you do that,' she said.

'Do what?'

'Stop talking right in the middle of a sentence. It's annoying.'

'I know. I'm sorry. It's just . . .'

'There you go. You're doing it again.'

'No, I'm not, I just . . .'

Mrs Flood leaned against the back of the armchair and closed her eyes. The conversation, such as it was, was over. Dara moved to the door of the sitting room. From behind, she heard her mother talking. She turned around. Mrs Flood sat in the armchair, shaking her head, her knitting discarded on her lap in a woolly knot.

'Sorry?' Dara asked.

Mrs Flood looked at her, as if surprised she was still in the room. She shook her head. 'It just doesn't seem fair, does it?'

'What do you mean?'

'I mean, why *Angel*? Why does this have to happen to *her*? When she's got so much to live for?'

When she replayed the comment back in her mind in the middle of the night, it was difficult not to conclude that Mrs Flood would have preferred it if *Dara* was the one with the end-stage renal failure.

Dara did not answer. Instead, she escaped to the kitchen to make pastry, kneading the dough with the weight of her whole body, both hands curled into fists.

'Isn't it well for you, Dara?' said Mrs Flood when she came into the kitchen to make a cup of tea. 'Nothing to worry about, only apple tarts? Of course, your father was like that. Carefree.'

Dara felt a gush of relief when the doorbell rang.

'I'll get it,' she said, wiping her floury hands on her jeans as she made a dash for the door.

It was Joe. Dara smiled when she saw him. Everyone did. 'Ridiculously handsome,' Tintin had tutted after his first introduction to the fireman. And he was. He was the type of handsome that would make you believe in fairy tales. In happy-ever-afters. Tall, with long legs, a long body and wide shoulders. Cropped hair, nearly as dark as Dara's.

He only ever wore jeans and T-shirts when he wasn't at work, but even these modest threads looked like they'd been made to measure.

'A great sense of *style*,' Miss Pettigrew had sighed, her eyes sliding down Joe's body after he'd installed the smoke alarm in her hall and landing. Her eyes watered as they settled on the outline of Joe's bum against the faded denim of his jeans. She smiled, like everyone did.

'Handy,' Mrs Flood conceded after he'd fixed her favourite but ancient hairdryer with nothing more than a piece of elastic and a hairclip.

His eyes were the colour of the sea in a brochure for someplace hot and exotic. Today, Dara noticed that they didn't crinkle into slits as they usually did. He looked tired. And uneasy, standing on the step with his hands jammed into his pockets.

'Joe, it's lovely to see you,' said Dara, opening the door wide. 'Come on in.'

'Hi, Dara,' he said. He had to bend slightly to get through the front door. The hallway narrowed as he stepped inside.

'I'll tell Angel you're here,' said Dara. 'She'll be delighted.' Joe dragged his hands down his face. 'Are you all right?' asked Dara, pausing at the stairs.

'I'm grand,' said Joe, stuffing his hands back into his pockets. 'I just . . . I haven't seen her since the hospital. I suppose I'm a bit . . .'

'She hasn't seen anyone since then,' Dara hurried to reassure him. 'She hasn't been herself. But maybe she's getting back on track. She wants to see you now. She called you.'

'She e-mailed me,' Joe said in a low voice.

'Oh.'

'Joe, how lovely to see you.' The kitchen door opened and light fell through the hall, landing on Joe like a spotlight.

'Kathleen. How are you?' Joe was the only man Dara knew who called her mother Kathleen. After her initial scepticism about the fireman – and indeed about any of the boyfriends her daughters brought home – Mrs Flood had allowed her reserve to wane and even went as far as to declare Joe a 'dote'.

'Good. I'm good. And you? How are you?'

'I'm OK. Angel asked to see me.'

'Great. That's great. She's coming around. I knew she would. I was just saying to Dara earlier how much brighter she seems.' She smiled and nodded at Dara, who smiled and nodded back. Even Joe was at it now, the three of them standing in the hall, smiling and nodding. Like if they smiled and nodded enough, everything would be all right. Everything would go back to the way it had been before the found-and-lost kidney.

'Joe.' Angel's voice reached them from the top of the stairs. They looked up. In the dark of the landing, her face appeared as pale as a moon, her eyes huge in her face that was gaunt now, in a way that it had never been.

'Joe's here to see you, love,' Mrs Flood called up the stairs, still smiling and nodding. Her voice was strained and anxious. It pulled at Dara.

'Could you come up?' asked Angel before she turned and walked into her bedroom. Joe looked at Dara and Mrs Flood. His smile was gone, his head no longer nodding.

'I'll bring you both a nice cup of tea,' said Mrs Flood, ushering Joe towards the foot of the stairs. 'And some apple tart. Dara's making some.'

'I'm not sure if I'll be here long enough,' said Joe quietly.

It turned out he was right.

Five minutes later, Dara heard footsteps on the stairs. Then Joe's voice, echoey in the hall.

'Angel, please, this is mad. Nothing's changed. Why can't we—'

'I'm holding you back,' she heard Angel say. The tone of her voice was firm. Rigid. She recited the words like they were lines she had learned.

'You're not. I *love* you, for God's sake.'

'I'm sick.'

'You'll get better.'

'I won't.'

'You will.'

'I won't.'

A pause. A long sigh. Joe's, Dara thought. When he spoke again, his voice was softer. Pleading. 'I love you,' he said.

There was no response to this.

'I said I love you,' said Joe, louder this time.

'I'm sorry.' Dara could barely make out the words. Her sister's voice was a whisper.

'Tell me you don't love me and I'll go. I'll never call you again.'

Dara squirmed in her seat in the sitting room. She crossed her fingers and sat on them. She held her breath. She waited.

'I don't love you.' Angel didn't sound like herself when she said that. She sounded like someone else. Someone Dara did not know.

The front door opened and closed and Dara heard the heavy sounds of Joe's footsteps, fading and fading, until they were gone.

9

'When are you coming back to work?' Tintin asked when he phoned on the Thursday. 'The hounds grow restless.'

'Tomorrow,' Dara said, surprising herself. She suddenly realised that if she spent another day in the house, waiting for Angel – the old Angel – to come back, waiting for things to get back to normal, and trying to dodge the full-on stand-up row her mother seemed set on, she'd go mad.

'I've missed you. Everyone has,' said Tintin, before shouting at someone – probably Anya – to *spark up the roasting spit, she's coming back to us.*

In the background, Dara heard the usual cacophony of barking and whining and the rattling of cages and the pitter-patter of tiny paws – probably Scrappy Doo – against the metal steps leading up to the Portakabin that Tintin called *the reception area.*

Dara could nearly smell the pound down the phone. A damp smell, sweet and strong. In her mind's eye, she saw the dogs – her charges – gathered at the gate, waiting for her. Her welcoming committee. And Tintin and Anya. Her friends. The first ones she'd ever really had, if she was honest about it. Before that, she had mostly shared Angel's friends. In school, out on the road. Everybody wanted to be Angel's friend, and because Dara came as part of Angel's package, they were friends with Dara too. That was the deal.

Dara began volunteering at the pound when she was seventeen. She had always wanted a dog, a puppy really, but Mrs

Flood had said no, it was hard enough trying to raise two women on her own, without having to clean up after a dog too. It was Angel's idea. Volunteering at the pound. She'd seen an ad in a local newspaper. Volunteers needed, with a list of things they would be expected to do. Lovely things, like dog walking and grooming and cleaning out kennels and feeding. It would be better than having a dog of her own. It would be like having lots of dogs of her own. Of course, the tricky part was saying goodbye to them when a family came to take them away. Or worse, when nobody came to take them away and the vet arrived to put down the ones that nobody wanted.

But, Dara reasoned, there's a down side to everything, and perhaps, some day, she might come to accept the transient nature of the pound. Of course she never did. Not really. But she became more used to the comings and goings of her charges.

'Our job,' Anya often said in her most serious voice, which sounded even more serious in her low purr of a Polish accent, 'is to find them their home.' Dara liked that. The idea that there was a home out there for everyone: it was just a question of finding it. Like Tintin said about OTLs (One True Loves). There was one for everyone, apparently. Except maybe Owen Wilson, Tintin said.

'What's wrong with Owen Wilson?' Dara felt this was unfair, being fond of the actor. One of her favourite films was *The Darjeeling Limited*. 'A bunch of misfits,' Mrs Flood concluded at the end of the DVD. Dara couldn't agree more.

'His nose. It's too much,' Tintin said, shaking his head.

'It's just been broken a couple of times, I think,' Dara told him. 'It gives him a bit of character.'

'It gives him a crooked schnozz is all,' Tintin said. 'And didn't he try to top himself?' He always sounded authoritative on the subject of celebrities, even though his main source of information was *Heat* and *Now*.

'He was just depressed. Are you saying depressed people with slightly crooked noses don't deserve a One True Love?'

'I'm not saying *all* depressed people,' Tintin conceded. 'But there's nothing slight about the bend in yer man's nose.'

Dara longed for a conversation like that now. Tintin had made her laugh right from the beginning. He said he loved making her laugh. That she laughed like a person trying not to laugh. Anya made her laugh too, although she would often frown whenever Tintin and Dara fell around the place at something Anya had said. Like the time she told them about the dinner party at her boyfriend's house. Her ex-boyfriend now, naturally enough, after someone at the table 'insulted my heritage'. Anya picked up the box containing the strawberry cheesecake she had made ('I bought it in deli, but still . . .') and headed for the door, pausing at each guest to pick up their portion of cheesecake and throw it into the box.

'Vat is so funny?' she would ask, frowning at the pair of them. 'I haf not told joke.'

'I've missed you too,' Dara told Tintin down the phone.

'Jaysus, that's a bit *Lassie Come Home*, isn't it?' Tintin said. 'The gallops have turned your insides to mush as well as your—'

'The gallops?'

'The gallops, the runs, the trots, call it what you will, so long as it's some form of horse's gait, apparently.'

'Oh yeah.' Dara bit her lip.

'How's Angel, by the way?' Tintin's voice softened. He loved Angel nearly as much as Dara did.

Dara did not answer immediately. Angel was out. Gone to dialysis. Since her conversation with Joe last night, Dara felt that her sister, for the first time ever, looked like a proper sick person. Wan and thin. Bloated and yet drained somehow of some essential part of herself that had made everyone call her Angel.

'I'll grab my coat,' Dara said to her, as she made her way down the stairs with one hand gripping the banister.

'Dara,' said Angel, and Dara knew what she was going to say. Still, she reached for her coat in the cloakroom under the stairs. 'You don't have to come. It's OK.'

Dara turned around, her coat in her hand. 'It's all right. I want to come. I'll keep you company.'

Angel shook her head, avoiding Dara's eyes. 'No, Dara, it's . . . I don't want you to come. Not any more. You've other things to be doing.'

Dara put on her coat and zipped it up to her chin, like a statement of intent. Angel shook her head again. 'I'm going on my own,' she said. She picked her keys up from the hall table and moved to the door.

'But I always come with you. When I'm not working.' Dara hated the way she sounded. Petulant. Needy. But it was true. She often went to the hospital and kept Angel company beside the dialysis machine. They read books or shared a set of earphones plugged into Angel's iPod. They played cards. Gin Rummy, usually.

'There's too much waiting around. You've done enough waiting on my account. I . . . I'll be fine on my own.' Angel opened the front door.

'But nothing's *changed*,' Dara insisted. She wanted to grab Angel and shake her.

'It's lovely of you to want to come. I appreciate it. Really I do. But I could be on dialysis for a long time. Years. I think that's likely. It's too much to expect you to spend all that time with me. And I don't. I don't expect you to. There's no point in the two of us wasting our time, is there?' The car keys hung from Angel's fingers. They shook slightly, making the keys rattle against each other. A grinding, grating sound.

Angel turned and walked out. Dara, still in her coat, followed her. Angel opened the car door and arranged herself behind the wheel. For a moment, she looked like she wasn't sure what to do next. Dara leaped into the pause.

'But I took the day off so I could come and keep you company.'

Angel concentrated on the steering wheel in front of her. 'You shouldn't have done that. I never asked you to,' she said. It sounded like an apology, the way she said it.

Dara waited, but still Angel would not look at her.

'I'll be late.' Angel reversed down the driveway, her mouth tightly closed, as if she was fighting an urge to scream out loud.

There was nothing Dara could do but watch her leave.

'She's gone to dialysis,' was all she said to Tintin.

'You sound funny,' said Tintin, using his ordinary voice, which he did occasionally when he was being serious. 'Is everything OK?'

'Yes, of course. I just need to go and . . . iron some clothes for tomorrow.'

'Iron clothes? Now I *know* something is up. Next you'll be telling me you took my advice and bought yourself the Mac eyeshadow I was raving about. *Nobody* does shimmery green like Mac.'

'No, I haven't.'

'You haven't what?'

'Bought the eyeshadow.'

'Well, that's a relief then. I was starting to get worried. So there's nothing you need to talk to Tintin about?' Even Tintin called himself Tintin.

'It can wait.'

'So there *is* something?'

'I'll see you tomorrow, OK?'

'You can't leave me like this!' Tintin shrieked down the

phone. 'There can't be something that Tintin doesn't know. It's not right.'

'Goodbye, Tintin.'

He was still protesting in the strongest terms as she hung up the phone.

IO

Stanley finally settled on Newbridge candlestick holders. He felt they were impersonal enough so that nothing could be read into them. And yet thoughtful. He knew Cora was fond of candlelight. She said she looked her best in candlelight and he had to agree that she *did* look very well. Although, now he thought about it, perhaps they weren't impersonal enough. Wasn't candlelight a little intimate? In the circumstances.

By the time he got home, he'd managed to convince himself that the candles were fine. Grand. They would do. At least he wouldn't have to worry about a gift any more.

'What's wrong with you?' Sissy asked him when he came in the door.

'Nothing. Why?' It was difficult to make out what Stanley was saying, as Clouseau got a hold of him and slow-danced him across the kitchen, his massive front legs in their usual choking position around Stanley's neck.

'You were sort of smiling when you came in.' That might be true, Stanley thought. He had a habit of sort of smiling when he felt relieved, as he did now. He wouldn't have to think about the engagement party again until he had to go to it.

'It was your idea, remember? Smile, and the world smiles back at you type of thing?' Stanley wrestled with Clouseau and finally managed to set him down on the floor in the more traditional all-fours stance. To keep him there, he had to pull at the dog's ears and keep his own face within licking distance of Clouseau's mouth. He wasn't fond of the scratchy feel of the dog's long flat tongue up the side of his face, but he hadn't worked out any other way to calm him.

'Yes, but I've been saying that to you for ages. You've never actually taken me up on it.'

Out of the corner of his eye, Stanley saw Sissy examining him closely. She got off the couch where she had been *zinging* herself, as she called it, with the Ab Rocker strapped around her middle as she watched *EastEnders* and ate chocolate fudge ice cream straight out of the tub.

'You've had a good day, haven't you?' she said, circling him now, stroking her chin with her fingers.

'Eh, yes, I suppose so, I mean it was grand, nothing startling.' Clouseau, bored with the face-licking and the ear-pulling, now pushed Stanley onto the floor with his massive head and stood over him, his four gigantic paws arranged like tree trunks around Stanley's pinioned body.

'Clouseau, heel!' Sissy said in a bored kind of a voice, as if this was something she'd said many times before, which it was. The dog gave her his sullen look before moving away from Stanley and coming to heel beside her. She didn't even pet him or say 'good dog' or give him a dog biscuit, like they tell you to do in all of the dog training books that Stanley read.

'How do you do that?' asked Stanley, getting up as quick as he could before Clouseau changed his mind.

'You're just too soft with him,' Sissy told him – and not for the first time either. 'I'm going to make us some dinner-ding and then you can tell me what that smile is doing skulking around your face,' she added, leaving the room at a gallop.

Stanley hated 'dinner-ding', but with the recent move to the office on Abbey Street, he hadn't had time to do his usual grocery shopping.

Sissy loved when Stanley didn't have time to do his usual grocery shopping because then he didn't cook and bake, which meant that she could indulge her passion for dinner-dings.

Ciara Geraghty

Not that she didn't love Stanley's cooking and baking, but he did it so laboriously and with such care, it took much longer than Sissy – an instant gratification type of a woman – liked. With dinner-ding, it was four minutes in the micro-wave, *ding,* and then served on your knees in front of the telly.

'Tell me everything,' Sissy commanded, setting the plastic container of beef stroganoff on Stanley's knees.

'There's nothing to tell, I . . .'

Sissy leaned over to the coffee table, picked up the remote and switched off the telly. Then she fixed him with the look she called *stoic* and pointed at him with a loaded fork.

'Tell. Me. Everything,' she repeated.

Stanley really did not want to tell Sissy the reason for his smile. A pair of fecking Newbridge candlesticks, for Christ's sake. People don't smile for candles. Not even when you've finally managed to decide on an engagement gift for your brother who's marrying the woman you used to go out with. The woman you used to love. Until your brother decided that *he* would love her instead. And she agreed. Not even then.

He sighed and set the plastic tray on the floor, forgetting about Clouseau, who wolfed up the beef stroganoff with one long lap of his tongue.

'That's a terrible waste, Stanley. That was a Marks & Spencer's dinner-ding, you know. They're not cheap.'

'I know, I know, I'm sorry,' said Stanley. 'I keep forgetting about his insatiable appetite.'

'You'll have to do something about that dog,' said Sissy, quickly spooning her dinner into her mouth before Clouseau got any ideas. 'He needs a stern hand and that's not something you possess.'

Stanley shook his head and sighed. This was true. But June Robinson had been most insistent when she told him she'd leave him the dog in her will. 'Every private detective needs a dog,' she'd said. 'You'll be like Turner and Hooch.' As this was one of the very few films that Stanley had not seen, he couldn't comment. And while June Robinson was a little old lady when she'd said it, Stanley could have had no way of knowing that she would shuffle off her mortal coil quite so soon.

'Actually, I was thinking of hiring someone,' Stanley said, settling himself on the couch and scraping out the last of Sissy's ice cream.

'Who? A hit man for Cora? I'm sure you're not the first man to think that particular thought. It's a gem, by the way. You have my support.'

'Someone for Clouseau. A dog trainer. Or a psychologist maybe. Are there dog psychologists? I'm sure there must be.'

'Yer man doesn't need therapy. He just needs a firm hand, Stanley. A firm hand.'

'Yes, but you've already said I don't happen to have one of those.'

'So, why were you smiling when you got in from work today?'

'I have no idea. It just happened.'

'Stuff like that happens to other people,' Sissy told him with her trademark conviction. 'Not to the likes of you.'

There was no getting away from her. He told her about the candlesticks.

'Jaysus. I can't believe you got them Newbridge. It's not too late for me to melt them down and make earrings for us.'

Stanley smiled at her. 'So, what do you think about my idea?'

'What idea?'

'About a dog trainer. For Clouseau.'

'Grand, grand,' said Sissy, 'I'll get a name and number for you. Samantha at work just got a Pomeranian. They usually need therapy, don't they? Small dog syndrome probably. I'll ask her.'

'Thanks.'

'But to get back to the Newbridge . . .'

'Aw Sissy, come on. I got them a present. That's it. I had to. You know that.'

'I know, I know, calm down. All I'm saying is . . . it's time.'

'For what?' He checked his watch. He didn't think *You Are What You Eat* was on for another hour, at least.

'For you. To move on.'

'Move on?'

'Yes, Stanley. Move on. You were smiling when you came in here tonight. I haven't seen you smile in ages. Months. It's time.'

'It's too soon. I'll get over the hump of the engagement party and the wedding and then—'

'It's time, Stanley,' Sissy told him grimly. 'Now pass me the remote. *Operation Transformation* is starting.'

11

Dara found it difficult to concentrate at work. This was the first day they had left Angel alone in the house, although Mrs Flood said she'd just give Mrs Butcher her weekly frizz control treatment and be home by lunchtime. Angel's doctor had given her a sick cert for a week, and even though the week was nearly up, there had been no mention of a return to her much-loved job as special resource teacher at the local primary school.

'I'm fine. Just a little tired,' Angel told Dara every time she rang.

Dara knew why she was tired. She heard her, every night. Now, it seemed, there were two sleepwalkers in the house. Although Angel wasn't asleep when she walked. She was wide awake.

It was hard to accept that, for everyone else, it was just another day. Dara hadn't yet told Tintin and Anya about the found-and-lost kidney. She would. Right after Tintin finished talking. She thought he was debating the pros and cons of taking *a lov-air* versus sustaining a long-term, stable relationship. The latter appealed to Tintin in theory. It was the reality that never lived up to his expectations.

'Take you, for instance,' he said as Dara shed some of her layers in the Portakabin, which was always either too hot or too cold. With the sudden onslaught of spring in the past few days, the precarious little hut was veering towards too hot.

'What?'

'Well, *you've* taken a lov-air. How does it compare to your basic Monday-to-Friday, nine-to-five type of relationship?'

'I've never taken a lov-air in my life,' Dara told him. 'I'm not that type of person.'

Tintin disagreed. 'Ian Harte is older, he's got a proper, grown-up job and he talks to you after *considerate* sex. That makes him a *lov-air,*' he told her, with his usual flourish of authority.

It was Friday morning. One of the busiest days at the pound.

'Kimberley is off her grub this morning,' Dara said, picking up the mound of clothes that she had removed from her person and shoving them into the cupboard they called the cloakroom.

'No, she's not,' Tintin told her. 'She's just full.'

'What did you give her?'

'Nothing. The bitch stole my full-Irish-in-a-bap from the pocket of my jacket when I arrived. She got Fleur to distract me with her Pilates routine.' Tintin shook his head, equal parts disgust and grudging admiration.

Fleur had been left at the pound some weeks earlier by a Frenchman, whose gay lover had switched back to the more conventional hetero status on meeting a woman whose father owned half of Munster *and* a thriving thermal-underwear business. "Ow can I compeeet wiz zat?' he had asked Dara that day, his tears raining down on Fleur's shaggy perm. 'Zay are loaded. Everybody in zis kip is wearing zee thermal un-dies, no?' Dara could only nod and take Fleur's lead as the man left to get the next flight home. He hadn't mentioned Fleur's penchant for Pilates, but it didn't take them long to notice her capacity for painful bodily contortions. She was especially good at the shell stretch.

'Anyway, I thought you were a vegetarian now,' Dara reminded Tintin, opening a packet of chocolate chip cookies and tossing one to him.

'Didn't work out,' said Tintin airily, making no mention of

his passionate monologue about the savagery of the meat-production industry the previous week. 'Too much peeling and chopping.'

Dara felt a little better now that she knew Kimberley wasn't sickening for something. Tintin changed the subject, not wishing to dwell on his brief brush with vegetarianism.

'I saw Ian last Saturday,' he said, concentrating on scraping a fork against the bottom of a tin of Pedigree Chum. The noise was high-pitched. Harsh. Saturday seemed like such a long time ago now. Back when Angel still had hope. And faith. Dara struggled to remember it.

'In M & S,' Tintin said. He opened his mouth as if to add something, but yawned instead. A great theatrical performance of a yawn.

'What were you going to say?' Dara asked him.

'What do you mean?'

'That was a fake yawn. You were just about to say something.'

'That was *not* a fake yawn.' Tintin looked suitably appalled at the notion. 'I'm exhausted, so I am. I've been working as hard as a cricketer's bat all week, no thanks to you, my sick little soldier.' He stopped briefly to pat Dara's head. 'I had to stay up most of last night to catch up on the soaps.' Tintin watched all the soaps. *Emmerdale* was his favourite. 'It's nothing to do with farming,' he'd told Dara, more than once.

'Well?' Dara said when Tintin had drawn out his yawn for as long as his breath would allow.

Tintin didn't meet her look. 'It's just . . .' he began, and Dara waited.

'He was with a woman,' he finally admitted.

'Oh, that's just Irene, the home help,' Dara said. 'They often go shopping on a Saturday morning. Grocery shopping, I mean. Ian hates it and Irene knows exactly what his mother likes to eat.'

Tintin looked relieved at this explanation, not being great at subterfuge. 'Although,' he added, 'I have to say that she didn't look much like a home help.'

'What do you think a home help should look like?' Dara was interested in Tintin's response, despite herself. He was a *brilliant* stereotyper.

'I don't know,' he said. 'Dowdier, I suppose. Flatter shoes perhaps. A thicker waist, definitely.'

'So she's pretty?' Dara said, before she realised that the aesthetic qualities of Ian Harte's live-in home help were not something she'd ever really considered. And today she found herself unable to rouse even a modicum of interest. Instead, she sighed and continued pecking away at the keyboard, updating the database.

Tintin considered Dara's question, rubbing his chin with the tips of his fingers, the way he did when he was deep in thought.

'Well-preserved is the way I'd put it,' he said finally. 'She's about the same vintage as him. Good bone structure. You can't underestimate the value of bone structure.' He shook his head sadly, as if this was something people did all the time.

Dara pushed her face into the tight pelt of the Jack Russell they called Jack Knapp, who had padded into the Portakabin, climbed into her lap and now lay in her arms, fast asleep. Dara closed her eyes too. For the first time since it happened, she felt she could sleep.

'Was it a late night last night?' Tintin asked.

'What?'

'Thursday night? You were out with Angel, weren't you?'

It was true that Thursday night was Dara's favourite night of the week. It was the night she and Angel went out. Or stayed in, if Mrs Flood was working late. Dara preferred staying in. That way, she could cook meals that Angel liked, without getting tangled in complicated conversations with bored waitresses in restaurants about what Angel could or could not eat. Not that Angel minded. She preferred going out. They dressed up. Well, Angel did. She liked to wear dresses. Sleeve-less ones, with bright colours and scooped-out necklines. In these dresses, the scar on her right arm – an AV fistula that hadn't gone to plan – and the one at the base of her neck – a venous catheter she had needed as a temporary measure while the permanent access in her left arm developed – were noticeable. People stared. Dara hated the way they did that. Angel laughed and insisted it was her tits they were looking at. The scars had faded from an angry red to a pale pink, and then to a silvery white, the skin creased across them like the skin of a person who was older and had been through a lot. Then there was the fistula in her left arm, not all that appar-ent unless you looked closely, and then you could see the skin there bulge and twitch with the vibration of her blood through the tube buried beneath her skin.

Dara shook her head. 'We didn't go out,' she said slowly.

'Oh my God,' said Tintin, swivelling in his chair to face her, both hands clamped to his mouth. 'I mean, I knew *something* was wrong when you didn't comment on my hair that I spent a *fortune* on at Brown Sugar's. You didn't even give out to me for eating more than my fair share of the peach Mazurka that Anya brought. *And* you weren't suitably interested in my sighting of your boyfriend and his home help.'

'He's not my boyfriend,' Dara corrected him. 'We just see each other occasionally. You know that.'

'Whatever. The point is, something is up and you're going to tell Tintin all about it.'

'All right,' said Dara, standing up and passing Jack Knapp to Tintin, careful not to wake him. 'But can I tell you outside?'

'Christ, it's bad, isn't it?' Tintin said, following her down the steps and pulling his flimsy little corduroy jacket across his chest for warmth.

Dara sat on a gigantic bag of dog biscuits and leaned against the bumpy pebbledash wall. Even though the bag was lumpy and unsteady beneath her and the wall was cold and rough against her back, she felt her body slacken and her eyes droop. She reached a hand into her coat pocket and took out the packet of Silk Cut she'd bought the day before.

'Jesus,' whispered Tintin before turning and cupping his mouth with his hands. 'Silky Sluts!' he roared across the yard, as if Dara had pulled the pin out of a grenade. He turned back to Dara then, making a dive for the cigarettes. Dara pulled her hand back. It glanced against the pebbledash. The pain was sharp. Insistent. Exactly what she needed to propel her off the bag and away from Tintin. She began to run, her hand clamped around the packet like a vice. She could run faster than Tintin, especially today, when he was a little sluggish after his omnibus session last night.

She would have gotten away, had it not been for the quick-witted action of Anya, who bore witness to the scene through the tiny window of the Portakabin that Tintin called her *corner office*. Anya clattered down the steps of the cabin, shouting, 'LOCKDOWN!' She ran fast, considering her attire. Today she wore strappy high-heeled sandals, with toenails painted the exact same colour of pink as her dress, which was a short, tight affair and would have been more at home at a cocktail party than a dog pound. Still, neither the shortness nor the tightness of the dress had any effect on Anya, whose collection of bracelets jingled up and down her arms as she ran. She stopped in the narrow passageway created by dog cages on either side and blocked Dara's way with her bejewelled arms outstretched, her dangly earrings careering around her lobes. Dara ran towards her, a streak of navy, apart from the hand that gripped the cigarettes. That hand was panic-white. Anya stood her ground, knowing that Dara would not try to bypass her, given the space constraints. Dara streaked up the passage, and for a moment Anya thought she had underestimated her need for a cigarette. For a moment, she thought Dara would run right through her.

'Easy, girl,' said Anya with her hands up, as if Dara was a horse she was trying to break. Dara slowed to a jog before stopping altogether. Her breath was ragged, her chest heaving with the weight of it. 'That's it,' coaxed Anya, taking a discreet step forward. 'Just gif me packet of cigarettes and nobody gets hurt, OK?' Dara looked behind her. Tintin was closing in, the Jack Russell still asleep in his arms. Small wonder they called him Jack Knapp.

'The thing is,' began Dara, looking from one of them to the other. 'I've given up giving up. I mean, I'm not a quitter, right?' She was the only one who laughed. Tintin and Anya stood on either side of her, waiting.

'Fine,' shouted Dara, petulant as a four-year-old. She threw the cigarettes on the ground and beat them to a pulp with the heel of her Doc Marten. 'There,' she said. 'Happy now?'

'Delighted,' said Tintin, between gasps.

'Thrilled,' agreed Anya, picking up the pulpy packet and pocketing it. Just in case. Dara closed her eyes and thought about the packet she'd hidden in an inside pocket of her bag that morning.

'Just hand over that other packet you have in your bag and I'll make us all a nice cup of tea,' said Tintin. Dara opened her mouth to contradict him and then closed it again. Damn Tintin and Anya. For being such great friends and doing only what Dara had asked them to do, six weeks ago, when she'd held the burning ceremony at the back of the pound. Everything went into the barrel that day: cigarettes, lighters, books of matches, photographs of her with a cigarette in her hand, a nicotine-yellow T-shirt she'd had since she was twenty-three that said, *Non-Smokers Die Too*. Even the beautiful silver cigarette case she'd been given by a grateful owner whose pound puppy she had trained in her spare time.

They returned in a solemn procession to the Portakabin. Tintin made tea while Anya force-fed Dara strawberry bonbons. 'Goot for disappointment,' she told her, with her usual conviction.

Tintin handed her his mug that he let her drink out of occasionally, when he felt she needed some pampering. In fairness, the mug was big and bright, with pictures of puppies chasing each other's tails around and around the base of it. 'Thanks,' said Dara.

'So?' Tintin said.

'Go on,' urged Anya, even though Dara had not said anything yet. 'Tell us about relapse.'

Dara sighed. There was no getting away from this pair.

'It was last Monday night,' she admitted. Tintin's mouth was a perfect circle of horror. Anya just shook her head in the resigned way she had, as if she hadn't expected much more.

Dara had brought Edward with her that night. Her cover. She picked the poodle up when she crossed the road, taking comfort from the solid warmth of him in her arms, and silenced her conscience by talking loudly to the dog. In this way, she made it all the way to the counter and managed to tell the shop assistant what she wanted, before her conscience was able to get a word in edgeways.

'Aw, for the lovin' honour of all dat's holy.' The voice of Dara's conscience was always the same: a man's voice, hoarse and low, with a thick Dublin accent. Dara ignored it and pulled Edward out of the shop. She tied his lead round a lamp post and tore the wrapper off the packet of Silk Cut. 'You've been off dem for nearly six weeks now, Dara. You were doin' so bleedin' well, so ya were.'

Dara pushed her hand inside her jacket and down the left sleeve until her fingers reached the patch. She picked at it until it came away. The second patch was more difficult to get at, plastered as it was to the back of her leg, just below the knee. She had to tug at the leg of the skinny jeans Tintin had insisted she buy. 'They'll make your legs look really long,' he'd said in the shop, pressing the jeans up against her lovely comfortable tracksuit bottoms.

'Long?'

'Well,' he said, looking her up and down. 'Long-*er* . . .'

But even though parts of her legs went numb when she wore them, due, she supposed, to the restricted blood circulation, she had to admit that the jeans did in fact make her legs look a little longer than they deserved to.

Dara had pretended to be tying her shoelaces as her hand crawled up the leg of her jeans. She tried to remember if she'd stuck any other patches on that morning. She didn't think so. She lit up the cigarette and breathed it in. The vile taste of it. The acrid smell of it. The filthy looks people shot her, as she stood there beneath the mushroom cloud of poisonous smoke. Her eyes watered and she felt light-headed with a faint possibility of vomiting. It was *gorgeous*. She leaned against the wall and took another drag, this time with her eyes closed. Fabulous. Edward sat on the pavement with his head on his paws and watched Dara. His expression was one of reproach.

'But *why*, Dara?' Tintin asked. 'I mean, why Monday night? Was it because *The Apprentice* is over?'

'Something bad must haf happened,' Anya told them both, as she often did.

Dara looked at Anya and nodded. She took a breath and began. She told them about the kidney that had been found and then lost, and about the journey back from the hospital and about Mrs Flood, who hadn't even brushed her hair since Saturday night, as far as Dara could tell.

'Jesus,' whispered Tintin, shaking his head.

'She must haf *combed* it at least?' said Anya, her voice shrill with shock. Tintin and Anya knew how proud Mrs Flood was of her hair. She called it her stock-in-trade.

Dara shook her head.

'But that's not the worst bit,' she said, popping two bonbons into her mouth at the same time and making her cheeks bulge like a frog. Tintin and Anya leaned forward, their eyes like saucers in their heads. 'It's Angel,' Dara went on. 'She's ... taken it really badly.'

'Of course she has. That's only natural, isn't it?' Tintin said, looking at Anya, who nodded solemnly.

'No,' said Dara, struggling to explain. 'It's ... it's serious. She hasn't really talked since it happened.'

'She probably needs a bit of time,' said Tintin, patting Dara's arm. 'To get used to things. She'll be fine in a while. Once she's had a bit of time.' His head swivelled from one of them to the other as he said this. Anya concentrated on Dara. She looked like someone waiting for something awful to happen.

Tintin tried again. 'I mean, come on, I know it's Angel, but ... still ... people get knocked back by disappointment all the time. Don't they? Even Angel?'

Nobody spoke. Anya continued to concentrate on Dara's face. Tintin continued to look from one of them to the other.

Dara kneaded her neck with her fingers. Her head felt heavy. Too heavy for her neck to support. She supposed it was tiredness.

'There is more,' Anya suddenly said, standing up. 'You haf not told us everythink, haf you?'

Dara looked at Anya. Tintin stopped swivelling his head and stared at Dara. In the pause that followed, Dara felt the weight of their worry, the depth of their concern. She shook her head. Rubbed at her eyes with the tips of her fingers. There was no other way to say it.

'She broke up with Joe.'

'WHAT?' Anya and Tintin shouted the question in unison, like they'd practised it. Then they waited, as if convinced that Dara would say something else now. Something different.

Dara took a breath and said it again, louder this time.

'Angel broke up with Joe.'

'Oh Jesus,' said Tintin, his voice smothered by his hands that cupped his face. He sat on the edge of a filing cabinet.

'Nobody would break up with Joe,' Anya said grimly. Even Anya shared the universal view about Joe.

Dara nodded. She agreed.

'She can't mean it,' said Tintin. The fact that he made no quip about Joe being available now underlined the ominousness of the development.

Dara shook her head. 'She does.'

Tintin stood up. 'No,' he declared. 'I won't allow it. I'm going over to see Angel right now. Tell her how wrong it is to break up with firemen. I mean, who *does* that? It's . . . it's unacceptable.'

Looking at his flushed face and his chest straining against the thin fabric of his shirt, Dara felt a charge of something positive. If anyone could make Angel feel better, it was Tintin. Then she remembered what Angel had said. *I'm holding you back*, she'd told Joe. *I don't love you*, she'd said. Dara shook her head. 'She won't even take his phone calls. He's been calling and calling since she told him. It's like she doesn't care any more. About anything.'

'But she's still going to dialysis,' Anya said, and Dara was grateful to her, knowing how hard it was for Anya to point out the positives. She was much better with the negatives.

'Yes, but it's like she's going through the motions. Just for the sake of it. Like she doesn't believe that anything good will happen anymore.'

Both Tintin and Anya looked stunned, and Dara couldn't blame them. She'd had nearly a week to get used to Angel – the old Angel – not being around.

'There must be something we can do,' Tintin said in a loud voice. Then, his voice quiet now, 'What can we do?' He looked like he might cry.

Dara shook her head. 'I don't know,' she said, reaching into her pocket for a cigarette before remembering that they were in Anya's custody, squashed flat.

'Look,' said Anya suddenly. 'She just needs a few days to vallow and then she vill be back to her old self before you can say kidney transplant, right?' Anya could be a spokesperson for the art of wallowing. She knew a lot about it and sought opportunities to engage in the practice as often as possible. In truth, she *enjoyed* the opportunity it afforded her to do very little. She looked from one of them to the other. 'Right?' she repeated, giving Tintin the benefit of her plucked-to-within-an-inch-of-their-lives eyebrows.

'Right,' supplied Tintin, looking unconvinced at best.

Dara said nothing.

A long, thin man came up the steps of the Portakabin and poked his head around the door. In his arms lay a quivering mess of shiny black fur in the shape of a Labrador puppy. About three months old, Dara thought. A dog-is-for-Christmas-not-for-life kind of dog. The man looked like they all looked. Apologetic mostly. He shifted from one foot to the other. 'It's the wife, you see,' he told them, biting his bottom lip, begging them to understand with his eyes. 'She just can't cope with Sherlock.' He nodded towards the puppy. 'He's wrecked the fecking garden – front and back, eaten all her daffs and tulips, chewed a hole in the fence and made flitters of the trampoline. And the garden is riddled with shi— . . . eh . . . droppings,' he said in a way that suggested he'd never used the word 'droppings' before. He recovered well. 'And the residents' association have been on to us about the barking. Night an' day he's at it.' The man – like most of the people who came to the pound with their leftover dogs, as Tintin called them – concentrated mostly on Dara as he spoke. Dara made it easy for them to leave with their consciences clear.

'Why do you do that?' Tintin often asked.

'They're going to leave their dogs behind, no matter what anyone says,' said Dara, and Tintin had nothing to say to that, because he knew it was true.

She stood up and reached for Sherlock. His nose was warm and wet. 'You're not going to . . . put him down?' asked the man, allowing Dara to take the dog from him with that familiar guilty relief.

'We may have no choice,' piped up Tintin.

'Is possibility,' offered Anya, shaking her head sadly.

'I think we could find a home for him,' said Dara, bending to bury her nose in Sherlock's glossy coat. 'He's a beautiful-looking dog. Plus he's a puppy. People love puppies.' This was true, even if it was a fact that broke Dara's heart when the vet came to put down the hundreds of fully grown mongrels that ended up at the pound every year.

The man couldn't get out of the Portakabin quick enough after that, nearly falling down the stairs backwards in his hurry to get back to his pre-Sherlock life. It didn't matter how long you worked in this business, thought Dara, who had worked there for a very long time indeed. The arrival of an unwanted dog had a way of getting in at you. The three colleagues each had their own method of dealing with new arrivals. Dara concentrated on Sherlock, unwrapping a Penguin from her pocket and feeding it to him. Tintin took charge of the administration, pushing at the keys of the laptop a little harder than necessary. Anya rang Domino's and ordered pizzas for lunch: the Mighty Meaty for herself, a Tandoori Special for Tintin and the classic tomato and cheese for Dara. It was during this phone call – *absolutely no cheese or tomato on Mighty Meaty, please* – that she had the idea.

'Oh! My! Got!' she shouted down the phone, pulling at her hair the way she did when one of the pound dogs was adopted.

And then: 'No, no, sorry, I was not to you speaking.' Anya's normally excellent English sometimes let her down when she became excited. 'I just . . . I haf idea and I . . . Vat? No, I have not just seen promotion on garlic bread and Coke. Yes, that sounds not bad. Yes, we vill have some of that. But I haf to go now, OK? . . . Yes? . . . Goodbye.' She banged the phone down and spun around to face the other two, whose undivided attention she already had.

'Dara, I haf it,' she said, and her dimples shuddered as if entertaining the notion of puncturing her cheeks with a smile.

'You have what? What are you talking about?' Dara set Sherlock gently on the ground.

Tintin's pale face rose over the top of the monitor, like a full moon. 'Is it about my surprise thirtieth?' he asked, even though he wasn't going to be thirty for another two-and-a-half years. But he was adamant that he wanted a big bash. A big surprise bash. So he brought it up as often as he could, so no one could be forgiven for forgetting.

Anya looked like she *had* forgotten. 'Vat? No, it's . . .' She turned to Dara. 'Is about Mr Flood.'

Dara wasn't sure she'd heard her properly.

'*Mr* Flood?'

Anya nodded.

'What about him?' Dara set a bowl of water on the floor beside Sherlock.

'You cud find him,' Anya said.

'Why would I want to do that?' Dara was genuinely confused.

'He could be match. For Angel, I mean. He could have kidney she needs.'

Dara shook her head. There were so many reasons why this couldn't happen. Anya *knew* all that. 'Why would he want to donate one of his kidneys to Angel?' she began. 'And that's even presuming that he *is* a match. And that's presuming that

I could find him, which I couldn't, because, well, I mean, he's been gone so long and I wouldn't even know where to begin looking.' She stopped there and looked at Anya. 'Why are you even suggesting this? It's mad. And completely out of the question.'

Anya nodded with great gravitas, as if Dara's response was exactly what she had expected. 'Is long shot and it probably won't work,' she agreed, still nodding. 'But,' she added, '*it might*.' She whispered that bit, leaning close to Dara and smiling her rare smile. 'If nothing else, it could give Angel bit of hope,' she conceded.

'But it's a false kind of hope,' said Dara, shaking her head. It was a crazy idea. She didn't even know why they were discussing it.

'But is hope all the same,' insisted Anya in her grave way, and for a moment Dara felt it. A faint tug on her line. A possibility, as remote as the Galapagos Islands. But a possibility all the same. She tried to ward it off, but Anya pressed home. 'What haf you got to lose, Dara?' she asked.

The solemnity of the Portakabin was rudely interrupted by the foul stench of Sherlock's *droppings*, which sat in a mound in the corner. Sherlock stood beside it, his head high, the proud owner.

'I'm on it,' said Tintin, rummaging in the drawer for the nappy bags and the shovel.

'You should at least think about it, Dara,' said Anya, placing her warm hand on Dara's arm.

'We-ell . . .'

'You should, Dara,' said Tintin, looking at her from his kneeling position on the floor in front of the mound.

'The thing is,' said Dara, clearing her throat, 'I think I could think about it much better if I could have just one cigarette.'

'NO!' they shouted together. And that was that.

★　　★　　★

I tell the days of the week by the dinners. Today is Saturday. They call it Irish stew, but really, it bears no resemblance to the stuff my mother used to make, God rest her. I don't know how long I've been here. I can't keep track. Weeks, definitely. Maybe even months. A long time, at any rate. The minutes and hours bleed into days and somehow the days become weeks and maybe even months, who knows? Time is relentless that way. It just keeps going.

Still, the ward is warm and there's three meals a day, even though I can't eat them myself. They spoon-feed me, like a baby. Fidelma, the nurse, does it quickly. Efficiently. I imagine she has children at home. Porridge dribbles out of the corners of my mouth and she scoops it back in with the edge of the spoon. She has big hands but is deft all the same. A good woman to have around in an emergency, I'd say. She picks my head up with one of her big hands and beats at the pillow with the other, as if it has done her a disservice. Her breasts are low-slung and heavy, the kind you'd have to lift with both hands. The old excitement that fizzed around my body has dulled, like everything else. Those days are long gone.

She gives me a bed bath. The sponge is soft and warm against my skin. Her movements are brisk. Economical. Under her breath, she hums a tune that I don't recognise. Her nails are short and square. A thick gold band pinches the skin around her wedding finger. She'll have a hard time getting that off, when the time comes. The sponge rummages between my legs. Her tune never falters. Why should it? Just another old prick, lying here, waiting.

She combs the last few strands of my hair across my scalp. There is no need to shave me. There was a time when I'd have to shave twice a day. Now, it's once a week, whether I need it or not.

She leans back, surveys me, nods.

The trolley leans and rattles as she pushes it away.

Tea will be in four hours. I lie here and wait. To pass the time, I

look out the window. The Manchester sky is like this place, differ-
ent shades of grey. It might rain later. I close my eyes. It seems that
the less I do, the more tired I become.

　　I am like an old building, reduced to rubble. People might look
at the space where I used to be and scratch their chins and shake
their heads and try to remember what had been there before.

12

Nobody really understood what Dara Flood saw in Ian Harte. Yes, he was quite good-looking, in as much as a middle-aged, balding man could be, with the beginnings of a Guinness paunch and the shy tips of some nostril hair pushing their way out of his otherwise handsome nose. They also agreed that he was a man of means, driving around as he did in a Mercedes jeep, dressed in a stiff Louis Copeland suit.

'He's olt,' Anya complained.

'Old-*er*,' Dara corrected her. 'He's not even fifty yet.'

'He will be in a few months,' Tintin pointed out.

'Fifty is the new forty,' Dara told them. 'Besides, age is just a number, Tintin. You've said it yourself.'

'Age is just a number when you're in your twenties,' Tintin told her. 'It's a fecking deathtrap when you're nearly fifty.'

But the relationship – such as it was – suited Dara Flood. Because Ian travelled a lot for business – he worked for some international bank in the IFSC – Dara saw him once a week. Perhaps twice, if his schedule allowed. Usually on a Saturday night. The cinema. Walks along secluded beaches. Occasional dinners in some softly lit, out-of-the-way restaurant.

'But you've never even been to his *house*,' Anya said. 'Where do you mate?' Even though Anya's English was excellent and she was well aware of the phrase 'have sex' or even 'make love' (not that she would ever use an expression like that), she was fond of using the term 'mating'. People smiled at her when she said it, indulging her use of the phrase, which they associated with her rather melancholy Polish accent.

The cinema or the walks along secluded beaches or the occasional dinner in some poorly lit, out-of-the-way restaurant were always followed by long, complicated exchanges in the apartment Ian's company owned in the IFSC. Because of the recession (Ian always paused before he said the word, and then whispered it, afraid perhaps that if he said it out loud, it might notice him and deal with him as it had dealt with many of his colleagues), the apartment was often empty on a Saturday night. No overseas clients to bring to l'Ecrivain for dinner followed by elaborate cocktails at The Morrison and of course the inevitable slippery slope to Leeson Street in search of young women whose high hopes at the beginning of the night had dwindled to a flatline of grim acceptance.

Ian Harte prided himself on his sexual prowess, and while Dara had to agree that his technique was flawless, she sometimes wished that he took it a little less seriously and didn't always approach her body like it was an obscure 1,000-piece jigsaw puzzle that he was determined to fit together.

'I can't go to his house. He lives with his mother. She's not well. I told you that.'

'A fifty-year-old man who lives with his mother,' Tintin repeated. 'I mean to say . . . what kind of . . . how could it . . . ?' He gave up, unable to articulate his bafflement at Ian Harte's domestic arrangements.

'His mother is in a wheelchair,' Dara reminded them. 'He minds her.'

'But he's never there,' Anya rightly pointed out. 'He's always away. *On business.*' She emphasised that bit, to convey her cynicism. But because Anya was cynical about most things, Dara didn't pay it much attention.

'She has a home help, when he's not there. I already told you that, remember?'

'Hmmm,' was all Anya could say.

Dara never stayed the night in the apartment. She enjoyed the dinner bit and the walking along the beach bit and the watching films bit and yes, even the complicated sex-marathons bit. But waking up in the morning in a bed beside Ian Harte was something that did not appeal to Dara Flood. There was something a little too intimate about it. Domestic. She felt things were just fine the way they were. So no, she didn't mind 'mating' in the impersonal uniformity of a company flat. Nor did she consider their once-a-week meetings insufficient. The fact was, the relationship was not going anywhere and that was just the way Dara liked it. There were no expectations. Which ruled out things like *disappointment* and *uncertainty* and eventual, inevitable *decline*. Even Mrs Flood might approve, had she known about it.

In the past, Dara had felt that her boyfriends' expectations had been too high. Anya had a theory. 'You attract needy men,' she told Dara over pints in the Doghouse one Wednesday night.

'I don't mean to,' said Dara, in an apologetic voice.

'Is because you are kind and you listen to all dee bullshit they talk. Instead of saying SHUT THE CAKEHOLE' – Dara jumped when Anya shouted this bit, oblivious to the looks she attracted from all corners of the bar – '. . . like I do.'

'So, what do you advise?'

Anya leant across the table. 'You have to be cruel to be kind,' she said. But Dara couldn't be cruel. She didn't know how.

She had to concede that Anya was right. She did attract needy men. Not that she called them needy. 'They've been hurt in the past,' she told Anya and Tintin.

'Bollox,' said Tintin. 'They just need to learn to drink milk straight from the carton instead of their mother's tit. You get them at the weaning stage, Dara. That's always difficult.' Tintin knew what he was talking about. His mother had nursed him until he was four.

In secondary school, there'd been Eamonn Tweedy. 'Needy Tweedy', Anya dubbed him when Dara got around to telling her about him. He cried a lot. He cried when Dara agreed to go out with him, he cried when she tried to break up with him, and again when she agreed to take him back. When he did the dirt on her with a girl called Penelope Gavin, he confessed gladly to Dara, crying all the way through.

'He was a very sensitive man,' Dara told Anya, trying to be fair.

'He was a fucking pussy,' Anya declared with conviction.

Then there was Seamus Delaney, the only man on Dara's secretarial course. Fresh stock, up from the country, lonely as hell and gay as Christmas, although he did not know that yet. It was Dara who would lead him to this realisation, with her soft voice and her endless patience and the way she could listen to him. For *hours*. Without interrupting. Seamus couldn't believe his luck. He'd heard that Dublin girls were high-maintenance bitches. In fact, he still kept in touch with her. Him and Norman. Living in San Francisco now, with a baby on the way.

Then came Oliver Browne. 'Melancholy Olly', Tintin called him from the start. 'Oliver Browned-Off' was Angel's pet name for him.

'He's just . . . he's going through a lot at the moment, ' Dara told them. Oliver Browne was a man who couldn't get the hang of being forty. In fact, he was forty-three when Dara met him and he still hadn't mastered it. Recently divorced, he was a tall, thin man with vague features and light blue eyes that were always fixed on something in the middle distance. He arrived at the pound one day, looking for a puppy.

'I need some company, to be honest,' he confided to Dara. 'The house is awful quiet since she took the kids to live with That Man.'

That Man turned out to be Gerry Strokes, a self-made millionaire who had made his fortune by supplying toilet paper dispensers and sanitary bins up and down the country. Also toilet brushes and soap dispensers. If it was in the toilet of a hotel or bar or restaurant, there was every chance that Gerry Strokes had put it there.

'I wouldn't like to tell you where I'd like to stick one of his toilet brushes,' Oliver said, more than once. Dara nodded. She was glad he wasn't going to tell her. She had a fair idea.

Oliver wasn't afraid to let his guard down with Dara. In fact, he dismantled it completely. He laid bare every single sad, shoddy detail of his life with the woman he referred to as *she* or *her*. Her name was Jane, which Dara felt was a blameless kind of a name for a woman who could inflict such grave wounds.

'That's not a relationship, it's a fecking therapy session,' Tintin told her.

'Move in with me,' Oliver asked, on more than one occasion. His voice was muffled, probably because of the position of his head, which was burrowed in between Dara's breasts. Men seemed to be especially fond of Dara's breasts, she couldn't help noticing. Perhaps because they were surprised to discover they were there at all, after they'd struggled through her layers of fleece jackets, baggy jumpers, T-shirts and sports bras.

But Dara always shook her head and nipped his earlobe lightly, just the way he liked, to distract him. Which usually worked, but not this time.

'It's been six months,' he told her. 'It's time to move on to the next level.'

'It's *only* been six months,' she corrected him. 'And we're fine as we are. Aren't we?'

But it seemed they were not fine as they were. Not for him. He looked *disappointed* and *uncertain* for a few weeks, before their relationship bowed under the weight of those wretched sentiments and gave way to eventual, inevitable *decline*.

If that had been the end of the story, Dara might have been OK. But it wasn't. Oliver took to ringing her in the middle of the night. Sometimes more than once. Begging her to take him back. To move in with him. To marry him. To have children with him. He'd always wanted four kids. But *she* had left him after only giving birth to two.

To each of these suggestions, Dara said no. As kindly as she could. Oliver began to talk in a way that worried her. About life not being worth living. About taking a dive off O'Connell Bridge. About throwing himself under the DART. In the end, he managed to swallow a mouthful of Disprin, washed down with half a bottle of Jack Daniels. He couldn't wait to tell Dara, calling her from the hospital, his voice weak and hoarse from the tubes they had pushed down his throat to pump his stomach out.

'I didn't want to live without you, baby,' he told her, when she arrived at his bedside.

'I'm afraid you're going to have to,' Dara told him gently, before getting up to leave. Even though his suicide attempt was more like a whimper for help than a cry, it had left her nerves in pieces. She knew she couldn't see him again. She walked out before she could change her mind. Tintin and Anya took her to the pub that night.

'We are so proud of you, Dara,' said Tintin, patting her hand. Anya nodded and smiled. They both looked at her as if she were theirs and had done something amazing, like brokered peace in the Middle East.

'What if he tries to do it again?' Dara worried.

'Let's hope he makes a proper stab at it next time,' Anya said, taking a grim slug of her pint.

'This is serious, Anya,' Dara said. 'He could have *died*.'

'Death's too good for that eejit,' Tintin told her cheerfully.

'That fucker will never die. He's not able for it,' was Anya's conclusion.

Dara avoided relationships for a long time after that.

Then she met Ian Harte.

Ian Harte was different.

Because his mother was old and infirm and incapacitated, and Ian was her only child, there was no question of him moving out. Moving on. He told Dara this on their second meeting, which happened to be their first date. Their first meeting took place in the park, the rose garden in St Anne's Park, one Saturday morning. Edward had slipped his lead and was making loose with a skinny chihuahua who was ageing badly. Edward had a thing about skinny dogs and was generally non-ageist in his approach. 'Edward!' Dara shouted, running. Edward darted away, his tiny tail a blur of slutty wags. Dara made a dive for him, which Edward sidestepped in his meticulous way, leaving Dara sprawled in a freshly-dug flower bed. She sat up and spat a chunk of muck out of her mouth.

'"A rose by any other name would smell as sweet",' quoted a voice from behind.

Dara turned and saw his legs first. Long and sturdy, in a pair of beige chinos. Her eyes travelled up and up, past a baby-pink shirt underneath a brown jacket. *Snazzy*, her mother would have called the jacket, with its buttons shining like a brass band in the sun. Up again and there he was. Ian Harte. Quoting Shakespeare at her, his voice rising and falling along the cadence of the line.

Dara didn't know quite what to say.

'Here,' said the man, offering her his hand. 'Let me help you.' His hand was fleshy and warm. He smelled of the aftershave in the bottle Mr Flood left behind, which still sat in the bathroom cabinet, shrouded now with the dust of years. Something spicy. His hair was brown with a smattering of grey at the temples, where it was thick, unlike the top, which was thinning and sparse. *Distinguished*, Dara thought.

He reached over and pushed his fingers into her hair, and Dara found herself wishing she had brushed it that morning.

'There,' he said, handing her a leaf.

'Eh, thank you,' said Dara, taking it.

'It was in your hair,' he explained, leaning towards Dara. His breath was minty with an undercurrent of cereal. Weetabix, perhaps.

'Oh,' said Dara.

The conversation was interrupted by Edward's excited grunting. The man's head snapped around. 'Stop it, you brute!' he roared. Dara turned to look. The skinny chihuahua stood like she was waiting for a bus. Patient and bored. Edward towered behind her, wrapping his front paws around the delicacy of her back as he prepared to mount her.

'Gerroffher!' yelled the man, running towards them. 'She's a very rare pedigree,' he shouted to Dara, still running.

Near them, a park ranger watered a bank of blood-red roses. Dara apologised before she yanked the hose out of his hands and turned it on the dogs. Edward took not the blindest bit of notice, head bent to the task. But the chihuahua yelped as Dara knew she would. Chihuahuas were not great fans of water. Especially cold water. Still Edward refused to move, until the chihuahua tossed her head back and sank her tiny sharp teeth into the poodle's white pelt. This worked. Edward emitted a high-pitched, girlish scream and, in his confusion, ran between the man's legs and urinated all over his suede loafers. Edward's bladder was weak and tended to let him down in stressful situations.

Now it was the man's turn to howl, and he stumbled backwards. For a moment, Dara thought he intended to kick Edward on his high, pert bottom, and instinctively she reached for the dog. But the man just took his shoe off and wiped it on the grass before using the hose, still trickling water, to wash the hand that had held the shoe in a most meticulous fashion.

Dara returned the hose to the gardener, who discarded her apologies with a resigned shake of his head. 'Horny dogs,' he said, almost to himself. 'The bane of my bleedin' life.'

'I'm really sorry about all that,' said Dara. She had to raise her voice to be heard, although Edward's howls had been replaced by long, shaky whines that would tear the heart out of you.

The man said nothing for a time, concentrating on drying each finger of his hand with a huge linen handkerchief. Then he folded it, replaced it in his pocket and turned to Dara, dazzling her with the force of his smile and the whiteness of his teeth. Celtic Tiger teeth, her mother would have called them.

'Ian Harte,' the man said, extending his hand again. He quoted his name rather than said it, like it was a sonnet.

'Dara Flood,' she replied.

'Oh,' he said. 'Is that not a boy's name?'

'It can be,' said Dara, shrugging her shoulders. 'In fact, I was called after a man. The nurse who delivered me in the Rotunda. I was named after her grandfather who was killed in the Second World War. On the beach during the D-Day landings, in fact.'

'Didn't your mother already have a name picked out for you? Before she got to the hospital, I mean?'

In fact, she had. Before Mr Flood had walked up the road for a packet of cigarettes and never come back, he had insisted on the name Meryl if she'd been a girl (Mr Flood being a *huge* Meryl Streep fan), and Eugene if she'd been a boy (Mr Flood being a *huge* Mr Flood fan, according to Mrs Flood). There weren't many positive things you could say about your father leaving your mother thirteen days before you were born. But not being called Meryl was definitely one of them. 'She did,' said Dara. 'But she changed her mind.'

'How . . . interesting,' said Ian, who looked more confused than interested.

'But it's a girl's name too,' Dara told him, and with this, Ian Harte appeared to collect himself.

'You're much prettier than your name,' he told her. 'In fact,' he continued, studying her face now like a map, 'has anyone ever told you that you're a dead ringer for Jodie Foster?' Dara nodded, even though up until that moment not one single person had *ever* told her she was a dead ringer for anyone other than Mr Flood. Ian Harte was still speaking: '. . . often been told that I resemble a younger Anthony Hopkins. They were both in *Silence of the Lambs*, remember?' He waited for Dara to agree.

'I don't think I saw that film,' Dara had to admit.

'Of course you didn't,' said Ian, looking at her closely now. 'You're far too young, aren't you?'

'Well, I . . .'

'Please forgive me. I'm forgetting my manners,' he said, extending his hand. I'm delighted to meet you, Dara Flood.'

He invited her for dinner the following week and took her to a softly lit, out-of-the-way restaurant on the banks of a slow-moving river somewhere in Wicklow.

'I know this conversation is a little premature, given that we've only just met,' he told her through the stems of two flickering red candles on the table between them, 'but I want you to know my position. I want to be as upfront as I can.' His position was that with all the travelling he did for his job, in between taking care of his ailing mother, Ian Harte declared himself unable to sustain a relationship in the manner in which a young woman such as Dara Flood should expect. Their meetings might be sporadic, he explained. Sometimes brief. He might have to cancel arrangements at short notice. He wanted Dara to understand all of that.

Dara nodded. She appreciated this grown-up approach to relationships. In this way, there could be no misunderstandings. No disappointment or indeed uncertainty. And, three months on, no mention had ever been made by Ian Harte of their need to *move on*, to bring the relationship to the *next level*.

Anya and Tintin concluded that Dara was a commitment-phobe.

'Is not your fault, Dara,' Anya told her. 'I would be commitment-phobe too, after Melancholy Olly.'

But Dara knew that this wasn't true. She *was* committed. To Angel. Angel needed her. Dara wasn't going to abandon her. There had been enough of that already.

Ian Harte spoke to her about things like her *career path*. 'Let them know that you are keen on securing a managerial position in the, eh, dog pound,' he advised her.

Dara nodded but did nothing about it, not entirely sure how Anya would take the news.

He encouraged her to further her education. 'You could do a business course,' he enthused. 'Set up on your own. A dog-training school with kennels for short-term stays and a grooming salon on the side. There's *huge* potential in the market for services like that. You'd be brilliant. I mean, this *recession*' – he lowered his voice at the word – 'can't last for ever, can it?'

Dara didn't comment. She knew she'd never do anything like that. Why would she? Weren't things fine the way they were? But still. It was nice to think that someone thought she could.

It was Ian who advised her to learn how to drive. 'What have you got to lose?' he'd said. And Dara – who up until then had always depended on her bike and public transport to get her where she needed to be – graduated from being a nervous passenger (she had a tendency to cower and cover her face with her hands and stamp her foot down on an imaginary brake in the front passenger seat), to being a nervous learner driver.

Ian supplemented her professional driving lessons – which were very expensive – with some of his own, and even though the jeep was an automatic, Dara appreciated the gesture, knowing how very fond he was of the vehicle.

It was Ian who encouraged her to apply for a car loan, even offering to help her fill out the long and tedious form. Dara wasn't keen on form-filling. With her large, loopy writing, she found it difficult to fit the words into the cramped constraints of the boxes provided. She also found it difficult to look at her mother's face when she read her writing. 'Is that a word?' Mrs Flood asked, every feature on her face tightening.

'I'll have it done in a jiffy,' Ian told her. He said things like that. Things like 'in a jiffy'. There were other oddities. Like the way he blessed himself whenever they drove past a church. Like the way he read the obituaries in the paper. That was the first page he went to. 'Because you just never know, do you?' he told Dara, who nodded, even though she was unsure as to what it was that he just never knew. He sometimes mentioned bands she'd never heard of (the Bay City Rollers?), books she'd never read (*Catch 22 – a classic*) and odd-titled films (*Terms of Endearment – I'm not ashamed to admit I cried*).

He encouraged her to set up a pension fund, even though, with her paltry monthly contributions, she'd be lucky if she had enough to retire to Blackpool, when the time came.

Dara knew that the situation was not everyone's version of ideal.

'It vill not end well,' Anya declared, darkly.

'I wouldn't classify him as Mr *Right*, exactly,' Tintin had to admit. His own search for Mr or Ms Right was well documented and discussed among the three of them at almost every lunch break, coffee break and Wednesday-night drinking session in the Doghouse, the pub across the road from the pound. Tintin described himself as bisexual. 'Why limit myself?' he said when Anya argued that he should be one thing or the other. 'I just want a bit of whatever's going round, that's all.' When he put it like that, it sounded entirely reasonable. Practical, even.

Yes, Dara did concede that Ian Harte probably wasn't her Mr Right. To be honest, she didn't believe in such a sentiment. But he was definitely Mr *All Right*. Better than all right, really. And it was nice to have a warm body to press herself against on a Saturday night. Someone who cared enough to Google motor insurance deals for her. And then there were the gifts he showered on her. Suspender belts and stockings and high heels, and bottles of champagne that he loved to pour into the deep well of her belly button and then empty with his tongue, that was as pink as Edward's.

13

Dara waited a whole week for the right moment to tell Mrs Flood and Angel about Anya's idea. She knew that it was a preposterous idea, a crazy notion, with very little chance of success. But it buried itself in her head and refused to go away. It kept tapping her on the shoulder. Because there was a *chance*, however small, that it might just work. Wasn't there? And there was something else as well. Some small curiosity that perhaps had always been there. About Mr Flood. Her father. The man who walked up the road and never came back. There was that same question that buzzed around Dara's head, like a fly banging itself against a closed window. *Why?*

But the right moment never presented itself. Since Angel's loss of faith and hope, something had happened to them. To all of them. They were still moving forward, but limping now, unsettled by the loss of Angel's confident stride. Without the positive, life-affirming energy that Angel supplied in buckets throughout their home and their lives, everything seemed quieter. Emptier, somehow.

Yes, Angel was going to dialysis three times a week, just as she had done before. But that was all she did. She hadn't returned to her job at the school. In fairness, the principal – a gentle, kind woman who went by the unlikely name of Dorothy Stern – told her not to, but this had never stopped Angel before. Now she spent her time lying on her unmade bed, watching a never-ending loop of mindless television programmes. Repeats, most of them, but Angel had never seen them before. She'd never had any spare time before, because of her life and the way it strained fit to burst with all the things she used to do. She listened to music too. Dara could hear the faint strains of it through Angel's closed bedroom door. Maudlin pieces by Joy Division and Leonard Cohen and Morrissey and The Smiths and Radiohead. It was enough to make anyone lose their will to live.

Without ever discussing it, Mrs Flood and Dara kept a vigil over Angel. Dara started work earlier in the morning, so she could come home earlier to relieve Mrs Flood, who then set off in her Bobs Away van to tame the hair of the women of Donaghmede, Kilbarrack, Edenmore and Raheny. They took turns. They kept watch. Angel didn't seem to notice.

Dara considered discussing the matter with Ian Harte. But it was difficult to know where to start, given that Ian knew very little about Dara's family life. They talked. Of course they did. But their conversations were rather generic in nature. Books, films, Penelope (Ian's chihuahua), Dara's charges at the pound, a rogue trader at the bank, places that Dara would love to visit and Ian already had.

'Paris,' Dara told him.

'Overrated,' Ian replied.

When they weren't talking or watching films, they were having complicated sex, although Ian managed to monologue through much of these couplings as well.

Before sex: 'Baby, I'm so hungry for you, it's like I haven't eaten in days and you're this . . . this . . .'

'Big Mac and chips?' Dara grinned at him.

Ian looked at her whenever she interrupted his soliloquys, as if he knew her from somewhere but couldn't quite remember where. 'God no, you're like a . . . a smorgasbord of delectable treats. Your breasts are like those gorgeous pink marshmallows melting on top of a hot chocolate . . .'

Whispering in her ear during sex: 'Oh baby, your skin is

so soft, it's like . . . like . . . clouds.' Dara was pretty sure that clouds would feel wet and cold, but she didn't mention it.

And of course afterwards: 'Baby, that was . . . that was . . .'

'Good?' Dara supplied.

'Christ, no.' Ian looked offended. 'It was much better than good. It was . . . it was *magnificent*.'

Yes, Ian Harte was a man who loved to talk. When she was with him, Dara never had to rummage around in her head for something interesting or outrageous to say.

The problem was that, in spite of all this talking, or more accurately, because of it, there never seemed to be a spare moment for Dara to tell Ian about Angel and the found-and-lost kidney. About the crazy notion of finding Mr Flood.

So their impromptu Wednesday night meeting – Ian's trip to Geneva had been cancelled at the last minute – passed without Dara mentioning it.

It was Friday before Dara allowed herself to acknowledge that the right moment was never going to present itself. The house was empty when she got home. There was a note on the kitchen table.

Gone to the hospital with Angel to keep her company. We should be back by 8 p.m.
Your mother (Mrs Flood)

Dara had long ago given up wondering why Mrs Flood signed all her notes like that. Even the ones to Angel were signed off like that. *Your mother*, and then, in brackets beside it, *Mrs Flood*.

Dara struggled out of her duffel coat, poured herself a beer and sat on the ancient swing in the garden, smoking one cigarette after the other until she hated them enough to want to give them up again. Then she made her way to the tiny narrow kitchen at the back of the house. She'd make something special for dinner. Something meaty. Something that would perk them all up, give them a bit of pep, as Tintin was fond of saying. She looked in the fridge and the cupboards and decided on lasagne. They all loved Dara's lasagne. And upside-down apple cake for dessert. It seemed apt. There was no cream in the fridge, but it would taste good with Dara's home-made custard: thick and yellow and sweet.

Soon the little kitchen was filled with the sounds and smells of cooking, and despite everything, Dara could feel the strain of the last two weeks ebbing and waning. She beat eggs and grated nutmeg. She crushed garlic and sliced onions, loving the clean sweep of the blade through the layers. She browned meat and washed basil leaves. She added raisins and cinnamon to the pulpy pleasure of the stewed apples. Unbeknownst to herself, she hummed the theme tune from *Animal Rescue*. She didn't think about cigarettes. Or about Angel's end-stage renal failure. Or about Anya's suggestion about Mr Flood. About finding him. No. Dara Flood stirred and poked and prodded and chopped and grated and hummed the theme tune from *Animal Rescue*, and thought about absolutely nothing. She could never really say why she liked cooking and baking so much. But here was the reason. It was her worry-free zone. And when you're the kind of worrier that Dara Flood was, a worry-free zone was not just advisable. It was *essential*. She lifted the box of sea salt, spilling a few grains as she shook some out on to the palm of her hand. She threw the spilled salt over both shoulders – just to be sure.

By the time Mrs Flood and Angel arrived home, dinner was prepared, the lasagne's cheesy top bubbling in the main oven, the cake rising shyly in the bottom one, and the table set. Properly set, with the silver cutlery Mrs Flood had received as a wedding present from her grandmother, and candles left over from last Christmas. Dara had even changed out of her work tracksuit (only into her home tracksuit, but still) and dabbed some perfume behind her ears to ease the smell of dog that Mrs Flood hated.

Mrs Flood struggled out of her coat and pulled Angel into the kitchen behind her.

'Isn't this *lovely*, Angel?' Her voice was airy and light. Cajoling. Dara turned back to the oven. It was hard to look at Angel's face now. There was something sunken about it. Defeated. She stood beside the fridge, fiddling with the magnets Mrs Flood liked to collect, her coat still on.

'I think I'll just have an early night,' Angel said, without looking at Dara.

'No,' said Dara in a way that made both Mrs Flood and Angel look at her, startled.

'I mean, please, Angel, stay and have some dinner with us. And I've made your favourite dessert.'

'I'm sorry. I'm just not very hungry,' Angel persisted, moving towards the kitchen door. Dara got there first and closed it. Firmly.

'I need to talk to you,' she said, her hand wrapped around the door handle like a lock. 'To both of you, in fact,' she added, nodding towards Mrs Flood.

Angel said nothing. But she sat at the kitchen table. Right on the edge of a chair, as if she wasn't staying long. With her coat buttoned up. But still. She was there. It was a start.

Mrs Flood sat beside her and looked at Dara, waiting. Dara could feel her mother's eyes boring holes into her back as she bent to lift the lasagne from the oven.'

'What did you make?' Mrs Flood asked finally.

'Lasagne.'

'Angel can't have too much cheese. You know that.'

'I only put cheese on the top,' Dara said. 'Hardly any. I've made a cheese sauce, though. You can pour it on your piece, OK?'

'I suppose so,' said Mrs Flood, with a tired sigh.

It was during this exchange that it happened. Angel's head lowered and lowered, until her face nearly touched the table. And then a tear splashed on to the empty dinner plate in front of her. Dara saw Mrs Flood bite her lip. No one said anything. This was uncharted territory. Crying at the kitchen table. The fear that had dogged Dara for the past two weeks squeezed a cold hand around her heart. She sat down in the chair beside Angel and lifted her sister's limp hand.

'Please, Angel, don't cry.'

'I'm sorry, I don't know how to stop.' More tears landed on the plate, making a small puddle.

'We've still got each other, haven't we?' Dara said to Angel. 'We're all in this together, aren't we?'

'I'm the only one with the end-stage renal failure, amn't I?' Angel's voice was like someone else's. Sour. Bitter.

'This is a setback, that's what this is,' said Mrs Flood. 'That's all it is.' She banged her hand on the table when she said this and it made the cracking noise of a judge's gavel. Dara jumped.

Angel spoke as if Mrs Flood had said nothing. She said, 'I'm never going to get a kidney,' and the quiet resignation in her voice hit Dara like a slap. For a moment, nobody said anything. But after a week of waiting for the right moment, Dara suddenly realised that there was never going to be a right moment, ever again. And even though this might just be the worst moment of the week, the lowest ebb, in fact, Dara decided that it was now or never. She jumped out of her seat, surprising herself as well as her mother and sister.

'YOU ARE GOING TO GET A KIDNEY!' she shouted.

Angel lifted her head and looked at Dara – really looked at her – for the first time that day. Maybe the first time that week.

'I have a plan,' said Dara with as much conviction as she could muster. There was a faint flicker of something in Angel's eyes that might just be hope. Or the memory of hope, perhaps. Dara grabbed at it before it could get away. 'First,' she said, eyeballing the pair of them in turn, 'you have to promise me that you'll hear me out and not say anything until I've finished, OK?' She fixed them both with a ferocious glare, and sure, what could either of them do, but nod mutely and wait. Dara never shouted. Or fixed people with ferocious glares.

There was no easy way to say this, so Dara took a deep breath and just said it in her ordinary voice as if it was something entirely normal.

'I'm going to find Mr Flood,' she said.

If she had picked a hand grenade out of the cutlery drawer, removed the pin and lobbed in on to the table between them, they could not have looked more shocked. Mr Flood was not a common visitor to their conversations around the dinner table. Dara pushed on. 'It was Anya's idea really. And at first I thought no. What would be the use? And where would we even begin? But I've been thinking about it all week. And you know what, it's highly likely that he's got the same blood type as Angel, isn't it? And you never know, maybe it would be an opportunity for him to atone for . . . for . . . leaving, I suppose. Maybe he's different now. Maybe he'd jump at the chance.' Her voice got slower and slower until it stopped altogether. Saying it out loud made it sound a bit, well, ridiculous. Like a dream you have that makes perfect sense, until you relay it to someone else and realise how preposterous it really is.

Still Angel and Mrs Flood said nothing, although her mother's arms were tightly folded across her chest and her mouth had disappeared completely behind the thin line of her lips. Dara pressed on. What else could she do?

'OK, so it's unlikely. Even that I might find him. Or that he's a match. Or that he would be willing to give Angel one of his kidneys. But it's *possible*, isn't it? It's a *possibility*.'

Mrs Flood finally managed to open her mouth, but Dara stopped her with another roar. 'WAIT!' Mrs Flood closed her mouth again, and even though she looked at Dara like she'd never seen her before, she waited.

'Here's the plan,' said Dara. 'We'll have dinner, then dessert – it's upside-down apple cake – and only then will we discuss this idea. Deal?'

Maybe it was because they were hungry. Or perhaps they were wrong-footed by Dara's vehemence that was so vehement, it was close to rage. Whatever the reasons, they did exactly as Dara bid. And for a moment, it was like old times, the three of them at the small square table in the narrow confines of the kitchen, with the sounds of dinner all around. Even Angel managed to eat some of the lasagne Dara spooned onto her plate – taking care to wipe off Angel's puddle of tears before she dished up.

Dara found that she couldn't stop talking. She beat at the silence that had penetrated the house over the last week with both hands, telling them anything she could think of. She told them about Sherlock and how he could whine to the tune of Whitney Houston's 'I Will Always Love You'. This particular nugget had been discovered by Tintin, who said he only ever listened to Whitney when he was depressed, which couldn't be true because he listened to Whitney all the time, and he had a generally affable disposition.

When this didn't generate much of a response, Dara rallied with an edited version of Tintin's date last week with a teacher who had only recently come out and was in no way ready for a date with Tintin, who had revealed his own bisexuality to his parents when he was a mere eleven years old. But the editing process snipped away most of what was great about the story, so when Dara got to the punchline ('I'm going to have to give you a 'C' minus for that'), only Mrs Flood made a stab towards laughter.

Nevertheless, Dara's one-sided attempts at conversation managed to get them through dinner, then dessert, and it was not until she put the kettle on for tea that Angel brought up Mr Flood.

'It's never going to work,' she said.

'Probably not,' agreed Dara. 'But it might. It just might.'

Angel shook her head.

'Maybe he's changed,' Dara said.

Mrs Flood laughed then. An ugly, harsh sound that distorted the features of her face, twisting them with her bitterness.

'Angel's right, as usual,' she said. 'A leopard doesn't change its spots.'

Dara tried again. 'He was a good man once. You said so yourself. When you were first married. You said he could be kind. You were happy then.'

Mrs Flood shook her head. 'That was a long time ago.'

'Mam, I know this is hard for you. And I'm sorry. But I have to try. Can you understand that?'

Mrs Flood shook her head again. 'He didn't just leave me, you know. He left *all* of us.' There was anger in the eyes she flashed at Dara. 'He didn't even wait around long enough to see you,' she went on, as if Dara had not spoken. 'Thirteen days. Thirteen days before you were born and he was gone, just like that. I was young back then. With two small babies. And no one to help me.' It was a speech the girls had heard many times before. There was more to come, but Dara reefed the conversation off her and did her best to steer it back on course.

'It's worth trying, Angel?' She turned to her sister. 'Isn't it?'

'I don't think it will work,' Angel said.

'But it *could*,' Dara shot back.

'It's unlikely,' Angel continued.

'Unlikely, yes. But not impossible, right?'

Angel shrugged and Dara took heart. It was not impossible. Unlikely, yes. But not impossible.

Nothing more was said on the subject until Angel went upstairs a short while later, saying she was tired. Dara was left, once again, alone with her mother.

'Why don't you bring your wine into the sitting room and watch the *Late Late*?' she suggested. 'I'll do the dishes.' To this, Mrs Flood made no reply.

'You should have discussed this with me before you said anything to your sister,' she said instead. There was something laboured about her voice. She sounded exhausted.

'I knew you'd say no.'

'You're setting Angel up for a fall.'

'That's not my intention. I'm just trying to give her some hope.'

'You're going to disappoint her.'

'I'm only trying to help.'

'Happy endings are for books, Dara. They're not for real life.'

There was nothing to say to that, so Dara said nothing. Eventually Mrs Flood took her glass and the remains of the bottle of wine and repaired to the front room. Dara sank on to a chair. If she was honest with herself, she agreed with Mrs Flood and Angel. The quest to find Mr Flood was a dubious one at best. There was no getting away from that. But Angel had eaten some of her dinner. Even a little dessert. She had stopped crying. And Dara had seen a flicker of something that might just be hope in her eyes. Or the memory of hope at least. Finding Mr Flood was the distraction Angel needed to get her through the dialysis and the endless waiting. It could take weeks to find him. Months! And a suitable kidney could come along before that, couldn't it? Any day. The hospital might ring at this very moment. But in the meantime, Angel could take comfort from the fact that there was a Plan B, however tenuous. It could work, couldn't it? And if it didn't, well, they had nothing to lose, so it didn't matter, right?

Dara set her shoulders and braced herself. What was the worst thing that could happen?

14

For someone who led such a contained kind of life, Miss Pettigrew knew a lot of people.

'I know someone who might be able to help,' she said when Dara called the next day to collect Edward.

'Help with what?'

'Finding Mr Flood, of course.'

There wasn't a lot that got past Miss Pettigrew. She had weaseled the story out of Mrs Flood when she popped in that morning to apply a purple rinse. 'Purple is *in*,' Miss Pettigrew told Mrs Flood.

'She doesn't think it's a good idea,' Dara admitted.

'That's one way of putting it,' Miss Pettigrew agreed.

'What do *you* think?' Dara asked, curious.

'You have to do something, Dara. That's what I think. You've had a face like a long wet weekend in Blackpool these past two weeks. Not to mention the cigarette smoking and the drinking in the garden last night.'

'I had *one* beer,' said Dara, stung.

'Nevertheless,' said Miss Pettigrew, 'it's the slippery slope all the same. Next thing you know you'll be on a park bench smoking, I don't know, *horse* or whatever they're taking nowadays, with some cheap bottle of ghastly wine – a Bordeaux perhaps.' Miss Pettigrew hated everything French.

When Dara didn't respond – she couldn't think of a thing to say – Miss Pettigrew peered at her from underneath her drawn-on eyebrows and said, 'I know how these things go, Dara. I watch the documentary channel, you know.'

'So who do you know?' asked Dara, anxious for a change of subject.

'A private eye,' said Miss Pettigrew. She also watched quite a bit of *CSI Miami, New York, London* and the rest.

Miss Pettigrew tapped her nose three times with a quivering index finger and winked at Dara. 'I have contacts,' she said.

Her contact in this instance was a fellow little old lady she played bridge with – online, of course – every afternoon at four. The Merry Widow was her online handle, although her real name was Ita O'Brien. Ita's youngest sister – Mabel – was acquainted with a man called Peadar Davis (*'We're just good friends, mind,* she insisted, even though nobody had ever suggested otherwise) and Peadar had an American cousin whose daughter – Cora – had disgraced herself by getting pregnant *out of wedlock,* although was now respectably engaged to the father of the child, a recently promoted detective, according to Miss Pettigrew's sources. Anyway, this Cora's husband had a younger brother called Stanley Flinter.

'*He's* the private eye.' Miss Pettigrew was a little breathless after this monologue and had to lie on the couch for a moment.

'Well?' she said after a while, raising herself up on bony elbows.

'Well what?'

'What do you think about Stanley Flinter?'

'I don't know anything about him. And neither do you, by the sounds of things.'

'Well, he found Spinach, didn't he?'

'Spinach?'

'Ita's cat. An almost pure-bred Persian cat. He's got an unfortunate greenish tinge about the jowls. Ita posted a photograph of him on Facebook.'

'He finds people's *cats*?'

'I'm sure he finds people too,' said Miss Pettigrew, worrying at her nails with an emery board.

'I don't know,' said Dara, tickling Edward behind his ears, which made his tail wag and his back leg twitch. 'A private investigator would probably cost a lot of money.' She thought about her paltry savings account.

'Ita gave him a silver photo frame for finding Spinach. Well, sterling silver, but still. I'm sure you could come to some arrangement with him.'

Dara, whose stock of sterling silver photo frames was about as paltry as her savings account, shook her head. 'I don't know,' she said again.

Miss Pettigrew ignored her, opened the lid of her laptop and began tapping away at a speed that belied the swollen arthritic knuckles of her hands.

'There,' she said after a while. 'Dara, be a dear and fetch me my writing pad and pen from the mantelpiece.'

Dara did as she was bid, taking care not to dislodge any of the myriad of china dogs that lined the ledge. With a shaky hand and her tongue poked out between her dentures, Miss Pettigrew wrote a number on a page and handed it to Dara.

'What's this?' Dara asked.

'Stanley Flinter's telephone number,' she said. 'Tell him I sent you. That'll probably get you a discount. No doubt he's heard all about me from that Cora's father's cousin.' Dara doubted this, but she pocketed the number anyway. 'You know, Dara, this could be the start of something for you.'

'What do you mean?' Dara was genuinely confused. All she felt at the moment was fear and uncertainty and, yes, a certain measure of foreboding. She just wanted everything to go back to the way it was before they got that bloody phone call from the hospital. Everything had been perfect before that. Well, maybe not perfect, but passable. More than passable.

Miss Pettigrew sighed at Dara's confusion. 'The great adventure that is life, Dara dear,' she said, shaking her head. 'You should try it sometime.' This coming from the neighbourhood recluse. 'You never know, you might even like it.'

Miss Pettigrew smiled the smile of a woman who knew all about the great adventure of life. And maybe she did. But that was a long time ago and the world was different now. Dangerous and disappointing and unreliable. And you didn't even have to experience these things. All you had to do was read the newspapers and look at the television to see how . . . how precarious everything was. Dara was alarmed to feel the sting of hot tears behind her eyes. She was not a woman who cried without a good, solid reason.

'Everything is changing,' she whispered to Miss Pettigrew.

'Yes, my dear,' agreed the old woman. 'But some changes are for the better, aren't they?'

Dara nodded, although she wasn't convinced.

'Now run along with you,' said Miss Pettigrew, rising stiffly from the hard-backed chair she had been sitting on. 'I've things to be doing.'

Dara didn't want to leave the warm comfort of Miss Pettigrew's house. But she did. Nor did she want to ring the number on the crumpled piece of paper in her hot fist. But she knew she would. She had promised Angel she would find Mr Flood, but the truth was, she had no idea where to begin.

So she squared her shoulders and took a deep breath and inched out towards the ledge of her lovely, steady, solid sort of a life. She hesitated – just for a moment – before she closed her eyes and stepped out. Out into the dangerous, disappointing and unreliable world. Out into the great adventure that was life.

15

Stanley Flinter got the call the following evening at 9.23 p.m. He was on a job. A proper job. For an insurance company. Which meant that he could charge a bit more and the chances of getting paid in actual cold, hard cash were considerably greater.

When the phone rang, Stanley was up a tree. A giant oak. The branches – thick as a sumo wrestler's thighs – afforded great protection against the *subject,* who, in this case, was suing a local pub for a significant six-figure sum because of a trip and fall he'd suffered on their premises after indulging one of his great passions, which involved the vast consumption of alcohol in the form of several cans of Beamish with nothing to eat for the day, apart from two packets of dry-roasted peanuts.

Despite this trip and fall (he tripped over an empty can of Beamish), he lost no time in contacting his solicitor and instigating a claim against the pub, called, funnily enough, The Daytripper.

Now this subject – Tommo-the-Thick Traynor, as he was known locally, more because of his girth than any perceived lack of smarts – lay on a bench press at the back of his house, lifting, as far as Stanley could see through his binoculars, 90 kg up and over his head without even breaking a sweat. Discarded on the ground beside him lay his neck brace, back brace, crutches and arm sling, like bits and pieces of a person. This was insurance-claim gold, Stanley thought, as he focused on the subject through the long lens of his trusty Nikon camera. He used the manual function of the camera, so there would be no flash to give him away. No matter how advanced technology got, Stanley loved the feel of the Nikon in his hands, the click and the whir of it, the stories it could tell, stored in the confines of its sturdy black body.

That's when he got the call. His ringtone was a loud and shrill rendition of the original theme tune to *Doctor Who*. In the silence, the noise was deafening. It reverberated through the trees, as eerie and menacing as the Daleks themselves. Stanley – already on tenterhooks, and not surprisingly, given Tommo-the-Thick Traynor's reputation for gratuitous violence – jerked, which was unfortunate because it was this jerk – more of a twitch really – that provided the domino effect for what followed. His body sort of jackknifed and began to slip off the branch he was straddling. If only he had let go of the Nikon, the outcome might have been different. But he did not. He held the camera tight against his chest, leaving him with only one free hand, which groped frantically through the empty space for a branch to grip.

As he fell, Stanley had time to curse himself for climbing so high up the tree. There'd been no need to go quite so far, but there was something about tree climbing that gave him access to his seven-year-old self in a way that was nostalgic and exhilarating, all at the same time.

He landed on a squashy bank of heather, and, while it was doubtful if the heather would ever blaze again, Stanley was remarkably uninjured. In fact, apart from the bruising to his buttocks and thighs, the lump rising like a head out of his left knee, a sprained ankle and a sharp graze down one side of his face where it had glanced against the rough, ancient bark of a branch, he was all right. But these injuries were the least of Stanley Flinter's problems. As he lay winded and disoriented at the base of the huge tree, he could hear footsteps. Running. Getting closer. Tommo-the-Thick Traynor could run quite

fast for a man of his girth. Of the shattered ribs, fractured leg
and torn ligaments cited in his insurance claim, there were no
signs. Stanley could hear him crashing through the hedge at
the bottom of his garden.

He gathered himself and sat up, every nerve in his body
screaming for Solpadeine, whiskey, a hot-water bottle and
a soft place to lie. He knew he couldn't outrun Tommo in
his current compromised state. His head thrashed this way
and that, looking for somewhere to hide. To his left, furious
breathing and the sharp crack of branches breaking as Tommo
roared through the wood. To his right, a tree, recently felled,
the trunk hollow and dark. Stanley crawled towards it, his knee
creaking and moaning every time he leaned on it. It was a
tight fit, but somehow he managed to squeeze himself inside.
The overpowering smell was one of damp and decay. A scuttling noise above his head and a rummaging in his hair may
or may not have been a curious mouse. Or a rat. Something
with a lot of legs strolled across his forehead and burrowed
into his fringe. Stanley held his breath and listened. Tommo-
the-Thick Traynor had arrived in the clearing, breathing like
a running bull in Pamplona.

'Where are ya, ya little fucker?' he roared, and in the silence
of the wood, his voice sounded like ten voices.

Ten angry voices.

'I seen ya, so I did. An' I'll find out who the fuck you are
and where the fuck you live and I will DEDICATE myself to
making your life a fucken MISERY.'

Stanley could hear Tommo kicking leaves out of his way,
then kicking something solid, perhaps a tree, before he
sighed – a tired sort of a sigh – and walked towards the felled
tree, his footsteps ominous and heavy in the stillness of the
wood. An owl hooted and Stanley wondered if this would be
the last sound he would ever hear. As last sounds went, it was
pleasant: high and plaintive and somehow comforting. Then

Tommo sat down. On the tree trunk. It rolled slightly under his weight, and now Stanley was on the flat of his back, looking up into the blackness, imagining Tommo's wide backside inches from his face, separated only by the decaying bark of the tree stump. Stanley hoped it would hold. A rustling sound now, like paper. Then the rasping strike of a match against wood and a silence, while Tommo inhaled for such a long time that Stanley was able to take a moment to admire the capacity of his lungs before remembering that he was moments away from being actually killed by somebody's bare hands and buried in a shallow grave in a wood in Wicklow.

It took Tommo a long time to finish his cigarette. Stanley had a terrible itch on the bridge of his nose, where a family of beetles were holding a reunion. There was one particularly dodgy moment when Tommo shifted his weight on the tree trunk and emitted a long, loud fart, followed by a moan that Stanley identified as one of pure pleasure.

'Good arse,' Tommo said.

Stanley fancied he could smell it through the bark. A hot, cheesy smell. This struck him as funny, even though there was nothing funny about the situation. He had to fight not to laugh, pinching himself on one of his myriad of bruises and biting down on his bottom lip until it hurt nearly as much as the rest of him.

Eventually Tommo got up and left. Stanley's immediate reaction was to crawl out of the hollow, but he forced himself to wait a full ten minutes before he began to move. There was one terrifying moment, when he thought he'd have to dislocate his shoulder to prise it past the narrow opening, but in the end he got away with a strain and some additional bruising. With the aid of a stick, he hobbled out of the wood, across the road, up a lane and over a narrow ditch until he reached his van, which he had parked behind a deserted petrol station.

Ciara Geraghty

He kept one eye on the rearview mirror all the way home. The Nikon sat in the front passenger seat. There wasn't a scratch on it.

It wasn't until later – when Stanley was in the bathroom of his flat, doing his best with cotton wool, antiseptic cream and a creased, nearly empty tube of Deep Heat – that he remembered his phone. It wasn't the first time he had forgotten to turn it off on a job. But it was definitely the last, he promised himself. Although this wasn't the first time he had made such a promise.

It was difficult to hear the message with the cacophony of barking in the background. And the girl spoke in a stage whisper, as if she didn't want anyone to hear her. She sounded young. Guarded. 'Hello, my name is Dara Flood. I got your number from Miss Pettigrew.'

The name meant nothing to Stanley.

'She's a friend of Ita.'

Still nothing.

'You found Ita's cat, Spinach, as far as I know.'

Ah yes, the mystery of the missing almost-pure-bred Persian cat, Spinach. Although it hadn't been much of a mystery, Stanley remembered. More of an exercise in tree climbing. Another one.

'So the thing is that I wondered if you might . . . hang on a minute . . . please, Edward, be quiet, I'm on the phone . . . sorry about that . . . anyway, could you ring me back? When you get a chance, I mean. My name is Dara Flood. Did I say that already? Sorry. And my number is . . . please, Edward, get down, I'll get you a biscuit in a minute, OK?'

Stanley held the phone away from his ear as the barking grew more frantic, then there was a thud, and a crack, and some rustling before the line went dead altogether. He suspected a missing dog case. He seemed to be getting a reputation as some kind of domestic pet finder. But still. In these recessionary times, he couldn't afford to be choosy. He knew how he'd feel if Clouseau went missing. Although that was unlikely, given the sheer width and breadth of the dog.

Stanley looked at his watch. Midnight. Too late to ring? Perhaps it was. But Stanley didn't like keeping people waiting. Dara Flood hadn't managed to leave her number. He checked his missed calls log.

The phone rang five times before it went onto voice mail. 'Hello, this is . . . ah . . . Dara Flood and I'll . . . I'll try to get back to you just as soon as . . .' (dogs barking, sound of running feet, then a door slamming) '. . . so leave a message,' (voice a little breathless now) 'and I'll call you back later. Or tomorrow if I don't get this message till it's too late to call back. Thank you for calling. This is Dara Flood. Thanks.'

Dara Flood's voice reminded him of Cora's, only because it couldn't have been more different. Hoarse. Gravelly. Worried. Cora's voice was high. Breathy. Carefree. Stanley sighed and wondered when he would stop being reminded of Cora. He'd thought he was getting better. Getting over it. Cora and Cormac had been together for fifteen months now.

'A year and a day, Stanley.' That was what Sissy told him. That was how long it took to get over someone. A year and a day. He was behind schedule.

He hobbled out of the bathroom and took the stairs in halting limps. In the kitchen, he poured himself a finger of whiskey before he took his wallet out of his back pocket and flicked it open. The photograph was a passport-size one. Tucked inside a book of stamps hidden behind some ripped lining at the back of the wallet. It had been taken only two Christmases ago. In a booth in town. The two of them. Him, grinning like the fool that he was, his heart splattered all across his sleeve. An easy target. A fucking eejit. Draped all over Cora, as she sat on the little stool with her blond hair falling across her face

so that only one of her green eyes was visible, clear and focused, staring straight ahead of her, straight into the camera.
Their last Christmas together. If he had known that, Stanley
would have tried to look a little more dignified in the photograph. A little less like a puppy who'd been rescued from a
pound. But that was how he had felt. At the time. And for the
two Christmases before that.

'At least you had a good run,' Sissy told him, more than
once. Sissy's longest relationship had lasted almost one year.
From the day after her twenty-fifth birthday to the week
before her twenty-sixth. 'Cheap bastard,' she'd sobbed on
Stanley's shoulder when it became clear that the watch Duncan had promised her for her birthday ('a D-D-Dolce and
G-G-Gabbana one,' she wept) was not forthcoming.

His mother couldn't say the usual things she said about the
women who had the *gall* to break one of her boys' hearts. The
situation was delicate, to say the least. Because of Cormac.
And the baby. 'There's plenty more fish in the sea,' was all
she'd been able to come up with in the circumstances. Stanley
knew she meant well.

He stood at the kitchen counter, drank the whiskey and ate
his way through two Penguin bars without really tasting them,
which was a shame when you considered how much he loved
Penguin bars. He'd been doing so well too. Well, better, at any
rate. It was Cormac's announcement that had thrown him off
course. The invitation to the engagement party. Cora would
be Mrs Flinter, after all. If she had been marrying anyone
else, Stanley didn't think he would mind all that much. He
and Cora did not have anything in common. It was easy to
see that now, from his position on the sidelines. No, it was
the fact that she was marrying Cormac. That Cormac was
marrying her. His big brother. The biggest of them. Despite
Cormac's arrogance, his bossiness, his absolute certainty and
belief in himself and in everything he did: despite all of those

things, Stanley had loved him. Had looked up to him. The way brothers do.

He cleared his throat and left a message for Dara Flood. Keep himself busy, that was the trick. He decided to take Clouseau for a walk even though it was late. The dog had to be walked twice a day, and although it was, technically, to-morrow, and Stanley's body jarred with every small move he made, he reached for the lead. 'Clouseau!' he called in a low voice so as not to wake Sissy. Then he braced himself against the kitchen counter as the mighty canine tore down the hall and flung himself against him, before arranging himself on his back legs and wrapping his front legs around Stanley's neck, like a lover.

'Eh, would you like to go for a walk, Clouseau?' Stanley hadn't quite worked out the correct way to address the dog. Clouseau barked his high-pitched, excited bark before howl-ing, a long, mournful howl with the weight of the world in it. As a response, it was a confusing one.

Stanley took him for a walk anyway. Keep busy, keep mov-ing. These were the thoughts in Stanley Flinter's head as he struggled to keep up with Clouseau. Whenever thoughts of Cora came seeping up through the drains in his head, like floodwater, he listed the ingredients needed for his summer berry pavlova, which held no memories at all of Cora, who hated anything sweet.

16

The building on Abbey Street was not ageing well. The door was a sorry affair, with peeling black paint and a rusting handle. Dara noticed the line of muck under her fingernails when she pressed the bell next to a handwritten sign that said 'Stanley Flinter'. Probably from helping Jeffrey, this morning, to recover the bone he'd gone to great lengths to bury the night before. Jeffrey was the new arrival. A massive St Bernard with a tendency towards forgetfulness.

The buzzer, when it eventually sounded, was as old as the building, and was a half-hearted, contrary wail. She pushed the door. Nothing happened. She braced her shoulder against it and pushed again, this time with both hands. The door flew open and she fell in, banging her hip against the corner of a hall table. The pain made her eyes smart and her bag drop, the contents scattered across the carpet, which was threadbare, the colour long gone.

The building did not improve with altitude, although the door to Stanley Flinter's office had benefited from a recent lick of paint. It was ajar, but she knocked anyway.

'Come in,' said a voice, and Dara recognised it as the voice on the phone. Quiet. Contained. She pushed the door open and stepped inside.

Dara noticed two things at once. A framed photograph of a dog – of undetermined pedigree, some type of lurcher – on the desk in the corner of the room. It was the dog's eyes that drew her careful attention. Big, sad brown eyes. Dara could hardly bear to look at them, they were that sad. The second thing she noticed was Stanley Flinter's eyes. They were *exactly* the same as the dog's. Big, sad brown eyes. There, the resemblance ended. The dog was *huge*. She could tell, even though he was sitting down in the picture. Whereas the man in the office ... well ... he was not a man who could have been described as lofty. Not even of average height. In fact, short was the only word that could be applied to him. Dara might even be taller than him if she wore heels, which she never did.

'Please excuse the mess,' said Stanley Flinter, bending over a chair and beating at the seat of it with a telephone book. Dust rose in thick, choking clouds and settled in Stanley's hair, which was short and black and could have been described as neat had it not been for the unfortunate position of the cowlick at the front. The cowlick played havoc with the fringe, which stood up and about, as if it were trying to get a better view. 'I've just moved in,' he explained, straightening and gesturing around the room with an air of quiet hopelessness. 'Here, take this seat, it's the cleanest one.'

He pointed at the chair he had just beaten the living daylights out of, and Dara sat down. Stanley turned and hobbled towards the only other chair in the room, winced as he sat down and looked at Dara. It was only then that she noticed the side of his face.

'Are you ... all right?' she asked.

'It looks worse than it is,' said Stanley, touching his fingers to his injured face. 'Just a minor ... ah ... accident last night.'

Dara rummaged at the bottom of her bag. 'Here,' she said, passing him a tube of cream. 'Try this. It's great for the pain and the inflammation.' Stanley hesitated, and the sadness in his big brown eyes turned to wariness. 'It's a natural remedy,' said Dara, who was no stranger to wariness.

'Eh, thanks,' he said, standing up and limping towards a mirror that hung crookedly on the wall. Dara could see him trying not to wince as he rubbed the cream on to the battle-field on his face.

From behind, Dara noticed his suit. The colour – melted chocolate brown – was nice, but it was crying out for an iron. Also, the trouser legs could do with being taken up three inch-es. To see his face in the mirror, he stood on the tips of his toes, and Dara could see a sticker on the soles of his shoes. He had bought them in Arnotts for €69.99. She stopped looking at him because she had the distinct impression that he was not comfortable with her scrutiny. Instead she looked around. If disorganisation were a place, it would be here, in this office. In fact, this office could be disorganisation's headquarters. The main hub. Central thoroughfare. Dara would have considered walking out, but for the thought of those big, sad brown eyes turning from the mirror and discovering the empty office. That, and the file on his desk. Pristine and flat with a white sticker on the front. The writing on the sticker was the tidiest thing in the office. In small, neat, steady print, it said 'FIND-ING MR FLOOD'. A declaration, rather than a question. The positiveness of it. Dara decided to stay.

'Actually, that's much better.' When Stanley Flinter smiled, everything changed. He seemed taller, his suit not quite so creased, the curse of his cowlick less pronounced. But it was his eyes, really. When his eyes lost their serious, hound-dog expres-sion, Stanley Flinter looked like a different man. A happy man.

'You can keep that tube, I've got another one at home,' Dara told him.

'Oh . . . thank you.' Again that look of wary surprise that told Dara Stanley Flinter was a man who did not expect much from people.

'Right,' he said, sitting down in a chair behind his desk. 'Where were we?'

'Eh, you were saying you had a minor accident last night,' offered Dara, who wasn't quite sure what the protocol for this meeting was, exactly.

'Was I?' Stanley pushed his fringe out of his eyes. It fell immediately back to its original position.

'Well, you mentioned it, at any rate,' Dara said.

'Coffee,' said Stanley suddenly. 'That's what I meant to say. Would you like some?'

'That would be lovely.'

'I'll put the kettle on.' He got up too quickly. The chair fell backwards and knocked against a shelf. This proved to be the last straw for the shelf, which was already crooked and clinging to the wall with the half-hearted assistance of two rusty nails. The shelf seemed to groan before it gave way, bringing its contents down with it. Box sets mostly. Dara saw *24, Mad Men, The Wire* and she couldn't be sure, but she thought Series Five of *Sex and the City*. The DVDs landed on a tray on the floor. The weight of them crashing down put paid to everything on the tray, which included a coffee pot, two mugs and a milk jug.

There was silence for a good while.

'Or tea?' he said then. 'We could have tea?'

'Tea is fine,' said Dara, hooking her feet around the legs of the chair to stop herself jumping up and helping Stanley with the broken delft. She felt the heat of his embarrassment, and knew that an offer of help would not ease it.

He picked his way carefully through the office and disappeared through a door. Dara heard a fridge opening.

'Eh, you don't take milk in your tea, by any chance?' he called out.

Dara hesitated for just a moment before she said no, even though she liked a good dollop. She just couldn't bear to think about Stanley tackling the several and sheer flights of stairs to get milk.

'That's good, I forgot to get some. I've only moved in. Did I mention that?'

'You did,' said Dara. 'Have you just started up the business?'

'No, I've been at it a year, but I've worked from home up until now.'

'Business must be good, so,' said Dara.

'Well, it's better, I suppose.' Stanley said this in a defeated kind of way, as if he wasn't sure if it were a good thing or a bad thing. He struggled out of the kitchenette with a mug in each hand and a packet of chocolate fingers clamped between his upper arm and his chest. Dara ran to help. Her nerves weren't up to any more . . . incidents.

She drank her tea – even though it was scalding and bitter – and told Stanley Flinter everything she knew about Mr Flood, which didn't take long because there wasn't a lot to tell. When she'd finished, Stanley said nothing. Maybe he was thinking. Or maybe his mouth was full of chocolate fingers. Dara didn't know. She chewed her bottom lip and thought about cigarettes, to pass the time and to stop herself from presuming the worst.

Eventually, Stanley looked at her. 'I'm not going to lie to you,' he said, and now his expression was as serious as a grave. Dara held her breath. 'This is not going to be an easy case.' Dara nodded. She knew that already. 'But . . .', he went on, and she leaned forward. Was that a trace of optimism? '. . . there's always hope.' This seemed like a funny statement, coming from Stanley Flinter, who looked like a man abandoned by hope a long time ago.

'Have you ever found a missing person before?' Dara asked.

Stanley shook his head. 'Not a missing *person*, no,' he said. He picked up a piece of paper Dara had given him on which she had written everything she knew about Mr Flood. Which wasn't a lot. His name (Eugene Flood), his age (59), his date of birth (1 November 1949), his nationality (Irish), where he was from (Bailieborough, Co. Cavan), his occupation (bricklayer) and the fact that he was left-handed, just like Dara. She wasn't sure if Stanley needed to know this, but with the paltry amount of information she had, she felt she should include everything she knew.

'I have a photograph of him, but it's very old. And creased, to be honest. It's probably no good to you.' Dara had found the photograph in the bottom of a drawer in Mrs Flood's bedroom. Mr Flood holds Angel in his arms. Like she is a parcel. Something delicate. Precious. Even back then, with the creases across the faded paper, Angel has the same eyes. Wide with the things that she holds dear. Things like faith. And hope. Mrs Flood stands beside them, her hand – small and brown – tucked into the bend of his elbow.

'He looks like you.' Stanley studied the photograph as he spoke. Dara looked at it again. It was true. It couldn't be denied. She looked like her father.

'Is that Angel?' Stanley went on. He traced her with his fingers. The pudgy roundness of her, all dimples and ribbons.

'Yes,' said Dara. 'This is her now.' She took out her phone and handed it to him. The picture of Angel – Dara's wallpaper – was a beautiful one, although it was difficult to find a photograph of Angel that wasn't beautiful. She was always photogenic. Always beautiful.

It was taken in the back garden. Back when George was there. Angel kneeling on the grass, washing him. George sits in a bucket of suds, his chestnut pelt gleaming in the slipping sun of evening. Angel looks up just as Dara takes the picture. Her expression is one of surprise. Interest. There is nothing vague about the woman in the photograph. She is not an impression of herself. She is just herself. Just Angel. Dara wished for her back, like a six-year-old wishes for a bike on Christmas Eve.

'That's a lovely photo,' said Stanley, handing the phone back to Dara. He slipped the page and the photograph of Mr Flood into the 'FINDING MR FLOOD' folder and closed it. 'I'll do some initial checking on the internet, and I have a few contacts in the Guards who might be able to help.' He nodded at a framed photograph on his desk. Dara looked at it. Six men, all remarkably similar in appearance to Stanley, apart from the fact that they were bigger. A lot bigger. All smiling at the camera, their uniforms straining to contain them.

'Your brothers?' she asked. Stanley nodded. 'All of them?' she couldn't help adding.

Stanley pointed to the man in the centre of the photograph. 'Apart from him. He's my father,' he said.

'Did you never think about becoming a guard yourself?' Dara asked, immediately regretting the question as something in Stanley's face emptied.

'I'm sorry, it's none of my business,' she told him.

'No, no, it's fine, it's just . . . well, I always just presumed I would, like the rest of them. But, well, it didn't work out, I suppose.' He said the words like he'd learned them off by heart. Like he'd said them many times before.

Dara struggled to change the subject. 'How much is this going to cost?' she asked, sitting on her hands to stop herself from biting her nails. She'd wanted to ask this question from the start but was afraid of the answer.

'It depends,' said Stanley. 'I usually charge €100 a day plus expenses.'

'I have about €450,' said Dara. In fact, she had exactly €412.37 in her savings account.

'Well . . .' It was clear that Stanley was wondering if a man like Mr Flood could be found in four and a half days. His grave disposition suggested he could not. 'You mentioned that you train dogs,' he said.

'Just in my spare time,' Dara told him. 'In the evenings and at weekends.'

'Perhaps you could help me with Clouseau?' said Stanley, nodding at the photograph on his desk. 'I sort of . . . inherited him recently. From a client who, eh, passed away, I'm afraid. He can be a little . . . unruly.'

'I'll certainly help you with your dog, but I'll pay you as well. I insist.' Dara imagined Stanley Flinter's house, cluttered with sterling silver photo frames and God knows what else he accepted as payment for his services. No wonder his office was such a sorry affair. 'Agreed?' she asked.

Stanley nodded. 'Agreed,' he said, almost smiling again.

Dara held her hand out towards Stanley Flinter. He proffered his slowly and she remembered not to grip it too tightly or shake it too vigorously. She ended up holding his hand rather than shaking it.

Afterwards, as she walked through town, she felt something odd trickle through her. She thought it might be optimism. Or some feeling distantly related to optimism, she wasn't sure. She couldn't work out why. Perhaps it was because she'd taken her first steps out into the great adventure that was life, as Miss Pettigrew had suggested. Perhaps it was because, despite Stanley Flinter's cautious reservations about the case, she sensed some quiet confidence under the wary surface of him that made her feel more hopeful than she'd felt in a while.

Whatever the reason, it felt good. She held on to it.

★   ★   ★

Fr Michael comes by most days. 'Have you any aul' sins you'd like to confess?' he asks, always his first question. His voice is the belt of a drum. Loud. Tuneless.

'Impure thoughts, Father,' I tell him.

'Lord above, but isn't it well for you, a man of your age?' he says, perching on the edge of the bed and worrying at the rosary beads in his hands.

He doesn't know my age. But I know I'm younger than he thinks I am. Younger than I look. The months of treatment have drained the last traces of myself from my face. I don't know who that old man is, staring at me from the speckled mirror in the bathroom. My features are diluted. Watered down. I try not to look, but sometimes you can't help it. It's like looking at someone else. My eyes are the worst. Hooded and pale. A bleached blue now. No trace of the navy that the women used to love. My hands shake when I cover my face with them. These hands that have trailed across the peaks and troughs of women's bodies. Their names and faces fade from my memory. Some day soon, they'll all be gone and even I won't believe my tall tales.

Today, there is a man with Fr Michael. I recognise him from before. He wears a tape measure around his neck.

'Keep your eyes to yourself,' I tell him. 'You'll be at me soon enough.' I know undertakers have a job to do, like everyone else, but there is something in the high ridge of his nose and the beady set of his eyes that lends itself to a vulture, swaying on a telephone wire, waiting. Fr Michael nods at the man, who smiles a quick, nervous smile and backs away.

'It's poor Mr ...' he consults a narrow black notebook, 'Jones next door,' he whispers down at me. 'He passed during the night.'

Fr Michael does not say 'died'. Perhaps he thinks it is a little indelicate, given the transient environment where he peddles his wares.

'Isn't it well for him,' I say.

'A happy release,' agrees Fr Michael, nodding his head up and down more than is necessary.

'Could you pass me my cardigan?' I ask, and Fr Michael reaches for it and pulls it around my shoulders.

'Is that better?' he asks, and I nod, not speaking. I knew Mr Jones. At least as much as anyone knows anyone in this Godforsaken place. He loved to read. The classics. I decide to think about him sometimes and remember that about him. Reading the classics. Not everyone does that. That has to mean something. Doesn't it?

It takes me a while, but eventually I manage to fasten each button on the cardigan. I pull the collar of it up around my neck. Even though the ward is hot and stuffy, there are days when I can't get warm.

Fr Michael is gone now. He asked if I would like him to read a passage from the Bible. Something soothing, he said. Something from the New Testament. St Paul maybe. I gave him short shrift. He takes it well, considering his vocation. Just smiles and says he'll see me tomorrow.

There's no chemotherapy now. No need. Just this waiting. I wish it didn't take this long. So long as you're alive, the thoughts come at you like trucks down a motorway. And when you're a man like me, the thoughts are the kind of things that do a body no good. No good at all.

'You'll be in better form tomorrow, Mr Waters,' Fr Michael says, even though we both know how unlikely that is. I say nothing and he nods before he turns to leave. I look at my watch. Four hours till teatime. My eyes flick to the window.

A bank of grey clouds crouch on the horizon.

There may be rain later.

I close my eyes.

17

On Friday night, Dara walked up the stairs towards Angel's room. She didn't think Angel would say yes. But she asked anyway, being perhaps more optimistic than she'd thought.

'I'm too tired,' Angel said, when Dara knocked on her bedroom door. When Dara didn't respond, Angel looked up from the book she was pretending to read, her face set in defensive lines. 'I had my dialysis today,' she said. 'I'm *supposed* to be tired.' This was true, but only in theory. Until now.

Dara massaged the sole of her trainer against the saddleboard at the doorway of Angel's room, unsure of what to do or say to make things different. Or at least to get back to where they'd been before. On Angel's locker, was a photograph of the three of them, last month, at the salsa dancing show they'd attended. Angel in a red dress, her head thrown back in a laugh, her arms wrapped around Dara and Mrs Flood, who looked up at her, sandwiched between them, smiling like they'd just come first in a competition they never thought they'd win. Happy. That's what Angel had been. Against all the odds. She'd been happy. In spite of being born with only one kidney. In spite of Mr Flood and his one-way ticket up the road. In spite of the infection and the diagnosis and the years of dialysis. And even with Dara's cautious approach to such things as happiness, she had never fully appreciated how precarious it all was. How quickly the cracks could appear. How shaky the ground beneath your feet really was.

Dara swallowed hard and cleared her throat. 'Well, maybe next time?' she said lightly, as if it didn't matter.

Angel tried to arrange her face into a smile, which was worse than no smile at all. 'Maybe,' she said, turning from one unread page to the next.

'Would you like me to make you a hot chocolate before I go?' asked Dara.

'No,' said Angel, putting her finger under a word on the page. 'Thank you,' she added, old habits being difficult to abandon completely.

'OK then, I'll just . . .' Still Dara lingered by the door. 'But if the hospital rings . . .'

'They won't.' Angel delivered this statement in a dull monotone, which Dara ignored.

'But if they do . . .'

'I'll ring you,' said Angel, and that was that.

Dara Flood loved to salsa dance. It was true to say that when Dara danced, it was the one time she let herself go completely. She didn't do it on purpose. No. Not at all. In fact, you could say that once she began to dance, she *forgot* herself. She danced like she was barely there. Like no one was watching. Except everyone watched. Because she was so good. Perhaps it was her height. Dara was five feet one-and-three-quarters, and even though the three-quarters was a dubious addition, people let her away with it. Possibly because of her diminutive size. Being short, her centre of gravity was perhaps more solid, being closer to the ground than most people's. That was one theory anyway. Of course Mr Flood had been an excellent dancer. Even Mrs Flood had to concede that. Before he walked up the street and never came back, he and Mrs Flood used to go to 'hops'. That was what Mrs Flood called them. They did things like jiving and jitterbugging, and while Mrs Flood was never what you might call fleet of foot, she remembers the way she wore her hair, in a towering beehive of backcombing engineering that took *hours* to achieve.

This Friday night, Mrs Flood was in a mood Dara could only describe as unsettled. 'I don't think I should go to the salsa dancing class,' she said. 'One of us should stay and see to Angel.'

Dara had guessed she would say this and had made provisions. 'I've asked Tintin to come over while we're out,' she told her mother. She wasn't looking forward to going out dancing with her mother, alone, without Angel. But it had been a long, hard week and the strain of it was visible on Mrs Flood's face, the skin pulled tight across her features. She was pale apart from under her eyes, where the skin turned to shadows, dark and weary.

In spite of everything, Mrs Flood smiled. She was fond of Tintin, calling him *the son she'd never had, thank God*. He flirted outrageously with her, of course, and she cuffed him affectionately on the ear, telling him that he wasn't too old for a good spanking, to which Tintin would whoop and say: 'With the wide-bottomed brush?'

'I don't think Angel is up to company, do you?' Mrs Flood asked in that dry, sceptical way she had.

'She won't even know he's here,' Dara said. 'She'll be in her room and I've told Tintin to be quiet.'

'Ha,' said Mrs Flood, and Dara had to agree with her. The only time Tintin had ever been quiet was last year, in the park, when he'd been knocked unconscious by the low branch of a tree while rollerblading. Still, Mrs Flood went to get her coat.

At the club, Dara found them a table with two chairs. She pulled one back for Mrs Flood to sit on, then went to the bar. Stanley Flinter had asked her to find out more about Mr Flood. He made it sound like such a plausible thing. A normal conversation. Up there with humdrum Irish dialogue about the weather. Or the recession. Or *The X Factor*.

Mrs Flood had not mentioned the subject since the night of the lasagne and the upside-down apple cake. The night that Angel cried in the kitchen.

Instead, she had reverted to a more pronounced version of her usual self. Stoic. Getting on with things, she would have called it. Bearing up. Dara had to admit that she was good at it, having had great practice, especially in the early years, when being abandoned by your husband was what happened to wives who did something to deserve such treatment.

But the only person she could ask about Mr Flood was her mother, so in theory, now was an ideal opportunity to ask her. When they were alone. Together. Away from the house, where neither of them could think of anything but Angel, and how different everything was now.

Still, Dara delayed at the bar, standing there even after the barman – Miguel – had served her drinks. Her beer grew warm from the heat of her hands wrapped around it, as she stood there trying to come up with the least contentious way to introduce the subject. Nothing occurred.

She returned to the table and gave Mrs Flood her drink. Mrs Flood brought it to her lips and held it there, for a long time. When she put the glass down, it was half-empty. Or half-full, as Angel used to say. She didn't smack her lips as she usually did and declare it to be 'just the tonic'. Dara wished she would. So there would be words between them. Some kind of communication. Something that would make them smile at each other or maybe even laugh, like two normal people out on a Friday night.

While she looked like she was enjoying watching the tight knots of dancers wrap themselves around each other on the dance floor, Mrs Flood didn't dance herself, admitting to some slight swelling of her ankles after standing around a particularly tedious perm and colour this afternoon. Her fingers worried at a loose thread on the button of her cardigan until the button came away in her hand. She threw it in the bin afterwards instead of stashing it as she normally would in the coin section of her purse, for sewing on later.

In spite of the throb of the music all around, the silence between Dara and Mrs Flood stretched, like a thin piece of elastic about to snap. Dara struggled for an opening that would lead them, like dancers, into a conversation about Mr Flood. Instead, she felt her body move to the hot pulse of the music.

'Go and dance, Dara. You're making me nervous with your twitching,' said Mrs Flood, nudging Dara's arm with her elbow.

'Sorry?' The music was as good a reason as any not to have a conversation. Dara felt like it was inside her, stroking her insides in a way that was distracting. Also loud. Much louder than it needed to be, but all the better for that.

'GO AND DANCE, I SAID!' repeated Mrs Flood, pointing at the dance floor and simulating a feisty dance partner with her arms in a semicircle in front of her body. She stopped in mid-simulation and dropped her arms in a hurry. 'Oh, good Lord of all that's holy and honest,' said Mrs Flood in a rush.

'What's wro—' began Dara, but Mrs Flood had already reached for Dara's wallet, making a great show of knocking it accidentally on to the floor, which gave her the perfect opportunity to slip off her chair and disappear under the table, where she crouched on her hands and knees in a way that was reassuringly nimble for a woman of her age and ample girth. For a moment, Dara imagined it was Mr Flood. He was behind her, with a packet of cigarettes in his hand and an apologetic smile on his face. 'Sorry I took so long, love,' he would say. 'The queue was out the feckin' door.' Even though this was a crazy notion, Dara entertained it for a moment, in a way that made her shoulders reach higher than usual until they almost touched the lobes of her ears. The sound of the music fell away until it was a dull thud, much slower than the frantic beat of her heart. She turned around. But it was only Charlie-call-me-Charles.

'If only you'd wear a dress, my sweet Dara Flood,' he crooned, moving towards her, 'we'd have no need for a defibrillator around here, let me tell you.'

'Charlie!' said Dara, extending her arm to shake his hand. He was much more of a Charlie than a Charles, with his hair that always looked like it needed a cut and his trousers that he called his 'dancing pants' that strained uncomfortably around his . . . upper thigh area.

'Please, Dara,' he said, bending his head to kiss Dara's outstretched hand and moving his body forward and back in time to the music, 'call me Charles.' He winked at her. 'And where is your delightful mother tonight?' he asked. 'I know she's here. I caught her scent as soon as I came in the door.' This was just possible, given Charlie's monument of a nose, and Mrs Flood's penchant for Lily of the Valley talcum powder, which she shook liberally about her body before she went dancing.

'She's . . . eh . . .' Dara began, wincing as Mrs Flood pinched her shin from underneath the table.

'Never mind,' interrupted Charlie. 'There's Mrs Moran. Recently widowed, the lamb. I'll just go over and convey my sympathies. Nothing like a good stiff cock . . .' He stopped, momentarily distracted by a dancer, whose breasts were threatening to leap out of the front of her dress with each twist and turn. Then, with the neckline of the dress tantalisingly down at almost nipple level, the crowd closed around her like a curtain and she was gone. Charlie sighed and turned back to Dara.

'Where was I?' he asked.

Dara paused only briefly. 'You were just saying that there was nothing like a good stiff, eh . . .'

'Oh yes, a good stiff cocktail to take the sting out of a recent bereavement,' he finished, setting his sights again on the unfortunate widow. Dara had to admire his tenacity. Also, he knew a thing or two about mourning, having buried two of his three wives. The third one hadn't had the decency to wait for death to claim her: she left him for a man who came to prune her overgrown privet hedge one spring morning last year.

'This is no way to spend a Friday night,' gasped Mrs Flood, struggling up from the floor when Charlie-call-me-Charles had finally taken his leave.

Dara peeled a piece of chewing gum off the back of her mother's skirt.

'He's right about one thing, though.'

'Who?'

'Charlie-call-me-Charles.'

'What?'

'You should wear a dress. Show off those skinny little legs of yours for a change. And that tidy chest. Such a waste. Some day they're going to go south for the winter, like Brent geese, and then it'll be too late.' Mrs Flood shook her head and drew a cardigan across her own heavy breasts – which had headed south many years before. And never bothered to come back for the summer either.

This was a conversation. Wasn't it? One that didn't involve Angel or kidneys. Wasn't it? It wasn't brilliant but it was a start. Dara took her chance.

'Mam, I was wondering . . .'

'What?' Mrs Flood didn't look at Dara. She concentrated instead on the dancers.

'Did you ever think about going out with anyone?'

'What do you mean?'

'I mean, you know, after Mr Flood left. A good bit after, I mean. Did you ever . . .'

'I am a married woman,' Mrs Flood said, drawing herself up stiffly in her chair. Dara was positive that her mother was not aware of how she reached for her wedding ring with the fingers of her right hand, twisting it around her finger. The ring that said 'For Kathleen, my love', the engraving faded now, on the underside of the band. 'That may not mean much nowadays, but I took vows. They meant something. To me, at least.'

Dara backtracked. She took a different tack. It was easier when her mother wasn't looking at her. She surprised herself by asking a question she'd always wanted to ask.

'Why did you never report Mr Flood as a missing person?'

Mrs Flood's head whipped around. Her eyes flashed and colour roared into her face, like blood from an open cut.

'To the police, I mean? Why didn't you report him?' Dara tried to make the question as casual as possible. It came out like the tip of a sword, it was that pointed.

'You think I should have?' Mrs Flood's voice was high. Tight. Like there was a hand around her throat.

'Well, no, I'm not saying . . .'

'You think there should have been a manhunt for him, perhaps?'

'No, not a manhunt, of course not, but . . .'

'People combing St Anne's Park, perhaps, sweeping sticks through the long grass?' Each word was a staccato, coated in bitter cynicism.

'No, I didn't mean . . .'

'He walked up the road, Dara.'

'I know, that's what you told—'

'Nobody dragged him.'

'Yes, but . . .'

'He chose not to come back.'

Dara's resolve slipped. Faltered. She had a bit left. Only a small piece. 'But how did you know? For sure, I mean?'

'I just knew. I was there, remember? You weren't even born.'
She said this like it was some failing on Dara's part. Something thoughtless. At least, that's how it sounded to Dara. As
for something else to say, nothing occurred.

Mrs Flood pressed her back into the chair. She reached for
her drink and drained it. Dara picked it up quickly. Thankfully. 'I'll get you another.' She was already on her feet.

'No,' said Mrs Flood, reaching for her bag. 'I want to go.'

'No,' said Dara. Sometimes that happened. She said exactly
the opposite of what she wanted to say to her mother. Because
she wanted to go too. Back to the house. Where they could
get back to worrying about Angel. Angel was what they had
in common. Angel was someone they could agree on. Share.
But she didn't say that. Instead she said, 'It's early yet. Let's
stay. Charlie's distracted with Mrs Moran. We could dance, if
your feet aren't too sore now. I'll be your partner if you'd like.'

Mrs Flood looked at Dara. 'You're too short. I'd have to be
the man. I hate being the man.'

'I could be the man,' Dara persisted. 'I could be a short man.'

'I hate short men,' said Mrs Flood. 'They always have such
a chip on their little shoulders.'

Dara thought about Stanley Flinter then. He was a short
man. So far, though, she had seen no evidence of a chip on
either of his shoulders.

'If Angel was here, I could dance with her. She's a grand
height, that one,' said Mrs Flood.

Dara decided to give it one more stab before she relented.

'If you don't dance with me, I will march over to Charlie-
call-me-Charles and tell him that you can't sleep nights for
thinking about him and his . . .'

'All right, Dara,' said Mrs Flood in a quiet voice, as she
reached down to pick up her handbag.

'. . . his bulging thighs and his long . . .'

'I said all right, didn't I?'

'. . . hair and his twinkly *come-to-my-water-bed* eyes and—'

'I'M COMING!' roared Mrs Flood, which was unfortunate, because the music changed at that moment to something hushed and sultry, and everyone turned to look at Dara and her mother, including Charlie-call-me-Charles, whose face changed from frustrated – Mrs Moran was having none of his agenda-driven benevolence – to long-standing hope. While Mrs Flood declined his repeated offers of dancing and dinners and peeks at his train-set collection, she had never shouted at him or threatened him with a barring order and, being a positive kind of individual, Charlie took this as a tentative promise of a possible dalliance, at some unspecified time in the future.

'Oh blessed Virgin of the divine sanctity of all that's holy,' breathed Mrs Flood, as Charlie pushed his way through the thickening crowd towards them. Dara – who had caught Miguel's eye behind the bar – grabbed her mother by the elbow and hustled her towards the counter, where Miguel raised the flap and ushered the pair of them through the storeroom and out an emergency exit into an alleyway littered with crates and kegs and one couple, up against the wall, taking salsa to the next, inevitable level, as Tintin would say. Tintin only came occasionally to the salsa dancing sessions. It made him too horny, he admitted.

Without saying anything, the two women turned in the same direction and walked away.

18

At around the same time that Friday night, Stanley Flinter got a phone call. The woman was crying and Stanley couldn't make out anything she said.

'Take your time,' he said, switching off the film he'd been watching – *Unforgiven* – and not for the first time either. A loud noise like an out-of-tune trumpet roared down the phone as the woman blew her nose and tried to compose herself. Then the sound of glass clinking against glass and a drink – Stanley assumed it was wine: it nearly always was with these women – pouring in an unsteady freefall. Some gulping, a little bit of slurping followed by a long, shaky sigh. Then there was silence.

'Are you OK now?' asked Stanley, tentatively.

'You sound so kind,' said the woman, and Stanley could almost hear her tears gathering, ready for a fresh onslaught. He headed them off at the pass.

'What did you want to talk to me about?' he asked, trying to sound more professional and less concerned. Experience had taught him that these women – and they nearly always called on a Friday night, late, after too much wine – responded less emotionally when he assumed his professional voice.

'It's my husband,' the woman managed to whisper down the phone, before her voice broke and she was off in a great gale force of a wail. Stanley waited until she ran out of breath.

'You think he's having an affair?' he said.

A stunned silence.

'How did you know?'

'Just a hunch,' Stanley conceded.

'Moya said you were intuitive all right,' the woman told him.

'Moya?' The name rang no bells.

'Yes. She thought her husband Gerald was having an affair but it turned out he was just sneaking off to a cross-dressing club in Monaghan the odd Friday night. She was so *relieved*.'

Stanley remembered the case, but the woman's name was Cassandra. He was sure of it.

'Although you might remember her as Cassandra. She sometimes calls herself that, depending,' the woman said. Stanley decided not to ask what it depended on. Now that the woman had composed herself, he detected a chatty disposition.

'So what makes you think your husband is having an affair?' Stanley steered the conversation back to the point.

'Well,' said the woman, flicking through what sounded like a notebook. 'It started last November. The twenty-sixth, to be exact. He said he was going down to Manly Makeovers and—'

'Manly Makeovers?' Stanley had to ask.

'Yes, it's our local beauty salon for men,' explained the woman, who would have gone on to give a detailed description of Manly Makeover's range of services, had Stanley not interjected with a timely 'Go on.'

'Well, when he came back, I knew *immediately* that he hadn't been anywhere near Manly's.'

'How come?'

'His pores, of course. Still as clogged as a smoker's arteries, they were. And the *whiteheads*. He suffers with whiteheads, you know. Mostly across the bridge of his nose. But there they were. And Celine is usually so good with him. Really understands his skin requirements.'

'Celine?'

'The head therapist.'

'At Manly Makeovers,' finished Stanley, writing it down. 'So, what else has he done to rouse your, eh, suspicions?'

'Isn't that enough?' the woman said in a low voice cluttered with hurt. Even though it wasn't nearly enough, Stanley couldn't help feeling sorry for her.

'Maybe he just got distracted on his way to the, eh, salon, and . . .'

'My husband would *never* forget about an appointment at the salon. He knows how important regular facials are. Especially with the whiteheads . . .'

Stanley scribbled down the word 'whitehead' and underlined it three times, although he couldn't be sure why. He put his pen down and waited.

'There *is* more, but it's a bit . . . personal,' the woman finally acknowledged. Stanley picked up his pen.

'I'm listening,' he told her.

'Well, it's just that my husband is . . . was . . . such a *considerate* lover. You know what I mean, don't you?'

'Yes,' said Stanley, louder than necessary in an effort to assure the woman that, not only did he know what she meant, but also that there was no need to elaborate on the subject. His efforts in this regard were fruitless.

'It's just that he always . . . you know . . . takes care of my . . . needs . . . before he sees to himself, if you know what I mean.'

'Yes, yes,' said Stanley in a strangled kind of voice. The woman sounded as old as his mother and he really didn't want . . .

'You name it, he did it,' the woman continued, as if Stanley had not spoken. 'I mean, I don't want to be indiscreet but really, there was no end to the lengths he would go to make sure that I—'

'So that's changed, has it?' Stanley interrupted, desperate now.

'Oh yes,' said the woman. 'He's not the ardent, attentive lover he once was. No doubt about it. I mean, we used to watch *The Thorn Birds* . . . you know . . . beforehand to . . . you know . . . get us in a romantic mood. Have you seen it?'

'Eh, no,' said Stanley weakly.

'Such a magnificent love story,' she said, in a reverential kind of a voice.

'So,' said Stanley, groping around for words that would steer them into safer waters. 'You haven't . . . eh . . . watched it in a while, then?'

'What?'

'*The Thorn Birds*.'

The woman stifled a sob. 'I can't remember the last time we saw it. There! Doesn't that tell you everything you need to know? Well? Doesn't it?' And the sob that she had stifled rose like a wave in a high tide and crashed against Stanley's ear. He held the phone away from him and waited.

'You must think me a foolish woman,' she finally managed.

'Not at all,' Stanley assured her. 'I think you're a woman who cares very much about her husband.'

'Oh I do, I do,' she moaned. 'He writes poetry, you know.'

'Does he?'

'Yes, very complex, deep poetry. It doesn't even rhyme,' she added, a note of pride in her voice now.

'Is he published?'

'God, no. He wouldn't taint his art with that level of commercialism.' She sounded scandalised.

'What does he do? For a living, I mean.'

'He's a banker. In the IFSC.'

'Oh.' Stanley decided not to comment on that level of commercialism.

'So what would you like me to do, exactly?' he asked.

'I want you to follow him,' the woman whispered. Underneath the pain of betrayal – real or imagined – Stanley could hear the illicit thrill of subterfuge. Which was not uncommon with these cases.

'Surveillance can be very expensive,' he told her, as he always did.

'Money is no object,' she said with the confidence of a woman whose husband is a banker in the IFSC.

'I'm going to ask you to think about this,' said Stanley. This was another thing he always said to these woman who invariably rang him on lonely Friday nights after one too many glasses of Chardonnay.

'No. I don't want to think about it,' she said. 'I just want to get on with it. I have to know. It's the doubt that's killing me. I've got hives, you know.'

'Hives?'

'Yes. All across my thighs. That's where I get them when I'm stressed.'

'Phone me in a week,' insisted Stanley. 'Next Friday. Morning if you can manage it. If you still want to go ahead then with the surveillance, I'll do what I can to help. I promise.'

The woman sighed. A long-drawn-out sigh with the weight of the world in it. 'You sound like a lovely young man,' she said, sniffing.

'Eh . . . thank you,' said Stanley.

'I hope your girlfriend appreciates you.'

'Well . . . I don't have a girlfriend, actually.'

'Have you never been in love?' the woman asked, shocked.

'Well . . . I . . .'

'Oh!' she squeaked suddenly. 'You have, haven't you? You've been in love and you got your heart well and truly broken, didn't you? I can hear the heartache in your voice. You poor lamb.'

Perhaps it was the sympathy in the woman's voice, as heartfelt as a handwritten love letter. Perhaps it was the fact that Stanley never expressed his . . . well . . . yes . . . heartache, that's what it was. Whatever the reason, he found himself nodding down the phone . 'We-ell, yes,' he said. 'I suppose you're right.'

'I usually am, my dear, about matters of the heart,' she said smugly. 'What happened?'

And Stanley told her. He figured he had nothing to lose because he thought he'd never hear from her again. And there was relief in it. In the telling. It was not something he voiced very often. 'It was my brother,' he began. 'My oldest brother.'

'What do you mean?'

'Cormac. That's his name. He . . .'

'Oh my goodness. No! He didn't!' came the woman's horrified voice down the phone.

'He did,' Stanley said quietly. The betrayal was still there. He could hear it. In his own voice. Even after all this time.

'Well, you're well rid of a woman like that, Stanley my dear,' she told him in no uncertain terms. 'Decent women know the bond between brothers. It's not something that can be broken. I'm sure you and your brother will come to terms with this. But *her*! She's a *rip*, so she is.' She was breathless after this declaration but she gathered herself nonetheless and carried on: 'Not worth another ounce of your time, believe me.'

Stanley tried to get a word in but could not.

'And I can promise you this. You'll be in love again. And this time, it will be different. In fact . . .' The woman paused as if consulting a crystal ball. 'In fact, I think this will happen quite soon. You may already have met her.'

Instead of dismissing this notion as fanciful and ridiculous, Stanley found himself asking, 'What makes you say that?'

'Some people say I have a gift,' she told him. 'I can tell things about people. Like my husband. Having an . . . an . . . affair.'

Stanley didn't mention that her suspicions about her

husband were more likely related to an acute case of paranoia rather than any psychic gift she might or might not have. That was not his job.

'So you'll ring back in a week, right?' he told her instead.

'I wish you wouldn't make me wait,' she sighed.

'I have a suspicion you might change your mind,' said Stanley.

'Are you a bit psychic too?'

'No, I've just been doing this job long enough to get a feeling for these things.'

'You know, I *do* feel a bit better,' she said, surprised. Stanley could hear her pouring the last of the wine into her glass. In the morning she would wish she'd never phoned him. He was sure he'd never hear from her again. For formality's sake, he wrote her name down in his notebook. 'Irene,' she told him.

'And your husband's name?' he asked, his pen poised.

'Ian,' replied the woman, with fresh tears choking her voice like weeds. 'Ian Harte.'

19

At work the following Monday, something happened to Dara Flood that had never happened before. She had to go to the emergency room at Beaumont Hospital to get a tetanus shot. Her first one. She'd been bitten by a dog. Her first time.

It was Tintin who had discovered the dog. Tethered to the gate at the entrance to the pound with a short, dirty rope. He strained against the rope that bit into his neck like teeth and growled a low, menacing growl that intensified any time Tintin approached him. Tintin rang Dara, who happened to be on her bicycle at the time.

'We've got a code red here,' he whispered down the phone. Dara could hear the ominous growling in the background. It wasn't a growl she recognised.

'A new arrival?' she asked, pedalling faster now.

'Abandoned,' Tintin told her. 'Tied to the gate. He's not in great shape.'

'Don't touch him,' Dara said, standing up on the pedals now, the phone clamped between her ear and her shoulder.

'Are you cycling and talking on the phone at the same time?' Tintin asked.

'I'm nearly there,' Dara panted.

'Get off the phone. It's dangerous.'

'I know that.'

'Well?'

'I bloody well will. Once you stop talking to me.'

'Fine. I've stopped.'

'Don't go near the dog,' Dara repeated, her breath coming in gasps.

'You already said that,' Tintin reminded her. He had no intention of coming within a swiping paw of the dog.

The stray was possibly the ugliest dog Dara had ever seen, even though she would never say such a thing out loud. He was ill-proportioned, with a huge body, a tiny head, long floppy ears, a stump of a tail, short legs and enormous paws.

'Praise the Lord, the Dog Whisperer has arrived,' Tintin said to Anya, who stood on the steps of her corner office with Jack Knapp in her arms, fast asleep.

Despite the lightness of Tintin's tone, Dara noticed a bead of sweat rolling down his face. She dropped her bike on the ground, released herself from the high-visibility jacket and the hat her mother had knitted for her, which made her head sweat and itch in equal measures. Then she knelt down and began to shuffle forward, keeping her eyes lowered and her hand outstretched. She passed Tintin, who touched her briefly on the arm. 'Don't get too close to this one, Dara,' he told her in a whisper. 'He's got anger issues.'

Dara conceded that the dog did seem aggressive. Foam gathered at the corners of his mouth and the hackles on his neck stood up, straight and rigid.

When she got close enough, she noticed the filth of his dark coat. There were bald patches on parts of his pelt – a sure sign of anxiety, Dara knew – and welts, some recent, running up and down the length of the dog's enormous body.

'He is olt,' said Anya, grim as a death sentence.

Dara nodded. The dog was at least ten, but perhaps as much as thirteen years old.

She eased closer. The growling of the dog was like an engine, ticking over. It seemed quieter than before.

'Hush now, hush now,' Dara whispered at the dog, like she was singing a lullaby to a newborn baby. She stretched her hand towards him.

'That's close enough, Dara,' said Anya, fishing her mobile phone out of her pocket.

'I'm just letting him smell me,' Dara told them, not looking around.

'You little minx,' Tintin said.

'You are dancing with death,' Anya told her.

'It's dicing,' Tintin explained.

'Wot?'

'Dicing with death. Not dancing. *Dancing at Lughnasa*, yes. *Dancing with Wolves*, grand. But no dancing with death. In Ireland, we *dice* with it, not *dance*.'

'He's got a name tag,' Dara said in an even, low voice.

'He doesn't look like a collar-and-tag kind of a dog,' said Tintin. 'What does it say?'

The name tag shuddered in tandem with the dog's growling. Dara concentrated on it until the letters cleared.

'Lucky,' she whispered, her hand nearly close enough now to touch the dog's head.

'There ain't nothing lucky about that poor creature,' said Tintin. Dara agreed. Nothing about the dog suggested that he was suitable for anything other than the short, one-way trip to the vet's long, sterile table.

And then the dog – still growling – leaned forward and pushed his nose into the fingers of Dara's outstretched hand so that they cupped it like a muzzle.

'Jesus!' shouted Anya and Tintin together.

'No, it's all right, he's just . . .'

'I'm calling the vet,' said Anya stoutly. All of them knew what the vet's diagnosis would be.

What happened next seemed to Dara to take place in slow motion. She remembers saying, 'WAIT!' and swivelling around, the sharp gravel stabbing the skin of her knees like pins. The arm that she had held out to Lucky swivelled too, but, instead of snatching it back against her body, as she had been trained to do, she left it outstretched as she turned towards Anya. The bite was sharp and insistent, but it was more surprise Dara Flood felt, as Lucky jumped and caught the delicate skin of her wrist between his teeth. It was a graze rather than a bite because of the rope tethered around Lucky's neck, which yanked him back almost as soon as he sprang.

Dara didn't feel the pain of it until she sat beside Tintin on the hard plastic chairs in the A & E. A steady, dull sort of pain. She shivered.

'Here, take this,' said Tintin, wrapping his jacket around her shoulders. 'You've probably got PTSD,' he told her with a certain amount of relish, Dara felt.

'What?'

'Post-traumatic stress disorder,' he explained.

'You've been watching too much *Grey's Anatomy*,' Dara said, trying not to look at the bandage that Anya had wrapped around her wrist in the office. It was slasher-movie red and Dara did her best to hide it from Tintin, who, she felt, was a more likely candidate for PTSD.

'You've gone very white,' Tintin told her, placing his hand against her forehead. 'And you're clammy, too.'

'I'm just hungry and hot,' Dara said, pulling her face away from Tintin's hand. 'I didn't have any breakfast this morning and it's like the fecking tropics in here.'

'You're not wrong,' Tintin agreed, nodding towards an overweight man whose face and neck looked like the front of a period house, it was that brick-red. 'I'll go and get you some breakfast. Mars bar do you?'

'Could I have a cup of tea too?' Dara asked.

'Christ, one dog attack and you've gone all *fetch me my*

smelling salts on us,' said Tintin, getting up and smiling down at her.

'It was hardly an *attack*,' Dara said.

'What would you call it?'

'It was more like . . . a nip,' said Dara, covering her bandaged wrist with her fleece jacket.

'You can call it what you like, Dara,' said Tintin grimly, 'but there's no way you're going to be able to save this one. Not this time.'

'Anya said she wouldn't make any decisions until I got back,' Dara reminded him.

'You can't save them all.' Tintin sat back down beside her and fixed her with what he called his *serious* look, which, to be honest, didn't suit him at all.

'Somebody loved him once,' Dara said. 'Somebody loved him enough to call him Lucky. He's just fallen on hard times, that's all. He just needs . . .'

'Dara, I think this one needs a little more than a dish of your canine stew, a hot-water bottle and a good night's sleep,' said Tintin.

Dara's canine stew was pretty much the same as her stew-for-humans, apart from the rabbit livers, which Dara never told Tintin (who had two pet rabbits) about.

When Tintin left to get breakfast, Dara rang Anya again.

'We haf given him shot and vet is going to examine him later. But . . .'

'Just don't make any decisions until tomorrow,' Dara begged.

'But he bit you . . .'

'It was nothing. Just a nip, really.'

'You cannot save all of them, Dara Flood,' Anya said, her voice fuller than usual of her trademark melancholy.

20

Stanley Flinter lived in a quaint two-up-two-down just off the main street in Baldoyle. He bought it shortly after the night he discovered how Cora . . . felt about Cormac. And, even though he'd closed the door on that scene, locked it, pulled the blinds down, stuffed tissue paper in the keyhole, he still saw it. Not all the time, like he used to. But at vulnerable moments, like when Clouseau pinned him to the ground in the living room and refused to get up, leaving Stanley with no choice but to lie and wait until, inevitably, the image would appear, uninvited and unwelcome, in the corner of his mind at first, seeping in until it took up the entire screen of his memory. An unfortunate widescreen. The picture still clear after all this time. And the sound. You can shut your eyes against the picture, but the sounds still make themselves heard. That was the worst bit. The sound of them. That was what he heard first but he kept walking towards it, towards the bedroom door, hearing it. But still not quite believing it.

He bought the house shortly afterwards, even though everybody told him not to because (a) the property boom, while stumbling towards its deathbed, was still well enough to whiten the knuckles of the wiliest property buyer and (b) even the estate agent had to concede that the house needed some work. A lot of work, in fact. A new roof, plumbing, rewiring, plastering, painting.

As well as being members of the Garda Siochána, Stanley's brothers were what you might call 'handy'. They all pitched in that summer, even Cormac, who was the handiest of them all. It was his version of flagellation. His recompense. Stanley didn't want him there but there he was anyway, crawling along the roof with nails poking out of his mouth like fangs, a broad tan across his back where a shirt should be.

The house, with its postage stamp of a garden, had been perfect when it had just been Stanley and Sissy. But all that changed last month with the arrival of one Chief Inspector Jacques Clouseau. The tiny little border where Stanley had planted fat, promising bulbs last autumn was now a juxtaposition of hills and holes where Clouseau dug as enthusiastically as he relieved himself, in between bouts of frantic barking whenever a recycling truck roared past on the road outside. Because of the lucrative nature of recycling, this happened much too often.

If the dog had concentrated on wrecking the back garden, it mightn't have been so bad. Yes, of course Stanley expected a certain amount of slipper-chewing and frivolity, given Clouseau's youthful disposition. But an entire suite of furniture? A patchwork quilt hand-sewn by Stanley's maternal grandmother, now gone to her reward? The trousers of two goodish suits? Clouseau couldn't reach the jackets, although he had tried, which resulted in the destruction of a chest of drawers in Stanley's bedroom that had toppled in the melee, destroying most of a DVD collection, as well as the only framed photograph Stanley had kept of him and Cora – standing on top of Errigal, the highest mountain in Donegal. As he often did, when he looked at that photo, he wondered why he had loved her. They had nothing in common. He remembered having to bribe her up the mountain.

'Wait till you see the view from the top,' he had urged as she asked – and not for the first time – what was the point?

'Fuck the view, Stan, look at my *hair*, for Christ's sake.' In fairness, her hair, usually a prime example of best practice in haircare, had been whipped by the wind into a tangle of briars around her head.

'I have chocolate,' he told her.

'Give it to me.'

'When we reach the top,' he promised, taking her hand and pulling her along behind him.

He thought perhaps it had something to do with the timing. He had only just received the rejection letter from the Guards. The disappointment was sharp. Keen. The grip of it was tight. Biting. And then Cora arrived. She sought him out when she came back from her round-the-world trip. He never really understood why. She took him on like he was a project. In spite of himself, he allowed the positive force of her to breathe into his life. The life he had not wanted. And with the sheer physical force of her presence, that life, that altered life, did not seem as bad as he'd thought it would be. She was bright, funny, and she always, always got what she wanted. She was simply unable to accept anything less. And for a while she had wanted Stanley. It was as simple as that.

'Good,' said Sissy when Stanley told her about the 'incident'.

'How is it good?' asked Stanley, genuinely curious.

'It's about time you got rid of that bloody picture. It even made *me* feel nostalgic.' Sissy fixed Stanley with a sceptical stare and Stanley nodded. It was true. Sissy was disinclined toward nostalgia.

'Still, a fair bit of collateral damage, wouldn't you say?' Stanley asked, surveying the wreckage of his bedroom.

'Well worth it,' was all Sissy said.

Stanley was attacking the bathroom with a cloth and a bottle of Cif when Sissy came in from work that evening. She stood at the door, watching him. 'We don't usually clean the bathroom until Thursday,' she told him. By 'we' she meant 'you', as Sissy liked to maintain a healthy distance from such things as toilet brushes and mops. Stanley let her get away with it, mostly because he was not fond of confrontation but also because Sissy took charge of washing and grooming Clouseau. After Stanley's first attempt, he would rather have scrubbed every toilet in the land than take to the dog again with a bucket of soapy water and a sponge.

'I know,' said Stanley, 'but I have a job on Thursday night and I mightn't get time.'

'But it's only Monday,' Sissy pointed out. 'And there's hardly any dirt in here. It's a bit of a waste, isn't it?' When Stanley didn't reply, Sissy propped herself on the edge of the bath. 'There's a funny smell downstairs,' she said, studying him closely.

'I, um, bought some air freshener,' he admitted, turning a bottle of Toilet Duck upside down and applying it liberally under the rim. 'The whole house smells of Clouseau. And not in a good way, either.'

'I see,' said Sissy, leaning down towards Stanley and inhaling. 'You smell pretty good yourself. New aftershave?'

'I was in Debenhams at lunchtime buying a bear for baby Cora. One of the saleswomen sprayed me with something when I walked through the Cosmetics section. There was absolutely nothing I could do.' Stanley pulled the lid of the toilet down, sprayed it with Dettol, dried it and sat down. His face was recently shaved and his cowlick had been pasted against his head with gel. Sissy's gel, as a matter of fact, but Stanley decided not to mention it.

'Hmmm,' said Sissy, studying him.

'What?' Stanley did his best to look confused.

'When is she arriving?' Sissy asked, tilting her head to one side and fixing Stanley with her best 'don't-shit-me' face.

Stanley sighed and leaned back against the cistern. 'They're just popping in for five minutes. On their way back from the pre-marriage guidance course.'

Sissy did her sceptical snort. 'It'll take more than one marriage guidance course to tame that pair, let me tell you.' Stanley closed his eyes. Sissy put her hand on his shoulder and squeezed. 'I wish you wouldn't make such an effort, that's all,' she told him.

'I haven't . . . I'm not . . . I just . . .'

'There's something in the oven, too. I can just about smell it, in spite of the air freshener. That stuff really is foul. Why do people want their houses to smell of pines? Why?'

'It's Caribbean Cooler, as a matter of fact.'

'In the oven?'

'No, the air freshener. That's what it's called,' Stanley explained. 'Chocolate brownies,' he went on. '*That's* what's in the oven.'

Sissy sighed and shook her head. Chocolate brownies were Stanley's speciality. Nobody made them like he did. Nutty and crunchy on the outside, soft and warm inside. This wasn't just making an effort. This was going *all out*.

'They're getting married,' she said softly, taking Stanley's rubber-gloved hand in hers and holding it as long as she could, before reaching for the tap to wash the rubbery, disinfectant smell off her skin.

'I am well aware of that fact, Sissy,' Stanley said, standing up with as much dignity as he could muster, which wasn't easy when you considered his rubber gloves and the fact that he only made it as far as her chin, although she *was* wearing heels. 'I will ask them about the wedding plans, I will give baby Cora her bear, and I will offer them a coffee and a chocolate brownie. That's it.'

The doorbell rang. Stanley jumped, banging his elbow off the edge of the sink. Even though it was his funny bone and should have hurt like a torture chamber at high season, he barely felt it. 'Shit, it's them and I haven't even washed the kitchen window yet.' He tore the rubber gloves off his hands and hid them in a drawer.

'It's bloody dark,' Sissy told him. 'Who's going to notice the fecking windows?'

Stanley had to concede that Sissy had a point.

'You know what, Stanley? The day she walks in here and the place is a kip and the only thing to eat with your coffee is a packet of Rich-fecking-Tea, *that's* when you get her attention. For what it's worth.' She flounced out of the bathroom, which was difficult to do, given the space constraints. 'I'll get the door,' she told him, 'and then I'm going to take a bath. You can let me know when the she-devil and her minion are gone.'

Sissy took her time getting to the door, stopping briefly to tell Clouseau to *get the feck off the couch*. Stanley, from his perch on the toilet seat, could hear Clouseau doing what he was told in the meek fashion he employed whenever Sissy addressed him, as opposed to the boisterous indifference he displayed around Stanley.

'Oh, hello. I was looking for Stanley Flinter.'

Stanley stood up, his backside stiff from the coldness of the toilet seat that had seeped through his trousers. The voice downstairs was hoarse. Gravelly. Worried. It was not Cora's voice.

'Who are you?' Sissy was not rude, as such. She just liked direct answers to her always direct questions.

Stanley took the stairs two at a time.

'Dara?'

'Hello, Stanley. You *were* expecting me, weren't you? You asked me to come over and meet Clouseau and we could talk about the case. Remember?' Dara's voice sounded more worried than usual.

'Of course I remember,' said Stanley, who had entirely forgotten. Dara's face was as worried as her voice and he felt shabby, like an ancient, creased overcoat. Even so, he struggled to peel the disappointment off his features and arrange them into a more appropriate expression.

'I'm Sissy, by the way,' said Sissy, extending her hand. 'That's not my real name, obviously, but that's what everyone calls me nonetheless.'

'Nice to meet you,' Dara said. Stanley noticed how her body shuddered as Sissy pumped her hand up and down with her trademark vim. He approached the door, trying not to scan the street outside for Cormac's car. But he scanned anyway. It wasn't there. He looked again at Dara, who continued to stand on his front step, unmoving. 'I could meet Clouseau another time,' she said.

Stanley had to incline his head ever so slightly to really look at Dara Flood. He'd say she was five feet one-and-three-quarters. He took it all in. The careful navy eyes. The arms folded tightly across the high-visibility jacket that smothered her chest. The way she chewed her bottom lip as she waited for him to say something. Then he noticed the bandage that looked bulky around her wrist. 'Are you all right?' he asked, nodding towards it.

Dara glanced down and pulled at the sleeve of her hoodie, covering the bandage. 'It's nothing,' she said. 'Just . . . a minor, eh . . . accident at work. Nothing to worry about.'

Now he felt like a heel. A really shabby heel. 'Sorry, Dara,' he said. 'Please. Come in.' He gestured her inside and ushered her towards the fire. 'I mean, I *am* expecting you. It's just . . . I'm expecting someone else too. Other people, I mean. Well, just two of them. My brother and his, eh, fiancée. Cora. That's his fiancée. That's her name, I mean.'

'Well, that's what *Stanley* calls her anyway,' said Sissy, and Stanley was relieved when she chose not to elaborate on the string of names she normally reserved for Cora.

'Weren't you going to take a bath?' he asked her point-edly, taking one last look up and down the street before he closed the front door. Sissy smiled at Dara, then headed for the stairs.

Up until now, Clouseau had sat by the hearth, warming his hindquarters with the heat of the fire and generally looking and acting like a buttered dog biscuit wouldn't melt on his long pink tongue. Sissy always maintained that the dog definitely had the capacity to act normally for at least five minutes a day, and when Stanley thought about it later, he had to concede that it had been at least five minutes since he'd separated him from the beanbag. Clouseau was fond of simulating a vigorous mating movement with various inanimate objects around the house. The beanbag was one of his favourites. 'He's just practising humping,' Sissy told Stanley, who already knew this but still felt uncomfortable about it, especially when he had visitors. Clouseau's five minutes of good behaviour had passed and Stanley realised that he hadn't even noticed it, let alone savoured it.

He started off by barking. Nothing new there.

'You must be Clouseau,' said Dara, and Stanley noticed that when she addressed the dog, her voice wasn't as guarded as before. She spoke to Clouseau as if Stanley wasn't even there.

Stanley held his breath. There was a curious chemistry in the room, as if something extraordinary was going to happen. Clouseau twitched his head in Dara's direction and cocked his ears. He whimpered, as if what he *wanted* to do and what he *should* do were two completely different things. It turned out that they were. He allowed a few seconds to lapse – during which time Stanley's hope grew in quite a disproportionate manner – before gathering himself on his haunches, lifting his head for a brief howl at the moon (full: always his worst time of the month) and launching himself towards Stanley in one single bound. Even Dara took a step back as Clouseau attached himself all down Stanley's front in a way that made Stanley stagger around the living room like a man who should have said no to the last shot of tequila. Because it was only a matter of time before Stanley succumbed to the might of the dog and fell flat on the floor, he gave himself up to it, wanting to get it over and done with sooner rather than later, so he could be back on all twos by the time Cora arrived.

It took Dara a while to coax Clouseau off Stanley's heaving chest. In the end she had to bribe him with dog biscuits.

'You see what I mean?' said Stanley, when he finally managed to pick himself up off the floor and brush a dark layer of Clouseau's pelt off his second best jumper. He would have worn his best one tonight, but Clouseau had eaten most of it at the weekend.

'The good thing is . . .'

'There's a *good* thing?' said Stanley, after he'd placed himself in a relatively safe position, behind the couch.

'Actually, yes,' said Dara with some surprise, as if this wasn't usually the case. 'Clouseau loves you.'

'He *loves* me?'

'Yes,' said Dara, and when she looked up, Stanley noticed that she was smiling. He realised then that he'd never seen her smile before. He'd have remembered it if he had. He smiled back, quite without meaning to. There was something a little infectious about Dara Flood's smile. Also, it was nice, he supposed, that Clouseau liked him. Loved him, even. After all the damage he'd inflicted. On the house. On the garden. On Stanley himself. It was nice to think he didn't mean it.

'The problem is,' continued Dara, her smile gone so suddenly that Stanley wondered if he'd imagined it, 'he doesn't *respect* you. I'm sorry, but he doesn't.'

'Oh,' said Stanley. Even though he knew this was true – and that it could in fact be a caption for the story of his life – he felt a sort of shame. As if there was something lacking in him that directly resulted in Clouseau's . . . well . . . cavalier attitude towards him.

'But it's only because you've been so kind to him,' Dara rushed on, as if trying to make up for the bluntness of her diagnosis.

Stanley thought about the night of the 'duck pond incident' (involving a disgruntled – and unfeasibly strong – duck, a thoroughly frustrated Clouseau, a belligerent park ranger and Stanley up to his hips in the brown sludge that passed as pond water). There had been a moment – fleeting but there – when Stanley thought about smothering the dog with a pillow when he got home. Instead, he made himself and Clouseau a hot chocolate, lit the fire and didn't curse when Clouseau fell asleep on his legs. Not even when the pins and needles came and no amount of encouragement could shift the dogged canine.

'I have tried to be tougher with him. It's just ... it's his eyes ... the way they look at me. They're so ... beseeching ...' Stanley was almost positive he'd never used the word *beseeching* before. But really, it was the only word that came to mind when he looked into the dog's huge, liquid brown eyes.

Dara nodded, as if there was nothing remotely odd about his use of the word. 'He's a handful,' she said, almost to herself, as she stroked Clouseau and pulled at his ears, just the way he liked. 'A beautiful handful, aren't you?' Stanley caught sight of the expression on Clouseau's face. It was close to rapt, he thought. Then Clouseau shook himself, as if he'd just remembered who he was and what he was supposed to be doing. He jumped up, placed his two front paws on Dara's shoulders and braced himself against her, trying to push her down. Stanley struggled to his feet to help, but all Dara did was make a curious noise, right down in her throat, and Clouseau stopped the messing and sat down on his bottom, with his front paws supporting the massive weight of him, straight and graceful, like he was a dog in a dog show, in danger of winning a medal.

'Good dog,' said Dara, feeding him a biscuit she lifted from the pocket of her jacket and giving him the briefest of pats on his head. She got up and backed away from him. 'Stay,' she ordered. Clouseau whined piteously but remained where he was. 'Stay,' she said again, coming to stand alongside Stanley.

Stanley stood there, feeling a little foolish, as Dara and Clouseau concentrated on each other, like there was no one else in the room. He wasn't sure what he should do, if anything. He could smell cinnamon and vanilla essence, in spite of the might of the air freshener.

'Did you bake those dog biscuits?' he asked.

'I did,' Dara said. 'They're much better nutritional value than the ones you buy. And they're way cheaper. George used to love them.' She looked surprised when she said this, as if she hadn't meant to say it at all.

'George?'

'Oh. Eh, he was my dog. He . . . he died.'

'I'm sorry.'

'Don't be. It was a long time ago.'

'And did you never get another one?'

'No,' said Dara, shrugging her shoulders and smiling a small, tight smile. 'I mean, I know they're just dogs, but . . . you get attached, don't you? And then they're gone and . . .'

'I'd feel the same about Clouseau,' said Stanley, surprised to realise that this was true.

Dara nodded but said nothing.

'You must give me the recipe,' said Stanley.

'Sure,' she said, and she must have stepped back because her voice was a little fainter now as she told Clouseau again to stay. By this time, Clouseau was nearing the end of his tether. He whined and shook and drooled all over the carpet Stanley had just hoovered. But he *stayed*. Stanley held his breath. If there was hope for Clouseau, then there was hope for them all.

'Is that chocolate brownies I can smell?' Dara asked from behind him.

'Eh, yes, they should be ready. I'll just go and check them.'

'Stay,' Dara said again, and while Stanley was nearly positive she was speaking to Clouseau, he couldn't be sure. He decided to err on the side of caution and remained motionless.

'What kind of chocolate do you use?' Dara asked.

'Eh, Bournville. I mean, I know it's only 40% cocoa but it's
the best. In my opinion, I mean.'

'I use that one too,' she told him.

'Do you?' Stanley sounded surprised.

'Yes, it's perfect for baking. The taste. And the consistency.
And, of course, the meltability.'

Stanley nodded and smiled. He was pretty sure meltability
wasn't a word but he agreed with Dara's prognosis nonetheless.

The dog training lesson was nothing like Stanley had imagined. For a start, he had never considered that any progress
would be made.

'You're right not to raise your voice at all,' Dara told him,
without Stanley having to mention that shouting at Clouseau
was not something he was comfortable with. 'An authoritative
tone will do.' Stanley looked sceptical but agreed to try.

'Stay, Clouseau?' he enquired of the dog. Clouseau barked
and wrestled Stanley to the ground with an ingenious weaving
action through his legs.

'Clouseau! Eh . . . stay. Please?' This produced a bark and a
series of excited yaps while the dog pranced around Stanley's
legs and stretched his mouth wide, so it looked like he was
laughing. And perhaps he was.

It was only when Dara stood beside him – she only came
up to his chin – that he managed it. 'Stay, Clouseau,' he told
the dog, raising the forefinger on his left hand as Dara had
shown him and injecting his tone with as much authority as
he could manage. And even though he had exhausted Dara's
entire supply of home-made dog biscuits and nearly half of

the chocolate brownies, Clouseau stayed, his head cocked to one side in a puzzled kind of resignation.

'He stayed,' Stanley said, turning to Dara Flood, his voice alive with wonder. 'That's the first time I—' but his words were cut off as Clouseau – who decided that he had done enough *staying* for one night – charged towards him like a bowling ball down an alley, scattering him like so many pins and leaving him in a winded heap on the ground.

Dara knelt beside them, coaxing Clouseau off Stanley's chest by bunching her mouth into a pucker and making a soft noise with her lips. A kissy noise. Stanley surprised himself by noticing that she wasn't wearing any lipstick. Instead, her lips had a fairy-tale blush about them, exaggerated by the pale transparency of her skin. He jerked his eyes away from her when she looked at him. 'That was good,' she told him, choosing her words with care. 'But we *do* have a way to go yet.' She picked herself up off the ground and smiled her slow, careful smile.

Stanley guessed – correctly - that this was not the first time Dara had witnessed premature exhilaration.

When the doorbell finally rang, it surprised Stanley to realise that he had forgotten he had been waiting for the doorbell to ring.

21

'Stanley, thank God. I need tea and chocolate. No, scratch that. I need a stiff drink and something deep-fried.' Cora handed Stanley her coat and marched into the house.

'Cora, what's the matter?' Stanley stood at the door cloaked in a cloud of Cora's powerful scent. Something sharp, like limes.

'Battered sausages. That's what that bastard has reduced me to.' Cora yanked herself out of her hat, scarf and gloves – all of which matched the coat draped across Stanley's outstretched arms – and flung them towards the couch, where they landed in Dara's lap. Even then she did not notice Dara. Clouseau began to growl, low down in his throat.

'Cora, let me introduce . . .' Stanley closed the door.

'He arrived late and left early. His beeper went off. Probably got one of his police cronies to call him. He just left me there. I had to sit through thirty minutes of *managing your household budget*. On. My. Own! And he *knows* how hopeless I am with math.'

It was only when Cora – perhaps spent by her brief brush with budgets – flopped down on the couch, that she finally realised someone else was there.

'Oh,' was all she said. Clouseau's growl deepened. Stanley saw Dara's fingers tightening around his collar.

'Cora, this is Dara Flood,' Stanley finally managed to say.

Cora looked at Stanley: a puzzled look. 'I didn't realise you had . . . company,' she said.

Dara lowered the hand she had extended towards Cora. 'I was just leaving,' she told them, picking herself up off the couch, her fingers still wrapped around Clouseau's leather collar. The dog continued to growl.

'Don't go on my account,' said Cora, taking off her shoes and tucking her feet underneath her so she looked very long and thin and utterly at home on Stanley's couch.

'Stay,' said Stanley, before he realised that it sounded like he was addressing Clouseau. 'I mean, if you like. You haven't tasted my chocolate brownies yet.'

'No thank you,' said Dara, already at the door. 'I'll ring you tomorrow, OK?'

Stanley nodded vigorously. 'Any time,' he told her. 'I'm around all day.' He watched her unwrapping her bicycle lock from a lamp post and stayed at the door until she was just a blur of fluorescent yellow, getting smaller and smaller until the dark moved across her and he couldn't see her any more.

He coaxed Clouseau – still growling in Cora's direction – into the back garden with a bribe of yet more brownies.

'That dog still doesn't like me,' Cora told him, when he had safely dispatched Clouseau.

'Apparently he loves me,' said Stanley, smiling a little to himself at Dara's observation. Cora looked at him carefully, like she was cramming him for an exam.

'Have you gone and gotten yourself a little girlfriend?' she asked. Her tone was playful. Teasing. Like she knew this could not possibly be the case.

'She's a dog trainer, actually,' Stanley told her, heading for the kitchen. He never discussed his cases with anyone. Sissy didn't count. He knew he could trust her. 'I thought you were going to bring baby Cora. I bought her a bear,' he called from the kitchen.

'Another one?' said Cora. 'You have to stop buying her stuff. I can barely fit her into the cot, with all the bears.'

'I'm her uncle. I'm supposed to buy her stuff. It's the rule,' said Stanley.

'I was supposed to stop by your mother's on the way home from the class, but I'm so annoyed with that brother of yours, I had to call in here first. I knew you'd calm me down.'

In the kitchen, Stanley gripped the counter and forced himself to let the comment go without thinking too much about it. Without thinking about it at all, in fact. Because Cora said stuff like that. Things that would give a person cause to hope. But he had learned the hard way that the things she said didn't cost her much of anything. There was no real investment in the words. They were fillers. Something to say. Something you think the other person would like to hear. They didn't mean anything. He knew that now.

He opened the fridge door. 'I don't have any sausage,' he said. 'But I have a bottle of gin, if you're happy to drink it with apple juice.'

'I'd drink it with formula right now,' Cora told him.

'There's no need for that.' Stanley had to raise his voice to be heard over the grinding of the juicer.

'Are you making *actual* apple juice?' Cora appeared in the kitchen, startling him. Stanley took a quick look around, trying to see it through her eyes. It was clean, that much was undeniable. But was it *too* clean? No, not when you took the window into consideration. There was a pretty obvious hand-print – one of Sissy's, by the looks of it. 'Hands like shovels,' her mother always told anyone who happened to be there.

'Eh, yes,' he said, nodding at the juicer. 'It's much nicer than the processed stuff.'

'Christ!' Cora threw herself down on a kitchen chair and held her head in her hands, her hair hanging down over her face like a curtain. 'Your house smells lovely.'

'It's the brownies,' Stanley told her, making no mention of the Caribbean Cooler.

'And everything is so clean,' Cora went on, as if Stanley had not spoken.

'Sissy did it,' Stanley lied. 'She's expecting a visitor later on.'

'Christ, has the he-she gone and bagged herself a boy-friend?' Cora asked, smiling, peering up at Stanley through a chink in her fringe, all traces of her earlier angst suddenly gone.

'I told you not to call her that. It's not nice.'

'*I'm* not nice, Stanley. But you already know that, don't you?' She looked at him then. Really looked at him. And just like that, something in the atmosphere in Stanley Flinter's kitchen changed. Something shifted. The hairs on the back of Stanley's neck stood taut as if straining towards Cora, and he knew, if he turned, that she would be there, right beside him, looking down at him with her curious green eyes, like a cat looks at a mouse it has been toying with. So he didn't turn around. Instead, he *busied* himself. He pushed too many ice cubes out of the tray and crushed them in the pestle and mortar his mother had bought him for his last birthday. He turned the juicer on again – full blast – even though the apples were more than mulched at this stage. He rummaged in the cupboard containing the glasses, making sure they clinked loudly enough to fill the kitchen with noise, but not so loudly as to crack them. All the while he hummed a tuneless melody, wrapping himself up in this cacophony of sound, as if it might somehow protect him against this shift in atmosphere that perhaps only he could feel.

Cora – who suffered with a low boredom threshold – soon tired of waiting for something to happen. She backed off and sat once again on a chair at the kitchen table.

'Nothing exciting happens any more,' she complained in a low voice, as if she were talking more to herself than anyone else. 'It's all dirty diapers and mashed banana sandwiches and teething and arguments about whose-turn-is-it-to-get-up-in-the-night. And it's always my turn, according to Cormac. The wanker.'

Stanley did not respond. Instead, he finished off Cora's drink with a sprig of mint, a paper umbrella and a cherry on top for good measure, and set it in front of her with a brief 'ta-da'.

Cora smiled her feline smile. 'You're so lovely to me, Stanley,' she said. 'You always were.' She looked surprised when she said that, like she'd only just realised it. She picked up the umbrella and stabbed the cherry with its sharp tip.

Stanley didn't sit down. Instead, he stood at the kitchen sink, poured himself a measure of gin that would have accommodated two people and tossed it back. It made his eyes smart and he was glad Cora could not see his face.

'Do you ever wonder, Stanley . . . ?' she began.

But she never got to finish her question, because Sissy breezed into the kitchen at that very moment, wrapped in Stanley's dressing gown that barely covered her knees – 'I couldn't find mine' – her hair forced into a towel arranged like a turban on her head. Stanley had never been so glad to see his big, beautiful friend.

'Sissy, sit down, sit down, join us, have a drink, have a brownie,' he said, aware that he sounded more than a little crazed.

'Hi, Sissy,' said Cora in a small voice, not quite looking at her.

'Cora.' Sissy acknowledged her in a voice devoid of emotion. As far as Sissy was concerned, she had already *dealt* with Cora. A long time ago. Only once, but once turned out to be enough.

'Brothers!' she had roared at her. 'Fucking brothers!' Neither of them commented on the pun, because none was intended.

'I . . . I couldn't help myself,' Cora whimpered. 'I never meant to hurt Stanley.'

'But you *did* hurt him!' Sissy shouted.

'He'll get over me. He'll find someone better than me. He deserves someone better than me.'

'You got that much right,' Sissy told her and left it at that, because as far as she was concerned, there was nothing more to say. There would always be women like Cora. And they would always break the hearts of men like Stanley. Sissy was practical enough to acknowledge this. But it didn't mean she had to like it. She refrained from causing any physical damage to Cora. Not because she didn't want to. She did. But she knew that Stanley wouldn't approve.

'No thanks, Stanley, I . . .' Sissy stopped when she noticed Stanley's face, contorted around an expression of pure begging. 'Oh, OK, just the one, thanks,' she said, accepting the glass with her 'you-owe-me-one' face. 'Is Dara gone?' she asked.

'Who?' Cora looked confused.

'The dog trainer,' Stanley reminded her, putting on the kettle to make some good, strong coffee, so Cora could drive safely home.

'You were right about her, Stanley,' Sissy told him, draining her glass and smacking her big, bee-stung lips with pleasure. She waited until she was sure she had their full attention before adding, 'She *is* attractive.'

Cora whipped her head around to study Stanley's face, which grew hot under her scrutiny.

'I never said anything about her being attractive,' Stanley said, stung by the accusation.

'Didn't you?' Sissy asked, assuming the innocent face she had that made her mother call her a *pet lamb*. 'Well, if you didn't say it, you definitely thought it. It was written all over your face.'

Cora studied Stanley's face. Stanley smiled at her and shrugged his shoulders in a helpless kind of a way. He knew Sissy was just trying to help. He just wished she was a little less . . . blatant.

He turned towards the counter and made a production out of grinding coffee beans.

'I can't even remember what she looks like,' Cora told them, examining her manicure with dissatisfaction.

'Attractive,' Sissy told her.

Cora stood up. 'I'm going,' she announced.

'I'm making coffee,' Stanley told her.

'I have to pick Cora up from your mother's house. I told her I'd be back by nine.'

Stanley checked his watch. It was nearly ten o'clock.

'You're late,' Sissy told her, even though there was no need.

'Brenda doesn't mind, does she, Stanley? She loves taking care of Cora.' This was true, a fact that Cora exploited regularly.

'I could make you a cup to go,' Stanley said. 'I'm sure I've got some paper cups around here somewhere.' He began rummaging around in a cupboard.

'Don't bother, Stanley,' Cora told him, picking up her car keys. 'It'll wreck my gin buzz, which is the only good thing that's happened to me all day.'

Stanley retrieved her coat and accessories and approached Cora, who stood with her back to him, her arms held out like a scarecrow's, waiting. 'Thanks, Stanley,' she said, turning to face him. Her breath smelled of gin and mint. Before Stanley could say anything, she breached the gap between them and kissed him. A soft kiss. On the corner of his mouth. A kiss that blurred the lines between platonic and inappropriate. It was Stanley who backed away first.

'I . . . I'd better go and get Clouseau,' he said when he couldn't think of anything else to say. 'He'll catch his death of cold in the garden.'

Cora ignored this, concentrating instead on Stanley's face and smiling her slow, knowing smile. 'I'll see you soon, Stanley,' she told him before she turned, flicking his face with the tips of her hair. He waited until she was in her car before he scratched.

'She left her scarf behind,' Sissy remarked as she came in from the kitchen.

Stanley jumped at the sound of her voice. He found that he couldn't quite look Sissy in the eye. His guilty conscience wouldn't allow him to. Although what did he have to feel guilty about? He hadn't actually *done* anything. Had he?

'The oldest trick in the book,' Sissy continued, oblivious to Stanley's discomfort.

'What do you mean?'

'I mean, dear friend, that Cora will be back. Soon, if I have surmised the situation correctly, and let's face it, I usually do. Alone, I reckon. When she knows I won't be here.' Sissy dangled the scarf in front of Stanley's face. 'To *pick up her scarf*,' she remarked, putting the sentence in inverted commas with her long fingers.

Stanley touched the part of his mouth where Cora had been. He could taste her there.

'She's getting married, remember?' he told Sissy, in a parody of what she had told him earlier.

'*I* know that and *you* know that, Stanley,' Sissy agreed, rolling Cora's scarf into a ball and throwing it in the storage cupboard under the stairs, 'but as we both know to our cost, Cora can be a little forgetful when it comes to the Flinter brothers, can't she? I'm telling you, her work here is not yet done.'

'That's a little melodramatic, don't you think?' Stanley pointed out. 'You sound just like that fortune-teller you forced me to go to last summer, remember?'

'Madam Zora,' said Sissy, staring into the middle distance. 'She told me I'd meet a man with royal blood and sideburns and we'd be married before the winter solstice.'

'She told *me* that I'd come into money and retire early, somewhere warm. The Mediterranean, she thought.'

'Well, you *did* find that fiver on the floor in the pub we went to afterwards, remember?'

Stanley looked at Sissy and shook his head. 'She was full of shite,' he told her.

Sissy sighed and nodded. 'You're right. She was full of shite.'

Sissy climbed slowly up the stairs, shaking her head and looking dubious. Stanley presumed she was still mulling over the ineptitude of the fortune-teller, when she stopped and turned around.

'I just want you to be careful,' she said. 'You're no match for the likes of her.'

'Thanks for the vote of confidence.'

'That's a compliment, Stanley, you daft berk. When are you going to realise that?' Sissy continued up the stairs, still shaking her head but now also muttering under her breath.

Stanley retrieved Clouseau from the garden and Cora's scarf from the storage cupboard under the stairs. He supposed he could have held it to his face. Perhaps inhaled its familiar scent. But he did neither of those things. He did, however, fold it before placing it in the bottom drawer of the tallboy, where it could be easily retrieved, should Cora return to claim it.

22

On Tuesday, Dara's mobile rang on her way back from the chemist to get more patches, via the Spar, to buy another packet of cigarettes.

It was Stanley Flinter.

'There's a cousin,' he said, sounding out of breath, like he was running and talking at the same time. In fact he was. Clouseau – who had been cooped up in the garden all day while Stanley waited at the Four Courts for a case that eventually settled on the steps of the courtroom at the last minute – ran the length of Dollymount Stand, straining at his lead and pulling Stanley along behind him, like a kite.

'What?'

'Eugene Flood. He's got a cousin.'

'Oh.' Mrs Flood hadn't said anything about a cousin. Then again, she hadn't said a lot. 'What's his name?'

'Slither Smith.'

Dara didn't respond immediately. 'Sliotar? Like the hurley ball?'

'No, Slither. Like a . . . a snake, I suppose.'

'I wonder why he's called that?' Dara couldn't think of any positive reason for anyone to be called *Slither*.

'I don't know,' Stanley admitted. 'I'm almost positive that's not his real name, but that's how the locals refer to him.'

'How did you find him?' Dara stopped at a garden wall far enough from her house not to be seen. She pulled the patch off her arm and lit up. Her smoking habit was now costing her a fortune, between the price of the cigarettes *and* the nicotine patches.

'The local librarian,' Stanley said. 'They're often good sources of information.'

'And did you tell her what you were up to?' Dara asked, her cheeks nearly inside out with the effort of dragging on the cigarette.

'I just said I was a family friend and that we were trying to locate Eugene Flood.'

'What did she say to that?' Dara wanted to know. There was a split second of hesitation before Stanley responded. 'She told me about Slither Smith,' he said, as if he had been going to say something else but settled on that instead.

Dara heard a door banging shut behind her and threw herself off the wall, crouching against it. No one except Tintin and Anya knew about her recent lapse. In fact, Tintin and Anya were convinced that that was all it was. Just a lapse. She hadn't told them she'd *re*-lapsed.

But it was only Electric Eddie, heading out to do one of his nixers. He had to do them, he told Dara. To bankroll his exotic animal collection. Behind the harmless painted wood of his front door lived a python, a tarantula, a lizard that he claimed was a distant relative of one of the Komodo dragons, and a stick insect that had apparently endured a narrow escape on *I'm a Celebrity ... Get Me Out of Here.* It was the one that Kerry Katona couldn't bring herself to eat. Dara and Eddie could see why.

Still, Dara remained on her hunkers. Just in case. She tuned back in to Stanley, but all she could hear was his tortured breathing as he struggled to keep up with Clouseau.

'Did you speak to, eh, Slither?'

Again that hesitation. 'Yes,' said Stanley.

'And?' The conversation was like pulling teeth, Dara thought.

'He'll meet us on Friday at lunchtime. In a pub. The Market Bar. In Bailieborough,' he told her.

'What do you mean? Us?'

'I think you should come with me.'

'No, I don't think . . . Why do you think I should come?'

'Well, he sounded a little . . . reticent on the phone, to be honest. He might be more open if you're there. You're family, after all.'

'Does he know where Mr Flood is?' Dara crossed her fingers, held her breath and tried not to sound anxious.

'No,' he told her quickly. 'Well, that's what he says. But people often know more than they think they know. At least, that's been my experience.'

'I can't come. I'm working that day.' She didn't add that for a mere cinema-sized packet of M&M's (the peanut ones), coupled with a respectable copy of *GQ* and a furtive copy of *Heat* tucked inside, Tintin – who was addicted to celebrity gossip – would agree to switch shifts with her, faster than he could say 'Brangelina'.

'At least think about it, Dara. OK?'

There was a grunt and a thud followed by barking and muted cursing. 'Are you all right?' Dara tightened her grip on the phone.

'I'm . . . fine.' Stanley's voice sounded far-off. 'Clouseau just got a little . . . carried away.'

'Remember that you're the boss,' Dara said, stabbing her cigarette against the ground and putting the butt in a plastic container she kept in the pocket of her jeans.

'Eh, yes, I'll . . . eh . . . try to remember that,' Stanley managed to say, before Dara heard a high-pitched yelp that could have been Clouseau or, in fact, Stanley.

The line went dead.

23

'Stanley Flinter thinks I should go to Bailieborough with him,' Dara told Tintin and Anya in the Doghouse the following night, after three bottles of Bulmers. She kept her wrist – with its telltale bandage – under the table. She had persuaded Anya to keep Lucky at the pound for a week. Long enough for Dara to tend his wounds and maybe even persuade a family to give him a home. Lucky, Dara felt, was a good dog to whom bad things had happened. Anya did not share this view.

'Is against better judgement,' she told Dara, shaking her head.

Even Tintin was pessimistic. 'That's a dead dog walking, Dara,' he said, keeping a safe distance between himself and the dog as Dara examined him.

It was their traditional Wednesday-night detox. Because they were people who often worked through weekends, they had settled on Wednesday as being their normal person's Friday. Dara had asked Angel to come, but she refused, saying she was a little tired. Dara was unsurprised by the response. It was becoming Angel's staple response to most questions these days. Still, it didn't stop her from feeling guilty. Initially she told Tintin and Anya she couldn't come.

'You've got the green light,' Tintin told her later.

'What do you mean?'

'I spoke to your mother. She says to tell you to go out. She'll be home to keep an eye on Angel.'

'How come you get on better with my mother than I do?' Dara wondered.

'It's normal,' Tintin told her with his authoritative tone. 'Mothers and daughters don't get along, as a rule. It's the menopause/puberty juxtaposition, you see. Messy.'

'Angel gets on with her.'

'There *can* be exceptions,' Tintin conceded. 'How is Angel, by the way?'

Dara sighed and picked up her beer. It seemed that every time he asked this question, there was something to tell him. Something bad.

'She's taking antidepressants. Dr Byrne prescribed them for her a few days ago.'

It was a testament to how much bad news Dara had given them about Angel recently that neither Tintin nor Anya put much into their reaction. Tintin nodded and Anya blew her fringe out of her eyes, which was the thing she did when she was unsettled but unsurprised.

Angel didn't refuse the prescription. Instead, she folded the piece of paper and tucked it into the pocket of Mrs Flood's ancient dressing gown.

'That's the girl,' said the doctor. If he was surprised by her unquestioning acceptance of his diagnosis, he covered it well. Angel usually expressed great interest in the kind of medication she had to take. What it did, what was in it, what the side effects were. She never took a painkiller if she had a headache or period cramps. She waited until the pain subsided. She was good at waiting. At least, she used to be.

'It's just a short-term measure,' the doctor told her, even though Angel had not asked. 'Just till you get the spring back in your step.'

'I'm really worried about her,' Dara found herself saying. She hadn't meant to say that. It was bad enough thinking it.

'What do you mean?' Tintin and Anya leaned towards her. They knew Dara worried. Of course they did. It was just unusual to hear her articulate it.

'Has something happened?' Tintin asked, his fingers pressed against his mouth.

'No, no, nothing like that,' Dara said in a hurry, wishing that she'd never said anything. 'It's just . . .'

'You haf fear that something will happen,' said Anya. It was a declaration rather than a question. Fear. That was what Dara heard. That was what she felt. Any time Angel was in the bath for longer than an hour and Dara could hear nothing through the door. Nothing.

When Angel sped down the road in her car — always alone now — on her way to dialysis, Dara thought about lamp posts and Angel's car, wrapped around one. The scenarios played out in her head. Always bad ones. Always full of fear. She would not articulate these fears. Not to anyone.

'The thing is,' she said, adjusting her tone and smiling at her friends. 'I think they might be working. The antidepressants, I mean. She came down for dinner last night.'

It was true. Angel had come down the stairs in that slow, careful way she had now, and ate one small potato — that Dara had double-boiled just in case, as she had done every mealtime since the phone call from the hospital — and half a chicken breast, steamed but tasty with the chunks of garlic Dara stuffed into the slits she cut into the meat. She had one floret of broccoli and half a glass of water and immediately Dara fancied she could see some colour bloom on her sister's face.

'That's my girl,' Mrs Flood told her, leaning across the table to squeeze Angel's arm. 'You'll soon be back on track, won't you?'

'Joe rang,' Dara told her. Again.

'I'm going to have a lie-down. I'm tired,' Angel said, standing up. She was gone before either of them could think of something to say to make her stay.

'No, they wouldn't kick in that quickly,' Tintin said, in a knowing tone.

'How do you know?' asked Dara.

'I took them once, remember?' He looked at Dara. 'After Fluffy died. I was in *bits*.' Dara nodded. She remembered the demise of Fluffy the rabbit only too well. Tintin had organised a full-scale funeral for him, complete with a piece of music he wrote and played (on a rusty tin whistle) called 'The Death Rattle', a touching eulogy delivered (again by Tintin) at the open mouth of the A4-sized grave and the Jimmy Choo shoebox that he laid Fluffy to rest in. *Nothing's too good for my Fluffy*, he told his mother when she expressed surprise that he was recycling the shoebox in this way: she thought the whole point of having a Jimmy Choo shoebox was so you could display it around the house in a quasi-careless manner to impress friends and random visitors.

'It took at least two weeks for the pills to have any effect,' Tintin added. Dara nodded. She remembered the two weeks with vivid intensity. The crying, the keening, the wailing and the endless discussions about the existence or otherwise of Heaven and what Dara's thoughts were on the accessibility of such a place to innocent rabbits such as Fluffy. She remembered it all.

'Tell us about private eye,' said Anya, bored now with Tintin's brief brush with depression.

'Stanley Flinter,' Dara said.

'I wish his name was Stan Flint,' said Tintin. 'Much edgier for a private eye, don't you think?'

'I'll pass on your suggestion next time I speak with him,' Dara said.

'What's he like, anyway? Stanley Flinter.'

'We ... ell ...' began Dara. 'He's ... realistic, I suppose. In a pessimistic kind of a way.' Anya and Tintin nodded. They both knew how Dara liked her realism: infused with a careful measure of 'just in case' pessimism.

'That's all well and good, Dara' said Tintin, interrupting her with an impatient wave of his hand. 'But what I meant was *what's he like?* As in, what does he look like?'

'What's that got to do with anything?' asked Dara.

Anya looked bored, but by the way her body leaned closer to the table, Dara could tell she was interested to hear the answer. Dara thought about it. 'He looks a little bit like his dog, Clouseau, to be honest.'

'Hairy?' asked Tintin.

'No, it's his eyes really. Big, sad brown eyes. They'd make Anya cry, they're that sad.'

Anya looked disgusted at this notion and Dara smiled, to show she hadn't meant it.

'And he's short. But he seems fairly together. Apart from his face, that is.'

'What's wrong with his face?' Tintin enquired, sitting up straight in his chair.

'Well, the first time I met him, it was all bruised and scratched and swollen,' Dara told him.

'Why? Was he in a fistfight?' Tintin leaned in, delighted now. He loved fistfights. Well, watching them and talking about them. As far as Dara knew, he'd never actually *participated* in one.

'No. I don't know. He said he'd been in . . . a minor accident,' she remembered.

'Unconvincing,' said Tintin, pursing his lips.

'Vot else?' asked Anya.

'Nothing else,' said Dara. She decided not to tell them about Stanley Flinter's wreck of an office. After all, he had only just moved in.

Anya shook her head slowly, several times. 'I don't know,' she said, her smoky grey eyes darkening with her very potent brand of concern. 'He sounds like the type of man who might latch on to you.'

'What do you mean?'

'Needy,' said Anya.

Dara shook her head. 'No, he doesn't seem like that kind of a person at all,' she said. 'Although there *is* a sense of sadness about him,' she conceded, 'but it's very contained, I think. Do you know what I mean?' She looked at Tintin and Anya but they both shook their heads.

'Contained sadness,' said Tintin, continuing to shake his head. 'That is not the mental image I had of our P.I.'

Anya nodded. A slow, sad nod.

'I don't suppose he has a *sidekick*, does he?' Dara shook her head and Tintin sighed. 'A trench coat?'

'I don't know,' admitted Dara. 'I've only ever seen him in his office and at his house. He wasn't wearing a coat.'

'He didn't talk about *cracking the case* at all, did he?' asked Tintin with a degree of hope.

Dara shook her head. 'He said it wasn't going to be easy but that he would do his best.'

Tintin slumped back in his seat. 'Well, they're my illusions shattered, so,' he declared.

'Is gut for you,' Anya told him, taking a tiny sip of her Guinness. She had not yet come to terms with the Irish tradition of 'drinking up' and 'keeping up with the round'.

'What? Guinness?' asked Tintin, confused.

'No,' said Anya, licking the white froth of the Guinness head from her upper lip. 'Having illusions shattered. Character-building, no?'

'Indeed,' said Tintin, while Dara tried not to laugh. Anya called a lot of things 'character-building'. Awful things, like heartache and homesickness and loss and disappointment. All these things, she told them with her characteristic gravity, were *gut for soul*.

'Anyway,' said Tintin, after a sufficient period of time had lapsed, 'I think it's a good idea.'

'What?' asked Dara, reaching for her glass.

'You. Going to Bailieborough.'

'Why?'

'Because I hear it's lovely this time of the year,' he shot back.

'Really?' asked Anya, always on the lookout for lovely places to visit on her days off.

'No, you eejits,' said Tintin, tossing back his peach schnapps with a neat flick of his wrist. He was always trying out different alcoholic beverages. He was the type of person that could never say 'the usual' to a barman.

'Because that's where Mr Flood is from, isn't it? And there's a cousin there. Slithery Smith. Isn't that what you said, Dara?'

'It's Slither,' Dara corrected him.

'Oh,' said Anya. 'So it's not nice this time of year, no?'

'I have no fecking idea. I don't even know where it is. In the midlands, probably. Nothing good ever comes out of day trips to the midlands, believe me,' said Tintin with the air of a man, who had been to the midlands many times and discovered things he never wanted to know.

'Oh,' said Anya, mentally crossing Bailieborough off the 'places-to-see' list in her head and making a footnote about the midlands at the bottom of the page.

'That's what Stanley Flinter said,' Dara told them.

'He said that?' said Anya. 'About midlands?' She put the footnote in bold and italics. It seemed important to remember never to go there.

'No,' said Dara. 'About Bailieborough. About going there, I mean.'

'Oh,' said Anya again, opening a packet of Tayto cheese and onion with one hand and guiding her glass of Guinness to her mouth with the other.

'You've really integrated into Irish society,' Tintin often told her, pleased and a little proud, as if this integration was something he himself could take credit for. And perhaps it was. After all, it was Tintin who bought her her very first glass of Guinness, coupled with her very first packet of Tayto.

'Is vile,' Anya told them.

'It is at first,' Tintin agreed. 'You just need to drink more of it. A lot more.'

'Smelly breath,' was Anya's summation after her first mouthful of Tayto.

'Yes, indeed,' Tintin had said. 'The trick is to make sure everyone at the table is eating them as well. That way, you'll *all* have smelly breath and everyone's happy, am I right?'

'So when are you and the private eye thinking about going to Bailieborough, then?' asked Tintin.

'Stanley mentioned Friday. But really, *I* don't need to go,' said Dara flatly. 'I can't see how it would help.'

'You should go,' said Tintin with that irritating certainty that he had.

'Why?'

'Because you're the spitting image of Mr Flood. People might recognise you. They might tell you things they wouldn't ordinarily tell some random stranger. You *have* to go and you know it.'

Dara shivered, as if someone had blown on the nape of her neck. Something *could* happen if she went to Bailieborough with Stanley Flinter. Someone *might* recognise her. Someone *might* have a story to tell. News to impart. An incident to recall. There was a chance – however slight – that Dara could actually find Mr Flood. Or find someone who could tell her how to find Mr Flood. This was exactly what she wanted, exactly what she had asked Stanley Flinter to do . . . wasn't it? But in spite of all these things, the very idea of making progress caused Dara to shiver, albeit involuntarily.

'I have only one further thing to say on the subject,'

announced Tintin, 'and then I want to talk about sex addiction (*what's the problem?*), Simon Cowell (*would you?*) and where we're going to go for our dinner, in that exact order, OK?' Dara didn't mention that, despite endless discussions about where they should go for dinner on a Wednesday night, they usually ended up at Melvin's, which, while it smelled a bit like an attic, served the best pizza this side of the Liffey and allowed them bring in bottles of wine from the off-licence next door without charging them corkage.

'I cannot contribute to any of dees subjects,' Anya told them, gathering her coat and bag. 'I haf date wid Irish man.' She delivered this with her usual gravitas, but had to fight against the smile that threatened to break out on her face like a rash.

'What?' Tintin and Dara said at the same time. Anya never had dates with Irish men. She said they were either too scrawny or too bloated and she had yet to meet one who shared her passion for charity-shop browsing.

'Hiss name is Fintan O'Connell and he is Irish dancer.'

'A professional dancer?' Tintin asked, interested now.

'No, he is debt collector,' she said.

'I'd say business is booming,' said Tintin.

'I met him at Irish dancing class. We are going to céilidh. He vill show me how to dance a jig.'

'I'd say he will, all right,' said Tintin.

'Be careful,' Dara warned. 'You don't know anything about him. Stay with the crowd, there's safety in numbers.'

Both Tintin and Anya inclined their heads towards Dara and smiled, in an indulgent kind of a way.

'You're such a *champion* worrier,' declared Tintin, patting her arm.

'You are familiar with my motto, yes?' said Anya, tucking her ears – the white tips of which had a tendency to stick out from the dark thicket of her hair – inside the tight band of her hat.

Dara nodded. So did Tintin. They were both familiar with Anya's motto, having heard it several times before. Anya paid no attention to this minor detail, and repeated it whenever she got the chance.

'While waiting for death, embrace life,' she said, closing her eyes and lowering her head – just an inch – to give the words the reverence she felt they deserved.

'Right . . . well, I'm sure we both feel much better after that,' said Tintin.

Anya, who was a newcomer to the Irish gift of sarcasm, nodded benignly and moved away from the table.

'Wait,' said Tintin, standing up. 'Don't you want to hear what *I* was going to say?'

'I already know,' Anya told him, moving towards the door now.

'You could be wrong,' Tintin shouted after her. But Anya was gone. Defeated, Tintin slumped back into his chair. He looked hopefully at Dara. 'I was just going to say . . .'

'You were going to talk about life and how it's like a packet of Revels.' Dara beat him to it.

Tintin had a love/hate relationship with Revels. He *loved* the chocolate ones and the toffee ones, but *hated* the coffee ones and the orange ones. As for the Malteser-like ones and the raisin ones, he was non-committal. But it wasn't always easy to tell which ones were which, so he had no choice but to bite into each one, alternately spitting and swallowing, depending on what he got.

'Exactly.' Tintin slapped the heel of his hand against the skinny black jeans that made his legs 'look like drainpipes', as he told them. 'Going to Bailieborough with Stanley might be, say, a coffee-flavoured Revel, but – and here's the crucial bit, Dara, pay attention – it could turn out to be pure toffee.'

'Let's go to Melvin's,' said Dara, finishing her drink.

'I don't know. I was thinking about Anjelo's tonight.'

'They've stopped doing side orders of chips, remember?'

'How about The Elephant's Trunk?'

'It's always empty now. And the waiter cried the last time, remember?'

Tintin shook his head and stared at Dara. 'Why would a waiter cry?' he asked.

'Lots of reasons,' Dara said.

Tintin nodded and continued. 'The Birdcage?'

'Tiny portions.'

'What about the Gazebo?'

'Too new. We haven't had sufficient feedback.'

Tintin sighed. 'You're right there,' he conceded. 'Will we just go to Melvin's then?'

Dara looked at him like she was considering the suggestion. She nodded slowly. 'I think that's a very good idea,' she said.

Tintin stood up and offered her his arm to link. Dara curled her elbow around his as she always did.

'Now, what should we order?' wondered Tintin as he swept her from the pub and headed for the restaurant.

'We always order the same thing,' Dara reminded him.

'You never know, I might break out and order anchovies on my pizza.'

'You hate anchovies.'

'I've never actually tried them.'

'You hate the way they smell. And the look of them. Like maggots, you said.'

'Maybe they taste better than they look.'

'But what if they don't?' Dara fretted for her friend. 'You'll be stuck with a lovely pizza that you can't eat because it's smothered in anchovies. The sheer waste of it. And you're hungry. You'll end up eating mine.'

'I'd never eat something as tedious as a Margarita, you know that.'

'We . . . ell,' began Dara, 'maybe I'll order something different too. The Florentine, maybe?'

Tintin's mouth hung open. He didn't look surprised. He looked appalled. The thing was that Dara Flood loved food. Preparing it, cooking it, serving it, eating it. But she wasn't a great fan of eating out. It was the disappointment she couldn't take. Ordering something that sounded gorgeous on the menu with words like *drizzle* and *diced* and *shredded* and *ground*. All the words she loved in cooking. But then it would arrive in front of her and – not always, but mostly – be nothing like she'd expected. Anticipated. It went without saying that it was absolutely never better than she expected or anticipated. Mostly it was worse. It saddened her much more than it should. She knew this about herself. So when she stumbled upon something that didn't disappoint – usually the most standard dinner in the restaurant – she stuck to it. Tintin told her she was missing out. 'You're right,' Dara agreed. 'I'm missing out on disappointment.'

Now he looked at her with his mouth hanging open and an overblown expression of shock on his face. 'But there's a fried egg on the top of that,' he said, his voice an octave higher than usual. 'And spinach, don't forget.'

'I know,' said Dara, looking worried.

'Does this mean what I think it means?' asked Tintin, pushing open the door to the pizzeria and ushering Dara through.

'What do you think it means?' She had to raise her voice to be heard over the usual cacophony of noise that was Melvin's on any night of the week, despite the recession. Dara put it down to the low prices and the great pizza, a good combination in any crisis.

Tintin stood beside her and put his hands on her shoulders. 'That you're going to bite into the Revel of life and see what flavour you get?'

Dara tucked her high-vis vest and duffel coat under their usual table and sat down.

'Wee ... ell, I suppose it mightn't be a bad idea if I go to Bailieborough with Stanley Flinter,' she said finally.

'Same thing,' Tintin told her, smiling as he caught the eye of their regular waiter, Dermot.

'The usual?' Dermot asked them both, not even bothering to take his pad and pencil out of his apron pocket.

'Actually, no,' Tintin said, enjoying Dermot's look of confusion as he fumbled for his pad. 'Dara is going to have the Florentine tonight.' Dermot crouched a little to get a better look at Dara – as if making sure that it really was, in fact, her – before he collected himself, licked the nib of his pencil and guided it towards the pad.

'Wait,' Dara said. The hand holding the pencil stopped inches from the page. Dermot lifted his eyes, resting them on Dara's face. 'Eh ... could I have the Florentine *without* the fried egg? Please? And ... and could I have the spinach on the side, if possible?'

'So let me get this straight,' said Dermot, tucking his pencil behind his ear once more. 'You want the Margarita with a side order of spinach? Yeah?'

'Um ... I suppose so ... yes,' Dara admitted.

'You're sure?' Dermot asked, reaching again for the pencil, which he hovered over the page, waiting. Dara nodded her head without looking at either of them. Dermot began to write.

Tintin lowered his menu and looked at her. 'I suppose you did well enough, even to consider it.' There was something about his tone that sounded like his normal tone except with a dish of what might have been disappointment on the side.

Dara poured herself a long glass of water and concentrated on drinking from it.

'I'm going to have my usual, but with some anchovies,'

Tintin declared as Dermot turned to him. 'On the side. They're not going to kill me, are they?'

'Are they?' he repeated when Dermot didn't answer immediately.

Dermot paused to consider the question. 'Eh . . . no. Not as far as I know, an-anyways.'

'Just a small portion,' Tintin rushed on. 'Tiny really. Just in case . . . you know . . . I don't like them.'

Dermot nodded and scribbled on his pad. He was unsettled but trying not to show it.

'And where's the bould Anya?' he asked, uncorking their wine. He seemed relieved to see that it was their usual bottle of Wally's Hut.

'She's on a date,' Tintin told him, pausing before delivering the punchline. 'With an Irish man.'

'Jaysus!' Dermot whistled. 'The wind of change is blowing a gale tonight, wha?'

Tintin glanced at Dara, who looked worried but nodded nonetheless.

'It certainly is,' said Tintin, handing Dermot his menu. 'But sure, isn't a change as good as a rest?'

'That all depends,' said Dermot ominously, gathering their menus and lighting the candle on the table.

Dara wanted to ask what it all depended on, but she didn't. Instead she drank her wine, concentrated on not biting her nails and waited for her side order of spinach to arrive.

24

Stanley Flinter felt pessimistic about the trip to Bailieborough. In fact, he felt it was going to be a disaster.

'But you're bound to say that,' Sissy told him, taking the nutmeg from the top shelf and handing it to him. 'Sorry, I forgot you can't reach that shelf,' she added.

'Why am I bound to say that?' asked Stanley, grating the nutmeg into the cheese sauce he was making.

'Because you're your greatest critic,' said Sissy. 'You know that.'

Stanley nodded. It was true. But that didn't mean he wasn't right. About the trip.

Stanley hadn't told Dara what the librarian had said about Eugene Flood ('*A waster and a scrounger and a ne'er-do-well and ...*' she'd paused. '*You're not related to him, are you?*'). He had also given her edited highlights of his conversation with Slither Smith. It had been a short conversation. A short, suspicious conversation.

'What's this you want Eugene Flood for?' Slither had asked. In the background, Stanley heard the sounds of a pub. A busy one. It was eleven o'clock in the morning.

'His daughter is looking for him,' Stanley explained.

'Why? Does she want something?'

'Eh ... no, she just wants to meet him and ... and talk to him. That's all.'

'Hmm,' said Slither Smith, taking a long draught of whatever was in the glass in his hand. Stanley was prepared to bet it was Smithwick's and a chaser.

'Dara just wants to talk to him,' Stanley said again. 'Her sister's not very well and—'

'Does her sister want something? Money for an operation? Because Eugene won't have it, I'll tell you that much for free. That fella barely had the arse in his trousers, back when we were gassuns stealin' lambs.' Slither's trip down memory lane was interrupted by a bout of coughing. A wet, hacking cough that needed the careful attention of a strong antibiotic, as far as Stanley could tell.

'Do you still keep in touch with him then?' Stanley asked, trying not to let even a morsel of hope seep into his voice.

'Haven't seen him this lock o' years,' Slither said, and Stanley could tell he was gearing up for a brief goodbye before getting back to his drinks.

'This Friday. We won't take up much of your time. Just a few minutes really.'

The pause was longer than the average telephone pause. Quite a bit longer. Stanley waited.

'I suppose we could meet here, in the pub,' said Slither with a drawn-out sigh. 'It's close to the day job.' He didn't add that the day job was next door in the bookie's (You Betcha!), filling yellow slips of paper with his curiously neat handwriting and handing them through the grid to Packie, the manager, more in hope than in anticipation.

'Great. Brilliant. Fantastic. We'll see you then,' said Stanley, anxious now to get him off the phone before he changed his mind.

'It's thirsty work, though,' Slither warned. 'Talking.'

'We could have a drink,' Stanley offered.

'A drink?'

'A few. And some food. If you like?'

'I never bother with lunch,' Slither told him. 'Sure isn't there atein' and drinkin' in the few pints of the black stuff?'

Not Smithwick's then, Stanley corrected himself. But close.

His mood was not helped by the fact that the insurance company were so impressed with the photographs he had taken of Tommo-the-thick Traynor, they had sent him a new brief. To trail and take photographs of Tommo-the-thick Traynor's current wife – Teresa Trinkets Traynor, so called because of her magpie love of gaudy jewellery – who was suing her local supermarket for a slip and fall on a banana skin in the personal hygiene products aisle of the shop. The fact that she herself had thrown the banana skin on the ground, once her toddler had finished mashing it along the handle of the trolley, was not mentioned in her statement of claim.

Stanley did not relish the idea of a second visit to the wood behind the Traynors' isolated monstrosity of a house. His bruises from the first trip were only now beginning to fade to an impressive range of colours, from pale yellow to gangrene green.

Still, it was work, and with the amount of rent he was now paying – the cost of which bore no resemblance to the standard of the office space – he could ill afford to turn it down. Besides, it kept him busy, leaving him little time to dwell on the upcoming engagement party. Although he managed to dwell on it nonetheless.

25

Dara asked Stanley Flinter to pick her up from the pound on Friday morning.

'I thought you were taking the day off?' he said, when he rang to make arrangements.

'I am. It's just that Lucky is . . .'

'Lucky?'

'He's a dog. A new arrival. He's a little . . . unpredictable.'

In fact, despite his rude introduction to Dara, Lucky refused to be fed by anyone but her. He wouldn't let anyone even *look* at him, unless that person happened to be Dara Flood. Dara thought that perhaps this was Lucky's way of apologising. Anya and Tintin weren't so sure.

Anya did everything she could. She put calls out to all the rescue centres around the country. She waited for a response, but not with any significant amount of hope. And, although this was how Anya normally waited for responses, Dara felt that this time she could be right. Lucky was old, had displayed aggressive tendencies, was in poor physical condition and took pleasure in unsettling the other dogs, by throwing himself against the bars of his cage whenever they so much as twitched their noses in his general direction.

Dara was no stranger to her clients being put down. She never got used to it, mind. But she accepted it as part of the job she did. She knew that Tintin and Anya were right. She couldn't save them all. But there was something different about Lucky. Perhaps it was the sheer breadth of the hopelessness of his situation. Or the mixed-up, confused appearance of him that made people look twice, to make sure that what they had seen the first time was right. It could have been his eyes: one green and one brown. The way they fixed themselves on Dara's face when she first approached him the day after The Incident. Eyes that seemed to say, 'Eh, terribly sorry about that misunderstanding, old girl. I'll jolly well make sure that it doesn't happen again.' Or it could have been his name. Lucky. The open-ended optimism of it, which had no bearing on the slow shake of Anya's head any time she received a negative response from one of the rescue centres.

Dara spoke to him as she fed him ham she had trimmed the fat off. 'We'll find you your home,' she whispered, pulling at his ears. She surprised herself with the things she told him. Raising his hopes. His expectations. Leaving him open to things like *disappointment, uncertainty* and, of course, eventual, inevitable *decline*.

Lucky did his best to wag his stump of a tail. He looked vulnerable but resigned. As if he hoped for the best but expected the worst. He reminded her a little of herself, perhaps.

'Good morning, I'm looking for Dara Flood.' Dara recognised the hesitant voice of Stanley Flinter.

'Why?' Anya was not rude, as such. Just naturally suspicious.

Dara made sure Lucky's cage was locked before she backed out of the room as quietly as she could. The dog jumped and cowered at any sudden noise or movement. Dara tried not to think about the reasons for this.

'Well, I'm here to pick her up, you see,' Stanley explained.

'Ah, yes, you are private inspector.'

'Well . . . yes.'

'Dara said you were short.'

A forced laugh. 'Yes, well, she was right there.'

'Anya!' Dara, hurrying towards the yard, could hear the

enraged tone in Tintin's voice. 'He may be short, but he's *perfectly* proportioned.'

'Eh, thanks,' said Stanley, squirming under Tintin's scrutiny.

'No trench coat, then?' Dara was running, but she could hear Tintin's disappointment.

'It's too warm for a coat, isn't it?'

'I suppose so.' Tintin was like a four-year-old being told it was time to leave the playground. Dara ran faster.

'Stanley, hi, sorry, I was just . . .'

'Don't worry, Dara, I'm a little early.'

'You've met Anya?' Dara shot Anya a look that she hoped would warn her not to mention Dara's reference to Clouseau and the resemblance he bore to Stanley. She'd meant that in a good way but was afraid that the compliment would be lost in translation, given Anya's solemn intonation.

Stanley nodded, smiling.

'Is nice to meet you, Stanley Flinter,' Anya said, shaking his hand briefly. 'I have never met P.I. before but I haf been followed by a few.' Nobody knew what to say to that, so nobody said anything.

'And that's Tintin,' Dara added, raising her eyebrows at him, which was code for 'don't be weird'.

'Tintin is delighted to meet you,' said Tintin, getting a little flirty around the edges. In fact, even Anya flirted with him. Dara could tell by the way she offered him coffee ('Is olt and colt but you are welcome to a mug if you don't mind washing one'), and the way she didn't tell him to mind his own business when he asked her what part of Poland she came from.

Stanley held the passenger door open and waited until Dara had settled herself in the seat, which took a while because of Clouseau and the rapturous welcome he insisted on lavishing on her.

When she had dried her face – Clouseau had the wet tongue and nose of a very well-cared-for dog – Dara noticed Stanley Flinter's van. It had the hopeless air of a van that would have been clean, had it not been for Clouseau and his dog hairs that stuck to the seats, and the smell of him – that curious mix of damp carpet and bone breath.

Stanley sat down beside her, put on his seat belt, looked in the rearview mirror and both side mirrors before swivelling around in his seat to check his blind spot. Because the van was an automatic, he didn't have to grapple with the gears and could, therefore, leave both hands on the wheel, which he did, in the proper 'ten-to-two' formation recommended by driving instructors. Dara stifled a sigh of relief and allowed herself to settle back against the warm fabric of the seat.

'Are you all right?' Stanley didn't look at her when he asked the question, but concentrated instead on the road in front of him. Another reason for Dara's relief.

'Yes, I'm fine, it's just . . . well, I'm a bit of a nervous passenger.'

'Don't worry, I won't speed.'

'No, I wasn't saying . . . I mean, you seem like a pretty safe driver. I don't feel as nervous as I usually do.'

'That's good, isn't it? That you feel safe, I mean.'

'Well, saf-*er*, at any rate.' Dara didn't want any misunderstanding.

'Well, saf-*er* is a good place to start, I suppose,' and because he was stopped at a set of traffic lights on red, Stanley glanced over at Dara Flood, who nodded in agreement before she smiled her slow, careful smile, which made Stanley Flinter smile right back.

The drive up to Bailieborough turned out to be the best part of the entire exercise. Perhaps if either of them had known this, the journey might have lost some of its sheen. But the warmth of the early spring sun seemed to melt some of Dara's natural reserve away. She found herself concentrating, not on the road ahead and its endless opportunities for carnage, but on the music (she hadn't taken Stanley for a Florence and The Machine man), even singing along to some of the songs, which was fine really, because she knew Stanley couldn't hear her over the heady howls of Clouseau, who, as it turned out, was also a big fan of Florence and The Machine.

'Do you mind if we stop for a while?' Stanley asked after they'd been driving for about fifty minutes.

'No, not at all.' Dara's patch began to itch, the way it did when she sensed an opportunity to smoke.

'It's just that Clouseau needs to, eh, relieve himself.' Stanley lowered his voice as if not wishing to embarrass the dog. Dara felt it was too late. Clouseau lay on the back seat with his paws covering his eyes.

'How do you know?' She was curious.

'Well, he gets very quiet. Subdued almost. And he always looks a bit, well, embarrassed.'

They pulled into the grounds of a little church, set on a hill, in the middle of nowhere, which suited Clouseau just fine. He ran behind a tree to do his business and barked at Stanley until he had removed the hefty offering with an industrial-strength nappy bag and a garden trowel.

Dara took the opportunity to check her phone. No coverage. She moved towards the top of the hill, lifting the phone over her head and squinting at the screen for signs of a signal. Still none.

'I have a signal on mine, if you want to use it,' Stanley said, walking towards her, holding the bag of Clouseau's leftovers as far away from his body as he could.

'No, it's OK, I was just checking to see if my mother or sister rang. You know, in case the hospital . . .'

Stanley nodded and Dara felt a rush of gratitude towards this man who seemed to understand everything without her having to explain.

'I'll wait till we get to Bailieborough,' she said, putting her phone into her pocket so she could feel a message coming in, even if she couldn't hear it.

She sat down and lit up. She was surprised to see that spring had arrived. She had not noticed it until now. Swollen buds stood taut at the top of bright green daffodil shoots, and there was real warmth in the rays of the sun that reached her shoulders. Crocuses clustered around the base of trees, unlikely pockets of optimism in a world where Angel now needed tablets to encourage some spring in her step. Up to now, Dara always believed that the waiting would have a happy ending. Angel had made her believe that. Now it was more like a dentist's waiting room: draughty and full of fear, with nothing but out-of-date magazines and other people's worried faces to distract you.

By this time, Dara was halfway through her cigarette and braced herself for the inevitable comments, the replies to which were always the same (*Oh, about ten a day. Since I was twenty-two. Yes, I have tried to quit. A couple of times actually. You're right, they are very expensive. Hypnosis? Really? Oh, I must try that*).

But Stanley Flinter made none of those comments.

Instead, he asked Dara if she would like a cup of coffee and a Cornish pasty.

'I've never had a Cornish pasty,' Dara said, examining the golden-brown puff of pastry Stanley placed in her hands. It was big. She needed both hands to accommodate it.

'I wasn't sure if you liked savoury or sweet, so I made both,' Stanley told her.

'Which one is this?' Dara asked, bending her nose towards the pasty. It smelled delicious.

'It's both,' Stanley said. 'One side is apple and cinnamon and the other is beef and onion. They're separated by a wall of pastry. Inside, I mean.'

Dara bit into the pasty. It was the savoury side. Still warm. The pastry melted in her mouth. She closed her eyes. It was comfort food at its most comforting. But interesting as well. She could taste tomato and basil among the beef and onion. Perhaps some rosemary and chives too. There was nothing she could do but keep eating until the savoury part was gone.

She looked at Stanley, nodding her head and smiling as best she could, her cheeks bulging with the last mouthful.

'So you like savoury?' Stanley asked.

'Yes,' said Dara. 'Although I like sweet too.'

'That's what I thought,' he said in his slow, careful voice that suggested he had given the matter much consideration.

Before she began work on the sweet side, she took another drag of her cigarette – just to make sure he had noticed. He had. It seemed he was not going to comment on it. Dara smiled and bent her head to the pasty.

The coffee was in a thermal flask, and was made from coffee beans that Stanley had ground that morning. The smell reminded Dara of Italy. Or at least, how she imagined Italy might smell. Perhaps because of the holiday-campish mood she seemed to find herself in that morning, she shared this thought with Stanley Flinter. He agreed.

'Have you been to Italy?' she asked.

'Just once. To Rome. For my brother Declan's wedding.' There was a note of something that might have been sadness in Stanley's voice that didn't fit into the hope of this lovely spring day that felt like summer. Dara had decided to change the subject, when Stanley's mobile rang.

'Hello? . . . Oh yes, of course I remember you, Mrs . . . OK then, Irene if you prefer . . . Yes? . . . Oh really? I'm sorry to hear that. Although it doesn't mean that there can't be a rational explanation, you know . . . No, no, that won't be any problem. What about Monday? Say around 10 a.m.? . . . OK,

I'll see you then. Try not to worry, it mightn't be what you think at all . . . Goodbye.'

Stanley hung up. He looked worried, as if he was sure that there was *no* rational explanation and that the thing he told Irene not to worry about was exactly what she thought it was.

'Sorry about that,' he said to Dara, standing up and brushing pastry crumbs off his jeans. 'That was a client of mine.'

'She sounded upset,' Dara said. 'Not that I was listening or anything, it's just that . . .'

'She *was* upset,' Stanley agreed. 'She thinks her husband is having an affair.'

'And do you think he is?' asked Dara, shivering as the sun slid behind a cloud.

'I don't know,' said Stanley, reaching over to pat Clouseau. 'But in my experience, people's suspicions are often well-founded. About things like this, anyway.'

Dara suddenly felt sorry for Stanley Flinter. Having a job that forced you to dig around the soil of a person and keep digging until you unearthed something. Something they never wanted anyone to know.

26

Stanley wished that Mrs Harte – Irene, he supposed – had never rung. His conversation with her and his subsequent conversation with Dara had somehow burst the bubble of the day. Up until then, it had seemed like – he struggled to put his finger on it – well, almost like a day trip, he supposed. An air of excitement. No, not quite excitement, but something almost as good. Some kind of quiet optimism that perhaps it wasn't going to be as bad as he had predicted. It might have been the weather, the gentleness of the spring sunshine that smirked in the face of the weather reports he had listened to earlier that morning. Or the high sweetness of Dara Flood's singing voice that he could hear despite her efforts to hide it behind Clouseau's insistent howls. There was something about Dara Flood that made Stanley Flinter want to forget his trip to Rome for Declan's wedding. The last trip he had taken with Cora before . . . well, before he walked up the stairs towards the sound that brought him to the closed bedroom door that he decided to open for reasons that even now he couldn't explain. Stanley hated thinking about that trip because, looking back, he plagued himself with the worry that Cormac – who happened to be between girlfriends at that time – might have begun his affair with Cora there. If you're going to begin an affair, doesn't it make sense to do it in Italy?

'We'd better go,' he said, standing up from the bench in front of the grotto where they'd had their coffee.

'I suppose so,' sighed Dara, making sure her cigarette was out before she put the butt into some kind of plastic container. She reached for a packet of chewing gum and offered one to Stanley. He shook his head.

'Are you all right? You look a bit . . . worried,' he said.

'Oh, I always look like this,' she told him and Stanley nodded. He had guessed that about her. 'I mean, I'm not expecting much from today,' she began and Stanley, remembering his conversation with Slither Smith, felt relief at this admission. 'But,' she continued, 'there's still a chance, isn't there? However small?' Stanley nodded warily. 'That's what worries me,' she told him. 'Do you know what I mean?' Stanley nodded again. He knew.

At first glance, Bailieborough was a thriving market town with a long and wide main street, topped and tailed by a Church of Ireland church at one end and a Masonic Hall at the other, with shops, takeaways and pubs flanking each side of the main street. It was only when they began walking around the edges of the town – being a little early for their appointment with Slither Smith – that Stanley realised that Bailieborough was one of those towns that had been eaten up and spat out by the Celtic Tiger. Half-finished houses, propped up with rusting scaffolding on mostly empty housing estates, with rubble where the promised landscaped gardens should be. Even Stanley – who wasn't what you might call gifted at DIY – could tell that some of the houses on these estates were built with the *build 'em cheap and stack 'em high* approach favoured by developers during the Emperor's New Clothes era (the 'boom', some people called it), never seeming to worry if the narrow little gardens wedged in between the houses like rat-runs could accommodate important things like bouncy castles or trampolines. Still, children played as they always did, throwing rocks gathered from the unfinished road into a swampy-looking pool at the bottom of the estate, where frog spawn shuddered.

Stanley and Dara wandered up a road through the estate. At the top, Stanley stopped. 'Oh look,' he said. 'It's a fairy fort.'

'A fairy fort?' Dara looked around, confused.

'There,' said Stanley, pointing to an elevated ring of broom bushes that sat, undisturbed, on the edge of the estate. 'The builders mustn't have been allowed to touch it,' he said. The circle of shrubs were beginning to flower, their bright yellow buds leaking a ring of sweet, sticky vanilla into the air. They were prickly and Stanley used a stick to push aside branches, so that he and Dara could make their way into the middle of the circle.

'You might know it as a fairy ring?' he suggested to Dara, who shook her head.

'What does it *do*?' she asked, moving cautiously around the ring as if whatever it *did* might begin at any moment.

'Well,' said Stanley, 'some people think that if you run around it three times at midnight and make a wish, your wish will come true.'

'Do you believe that?' Dara asked.

'Well, no, not really,' he said after a moment's hesitation. 'But my father does. There was one in Tipperary, where he grew up.'

'What did he wish for?'

'It was for my brother Neal,' said Stanley, remembering. 'His hands were covered in warts when he was a kid. Twenty-eight of them he had, at the height of it.'

'That's a lot of warts,' Dara had to agree.

'It was,' said Stanley. 'Dad tried all the usual remedies at the time. You know, potato peel and rhubarb and the spit of a cuckoo. He even rubbed them with slug slime.'

Dara shuddered. Stanley nodded. He had nothing against slugs, per se, but had never picked one up. He imagined the feeling would be cold and wet. Rubbery perhaps.

'When nothing worked, Dad drove to Tipperary from our house in Dublin, waited until midnight, did the three laps of the fairy fort, wished the warts away and drove back to Dublin. When he got home, he checked Neal's hands and the warts were gone.'

'All twenty-eight of them?'

'Every last one.'

'Are you making that up?' Dara studied Stanley's face.

'No. I wasn't born at the time, but all my brothers remember it and my dad swears it's true.'

'Your dad sounds lovely.'

There was something wistful in Dara's voice that brought Stanley back to the task at hand. He looked at his watch.

'We should go.'

'If it was midnight, would you run around this fairy fort three times?' Dara asked him.

'I have nothing to wish for,' Stanley told her.

'Yes, but if you did,' she persisted, 'would you?'

'Well . . .'

'You would, wouldn't you?' There was a smile in Dara's voice.

'I suppose I would,' Stanley said. 'Sure, what would I have to lose?'

27

The pub was called The Market Bar and was one of only ten pubs still open in the town. It took Dara's eyes a while to adjust to the dark interior, which seemed oblivious to the change of season outside. Despite the warmth of the day, a fire burned in the grate, the peat sending up clouds of smoke along with its heavy, earthen smell. Dara's eyes watered. Stanley nodded to a table on the far side of the bar and she looked over. A man sat there, alone, bent over a newspaper open at the racing page, a pen gripped in one hand and a magnifying glass in the other. When he looked up as Dora walked in – still peering through the magnifying glass – his eye appeared grotesquely altered, spilling over the edges of his face. He lowered the glass and raised himself off his chair, in a manner that suggested he had been sitting on that chair for much of the morning.

'Oh, be the hokey,' he said, in the cracked tones of someone who spent a lot of time yelling at horses that never reached the finish line when he wanted them to.

He had a pale full moon of a face and one of those noses that told tales of drinking sessions that limped into the small, curious hours of early morning. It rose from his face like a bus coming over a hill; bumpy and swollen, peeling and purple. His nostrils flared, as his eyes – tiny little pinpricks of colour that were impossible to decipher – settled on Dara Flood.

'Well,' he said, smiling a smile that revealed teeth like old gravestones: long and grey and listing in different directions.

'If you're not Eugene Flood's lassie, I'll run down the main street with nothing but a smile on my face.'

For once in her life, Dara was grateful that Eugene Flood was her father.

She held out her hand. 'Yes, I'm Dara. Dara Flood. You must be . . .'

'Slither Smith,' he told her, taking her hand in both of his and squeezing. 'First cousin of one Eugene Flood.' He licked his lips and nodded at the chair beside him, before turning to Stanley. 'A pint of porter, if you please,' he told him. 'And better get me a nice little sidekick too, to wash it down. A Jameson will do.' He cocked his head towards Dara. 'And whatever your pretty little girlfriend is having.' His smile was a leer and Dara did her best to smile back, wondering when he would release her hand. She was beginning to lose all sensation in it.

'Oh, she's not my girlfriend,' Stanley seemed at pains to point out, but Slither had lost interest in Stanley now that he'd put his order in.

'You're a pretty little filly, aren't you?' he told Dara, pushing the wide expanse of his backside into the narrow confines of the chair. Because he still had her hand in the vice of his grip, Dara sat down too. She could do little else. 'Although I suppose your father was a bit of a peacock in his day.'

'What was he like?' Dara asked, pulling her hand as gently as she could. It came away from Slither's grasp with a sickening sucking sound. Dara shoved it into the pocket of her jacket, before Slither noticed it was gone.

'He was fond of the women, the jar and the horses, in no particular order,' Slither told her, draining his pint. 'We had that in common, the pair of us, although if I had to choose, I'd go for the women every time.' His voice lowered along with his face until Dara could smell the smoky, drinky smell of him that cloaked something else, something fetid, like rotting fruit. Dara nodded and Slither smiled. If he had eyelashes, she suspected he might bat them at her.

'So, is he still into the, eh, women and the jar and the horses?' Dara asked, noticing that she crossed her fingers as she did so. She wondered what it was that she was hoping for.

'Steady on, young Dara Flood, we'll get to that,' Slither said, lifting the finger of whiskey that Stanley had placed on the table and knocking it back in a way that was close to graceful, the movement was so fluid.

When Stanley came back from the bar again, Slither dragged his eyes away from Dara's face and glared at him as if he were a bad smell. Or a worse one, at any rate. Still, he accepted the pint Stanley carried, and while he did it grudgingly, he made a small pocket of space available for Stanley to sit at the table before turning his back on him and concentrating on Dara.

'Thanks, Stanley,' Dara said, stretching her neck past Slither's fleshy bulk to see him. She wrapped her hands around the mug of tea and sipped it as she listened to Slither's tales of himself and Mr Flood when they were *young bucks with great plans*.

'What kind of plans?' She found herself interested to know.

Slither looked confused, as if she'd asked the question in Russian.

He shook his head and reached for his pint, the sharpness of his Adam's apple threatening to pierce the surprisingly delicate skin of his neck with each gulp.

'Gettin' rich and ridin' women,' he said eventually, with a wink and a nod at Stanley, 'if you'll excuse me for saying so,' he added in a lower voice towards Dara, as if remembering that he was, in fact, talking about her father. 'As far as I know, neither of us got rich,' he continued, running his long yellow tongue around his mouth. He didn't elaborate on the success or otherwise of their collective pursuit of women, and for this, Dara Flood was grateful.

'Would you describe yourself as a lucky woman, be any chance?' Slither asked Dara at one point.

'We ... ell ...' She wasn't sure quite what Slither meant until she saw the yellow betting slip in his hand. 'Oh, well, I *did* win the lottery once.'

Slither's eyes widened, although not enough to tell what colour they were. 'How much?' he asked, his voice caught deep in his throat.

'Seven euros,' Dara told him.

'That's not even the price of a pack of Major,' Slither told her.

'I know,' she agreed. 'I spent it all on Creme Eggs for the three of us. My mother and sister and me. It was around Easter-time.

Slither's face was impassive, although Dara could tell he was unimpressed with her winning streak. Still, he must have decided that a win was a win, because he shook the newspaper in front of her and asked her to pick him a winner for the two-thirty.

'I couldn't.'

'You will, to be sure.'

'What if it doesn't win?'

'Sure, when do they ever win? Besides, it'll be nice to have someone else to curse for a change.'

'All right then.' Dara scanned the tiny print on the page. 'That one,' she said finally, her finger under the name.

'Him?' Slither's voice was dubious. 'That fella's mother was a donkey and his father was no better.'

'I told you I didn't have a clue.'

'But if a lotto winner is telling me to put a flutter on ...' Slither bent his head towards the page, 'Lord Lucan Returns, then I suppose I'd better heed her.'

Slither Smith could talk for Ulster. And he did. Any time his glass slid below the halfway mark, he sniffed the top of it and said the same thing. 'Jaysus, but there's a shockin' smell o' seaweed off that, isn't there?' The first time he said it, Stanley and Dara just smiled at him, the way polite people do when they've been told a joke they don't get. 'The tide's out,' Slither explained, swilling the remains of his pint around the glass.

Over the course of the next couple of hours, the tide went in and out several times. No matter how many pints Slither emptied, no matter how fast he tossed back the 'little sidekicks', his story-telling never faltered, his words never slurred. Stanley and Dara tried to steer his monologue towards Eugene Flood, but he resisted, as if he knew that once he spilled the beans about Mr Flood, his captive audience would be as gone as the group of empty glasses collecting at their table.

Dara saw Stanley hiding a yawn behind his hand. She thought about Angel, swallowing pills. About her mother, waiting at home, as she always did. She'd been waiting for longer than any of them. Dara had had enough. She stood up, the legs of her chair scraping against the tiled floor and interrupting Slither, who was lost in the midst of a complicated story about a horse that went lame and an overweight jockey who was last seen 'atein' a lock of chips on the bus to Shercock', his pockets bulging with Slither's hard-earned cash. Exactly what Slither had done to earn this cash remained unclear, but Dara didn't care any more.

'Don't you go gettin' me another drink,' Slither told her in a way that he would have described as gentlemanly. 'I've full and plenty here. For the moment, anyhow.'

'I can't buy you any more drink. I've no more money left,' Dara told him.

Slither sighed and shook his head at this admission. 'What's this you do, up above in Dublin?' he enquired, the first question he had asked since they arrived.

'I work in a dog pound,' Dara told him.

'Not too much money in that auld crack,' Slither told her, as if she didn't know that already.

'And I have to get back there.'

'I suppose I could buy you and your fancy man a drink,' said Slither slowly, as if the notion was a strange one.

Dara's eyes settled on Slither's. No, she still couldn't tell what colour they were. 'Are you going to tell us about Eugene Flood?'

Slither smiled and banged the flat of his hand against the table. 'I will, to be sure,' he declared before roaring to the barman for the same again.

'Actually, no,' said Dara Flood. 'I'll have a bottle of Corona.' She couldn't face another cup of tea.

'So will I, actually,' added Stanley, smiling at Dara.

Colour rushed into Slither's face, delivering it from white to red to puce before settling on a strangled purple, as if there was a hand wrapped around his throat.

'Right so,' he said in a voice several shades higher than his usual squawk.

It was only when Slither Smith stood up that he got the value out of the porter and the whiskey. Dara could nearly hear the drink sloshing up and down him with each unsteady step he took towards the bar. He leaned on stools and the backs of chairs, and for a moment it seemed like he would make it.

The fall, when it happened, was quite spectacular, as falls go. Slither reached for a stool or the back of a chair that only he could see. His hand leaned heavily on this imaginary chair, and, like a tree surprised by a woodcutter's axe from below, he fell through the empty space. He never made a sound as he fell. It took a long time for him to reach the ground, or so it seemed to Dara Flood, who could do nothing but watch. The noise his head made when it finally connected with the floor was a sickening crack that made her teeth clench in her gums. She ran to Slither and knelt down beside him. He was out cold.

'Quick, I think we need to . . .'

But the barman had already picked up the phone and dialled a number. 'Slither's after falling again,' he said in a bored voice. 'Yeah, out for the count.' He paused to listen, then leaned across the bar. 'Is he bleeding?' he asked Dara.

It was Stanley who picked Slither's head up, carefully, like it was a box of eggs. Dara looked underneath. There was a cut on the back of his head, out of which squeezed a few miserable drops of blood. She nodded.

'Not very much,' the barman said down the phone. 'You know him, he wouldn't like to waste it.' He sighed and hung up. 'Would you like a drink while you're waiting?' he asked them in a chatty tone, as if the body of a man wasn't strung out on the floor of his establishment like a fresh corpse.

'Eh, no, you're all right,' said Dara. 'Was that a doctor you were talking to?'

'Aye, Dr Mac,' said the barman. 'He'll be here in a—'

'Where's yon eejit?' roared a voice from the door. Dara turned around. The man at the door was so fat, he had to turn sideways to get inside the pub. He looked vexed, as if he'd had to leave in the middle of something lovely, like a strawberry cheesecake. He stopped when he saw Dara. 'If you're not related to Eugene Flood, I'll eat my own body weight in potatoes.' He looked like he'd already followed through on this promise. And not just once.

Dara nodded. 'I'm his daughter,' she admitted.

'Well, at least he got something right,' said the doctor, grunting as he knelt down on the floor beside Slither, who groaned and tried to lift his head off the floor.

'Lie down you, you're dyin',' the doctor told him, in no uncertain terms.

'Is he?' Dara whispered, her pale face growing paler.

'Not at all,' said the doctor, settling himself on a chair and taking a pipe out of the breast pocket of his jacket. 'He's just sleeping it off. Sure, hasn't he been here since the place opened?'

Dara looked at her watch. 'Ten o'clock?' It was now past lunchtime.

'November 1975,' replied the doctor, stuffing the head of the pipe with long strands of tobacco.

'Oh,' was all Dara could say.

'Jamsie, put a pot of coffee on for Slither. And fry him up a few auld sausages and rashers. And butter a loaf of bread for him, would you? He could do with a bit of soakage.'

As a diagnosis, Dara felt it was fairly accurate.

'What am I, his Jaysus mammy?' Jamsie – the barman – complained, as he filled a kettle and roared at someone in a back room to get busy with the pan.

'You're probably the closest thing he has to one, the craythur,' sighed the doctor, taking a long pull on the shaft of the unlit pipe.

Dara noticed that people in the pub were mindful of Slither, in that they either walked around him or stepped over him. Other than that, they ignored him completely, as if he were a broken fixture they were used to and careful to avoid, like a rickety table, or a three-legged chair.

She sat down.

'Did you know Eugene Flood?' asked Stanley, who had folded his jacket and slipped it under Slither's head.

'And who might you be?' said the doctor, without looking at Stanley.

'He's my friend,' explained Dara. 'We're looking for Mr . . . for my father.'

'What's he's done this time?'

'Nothing. It's just . . . I've never met him and I . . .'

'I haven't seen him this lock o' years,' said the doctor, shaking his head slowly so as not to dislodge the pipe, which hung from the corner of his mouth.

'But you knew him?' Dara persisted. 'Can you tell us any-thing about him?'

The doctor sighed and plucked the pipe from his mouth. 'He was fond of the women, the jar and the horses, in no particular order as far as I remember,' he told her. 'I'm sorry,' he added then. 'It seems like you've come a long way for noth-ing.' He nodded towards Slither, now curled into a foetal posi-tion on the floor, snoring like a train.

'Does Eugene have any other family?' Stanley asked. 'In the town, I mean. Someone who might be able to help us find him?'

The doctor shook his head. 'He was an only child,' he told them. It sounded like an infectious disease, the way he said it. 'His parents were old when they had him and young enough when they died. In a fire across the road.' He looked out the window and Dara followed his gaze to a building that might once have been somebody's house. Somebody's home. 'Eugene was in boarding school at the time, up above in Cavan town,' the doctor remembered. 'He was a bright enough lad, only seventeen when his auld pair died.'

He stood up and reached his arms above his head, stretch-ing. 'Well, there's real sick people around this town need fixin',' he told them, reaching for his bag, which Slither had curled his arm around, like a lover. The doctor released it from his embrace with a tenderness that touched Dara.

'But what happened to him then?' asked Stanley.

Dr Mac scratched his head. 'He didn't go back to school, as far as I remember. Got a few auld coppers for his father's pub and the house above it across the road and I'd say he wasn't long about spending it either.'

Dara didn't ask what he'd spent it on. She had a fair idea.

'And then sure didn't he go the way of most of the young men back then?' the doctor went on. 'He left and he never came back.'

Dara struggled to find another question to ask. There must be *something* to find out, someone who could tell her something.

'What about his parents?' she came up with. 'Are they buried locally?'

'They're buried in the cemetery out the Kells Road. Biddy and Slouch Flood.' His hand made the sign of the cross up and down and across his chest. 'God rest their souls,' he added.

'Slouch?' Dara had to ask.

'What's this his real name was?' The doctor's face creased in concentration. 'It was a bit of a fancy-dan name that didn't suit him, so everyone called him Slouch on account of his bad posture.' He slapped his hand against his knee. 'Walter!' he shouted. 'That was it. Walter Flood.'

As names went, Dara could think of fancier-dan ones. Walter and Biddy – Bridget? – Flood. It wasn't much after the morning. But it was something, she supposed.

'Give him his dinner and a lift home,' the doctor shouted across the counter at the barman. 'And don't serve him any more drink, d'you hear me? At least not today.'

'Aye, and would you like me to tuck him in and read him a bedtime story while I'm at it?'

'What you like to do in your spare time is your own business, Jamsie Cullivan,' the doctor said, taking his leave with a curt nod at Stanley and a warm smile at Dara.

'I'm just going outside for a cigarette, Stanley, OK?' She nodded towards Slither. 'Could you keep an eye on him? I'll be back in a few minutes.'

'OK,' said Stanley, looking at the sleeping Slither like a man who'd got the short end of the stick.

It took Dara's eyes a while to adjust to the natural light after the gloom of the pub. She walked across the road, unsure of what it was she was looking for and positive that whatever it was, she wouldn't find it here.

When she peered through the filth of the ancient, sagging net curtains, she saw that the house was derelict. Abandoned. There was a planning permission notice stuck to the window. Although even that was yellow with age and curling at the edges, as if whoever had put it there had long forgotten about it and their plans for the place. The back walls had either been demolished or just collapsed: either way, Dara could see straight out into a sorry little yard, overcome with sturdy weeds and broken pallets and one forlorn-looking goat, picking its way through the debris on dainty hooves.

She turned and pressed her hand against the windowsill before lowering her weight onto it. She slid her hand up the leg of her jeans, feeling for the patch, before remembering that she hadn't replaced the one she'd torn off at the little church.

In the time it took for her to smoke one cigarette, three people stopped and declared her to be Eugene Flood's daughter. The frustrating thing was that this was the bit she already knew. About Eugene himself, or his whereabouts, no one had anything useful to say.

28

The trip home was a much quieter affair Stanley felt. The weather, so bright and hopeful that morning, had dulled to a brick grey, and while it was dry, a chill wind had started up. The rain wouldn't be far behind.

Then there was Dara. While he hadn't expected much from their trip to Bailieborough, he felt the sharp edge of her disappointment, no matter how she tried to hide it. He suggested stopping at the cemetery on their way home. Dara hesitated, then nodded. Stanley turned the car into the graveyard.

Biddy and Slouch were buried together. The grave was a bit like the house: untended and overgrown. It had begun to sag in the middle.

In loving memory of Bridget and Walter Flood
Born 23 May 1924
Died 20 December 1966

'That's weird, isn't it?' Stanley said to Dara, who sat smoking on the little stone runner around the grave.

'What?' she asked, turning to look at him.

He nodded at the headstone. 'Your grandparents. They were born and died on exactly the same day.'

'Oh yeah,' said Dara, lifting a stick and throwing it for Clouseau.

'And your father loved them,' added Stanley, anxious to put some positive spin on the situation and make Dara Flood smile.

'What makes you say that?' She looked at him, curious.

'*In loving memory*,' he recited, looking at the headstone.

'They all say that, don't they?' said Dara.

'They died just before Christmas,' Stanley went on. He couldn't seem to stop. 'That must have been awful for your father. Seventeen. A boy, really.'

'Clouseau's doing his business behind Bat Reilly's gravestone,' said Dara, standing up, mashing the cigarette out with the heel of her Doc Marten and dropping the butt into that little Tupperware container she kept in the pocket of her jeans. 'Do you have a nappy bag?'

'I'll sort him out,' Stanley said, but Dara insisted. They left shortly after that.

The really weird thing, the thing that neither of them commented on, was what was written just below the names of Dara's grandparents.

Eugene Francis Flood
Born 1 November 1949
Died _____

Stanley shivered on the way back to the van, as if it were *his* name on a gravestone with the date of death left blank, just waiting for something to happen, so someone could fill it in.

After having made threatening noises for the past few weeks, the heating in the van finally threw in the towel and refused to blow anything but icy air straight into Stanley's face, reddening his nose and turning the tips of his gloveless fingers a chill white. They might have laughed about this on the way down. They didn't mention it on the way back.

Clouseau – not a great fan of cold weather – took to howling in the back seat and only considered stopping when Dara

Flood offered to sit beside him and fed him an entire packet of Bourbon Creams.

Stanley had to admit to being glad when Dara climbed into the back seat, somewhere around Kells. Perhaps it was the rain that lashed against the windscreen in sheets, obscuring the road ahead. Or the disappointment of the day that seemed to settle around them like low-lying cloud. Whatever it was, the reserve that Dara had shed like a skin on the way down returned, dragging her nervous-passenger disposition behind it like a shy child. He saw it in the whitening of her knuckles as she tightened her grip on the dashboard any time he had to do anything that wasn't driving in a straight line at a speed of no more than 60 kph. He had stopped overtaking as far back as Moynalty.

Then there was the *incident* just past Navan when they were pulled over by an overenthusiastic traffic corps garda who needed one more speeding ticket to fulfil his weekly quota. Stanley had been going 57 kph in a 50 kph zone.

'Stanley Flinter,' the garda said, looking at the driving licence Stanley handed him. 'You're not related to Cormac Flinter by any chance?'

'He's my brother,' Stanley told him, trying to encourage his frozen face into a smile.

'And . . . what's this the others are called . . . Declan, Lorcan, Neal and Adrian. Am I right?'

'You are,' Stanley told him.

The garda beamed. 'You're the one who's not in the force, isn't that right? You're deaf, aren't you? Jaysus, but you're great altogether at the auld lip-syncing. Fair play to you.'

'I'm only partially deaf in my left ear. I don't need to, eh, lip-read,' Stanley explained.

'You're not partially blind as well, by any chance?' asked the garda, reaching his head into the van and winking at Dara Flood.

'Eh, no. No, I'm not,' Stanley said.

'It's just that you were going 57 in a 50 kph zone,' explained the garda, all business now.

'Oh, I thought . . .'

'I know what you thought,' said the garda, taking a notebook out of his breast pocket and flicking through it with a wetted thumb. 'You thought you were above the law, didn't you? Being a member of the Flinter dynasty.' He began to scribble furiously on a blank page in the notebook.

'No, Guard, not at all . . .' Stanley began.

The garda lowered his notebook and winked again at Dara – or perhaps it was at Clouseau, Stanley couldn't be sure – before his head swivelled again towards Stanley and he smiled, revealing two rows of teeth that were so small and white, they might have been his milk teeth.

'Sure, I'm only coddin' ya, amn't I?' he roared, laughing at Stanley, jabbing his pencil in the air as his shoulders shook. 'Wait 'n' I tell the lads back at the station. The face on ya. It's class, so it is.'

Stanley had to wait quite a while for the policeman to compose himself. He laughed and shook and slapped the flat of his hand against his knee and finally wiped tears from his face with the back of his sleeve. It was only when the policeman stopped laughing that he realised he was alone in his mirth, although Stanley did his best to paste a sort of a smile across his face.

'I'm well within my rights to give you a ticket, Stanley,' the garda said, his features darkening with officiousness. 'But . . .' He paused for effect. Stanley waited. 'That brother of yours will arrange for me to be transferred to Limerick if I do.' Stanley guessed he was referring to Cormac. The garda tipped his hat at Dara and punched Stanley in the upper arm. Despite the throbbing, insistent pain in his muscle, Stanley was pretty sure the gesture was a playful one.

'I didn't realise you were deaf in one ear,' said Dara from the back, when they drove away. Her voice was louder than usual, like everyone's once they found out.

'Only partially deaf,' Stanley corrected her.

'Is that why you couldn't join the Guards like your brothers? And your father?'

Stanley nodded. 'I didn't realise anything was wrong until I went for the medical exam.'

'How could you not know you were deaf?' asked Dara, almost to herself. 'Partially deaf, I mean.'

Stanley laughed, even though he knew that being partially deaf in one ear was no laughing matter. It had robbed him of his dreams. Well, one of them, anyway.

'I suppose I didn't know any different,' he said after a while. 'I was born like that so I just presumed that it was normal, how much I could hear. And then I was the youngest of six boys. That helped, I suppose.'

'How?'

'You don't have any brothers, do you?'

'No.'

'I just did everything they did,' Stanley explained, taking one hand off the wheel before remembering Dara and the return of her nervous disposition. He replaced it before she noticed. 'I followed them around, I copied them: whenever they were sent to tidy their rooms, I went and tidied mine.'

'I'm surprised your mother never realised,' Dara said, stung by the idea of Stanley as a boy, trailing his brothers, who – if Tintin's tales of older brothers were true – probably spent much of their time trying out new torture techniques on him when they weren't trying to get rid of him.

'To be fair, she usually roared quite loudly at us,' said Stanley. 'I mean, she had to. To be heard. I never had any problem working out what she was trying to say.' He smiled at the recollection.

'You probably compensated,' said Dara.

'What do you mean?'

'Well, I'm just thinking about Reggie. He was a border collie we minded for a while. A blind one. But he had this amazing sense of smell. Tintin had to stop eating egg salad sandwiches while Reggie was with us. Not that Anya or I minded much. Eggy mix, he calls it. A heavy hand with the onion.'

'I'm quite partial to an eggy mix sandwich,' Stanley piped up.

'Well, I suppose they *taste* OK,' Dara conceded. 'But the smell off them . . .'

'A bit rank,' Stanley said, nodding his head.

This conversation brought them most of the way home and, Stanley noticed, managed to loosen Dara's white-water grip on the headrest of the front passenger seat.

'Can you drop me off at the pound?' Dara asked.

'I can wait for you and bring you home, if you like?' Stanley offered.

'No, I've got my bike. But thanks.'

'You'll get saturated in this weather.'

'You sound like my mother.' There was a hint of a smile in Dara's voice, but when Stanley looked at her, he saw in her face traces of the disappointment of the day, her long navy eyes dark with it. He watched her through the rearview mirror as she pulled gently at Clouseau's ears before letting herself out of the van. He rolled the window down and leaned out.

'Dara, I . . .'

'I know.'

'What?'

'There's nothing more you can do.'

Stanley opened his mouth and then closed it again. He felt that she was probably right. After all, he hadn't thought much of his chances to begin with. Finding Mr Flood would be his first unsolved case.

'I mean, you've looked everywhere, haven't you?' she continued. 'He's not dead, he's not working, he hasn't remarried, he's not in prison, he's just . . . gone.'

The resignation in Dara's voice was catching. Stanley wished things were different. He'd run around the fairy fort three times to make them different.

'Will you send me your bill?' Dara asked, lifting a notebook and pen out of her backpack. She used the van roof to lean on as she wrote. 'Here's my home address. And my e-mail,' she said, handing him a page through the open window. Her nails were tiny and pink, each one bitten down to the same length, in a careful kind of a way. She smelled of Clouseau and coffee.

'It won't be much,' Stanley told her. 'After I've factored in Clouseau's training and all.'

'Don't worry about that,' Dara said, straightening. 'That was nothing. That was my pleasure.' She smiled at Clouseau, who had tucked his head between his front paws in the back seat and was snoring gently.

'So, goodbye,' Dara said, extending her hand to shake his. 'And thanks. Thank you.'

'I didn't do anything.'

'You did what you could,' Dara told him.

'I might need to call you, though. If . . . if I need some more help with Clouseau?'

'I don't think you need any more help, to be honest,' she told him, picking up her backpack and slinging it on to her shoulder. 'He's so much better already, isn't he?'

Stanley nodded. It was true. Clouseau had taken to lifting his paw and shaking the hands of strangers every chance he got. Like he was the best-trained dog in the world. After one bloody session with Dara Flood. Stanley shook himself – mentally, so Dara didn't notice. This was what he wanted. Less thinking about Cora, and a dog who didn't try to strangle him with love every time he saw him. This was good. This was progress.

'But you can ring me if you have any questions or need any advice,' Dara told him, perhaps mistaking his frustration for uncertainty about Clouseau's miraculous turnaround. 'You have my number, don't you?'

Stanley nodded and turned the key in the ignition.

'Take care of yourself,' he called to her through the window. 'And I'm sorry things didn't work out better.'

'Don't worry. I wasn't expecting much.'

She smiled when she said it, but Stanley felt her words like the sting of a nettle. He knew that about her, somehow. That she didn't expect much. They were similar in this way, the pair of them. But he'd wanted to surprise her. He'd wanted to be more than she'd expected.

But he hadn't managed to do any of that.

Instead, he drove away.

PART TWO

29

'You're like a dog with a boner,' Sissy told Stanley, a few days later.

'It's a bone,' Stanley said, not looking up.

'What's a bone?'

'The expression. It's a dog with a bone,' he explained.

'I know that.'

'Right.'

Stanley returned to his notes.

'What are you doing anyway?' Sissy asked. She picked up the bundle of papers and sat on the desk beside his laptop. It shifted a little under her weight. The desk was a sturdy affair, left to him by his grandfather, who said that Stanley was the only one of his grandchildren who appreciated the ancient beauty in the furniture that he had spent his whole life making, when he was not on duty. Sissy got herself more comfortable and the desk creaked again. Stanley ran his hand along the smooth, burnished surface. The desk *was* sturdy. But was it sturdy enough?

'I'm finding Mr Flood,' he told Sissy, taking the bundle of papers from her.

Sissy's look was one of surprise. Stanley knew what she was surprised at. His positiveness. It felt strange, this feeling, like wearing your shoes on the wrong feet. But that's what it was. Granted, it was a quiet brand of positive, but positive all the same. This kind of feeling was an infrequent visitor to the hinterland of Stanley Flinter, which was probably why he didn't recognise it immediately. But once he realised what it was and accepted it – no, not just accepted it, invited it in for one of his chocolate brownies and a cup of fresh coffee – he felt better. Better than he'd felt in a long time. Ages, in fact. He supposed it was because he had made a decision. He had decided to find Mr Flood. That was what Dara had asked him to do. He had made this decision shortly after dropping Dara back at the pound after the trip to Bailieborough.

Sissy slid off the desk and circled him, her hand on her chin.

'You have a look of Cormac about you,' she said.

'I don't look anything like Cormac,' Stanley said. 'I'm too short, for a start.'

'You do. You look like a shortened version of Cormac. An abridged edition.'

Stanley supposed it might be true. He imagined that this was the way Cormac must feel. Every day. Positive. Decisive. Getting things done. Getting what he wanted. No wonder that smug smile was always hanging around his face, like teenagers on a street corner.

'Anyway, you said that it was a long shot. Finding Mr Flood. In fact you said it was hopeless. Where's *that* Stanley Flinter gone?' Sissy continued to study him, keeping a wary distance.

'I never said it was hopeless,' Stanley said.

'No, but you *thought* it, didn't you?'

Stanley ignored the comment. He swivelled his chair to face Sissy. 'It's too soon to mark him up as unsolved. I just want to make sure I've done everything I can to find him. It's the least I can do for . . . for a client.'

Sissy smiled indulgently at him when he handed her this explanation.

'Ah, I *see*,' she cooed.

'What?'

'You mean, it's the least you can do for Dara Flood.'

'Yes, that's what I said. For a client. Dara is my client.'

'She won't be your client forever. And she's lovely. And tiny.' Sissy's voice was wistful when she said that. Even her mother – who openly admitted that Sissy was her favourite daughter – called her 'a grand big *hoult* of a girl'. But like most grand, big hoults of girls, all Sissy wanted to be was tiny. Petite. Delicate. Even Clouseau, who was huge, only came up to Sissy's big – but taut – thighs. Because the thing about Sissy was there wasn't an ounce of fat on her. She was just a big girl. Tall and big-boned. 'An imperial bearing', Stanley told her, ducking immediately afterwards, as she made a swipe for him with one of her hands that she called paws.

'That's not the point, Sissy. I'm just not ready. You know that.' Stanley disagreed with Sissy when she told him he was a pessimist. He was a realist. There was a difference.

'It's time, Stanley Flinter,' Sissy told him, in that infuriatingly positive way she had. As if she knew him better than he knew himself.

'She probably has a boyfriend. Or a husband even.' Stanley did his best to distract Sissy from her *notions*.

'It's time,' Sissy repeated, maddeningly.

'It's not. It's too soon.' Even Stanley could hear the note of panic that had crept into his voice.

He returned to his notes. He had spent the last two days on the beat. Slither had mentioned that Eugene Flood liked the women, the jar and the horses, in no particular order. Stanley decided he would start with the horses. He began in Raheny, visiting every bookmaker between there and the city. It wasn't until he had reached Capel Street this afternoon that something happened.

The bookies was like all the others. The smell was the same. A thick, heavy smell. Sweat and bodies, hot with the kind of hope that never lasts. Counters ran along the walls, cluttered with newspapers, rolled-up balls of betting slips, blunt stumps of pencils, empty cigarette boxes, the occasional can of Red Bull, rolling on its side. When Stanley entered, the telly was on and horses thundered down a track, their breath roaring out of their nostrils in thick clouds. There were three men inside, eyes swivelling towards Stanley, before swivelling back to concentrate on the screen. Nobody spoke. Or cheered, shouted or roared the way his father and brothers did whenever they put a flutter on the Grand National. He supposed that was what separated the amateurs from the professionals.

Stanley approached the woman behind the counter. She was surrounded on all sides by thick panes of glass. She didn't look up as he appeared, perhaps sensing the amateur nature of his gambling experience.

'Eh, excuse me,' Stanley began.

She glanced up, her teeth and tongue working a wad of gum around her mouth. She came from the Sissy school of make-up – the more, the merrier – and Stanley blinked a little as she trained her paint palette of a face on him.

'Wha?' she said.

'Eh, hello,' Stanley began. 'I wonder if I could speak to . . .' He consulted the page he had printed out that morning, 'Harold Quinn.'

'Who?'

'Harold Quinn,' Stanley said again. 'The owner?'

'Oh, yeah, Harry,' the girl said, in a bored monotone. She blew a massive bubble that nearly covered her face, reeled it back into her mouth and shook her head.

Stanley said nothing, but waited. He felt sure the girl had more to say. She just needed time to position her chewing gum to facilitate a coherent conversation, he thought.

'He's no' in,' she said. Her cheek bulged.

'Do you know when he'll be back?' he asked.

'No,' she said. She seemed to have two settings. Monosyllabic and silent.

Stanley turned away from her and looked at the screen. The race was reaching its climax. He could tell by the excited timbre of the commentator's voice and the tightening of the three men's fingers around their pencils.

He turned back to the girl, who had removed the wad of gum from her mouth and placed it on a yellow sticky on the desk.

'Whatcha want him for an-annyway?' she said.

'I want to ask him a question,' Stanley told her.

'Abou' wha?'

'I'm looking for someone.'

'Whatcha think dis is? Lost and bleedin' fow-end?' The girl's voice was louder now and Stanley could feel the eyes of the men behind him settling on his back.

'Is it a woman you're looking for?' the girl asked, tilting her head and sort of smiling at him.

'No, it's a man.'

'Each to their ow-en, I suppose,' she conceded.

He reached into his bag for the photograph Dara had given him of Mr Flood.

'That's him,' he said, sliding the photograph under the gap in the glass partition. 'But you won't remember him. If he ever came in here, it would have been a long time ago. I thought Harold might remember him.'

She studied the picture for a while. 'He's no' bad-lookin', I suppose,' she said.

Stanley looked down. Everything about Mr Flood reminded him of Dara. The thick, dark hair falling around a pale face, the navy eyes – long rather than big – the small nose, the soft mouth.

He slid the photo back into his bag and closed it.

'Harry's inside,' the girl said then.

'In the office?' Stanley asked, nodding to a door that swayed in a draught.

'No, he's inside. Fraud and GBH.'

'Oh,' said Stanley.

'And extortion and arson.'

'Right,' said Stanley.

'And manslaughter, but he's definitely not guilty of da', is he fellas?'

The three punters shook their heads, never taking their eyes off the television screen.

'He *meant* to kill that fucker, didn't he, lads?'

Nods all round.

'Right, well, thanks,' said Stanley, picking up his bag.

'Why are ya lookin' for da fella, an-annyway?' Now that he was leaving, the girl seemed reluctant to let him go.

'It's his daughter. She's looking for him.' Stanley headed for the door.

'And?'

'Sorry?'

'What does she want?'

'One of his kidneys,' Stanley told her.

'Jaysus, she doesn't want much, wha?'

'It's a long story.'

'Is she your girlfriend, then?'

'Who?'

'The daughter of the fella whose kidney you're lookin' for. Keep the fuck up, wud ya?' She picked up the gum and put it back in her mouth, chewing up a storm before she blew another bubble. She kept blowing until it burst and spattered against her face. Then she peeled it off her skin and examined it before slotting it back inside her mouth.

'Eh, no, I'm just trying to help. That's all.'

'Bat might know something.'

Stanley jumped and looked round, but couldn't see where the voice had come from. It was a big voice, deep and full.

'Bat knows everyone, so he does,' the voice persisted.

Stanley looked down. The man came up to his elbow. He was either a tall dwarf or an exceptionally short fully-grown man. Stanley wondered about the word 'dwarf' then. Were you allowed to call people dwarves?

The mini-man smiled at him, revealing a row of gold-capped teeth and fleshy pink gums. 'Bat's been coming in here since before Molly Malone was lyin' back showin' everyone her cockles and mussels. No disrespect meant, Jacinta.' He turned to the girl behind the counter, who shrugged.

'None taken, Wally,' she said, not looking up from her magazine.

'Do you know where I might find this, eh, Bat?' Stanley asked.

'You'll get him in O'Donoghue's every night from six till closin',' Wally said. 'Apart from Tuesdays. He does his aqua-aerobics of a Tuesday. Never misses a class.'

Stanley looked at his watch. It was just past seven. He stood up. 'I have to go out,' he told Sissy.

'I'll come with you,' she said.

'You don't even know where I'm going. Besides, you can't. It's work.'

'People will tell you more if I'm with you. You know that,' Sissy said, jamming her feet into a pair of wedges. Her toes stuck out the front and her heels hovered out the back, but other than that, they were perfect. That was what Sissy said, anyway. 'Isn't that true?' she persisted and Stanley had to nod. It *was* true. People told Sissy things – Stanley suspected it was because they were frightened of what she might do to them if they didn't. But still. If Bat knew anything, Sissy would be the one to drag it out of him.

Wally's description of Bat was spot-on. His head *was* too big for his body. And he was right about his hair too. There was something suspicious about it. 'Coal-scuttle black,' Wally had said.

He sat where Wally had said he would be. Just inside the door, his head buried in a book.

'It'll be a Mills & Boon,' Wally told Stanley. 'He's mad for an auld bit of romance, so he is.'

The man was reading a book called *Love in Ward Seven*. Sissy confirmed later that it was indeed a Mills & Boon.

'Eh, excuse me . . . Bat?' Stanley said, approaching the table. Bat lowered his book, but it was Sissy he looked at. His eyes scanned the length and breadth of her. It took a while. Stanley coughed. 'Eh, Bat, look, I'm sorry to disturb you, but I got your name from Wally. Down at A Sure Thing. The bookmakers. On Capel Street.'

Still Bat did not take his eyes off Sissy. She took her chance and slid into the seat beside him. 'Is that the one where the doctor and the nurse meet and first they hate each other, then they fall in love, but there's that complicated misunderstanding with one of his patients that nearly scuppers them before they—'

'Don't go telling me the end, whatever you do. You'll spoil it for me,' said Bat, smiling at Sissy with a set of beautiful white dentures. Wally had been right about his voice. Loud as a drum and riddled with Kerry.

Sissy offered him her hand, which he held rather than shook. 'Sissy Clarke,' she declared.

'Brendan O'Malley,' he said, bending to plant a kiss on Sissy's hand that he still held. 'But everyone calls me Bat.'

'And this is Stanley Flinter,' Sissy said, pointing at him. Bat dragged his gaze from Sissy's face just long enough to acknowledge Stanley with a brief nod.

Stanley sat down. 'Bat, I'm sorry to disturb you, but Wally said you might be able to help. I'm looking for a man called Eugene Flood.'

This caught Bat's attention. He looked at Stanley again, but this time did not look away. 'Eugene Flood,' he said, shaking his head. 'Christ, there's a name I haven't heard in years.'

'You know him?' Stanley felt something peculiar tighten inside him. He thought it might be hope.

'I knew him as well as anyone can know a man like that.'

'Look, can I buy you a drink? I . . . I mean, we . . . won't take up much of your time.' Stanley nodded towards Sissy when he said that, blatantly dangling her like a carrot on a stick.

Bat nodded. 'That's very Christian of you altogether. I'll take good care of your lovely lady while you're gone.'

As Stanley made his way to the bar, he could hear Sissy telling Bat that she was *not* Stanley's lovely lady. 'Christ, would you look at the scutty little size of him. How's a girl supposed to look petite beside *that*?' What Bat's reply to this observation was, Stanley did not hear, but when he returned, the pair of them were wrapped up in an animated conversation, like they'd known each other for years. Well, Sissy was doing most of the talking. She was telling Bat about the cad who must not be named, aka Duncan.

'Ah, Sissy love, he's not worth it,' said Bat, as if he and Sissy had met years ago, maybe even slept together a couple of times before coming to the conclusion that they were better off as bosom buddies, rather than threatening their relationship with the vagaries of romance. 'I mean to say, a man who can make promises like that' – Sissy had already told him about the watch: the Dolce and Gabbana one – 'and renege on them, well, that's not a man who's fit to lick the soles of your shoes, is it?' He peered under the table then. 'Are they Stella McCartney wedges?'

'They are,' Sissy admitted. 'But they were on sale when I bought them. Nearly half price.'

'Even at half price, they're still a shocking amount of money, aren't they?'

'Yes, but I haven't taken them off my feet since I bought them. I'm going to get the value out of them that way, y'see?'

Bat nodded sagely. Apparently he *did* see.

Stanley sat down and handed out the drinks. He looked at Sissy with the look she called his private detective look. An *ahem ahem* sort of a look. She glanced down at her wedges to admire them one last time before she turned to Bat.

'So, Bat, what can you tell us about Eugene Flood?' she asked.

Bat lowered his head to his pint and drank deeply, his eyes closed. When he opened them again, his pint was past the halfway mark. He looked at Stanley. 'You're not the first people who have come lookin' for Eugene Flood,' he said. 'And I'm sure you won't be the last, either.'

Stanley wanted to get to the specifics. 'He was a gambler, is that right? Is that how you met him? In A Sure Thing?'

Bat smiled and leaned back in his chair. 'I've been going to A Sure Thing since I was a boy. Since before I was born really, if you think about it. My mother was a gambler too, God rest her. Handy she was. She owned her own house when she died. And half a greyhound. Not many people can say that, can they?' He paused to gauge Stanley and Sissy's reaction. They both shook their heads and waited for him to continue. 'You see, there's people like me and Mother. We're *professional* gamblers.' Bat sat up straight and jutted his chin. 'People like you' – he looked at Stanley when he said this – 'might not know it, but there's a world of difference between the likes of me and Mother and the likes of Eugene Flood. We know when to get in and, more importantly, when to get out. Poor Eugene had no such discipline. He was a compulsive gambler, God love him. He wasn't content to just make his living out of it, like I've done. Not much, but enough to pass the time of day on. Eugene was different. He wanted to make his fortune. He was looking for The Big Win. That's what he was after. One big win and then he said he'd give it all up. He was a book-maker's dream, so he was.'

'What happened?' Sissy asked, leaning forward and giving Bat the benefit of her 'puppies', as she called them, straining against the thin fabric of a low-cut top. In fairness to Bat, he lost the thread of his thought only briefly, before he continued with the story.

'He owed money. A lot of money. He made the mistake a lot of them did back then. Borrowed it from a loan shark who looked like he wouldn't shout *heel* at a puppy. Benny Byrne, God rest him.' Bat blessed himself, his head bowed.

'He's dead?' Stanley asked.

'He is,' said Bat. 'Felled by his own sword.'

'Suicide?'

'No, flattened by the 46A,' Bat told them. 'He took that bus every day of his life. Right up until the end.'

Stanley allowed what he felt was a respectful amount of time to lapse before he returned to the subject of Eugene Flood.

'So, the money that Eugene Flood owed Benny Byrne . . . ?'

'Benny sold that debt. Just a few days before he died, in fact. Almost like he knew.' Bat shook his head before he picked up his glass and leaned towards it. Stanley waited. He knew there was more. When Bat resurfaced, there was a new look in his eye. It was fear. 'He sold it to a man they call Con King.' He shook his head when he said the name. A reverential shake.

Sissy was impressed. 'Why do they call him Kong King?' she asked in a hushed voice.

Bat looked at her, confused. 'Because that's his name, like,' he explained. 'Con King.'

'Oh,' Sissy said.

'Anyway, the debt started to add up and up and Con got restless. Eugene stalled him as long as he could, which was pretty long when you consider what a psycho Con was. But there was something about Eugene, you know. He was the only man I ever met who was truly charming. Not lick-arsey charming, if you know what I mean, but proper, honest-to-goodness charming. He had a way of gettin' in on you, did Eugene Flood. Even Maurice-the-misery Mahon couldn't help smiling when Eugene spoke to him. And God knows, they didn't call him Maurice-the-misery Mahon for nothing.' Bat stopped to take another drink. Stanley pushed his chair closer to the table. He was getting somewhere. He could feel it in the taut hairs at the back of his neck.

'So,' he said to Bat when he set his glass back on the table, 'how much did Eugene owe?'

'They say Con King pulled an oak tree up from the ground with his bare hands when he found out that Eugene had done a runner. That's how much he owed him.'

'Do you know where he went?' Stanley asked. 'Where Eugene went?'

Bat shook his head slowly. 'No one knew. Somewhere far away, that's for sure. Con never stopped looking for him, I can tell you that much. He's probably looking for him still.'

30

Angel's reaction to Dara's news about the non-events of Bai-lieborough was one of low-key acceptance. 'Well that's that, then,' she said, pulling Mrs Flood's ancient dressing gown tightly around her narrow frame.

'That's what then?'

'That's an end to it,' Angel said, pushing her greasy fringe out of her eyes. She needed a haircut. And a good wash, to be honest. She'd begun to smell a little . . . lived in.

Dara stood on a chair to open the window in the sitting room.

'What are you doing?'

'I'm just letting a little fresh air in here. It's a bit stuffy.'

'Is it? I hadn't noticed.'

'You can't just give up,' said Dara, sitting beside Angel on the couch.

'I'm just accepting things as they are. It's about time. I'm not waiting for the phone to ring any more. I'm not worrying about Joe and all the opportunities he's missing. And as for you . . .'

'What about me?'

'Well, you can get back to your life. Such as it is.'

'What's that supposed to mean?' Dara felt a hot flush of anger rush to her face. This was a side to Angel she hadn't experienced before. There was a sneer in her voice that didn't suit her. Not the Angel that Dara knew.

'Your steady, comfortable job at the pound.'

'I *love* that job.'

Angel dismissed this defence with a wave of her hand.

'Your situation with that bloke you see once a week.'

Dara regretted ever confiding in her sister about Ian Harte. 'He's away a lot,' she reminded Angel. 'On business.'

'Whatever,' said Angel, picking up the remote and turning the telly on. 'It's going nowhere and that's just the way you like it, isn't it?'

'I don't know why you're being so cruel,' Dara said and it was true. She barely recognised Angel at this moment.

'Not cruel, just honest,' Angel said, flicking from one channel to another at speed. 'You never go anywhere, you never do anything, you might as well be as sick as me.'

'That's not fair.'

'Hadn't you heard, Dara?' said Angel in a flat monotone. 'Life's not fair.'

'I'm trying to help,' Dara told her.

'Don't bother,' Angel said, not looking at her sister.

It was the closest they'd ever come to a fight. It cut Dara to the quick. It didn't seem to have any effect on Angel though, not as far as Dara could see. When she left the room, Angel called after her, 'Can you close the door behind you?' Dara grabbed the handle and banged the door shut. Then she opened it and banged it shut again. She did that three times. They hadn't spoken since.

31

Con King looked like a man who might be able to pull an oak tree out of the ground with his bare hands. Even with the guard sitting in the corner of the room – a female guard, reading a copy of *OK!* – Stanley had to admit to feelings of fear. It was the sheer length and breadth of the man. Big was too small a word for him. And the colour of the skin on his face. Brick-red, like he'd poured chip oil all over himself and sat in the sun at midday in the Sahara desert. His face wasn't just roaring red. It was bawling. In shocking contrast, his hair was a thick bush of pure white. Which was weird, because his eyebrows were shaggy and dark and jutted like awnings over his eyes: tiny, pale blue slits that looked hopelessly lost in the bloodbath of his face.

'Cormac said you wanted to ask me a few questions?' Stanley guessed – correctly – that Con's voice had let him down badly over the years. It was not the voice of a gigantic man. A hardened criminal. A vicious debt collector who had been known to beat his victims with 5-irons. He was a golf fanatic. A violent golf fanatic. Never a good combination. Con's voice did not lend itself to a man like that, however. There was something thin and high about it. Dainty almost. A mouse. That's what came to mind when Con opened his mouth to speak. Stanley did not allow his face to betray these thoughts, although it was not as easy as you might think.

'Eh yes, I'm Cormac's brother. Stanley. Stanley Flinter.'

'Are you a fucken pig too?' Con asked before he turned – timidly, Stanley felt – to the guard sitting in the corner. 'No offence, Rosie,' he squeaked at her.

She acknowledged him with a brief nod, not looking up from her magazine.

'Eh, no, no I'm not,' said Stanley, who decided not to mention the fact that he was a private investigator. Con might take umbrage at this occupation too. He looked like the kind of man who took umbrage on a regular basis.

'Good man,' said Con, settling back in his chair and studying Stanley with his tiny, pale blue eyes, barely visible beneath the overhanging bushes of his thick dark eyebrows. 'Cormac said you had a question to ask me.' He looked at Stanley in a curious way, and Stanley shifted in his chair.

'I do,' he said.

'Go ahead, comrade. I don't bite,' he said, cradling the back of his skull in his huge hands. 'Much,' he added. When Con smiled, his eyes disappeared altogether, into the raw red landscape of his face.

Stanley cleared his throat. 'I'm looking for Eugene Flood,' he said.

Con was on his feet in an instant. 'That blackguard!' he roared before slamming his fist against the table between them – which, incidentally, was nailed to the floor. Stanley had checked before he sat down. The table shook with the beating Con gave it, but the nails held strong and it remained in place.

Rosie's face peered over the top of her magazine. 'Con?' she said, like it was a question.

The result was instantaneous. Con stopped thumping the table. He sat down. He smiled at the guard. 'Sorry about that, Rosie,' he said.

'That's quite all right, Con,' she replied, nodding encouragement at him before returning to the magazine.

'Anger management classes,' Con explained to Stanley. 'I don't know what I'd do without them, bein' honest with you. They're doin' me the power o' good.'

Stanley nodded and tried not to think about Con King before the benefit of the anger management classes. 'Eh, Mr King,' he began. 'I know that you bought Eugene Flood's debt. Off Benny Byrne, wasn't it?'

At the mention of Benny's name, Con dropped his head to his enormous barrel of a chest and crossed himself. 'Just a few days before he died. It was early, y'see, the bus. Took him by surprise, God help him.'

'How much did ...' Stanley didn't want to mention Mr Flood's name again, now that Con King seemed to have composed himself, 'did the man owe you?' he finished.

Con's hands curled into furious fists. He took a deep breath and expelled it, like a gale-force wind. His breath smelled of very strong toothpaste. Euthymol perhaps.

'Six large,' he said. 'And that was pounds, remember, none of your euro shite.'

Stanley nodded. He realised that six thousand pounds was a lot of money back then. A fortune, really. But even so, it seemed like a sad little pile of money when you compared it to the toll it had taken.

Con King seemed to read Stanley's mind. 'I never took him for a runner,' he said, shaking his head. 'Men with wives like that don't run. And the little one with the blond hair. Like an angel, she was. A little angel.' It was as if Con King had forgotten about Stanley Flinter. Even Rosie. For a moment, it was just Con in the room. And his memories, moving across his face like clouds, casting their shadows.

'Did you ever ... did you go and see Mrs Flood? Back then?'

Con sprang to his feet and gripped the edge of the table, as if he intended ripping it from the floor, in spite of the nails. 'What have ya heard?' he bellowed at Stanley.

'Nothing. I've heard nothing.' Stanley forced himself not to back away as Con's face moved towards him, even redder than before.

'Calm yourself, Con,' came Rosie's soft voice from the corner.

Con spun around to glare at her. 'He thinks I'm a fucking pussy, Rosie – excuse my language, love – just like the rest of them.'

Rosie studied Stanley Flinter. 'No he doesn't,' she said, 'do you?' She moved her head so Con couldn't see her eyes, which she trained on Stanley in a very deliberate way.

Stanley understood. He shook his head, more than once. 'No,' he said, 'I don't.' And it was true. Con King had been inside many times over the past 27 years and none of his crimes were unrelated to fairly spectacular bouts of gratuitous violence.

Con sat down. 'They said I lost me nerve after the Flood job,' he said, the squeak of his voice smothered in the hands he held against his face. 'Just because I'm a decent, compassionate man. I mean, I take pride in my work. I *enjoy* it. I'll beat any man to within an inch of his life with a golf club. But a woman? A heavily pregnant woman? I'm a *gentleman,* for fuck's sake.' He lowered his hands and glared at Stanley. 'That's what's wrong with the world today, Stanley. There's no lines that people won't cross. There's no *limits.*' He looked at Stanley then, a pleading look, begging him to understand.

Stanley nodded again. He knew about the lines that people crossed.

'*You're* afraid of me, aren't you?' It was a question rather than an accusation. There was something vulnerable about the way Con asked it.

Stanley nodded. He wasn't afraid of Con King, here, in the confines of this small room, with Rosie's quiet authority. But he felt pretty sure that if he met the man down some dark alley with a 5-iron in his hand, he'd be afraid. Terrified, probably.

Con almost smiled. Stanley could tell by the way the edges of his mouth twitched. 'I *am* scary,' he said, defiant. 'But I'm a family man, Stanley, do you know what I mean?'

Stanley nodded.

'Do you have any chizzlers yerself, Stanners?'

'Eh, no,' said Stanley. 'But I have a niece,' he added quickly, taking a photograph of Baby Cora out of his wallet and sliding it across the table.

The passport-sized photograph was immediately lost in the enormity of Con's hands. 'She's a fucken dote, so she is,' he told Stanley, handing the photo back, trying and failing to drag the smile off his face. He opened his own wallet then, bulging with the number of photographs it held. He spread them on the table between them. 'That's Kylie. And Charlene. And Con Junior, o' course. And Jasmin. And that's the baby there, Angelina.'

Stanley nodded and smiled as Con provided doting details of each of his children, in age order. He wondered how he was going to steer the conversation back to the choppy waters of Eugene Flood. In the end, it was Rosie who did it. 'Five more minutes, Con,' she said gently as Con neared the end of an anecdote involving Angelina, a local bonny baby competition, a second place, followed by a 'chat' with one of the judges, which was how Con came to be incarcerated in Mountjoy gaol this time round. 'You'd better tell Stanley whatever you know about Eugene Flood before he has to go.'

'That fucking fucker!' roared Con, but this time Stanley didn't even flinch. Instead he leaned forward.

'His daughter is looking for him,' he said. 'She needs a kidney. He might be a match.'

Con's face softened, as Stanley knew it would. He didn't look like a pussy, as such. More like an oversized teddy bear that you keep for years after you should have thrown it out. Stanley hoped that Con wouldn't catch sight of his reflection in the window. He felt sure that the debt collector wouldn't like what he saw.

'The little one with the blond hair?' Con asked. Stanley nodded. Con shook his head. 'I don't know where he is. If I knew, I'd be there meself, separating his bleedin' head from his neck.' Stanley didn't doubt it. 'To be honest wichya, the Celtic Tiger put most of us out of business, what with the banks giving the money away for free. I had to diversify. Automobiles. That's me main game now, stealin' and sellin', so let me know if you're ever lookin' for a little runaround, yeah?'

'It's time, gentlemen,' Rosie said, closing her magazine and standing up. Stanley felt desperation take hold of him and squeeze.

'I know it was a long time ago,' he said, 'but were there no leads at all? Back then, I mean?'

'Ah, there were rumours, Stanley, o' course there were. There's always rumours in my line o' work. London, Manchester, Leeds, Birmingham, Edinburgh. There were sightin's of that little rat all over the place. I lifted every stone a slug like that might hide under. There was one rumour he'd scarpered to Paris.'

'Paris?'

'There was no way I was goin' lookin' over there. They don't even speak English, for fuck's sake. Savages, the lot of them. They eat horses in France, did ya know tha?'

Stanley shook his head.

'I'm very partial to horses. Not eatin' them, mind. Just ridin' them an' the like.' Con stared into the middle distance. 'I remember, back in Hollyfield when I was a lad, we used to ride them bareback up and down the streets and in and outta the pub. It was only magic, so it was.'

'Con?' Rosie nodded towards the door.

Con leapt to his feet and smiled a deferential smile at her. Then he turned to Stanley Flinter and hesitated before offering his hand. Stanley took it. There was nothing else to be done with it. 'If you find that bollox, you be sure and tell me, won't you?' Con said. 'He's still on me books, there's no time limit. You can tell him from me that Con King is still waitin' for his money, yeah?'

Stanley nodded. He could make that promise to Con, because it didn't feel like it would ever come to that. The closer he got to finding Mr Flood, the farther away he seemed.

32

Dara didn't tell her family immediately about Stanley's news.

For a start, it wasn't what she had expected. It had taken her by storm. Left her winded. Wrong-footed. To discover that Mr Flood's leave-taking had had very little to do with her. Nothing, in fact. It had had nothing to do with her. She hadn't expected that. She thought he left because of her. Not *just* because of her. But she'd thought she was a substantial part of the reason. There were things that certain people couldn't face: the burden of responsibility, the drudgery of parenthood, the truth about money and how tight it could get, the scarcity of jobs. She'd had many theories over the years, and the common thread through all of them was her. Dara Flood. The baby that he never saw. The one he didn't wait for.

It seemed strange now to realise that she had nothing to do with it. Nothing whatsoever.

So she hadn't told her family yet. She couldn't bear to see Angel shrug in that careless way she had now, as if she expected nothing more. As for Mrs Flood, Dara hadn't worked out how to tell her that her husband had abandoned her and her two children for the want of six grand.

'Yes, but it was 6,000 *pounds*, not euro,' Tintin pointed out, trying to be fair.

Dara felt her mother would take it badly, whatever the currency.

'At least now you know why,' said Anya, rubbing at a paw print on the pale pink wrap she had worn over the Karen

Millen dress she had found in the bottom of a bargain bucket in a charity shop in Killiney.

'It's not the best reason for a man to leave,' Dara said.

'Is not worst one either,' Anya told her, removing the tube of Stain Devil she always stowed in her bag.

'You're uncharacteristically chipper today,' Tintin told Anya. He turned to Dara. 'She unloaded all the dishes in the dishwasher this morning. Not just the ones she used.' He turned back to Anya. 'What's the matter with you?'

Anya blushed. She turned away from them, but they could see her reflection in the Portakabin window. She was trying not to smile.

'Well?' Tintin persisted.

'We are supposed to be discussing Mr Flood,' Anya reminded him primly.

Tintin looked at Dara. 'You don't mind a little diversion, do you?' Dara shook her head. Ever since Stanley rang her last night to tell her, she had thought of little else. Apart from Stanley himself. He had surprised her with his persistence.

Her phone beeped and she grabbed it out of her pocket. But it was just a text from Ian. *Can't wait to see you at the weekend, my beautiful Dara. To sustain me until then, tell me what you are wearing ...*

Dara sighed. This was not an atypical text from Ian. But it was one that she could never quite get on board with. She texted back: *Navy tracksuit, white aertex top, hoodie, trainers.*

She knew this was not what Ian was after but she found it a little embarrassing to text about her underwear. Ian called them sex-texts and said they kept him going during the week when he could not see her. She pressed SEND.

Tintin was persisting with Anya. 'So, my Polish pessimist. To what – or whom, perchance – does your face owe the pleasure of your maiden's blushes?'

'Is none of your business,' Anya told him snippily.

'I know that, my dear Anya. When has that ever stopped me poking my nose in?'

Anya shrugged, which was her way of conceding the point.

'Is Fintan. Irish dancer. I allowed him to mate with me. Last night. Standing against fridge of kitchenette.' Anya was a stickler for details, but in fairness to her, she supplied as many as she demanded.

'You *mated* with an Irish man?' Tintin was appalled, and not at the fact that the fridge he shared with Anya had been used as a prop in a sex-related incident. 'In our kitchen?' he added, but Dara knew it was just for show.

Anya nodded.

'And?'

'I did not have orgasm,' she told them, her tone solemn. 'But it was ... acceptable, nonetheless. I have had worse. Much worse.' From Anya, this was high praise indeed.

'Jesus, Anya, what are you saying? Might you be in love?'

Anya shook her head, but the blush persisted.

'Well, I'm in love,' declared Tintin. When this did not garner much response, he elaborated. 'With two people. Siblings, in fact. A brother and a sister.' From anyone else, this might be deemed shocking, but from Tintin it simply wasn't shocking *enough*. He went for broke. 'They're twins. They're not identical obviously, but they look so alike. I just can't choose.'

'They're not sweets in a sweet shop, Tintin,' Dara reminded him.

'I know, I know, but I can't think straight when they're around. You know that's always been one of my fantasies: a threesome with a boy twin and a girl twin.' Dara nodded. So did Anya. Tintin hadn't shared *all* his sexual fantasies with them. There were too many for that. But still, he'd confided a fair few.

Dara smiled. Being at work was so much easier than anything else at the moment.

In fact, work was the one area of her life that was going well. The weekend had been productive, with homes found for Kimberley, Sherlock and even Jack Knapp, who had stayed awake long enough to charm the tweeds off an elderly lady looking for a sedentary type of a dog. 'It's my arthritis, you see,' she explained, even though there was no need. Dara could see it in the swollen knuckles of her hands and the slow gait of her walk.

Dara felt the usual mix of relief and regret as she handed Jack Knapp over. 'He's perfect for you,' she told the old lady, who already gazed at Jack with something like adoration in her eyes, as if she'd owned him since he was a pup. 'He likes snoozing and fun-size Crunchies.'

'Just like me,' the woman said, easing herself through the door of the Portakabin, clutching Jack to her like a long-lost son. Dara didn't watch them go. She never did.

Then there was Lucky. He seemed oblivious to the number of dead ends Anya, Dara and Tintin had been down in their search for somewhere to put him. Someone to take him on. In fact, it seemed to Dara that Lucky was thriving in direct proportion to the number of negative responses they'd had about him. The welts on his body were healing, his fur was reacting well to the regular treatments Dara applied. His appetite had improved, although he still refused to be fed by anyone who wasn't Dara Flood. Even his attitude towards the other guests was better, although there was a way to go yet. Dara felt he was developing a particular soft spot for Jeffrey, the massive St Bernard with the tendency towards forgetfulness. Possibly because Jeffrey kept forgetting to be afraid of him. Either way, Lucky didn't throw himself against the bars of his cage quite so furiously whenever Jeffrey waddled past.

'He's keen, isn't he?' said Tintin, setting his sights on Dara when it became clear that no one was that interested in his twins story and no further details were forthcoming from Anya about Fintan the dancer.

'Who?' Dara asked.

'Mr Stanley Flinter, that's who,' Tintin said. 'All this work he's been doing. It's a bit above and beyond, isn't it?'

'I'm going to pay him, you know,' said Dara, making a mental note to call Stanley and ask him – again – to send her a bill. So far, her €412.37 was still intact. She hoped it would be enough. 'He's just doing his job,' she said, moving towards the door. 'You should try it sometime,' she added, looking pointedly at Tintin, who swivelled in Anya's chair with his legs draped across her desk.

'I did try it once,' Tintin told her. 'It didn't agree with me.'

'If you help me feed the dogs, I might give you some of the cottage pie I brought in. There's enough for all of us.'

'Did you put peas in it?'

'Of course not.' Tintin ate most things but drew the line at peas, beans and lentils. He said the only pulses he liked were the ones that quickened in response to his advances.

Tintin leaped to his feet. He loved Dara's pea-less cottage pie. They all did.

'So what's next on the agenda for our super-sleuth?' he asked as they made their way towards the kennels.

Dara shook her head. 'He says he's looking at a few possibilities in Paris. I'm not holding out much hope, to be honest.'

'You do surprise me, Ms Flood,' Tintin said, wrapping one of his long, thin arms around Dara's neck.

She stopped suddenly and faced him. 'What am I going to say to Mam?'

'Just tell her,' Tintin said, his voice gentle. 'At least she'll know that he didn't leave her for another woman. Or because he didn't love her.'

'Well?' said Dara. 'He didn't love her. Did he?'

'He did,' Tintin said, picking up the bag of dog food. 'He just didn't love her enough.'

That seemed worse somehow. Hate seemed more passionate than being loved in a way that just wasn't enough. Dara walked on.

'How's Angel?' Tintin asked, as he did every day.

Dara shrugged. 'The same,' she said. She hadn't told him – hadn't told anyone – about the things that Angel had said. About Dara slamming the door. Three times.

Tintin tightened his arm around Dara's shoulders. 'You're doing everything you can,' he said. Dara nodded. She didn't think that was true, but even if it was, it was a bit like Tintin's take on her father's love for her mother: it wasn't enough.

33

Mrs Flood and Dara were downstairs in the front room. Angel was in her bedroom. Through the thin walls of the house, Dara heard the melancholic strains of Tears For Fears' version of 'Mad World'. She had a sudden urge to run upstairs, grab Angel's iPod and her docker and pitch them out the window, and then run downstairs and out to the front garden and jump up and down on the remains, just to make sure. But she didn't do any of those things. Instead she sat in one of the two armchairs in the front room and tried to read her book. She usually read in her room. But with Angel spending so much time upstairs, she didn't like to leave her mother on her own all the time. Besides, she wanted to talk to Mrs Flood. She had promised Tintin.

Mrs Flood sat in the other armchair, watching the telly. Or at least she pointed the remote at the telly and flicked from one channel to another. She'd been restless since she came in, moving between the front room and the kitchen, stopping to adjust a picture here, an ornament there. She was spoiling for a fight. Dara recognised the signs.

'I nearly tripped over these,' she told Dara, handing her the Doc Marten boots that Dara had left in the hall.

'I'll put them away,' Dara told her, hurrying upstairs

Angel ate in her room, which left Dara and Mrs Flood in the kitchen, concentrating on the vegetable stir-fry Dara had made, the table wedged between them like a referee.

'What's that?' Mrs Flood asked, poking at something on her plate with a fork.

'It's a water chestnut,' Dara explained.

'It doesn't really taste of anything,' Mrs Flood said in an injured tone. She poked through the mound of vegetables on her plate like it was rubble in a skip.

'There's a piece of broccoli there, look,' Dara said, pointing. 'And some carrot sticks. You like carrots.'

She wondered when the best time was to speak to her mother. Perhaps after she'd eaten her dinner – which she eventually managed, although she left all the water chestnuts on the edge of her plate like some kind of dirty protest. Or perhaps after the glass of wine she'd drunk had taken the sharp edge of the day off her. Perhaps then Dara could broach the subject. She waited.

'Do you have to read like that?' Mrs Flood asked later, nodding towards Dara's finger moving along a line of text on the page of her book. Dara moved her hand away from the page.

Mrs Flood returned her attention to the television. In spite of all the channels they had now, she had gone through them and was back where she started. She sighed, long and loud.

'There's never anything on,' she said finally, setting the remote on the arm of the chair.

Dara put her book down. She couldn't concentrate on it anyway, without her finger sliding under the words like a ruler. She reached for the remote. 'I'll turn it off. Maybe we could talk.'

Mrs Flood looked surprised at the suggestion. 'About what?' she asked.

'Well, the thing is . . .' Dara hesitated.

'What?' Mrs Flood's tone was impatient, but there was a flicker of something in her eyes that might have been wariness.

Dara backed up. 'I was just wondering if you could cut my hair? Just a trim.'

'I suppose you want me to wash it for you as well?' her mother said, using both hands to push herself off the couch and shaking her head as she went to retrieve her hair bag.

'Eh, yes please,' Dara called after her. She followed her mother to the kitchen and settled herself in a chair by the sink. There was something familiar – soothing almost – in watching her mother attach the rubber pipes to the taps, in listening to the water splash against her mother's hands as she adjusted the taps and waited for the water to heat. In leaning her head back, allowing the weight of it to settle in the cradle of her mother's palm, feeling the warmth of the water against her scalp and the sweep of her mother's fingers through her hair, kneading her head like dough. Deft. But gentle. Thorough. But careful. This was the place where Dara and her mother could communicate, even though neither of them spoke. There was no need. The snip-snip-snip of the scissors slicing through her hair was like a conversation between them. Quiet and clear. The soft glance of her mother's breath against Dara's face as she stood in front of her, sliding strands of Dara's hair through her fingers, holding it, cutting it, inspecting it, her tongue trapped between her teeth until she took a step back, nodded and moved towards her again. Her fingers sometimes brushed against Dara's face as she worked on her fringe. Warm and soft. They smelled of shampoo and Lily of the Valley. But something else too. Some sweet, fruity smell that Dara could not name but would always associate with her mother.

'There,' Mrs Flood said finally, stepping away to inspect her handiwork. She leaned towards Dara again and slid her hair behind her ears, then stepped away. She nodded. 'You'll do,' she said, as she always did.

'Thanks,' Dara said, standing up and looking at herself in the mirror. Nobody but her and Mrs Flood could ever tell she'd had a haircut.

Mrs Flood stood behind her, looking at her reflection in the mirror. 'You're so like your father,' she said, and Dara looked at her cautiously. The expression on her mother's face was distant, but there was a softness to it. 'He had that same silky black hair. The very same.'

'Did you cut his hair too?' Dara felt able to ask. Mrs Flood's comments did not seem to be tainted with any of the usual bitterness or vitriol.

Her mother nodded, and there was a trace of a smile around her eyes. 'Every Friday night,' she said, 'whether he needed it or not. He loved getting his hair cut. It was the only time he ever really relaxed.' She smiled then, at some memory only she could see, and for a moment it was like he was here, standing between the two of them. Dara felt awkward, like she was intruding on something she did not understand. But still, as moments went, it was about as good as it was going to get. She took her chance.

'Mam . . . ?' she began, taking a seat at the kitchen table.

'Yes?' Her mother's voice seemed to come from far away, from whatever memory she had wrapped around herself. Dara hesitated before she went on.

'You know Stanley Flinter?'

'That private detective?' her mother said, sharper now.

'Yes, Stanley. Well, he's . . . he found out something. Something about Mr Flood, I mean.'

Mrs Flood had her back to Dara. She stood at the draining board, sorting out her hair bag. But she was listening. Dara could tell. It was in the high ridge of her shoulders.

'Well, the thing is . . .' Dara went on, 'it seems that . . . before he . . . left, Mr Flood owed money. A lot of money. To a loan shark in Dublin,' she said, careful to keep her tone somewhere between neutral and informative.

Still Mrs Flood said nothing, but Dara could see her body stiffen. She fastened the straps on her hair bag and placed it on a chair. Only then did she look at Dara. Her expression was one of tired resignation. She sat down.

Realisation hit Dara like a slap. 'You already knew,' she said.

Mrs Flood laughed, a dry bark of a laugh that had no humour in it. 'I had an idea. Wasn't I married to the man, God help me?'

'Why didn't you tell me?' Dara asked. Her neutral tone slipped away. She felt hot. Felt the label of her T-shirt rasp against her skin. She pulled the material away from her neck.

'Why should I have told you? Told anyone? It was nobody's business but mine. Mine and your father's.' Her tone was defiant, and for a moment there was silence in the kitchen, punctuated only by Dara's heart hammering in her chest. Mrs Flood raised her eyes once again to Dara's face. 'How does this Stanley Flinter know that anyway?' she asked, her eyes flashing with suspicion.

'He's a private detective. He found out. He knew that Mr Flood was a gambler, so he—'

'Who told him that?'

'Slither Smith,' Dara said. 'When we were in Bailieborough.'

'Oh, of course, that reliable old miser,' Mrs Flood said. Bitterness and vitriol returned to her voice as if they'd never been away. The conversation was like double maths before Mr Horan came. Algebra. The worst kind. Dara wished it would end.

'So it's all true?' she asked. 'What Slither said? About my father being a gambler. And what Stanley found out. About him owing a lot of money.'

'It was a long time ago, Dara. What difference does it make now?' Mrs Flood's voice rose and rose and colour flooded her neck and face.

Dara tried not to see it. 'No, I know that, but . . . it would have helped,' she said. 'If you'd told me and Stanley in the first place, then—'

'I don't *want* strangers knowing my business,' Mrs Flood snapped. Dara swallowed hard.

'*I'm* hardly a stranger,' she said. 'Am I?' she added when her mother said nothing. Mrs Flood looked away. The tension in the room tightened around Dara. 'And Stanley is not a stranger,' she went on. 'He's a private detective. He's working for me. For *us*. And he's discreet. He's not going to tell anyone. I know he wouldn't, he's . . . I trust him.' The statement took her by surprise. The truth of it.

'I trusted a man once,' Mrs Flood said, smiling like she'd said something amusing.

'Mam, I know, but . . . they're not all like that,' said Dara.

'I suppose you're going to tell me that Stanley Flinter is not like that?'

'No, he's not.' Dara put her hands into the pockets of her tracksuit so her mother could not see them. Could not see the fists she had made of them. The conversation was as sour as a bottle of milk left in a car on a hot day. Dara could nearly taste it. Omitting the truth was the same as telling lies. Her mother had lied to her. A consistent line of lies that had not eroded with the passing years. Like why her father had left. Dara had thought it was because of her. Her mother had let her believe that.

But Mrs Flood did not notice Dara's hands. Her fists. Her anger. She was too busy being angry herself. With Stanley Flinter. 'What kind of a man snoops around other people's business? For money? It's such a *sneaky* way to make a living.'

'You should have told me,' Dara said. 'Instead of having me believe . . .'

'What?' Mrs Flood said. 'Believe what?'

'That he left because of me.'

'Jesus, Dara, I don't know where you got that notion.' Her mother's tone was dismissive.

'Because you told me. That's where I got that *notion* from.' Dara felt like she was surrounded on all sides by anger. Under siege. She was breathless with it.

'That was *one* time. One time I said that. Years ago. It's not fair to bring it up now. To throw it in my face like this. I was angry. God knows I was entitled to be.' Mrs Flood got up, as if to go then. Dara stood too, blocking her way.

'I WAS EIGHT YEARS OLD!' She shouted that bit. Dara, who never raised her voice, who avoided confrontation like Tintin avoided pulses. Dara, who had never mentioned again what her mother had said to her that day. Dara, who had thought about that day more than she should have, who had never forgotten. Any of it. Her mother arriving home. Dara standing in the middle of the kitchen floor, in a sea of broken eggs and spilled milk. She had wanted to make omelettes. Surprise her mother when she came home from work. But it was her mother who had surprised her. Coming home early, slamming the front door, marching down the hall, already angry. Dara moving carefully from the fridge to the counter, the six eggs cradled gently in a pouch she had made with the ends of her school jumper, holding on tight to the top of the bottle of milk with the tips of her fingers, pinched and white with the effort.

The kitchen door was thrown open and Dara jumped and everything fell. She still remembers the eggs, six of them, slowly falling. Almost floating. Her hands a blur, reaching for them. She knew there was nothing she could do about the milk. But the eggs. Right up until the end, she thought she could save some of them. Even one.

The slap. The only one she ever got. Dara still remembered the sound of it. She didn't remember if it hurt. It was the sound she remembered. That was something she never forgot. The harsh crack of it.

Later, Angel crept up the stairs with some bread and jam for her. She didn't bring a glass of milk. There was none left.

'Why is Mammy always so cross?' Dara didn't add 'with me'. She didn't need to.

'Because Daddy left,' Angel told her, in the matter-of-fact way she had.

'Where did he go?'

'Some place far away,' said Angel. 'India, probably.' Angel's class were doing a project on India.

'Why didn't he tooken me with him?'

'You weren't even born then,' Angel told her.

'Where was I?' Dara asked, in a whisper.

Angel sighed and pushed the plate under the bed where Dara hid with Cloth, a blanket she'd dragged behind her since she was a baby. 'Eat your bread and jam,' she told her sister.

Now Dara and Mrs Flood were standing facing each other in the kitchen, just as they'd done all those years ago when Dara was eight. But this time, there were no broken eggs at their feet, no spilled milk, no shards of glass. No one shouted and there was no harsh crack across Dara's face. In fact there was no sound at all. Even the music that came from Angel's room had stopped. There was something attentive about the silence that fell around them. Like the house was listening. Straining towards them. Waiting to see what might happen next.

'I suppose you've told Angel,' Mrs Flood said finally. Dara shook her head. Her mother moved towards the door. This time Dara did not stop her. She paused at the door, her fingers gripped around the handle. 'You know, Dara, that time, when you were eight . . .'

'I shouldn't have brought it up. It was a long time ago.'

Mrs Flood shook her head, her eyes casting about the room. 'Dara, I was . . . I wasn't well back then. I was working full-time, trying to raise you and your sister on my own, I felt tired all the time and I just . . . I lost my temper that day, I said things . . . things I shouldn't have said . . .'

Dara nodded. 'I know, I'm sorry.'

Mrs Flood paused at the door. 'You have nothing to be sorry for,' she said before she left the room, closing the door behind her.

It was nearly an apology.

34

The doorbell rang at eight o'clock the following evening. Dara was baking meringues in the kitchen. There was something uplifting about meringues, she found. The word *splendid* seemed to have been invented just for them.

'Can you get the door, Dara?' her mother called from the front room. 'My feet are in the bucket.' Since their conversation that had ended in something that was almost an apology, an unspoken kind of a truce had settled between them. The bucket was part of that. It was a foot spa that Dara had bought for her mother a couple of Christmases ago. Mrs Flood suffered with her feet, referring to this as collateral damage in the war against unkempt hair. The troops. That's what she called them. In spite of this, the foot spa had remained in its packaging under her bed ever since Mrs Flood had released it from its festive wrapping paper.

'It's . . . nice,' she'd told Dara, who waited for the delivery of the rest of the sentence. 'But, well, it's really just the same as the bucket I use, isn't it? It's a bucket with a plug really. Isn't it?'

This evening, Mrs Flood slid the unopened box out from under her bed. She wiped at the thick layer of dust covering it and opened the box. Now she sat in the front room, watching *Nationwide* and emitting little moans of pleasure as the bucket with a plug massaged her feet and warm bubbles tickled her splayed, grateful toes.

Dara turned the oven off and slid the meringues onto a wire

tray on the counter. She smiled at the snowy-white peaks of them. She couldn't help it.

Through the glass of the front door, she could make out the shape of a man. Probably one of the door-to-door bandits that Miss Pettigrew loved to torment. She wiped her hands on the apron Angel had bought her in Sicily last year and opened the door. It was Stanley Flinter.

'Stanley,' she said. 'I . . . I wasn't expecting you.' Now she could answer Tintin's question, and the answer was no. Stanley Flinter did *not* wear a trench coat. He wore a denim jacket. A black one. And black skinny jeans and a white shirt. She committed it all to memory. Tintin was a stickler for details.

'I know. I'm sorry. I should have called first. Is it a bad time?'

'No, no of course not. I was just . . . I'm in the kitchen. Come on through.' She opened the door wider and stepped aside, and Stanley walked past her, into the hall. The dark stubble on his face lent his skin a ghostly pallor, darkened his eyes. If her mother got a hold of him, she'd insist on a very close shave and a lengthy haircut.

'Something smells good,' said Stanley, moving down the hall towards the kitchen. 'Are you making meringues?'

'Yes,' Dara said, following his progress. Tintin was right about skinny jeans. Stanley seemed tall in the hall. Well, tall-*er*, at any rate.

'They're one of my favourite things to bake,' Stanley told her. 'There's something a bit . . . I don't know . . . uplifting about them.' He blushed a little after he'd said it. As if he was sorry he'd said it at all.

Dara nodded. 'No, I feel the same way,' she said. 'About meringues, I mean.' She pointed at a chair. 'Why don't you sit down. I was about to make a fruit salad to go with them. Would you like some?'

Stanley didn't sit down. Instead, he moved to the counter. 'I'll help,' he said, shrugging himself out of the jacket.

'No, there's no need, I'll . . .'

'I'll peel and you can chop, OK?' He draped his jacket over the back of a chair and rolled up the sleeves of his shirt. His arms – pale and long with a smattering of fine dark hair – came as a surprise to Dara. They looked like the kind of arms that could lift things. Heavy things. He found the peeler without having to ask and pulled the fruit bowl towards him, picking up an apple. He began to peel.

'OK,' Dara said. She reached for a bunch of grapes, rinsed them under the tap and began to slice them in half. For a while, neither of them spoke. Dara knew he had something to tell her. Something about the case. About Mr Flood. And she knew he would get to it. Eventually. But just for a moment, there was something comforting about her and Stanley standing there, close but not touching, not speaking, with the sounds of chopping and peeling all around, like the soundtrack of an old movie you never forget. Later, when she told Tintin about it, he would declare it *peculiar*, but there was nothing peculiar about it. In fact, it felt like the most natural thing in the world, Dara thought. There was something familiar about it, like they'd done it before. Many times.

Stanley whipped the cream. Dara took down the bowls. Stanley reached for cutlery. Dara made tea. Stanley spooned out the salad. Dara slid the meringues on to a plate and placed it on the table. Even though the kitchen was a narrow, cramped affair, they never once, throughout the entire process, touched each other. They didn't even brush against one another. There was a grace about Stanley Flinter, Dara realised, that was at odds with the shortness of his stature. His movements were fluid but defined. He could dance, she felt.

They sat down. Now the absence of conversation became a burden between them. Stanley must have felt it too, that burden. He cleared his throat. Dara held her breath and waited for him to say the thing he had come to say. Instead he said, 'These are the best meringues I have ever tasted. You've got the gooey/crispy ratio just right. How do you manage it?'

'The secret is the two Ts,' Dara told him, waiting until the piece of meringue in her mouth had melted on her tongue before speaking again. It was her favourite thing about meringues. The way they melted in her mouth. Stanley waited, as if he understood. As if it was his favourite thing too. 'Temperature and timing,' she said.

He smiled at her, which was when she noticed a dimple – just one – that dented the right side of his face. It was deep, as dimples went. She hadn't noticed it before.

The kitchen door opened. Dara looked up. It was Angel. Stanley stood up and moved towards her. 'You must be Angel,' he said, his dimple deepening. Dara was struck by how different Angel looked from the photograph she had shown Stanley that first day in his office. How fragile. Like she might break. She felt that Stanley thought that too. It was in the careful way he shook her hand. It was in the gentleness of the smile on his face.

'Angel, this is Stanley Flinter,' said Dara, standing up.

'You look different to how I'd pictured you,' Angel said to Stanley.

'Shorter, you mean,' Stanley said, grinning. 'I get that a lot.'

'No,' said Angel, and her face softened. She was nearly smiling. 'Just different.'

Dara felt a surge of gratitude towards Stanley Flinter. He had engaged Angel in conversation. He had made her smile. A hint of a smile, but still. It was something. It was so much better than the silence that had filled the space between them in recent times. Dara didn't want the moment to end. She pulled out a chair.

'Why don't you join us?' she said. Her voice was pantomime jovial. She lowered it. 'I've made meringues.'

Angel looked at the table, set for two. She shook her head. 'I just came down for some water,' she said, moving to the sink. Stanley got there first, letting the cold tap run before he filled a glass and handed it to her.

'Stanley has something to tell us,' Dara said, making a last stab. 'Something about Mr Flood.' She looked at Stanley and he nodded, slowly.

'Nothing good, I presume,' Angel said, and her smile hardened into something cynical.

Stanley's eyes darkened. 'Nothing concrete,' he conceded.

'I'll leave you to it,' said Angel, turning and moving towards the door. Dara watched her go. She was getting used to this view of Angel. The back of her. Leaving a room.

Dara looked at Stanley. She felt like some explanation was necessary. 'She's not usually like that,' she said. Stanley nodded. 'She's just . . . she's not herself lately.' Stanley didn't say any of the usual platitudes that people felt obliged to say. Like 'I'm sure she'll be feeling better soon,' or 'I'd say the hospital will ring again. Any day now.' Things that they said with the best of intentions, even though they never made you feel any better. If anything, they made you feel worse. You recognised the words because they were the same words that you had said to yourself. That you had tried to make yourself believe, with little success. Dara was grateful to Stanley for not saying any of those things. Instead he nodded and smiled and Dara felt, in his own quiet, contained way, that he understood somehow.

'So,' she said, sitting down at the table. 'You have something to tell me.'

The dimple vanished. Stanley reached for his fringe and tried to flatten it with his hand. The action had no discernible effect on the fringe, which sprang back as soon as he lowered his hand. Dara hoped her mother would not walk in on them. She wouldn't be able to resist the challenge of Stanley's cowlick.

Stanley slid his hand into the pocket of his jacket and pulled out a crumpled page, covered with his careful handwriting. He didn't look at Dara but kept his eyes instead on the page. He took a breath. 'Mr Flood ... your father ... was arrested in Paris in the spring of 2001. He was released on bail but before the case came up for hearing, it seems that he skipped bail and fled the jurisdiction.' He stopped reading, but did not look up.

It took Dara a while to gather her thoughts after this statement. There were a lot of questions she wanted to ask. The first question she asked was, where. Did Stanley know where Mr Flood had gone?

Stanley shook his head. 'I'm sorry, Dara,' he said, and he looked at her and she knew it was true. He *was* sorry. 'I don't know.'

'What was he arrested for?'

'Who was arrested?' Both Stanley and Dara jumped at the sound of Mrs Flood's voice. They turned at the same time and saw her, standing in the doorway, her feet covered in suds that soaked slowly into the carpet. Stanley got up and moved towards her, his arm outstretched.

'You must be Dara's mother,' he said. 'I'm ...'

'You're the private investigator,' Mrs Flood told him. She did not proffer her hand and Stanley lowered his.

'Yes, I'm Stanley Flinter, and I ...'

'Who was arrested?' Mrs Flood repeated.

Dara stood up. 'I'll get you a towel,' she told her mother.

'I don't want a towel. I want to know who was arrested,' said Mrs Flood, looking not at Dara but straight at Stanley Flinter.

Stanley's eyes flicked towards Dara and she nodded, a small nod, but enough for Stanley to understand. He reached for the crumpled page in front of him.

'Eugene Flood,' he said. His voice was low but the words were clear. There could be no mistaking them. 'Eugene Flood was arrested in Paris in the spring of 2001. There was a rumour doing the rounds that he had gone to France after he . . . after he left Ireland. One of my brothers has a contact in the French police and—'

'What was he arrested for?' Mrs Flood's voice cut through Stanley's explanations, sharp as a knife.

'Well, the thing was . . .' Stanley began, shifting a little in his chair.

'What was he arrested for?' Mrs Flood said again. She sat down with her legs and arms crossed, unmoving, apart from one foot that jiggled and twitched as if it were separate from her. As if it belonged to someone else.

Stanley put the page down on the table. He looked at Mrs Flood like she was someone he knew. Someone he cared about. He leaned towards her and for one awful moment Dara thought he was going to touch her. But he didn't. He cleared his throat. 'Armed robbery,' he said.

Mrs Flood's reaction was not what Dara had expected. She shook her head. 'No,' she said. 'Eugene was many things, but he was not a violent man. Stupid, yes, selfish, definitely, but violent? No. He'd put flies out of the house rather than squash them against the window with a rolled-up newspaper like I do. There's no way he—'

Stanley, who had been trying to interrupt her since she began, finally succeeded. He did it by shouting. 'It was a toy gun!' he roared, loud enough to stop Mrs Flood's defensive tirade. She stared at him.

'What do you mean?' she said.

'He held up a tabac. With a toy gun, apparently. But the woman behind the counter, turned out she had a heart condition, and when she saw the gun, she collapsed. Eugene revived her. He gave her CPR. That's how he got caught. The woman managed to press the panic button before she collapsed. The police arrived just as she was coming round.'

Throughout these revelations, Dara Flood stood at the kitchen table, one hand at her mouth so she could worry at her nails. She felt a sense of gratitude. To Stanley. That it had been him – not her – who had told her mother. She wouldn't know where to begin a story like that.

'A toy gun,' Mrs Flood said finally. The words sounded deflated. Withered. Like a balloon a week after a child's birthday party.

Dara sat down. She looked at Stanley, who concentrated on the page in front of him. She turned to Mrs Flood, but her mother's face was impassive. Unreadable. Dara felt her face would be like that too. If she had married a man like that. A man who had left with no forwarding address. A thief who took things that didn't belong to him. A fool with a gun that wasn't real. She imagined him, kneeling on the floor of the tabac, pressing both hands against the woman's chest, trying to jumpstart her heart as the sound of the sirens gathered and swelled.

'Did she die?' Dara said, looking down the table at Stanley.

'Who?'

'The woman. In the tabac. Did she die?'

'No,' he said, shaking his head. 'In fact, she wanted to drop the charges, but it was too late. Mr Flood had already skipped bail by then.'

'You said somebody bailed him out?' Mrs Flood looked at Stanley too. There was no curiosity in her look, more a wary resignation.

Stanley nodded slowly. 'Yes,' he said. 'A woman called Isabelle Dupoint. I have an address for her but I haven't been able to reach her by phone. I'm working on it.'

'Isabelle Dupoint,' Mrs Flood said, as if the name itself was something she had eaten. Something that did not agree with her. 'Who is she?'

Stanley coughed in the way that people do when they do not need to cough.

'According to the paperwork at the police station . . .' he began. He looked at Dara before he continued, and again she nodded at him. They had come this far, hadn't they?

'Isabelle Dupoint was his wife.'

35

Mrs Flood arrived home from work the next day with a roll of black plastic bags. She made herself a strong mug of coffee, snapped on a pair of rubber gloves, filled a bucket with hot soapy water and walked up the stairs with a rigid sort of resolve.

'What are you doing?' asked Dara, following her. There was something about her mother's dark determination that made her nervous.

'Something I should have done a long time ago,' said Mrs Flood, marching into her bedroom and opening the door of Mr Flood's wardrobe. She ripped a bag off the roll and shook it until it blew up, like a black balloon. With no recourse to ceremony, she began pulling at Mr Flood's clothes and throwing them into the bag. She dumped them, rather than threw them. Like they were rubbish and not clothes once worn by a man who used to stand in front of the house and rub the dust of the day off his trousers and say, 'It's well you're looking, Mrs Flood.' She rolled each item of clothing into a ball before she dumped it, her hands a blur of activity. She climbed onto a stool and, with one sweep of her arm, relegated the clothes on the shelf at the top of the wardrobe to a heap on the ground, before stuffing them into the black plastic bag. She didn't stop until they were all in, and even when she'd finished, the black bag wasn't full. Mrs Flood – her breath coming fast now – turned her attention to the bedside locker. Nothing there, but the tarnished cufflinks and the dust of years that she had allowed to collect in a way that reminded Dara of the unfortunate Miss Havisham in her withering wedding dress, her wedding bouquet on the table, green with mould and loss.

Mrs Flood looked at Dara. 'Do you want these?' she asked, dangling the cufflinks over the open mouth of the black bag. Dara shook her head. Mrs Flood dropped them and they landed inside the bag, making neither impression nor sound. The next stop was the bathroom. Mr Flood's comb with the one hair, snagged against a tooth, black as night, went into the bag. Followed by a bottle of aftershave so old, the lettering had worn away on the plastic of the bottle, peeling now. Dara had never known what it was called, but she remembered the smell of it. A spicy smell. A toothbrush, a spool of floss – he *did* have good gums, Mrs Flood once conceded – a rusting razor, a book of blades – unopened, tweezers, a tub of Brylcreem, a shower cap, a pair of ancient nylons he used to stretch over his head after he'd washed his hair to keep it flat, if Mrs Flood was to be believed, and a facecloth, hardened now.

When everything was in the bag, Mrs Flood lowered herself onto the lid of the toilet and struggled to get her breath back. She looked at Dara.

'You could make yourself useful and go and do the shoes.'

'All of them?'

'No, let's keep one pair to remember him by, shall we?' While the words were sharp, Mrs Flood's voice was quieter than usual, as if the wind had dropped from her sails.

Dara prised the black plastic bag from her mother's fingers that strained white in her grip. Mrs Flood took a breath and stood up again, reaching for the sponge floating on the top of the bucket of hot soapy water. She began to scrub at the rings in the cabinet, left by the standing stones of Mr Flood's things that were no longer there. Dara walked into her mother's bedroom, dragging the bag behind her. You could have fitted a lot more in the bag, but apart from the shoes, there was nothing left to throw away.

Angel didn't comment on the clear-out. In fact, she completely ignored it, as if it were something commonplace. Something that had happened before. Instead, she commented on something else when Dara came across her later, making toast in the kitchen.

'He's nice, isn't he?' Again that smile on her face. That hint of a smile.

'Who?' The smile – the hint of a smile – had distracted Dara.

'Stanley Flinter,' said Angel.

'He's been really helpful,' Dara agreed, handing Angel the jam from the fridge.

'Helpful?' Angel had not asked Dara what Stanley had told her last night. Dara felt this was her way of asking.

'He found someone in Paris who knew Mr Flood. Perhaps knows him still.'

Angel turned back to her toast. She shook her head. 'You're never going to find him. It'll be easier in the long run if you just accept that. I have.'

'We might find him,' Dara persisted. Again, she was struck by their role reversal. It seemed that *she* was the optimist now.

Take Mrs Flood's clear-out, for instance. She couldn't help feeling that, while it was years overdue, it was something good. Something positive. A line was being drawn. A full stop at the end of a sentence. It was time. High time.

Hot on the heels of this thought was a thought that would have been more at home in Angel's head. Before the found-and-lost kidney affair, at any rate. It was a thought tinged with hope. And perhaps a little bit of faith. That the finding of a woman called Isabelle Dupoint, in Paris, was a sign. A clue. As to her father's whereabouts. The possibility it afforded. Of finding him. Speaking with him. Perhaps even getting him to agree to help Angel. People could change. Couldn't they?

Wasn't it just possible that he might have changed after all these years?

Her phone beeped, interrupting her thoughts with their new-found optimism. It was a text. From Ian.

'*Thinking about your breasts in the new black lace bra I bought you today. Can't wait to see you at the w/end. x x x.*'

Dara couldn't think of a suitable reply, so she saved it in her pending folder until something occurred to her.

Mrs Flood marched into the kitchen, snapped off her rubber gloves and set the bucket of water, now dirty, on the ground. It seemed she had not noticed Dara. She gripped the edge of the countertop as if she might fall if she did not.

'Mam?'

Mrs Flood did not respond.

Dara approached her. She stood behind her. She thought about reaching for her mother, with both hands. Leaning into her. Letting her know she was there. That she understood.

But she did none of that.

'Mam?' she said again.

Mrs Flood's head shot up and she reached for the bucket and began pouring it down the sink, filling the kitchen with noise. Dara bit her lip and waited.

'I don't know why I'm surprised,' said Mrs Flood after a while. When the bucket was empty, she set it on the ground but still did not turn around, looking instead out the kitchen window, even though there was nothing to see in the dark.

'*Are* you surprised?'

Mrs Flood shook her head. 'That he took up with some woman in France? No.'

'Well, we don't know there was anything going on between Mr Flood and this woman. Isabelle Dupoint.'

'Apart from the fact that they were married, perhaps?'

'We don't know that for a fact. I mean, all we know is that

Isabelle Dupoint said she was his wife. She hadn't taken his name.'

'I think it's a bit late to be giving him the benefit of the doubt, don't you?' said Mrs Flood, in a strained voice.

Dara nodded. She supposed it was true.

'He hasn't changed. Not one bit. He was selfish and thoughtless when I married him, and . . .'

'Didn't you mind?' Almost immediately, Dara regretted the question. It was a stupid question. One that needed no answer. Mrs Flood answered anyway.

'Of course I did. But I thought, once we got married, had a couple of kids, he'd change. I was young back then. Naïve, I suppose. I loved him. That's how stupid I was. I thought he'd love me enough to stay.'

In twenty-seven years, this was the most revealing thing Mrs Flood had ever said about Dara's father. Her voice was high and taut, like a tightrope stretched between buildings.

For Dara, the delivery of this one, miserable sentence justified her entire philosophy of relationships. Here, along the shoddy, crooked line of this sentence, were the three things she had spent much of her life trying to avoid. *Disappointment. Uncertainty.* And, of course, eventual, inevitable *decline*.

36

'I have a Plan,' Miss Pettigrew told her with a flourish of both hands when Dara went next door to get Edward the next day. She ushered her into the front room and pressed a large glass of sweet sherry into her hand.

'I thought cocktail hour began at five?' Dara asked in a vain attempt to avoid the sherry.

'No matter,' Miss Pettigrew told her with a wink and a smile. 'Some things can't wait.'

'So, what's your Plan?'

'Oh yes, the Plan.' Miss Pettigrew sat on the piano stool and rubbed her long, slim hands against each other. She had a gleam in her eye, the likes of which Dara had not seen since the old lady had spied the ad in the *Northside People* for the poodle pups more than a decade ago. 'I've booked two first-class tickets to Paris. Next week. Return, of course.' She set this nugget of information in front of Dara like a banquet and stood back to watch her tucking in. For a moment, Dara said nothing. The news sank into her mind like a wellington boot in a swamp. She struggled against it.

'Wait,' she said. 'Wait a moment. What do you mean? Paris? Two tickets? Who's going to Paris? Why?'

Miss Pettigrew shook her head slowly and settled herself in the soft lap of the pouffe in front of Dara's chair. She took Dara's hands in hers and spoke slowly. 'Your mother told me what young Stanley Flinter found out. This morning. When she came in to do my nails.' She released Dara's hands and held out her nails for inspection. A French manicure. That's what her mother had done. Dara felt it was ironic, in the circumstances. Mrs Flood mustn't have told Miss Pettigrew that the manicure was French. Dara nodded and declared the nails *stylish*. Miss Pettigrew, pleased with the description, took a moment to admire them herself before she returned to the Plan.

'You're going to Paris. To find Mr Flood. Next week.'

There were a thousand questions clamouring for priority in Dara's head. 'But ... but why are you coming with me? You haven't been out of the house in years.' Miss Pettigrew's reclusiveness was something that neither of them ever mentioned. She took its brief appearance in their conversation quite well, considering. In fact, she just ignored it.

'My dear girl,' she said, '*I'm* not going. I can't. Edward would pine dreadfully. No. I've booked the tickets for you and your young man.' Miss Pettigrew winked when she said this and assumed a grin that might have been called 'cheeky', were it on the face of a younger woman.

'What do you mean? My young man?' As far as Dara knew, Miss Pettigrew knew nothing about Ian Harte. And while he was a pretty well-preserved man for his age, no one – not even someone as old as Miss Pettigrew – could mistake him for anyone's young man.

'Stanley Flinter, of course,' Miss Pettigrew said, peering at Dara's face in a worried kind of way.

The image of herself and Stanley Flinter in Paris was an odd one, like chocolate sauce poured over ratatouille.

'Isn't Stanley Flinter divine?' Miss Pettigrew said then. The abrupt change of subject threw Dara.

'What do you mean?'

'Oh, Dara Flood, you are a hopeless case.'

'Well, he has been helpful all right,' Dara said. 'He seems like a good person.'

'Good?' Miss Pettigrew was unimpressed at the description.

'How did you meet him?' asked Dara, confused now.

'We're friends on Facebook now.' Miss Pettigrew winked at her. 'I looked him up, told him how I knew him and what great pals you and I are, and now we poke each other and send each other tequila slammers on a Friday afternoon.' She looked pleased at this admission, and Dara had to admire the old lady. She might not have been out of her house in years, but she was still out there. Out in the world. Making friends and 'poking' people. Dara wondered what that involved. She'd heard of Facebook. Of course she had. But she'd left it alone, thinking it a little too intrusive for her liking.

'You were right about him,' Dara said.

'About him being divine?'

'No, about him being good at his job.'

'Of course he is. He found Spinach, didn't he?'

'Well, yes, there's that, of course,' Dara said. 'But I don't understand why you would want him to come to Paris with me.' Again, the thought jarred, the chocolate and the ratatouille.

'He's a private detective, isn't he? If there's any, I don't know, shadowing of the subject to be done, he'll know how to do it, won't he? All that hiding behind lamp posts carry-on. And looking at people's reflections in shop windows. All that malarkey.' She dismissed these skills with a flick of her wrist and stood up.

'Wait,' Dara said, panicked now. 'I can't just . . . go to Paris. I mean, it's such short notice, and . . .'

'Short notice would be today. I've booked the tickets for next week. It's buckets of notice.'

'But it must have cost you a fortune,' Dara said. 'First class?'

'It's the only way to travel, my dear,' said Miss Pettigrew, as if she travelled this way all the time. And perhaps she had. Long ago. 'Besides, I've pots of money and not much opportunity to spend it, do I?' She looked around at the four walls of the room as if realising, for the first time, the tight confines of her life.

'But, but . . . Stanley probably won't be able to come with me. He's . . . he's busy and . . .'

'Just ask him, my dear. I'm sure he'll be delighted to accompany a young lady such as yourself to the City of Romance.'

'But . . .'

'And I've booked two rooms in a very swanky hotel. At least, it used to be swanky anyway. Forty years ago. It's the Louis XIV.' Miss Pettigrew's smile dimmed and her face clouded over. She shook her head. 'Manus MacBride promised to take me there for our honeymoon. He said he would buy me a red dress and take pictures of me at the top of the Eiffel Tower. He said I looked beautiful in red. The Mona Lisa seemed homely compared to me. That's what he said.'

'Miss Pettigrew, I'm sorry, but . . .'

'You're right, Dara,' said Miss Pettigrew, her voice as firm as a green tomato. 'There is a but. One condition.'

Dara waited. She knew there had to be a catch.

'I'm going to buy you a dress for the trip and you have to promise me you'll wear it. I'm not having you calling to the door of a French floozy in one of your navy tracksuits. You'd be letting us down. All of us.'

'But . . .'

'Promise me.'

Something occurred to Dara. 'OK, I promise,' she said in a meek way that made Miss Pettigrew's face curl suspiciously.

'Aren't you worried about what kind of dress I'm going to buy?' she couldn't help asking.

'Well, the thing is, I mean, it's very kind of you and everything. But I don't think I can go after all. My passport is out of date.' In fact, Dara's passport had been out of date for five years.

'Don't worry,' Miss Pettigrew told her, touching the bridge of her nose with the tip of her finger. 'We can use the express service.'

'But that takes ten days.' Dara Flood might not have had a passport for five years, but she remembered how to get one.

'Don't fret, my dear girl.' Again the little touch of finger to nose, followed by a wink. 'I know someone.'

37

Mrs Harte – Irene – had been in Stanley Flinter's office for an hour. She'd arrived armed with a lifetime of photographs.

Stanley picked another one up. Mr and Mrs Harte on their honeymoon in the Maldives, fifteen years ago.

'He hasn't changed all that much since then,' Mrs Harte told him, gazing at the picture and running her thumb along the side of her husband's face. It was a tender gesture, and for a moment Stanley wondered what it would be like to be on the receiving end of that brand of love. 'I mean, yes, his hair may not be quite as thick, and there may be a bit more flesh around his bones, and perhaps his stomach is not quite as washboard as it once was, but *apart* from that, he looks exactly the same.' She looked at Stanley, and he didn't comment on the sharp glint of tears in the corners of her eyes. 'He's a handsome man, wouldn't you say?' It didn't seem to be a rhetorical question, and Mrs Harte waited for Stanley to answer.

'Eh, yes, he's very . . . nice.'

'Nice?'

'I mean, you know, well-preserved.'

'He's not ancient, you know. He's not even fifty yet. Although his birthday isn't too far away. I thought I might get him something red. A sports car, maybe. He looks great in red.'

Stanley studied a more recent photograph of Ian Harte. Immaculate pink fingernails at the end of short, fleshy fingers wrapped around the handle of a golf club. A grim set to a loose chin. A sprinkling of silver through thinning hair. The beginnings of a potbelly straining against a tight-fitting top that would have been more at home on a younger man. Vain. That's what came to mind as Stanley looked at the photograph. And tall, of course.

'Doesn't he have lovely long legs?' Mrs Harte persisted. All Stanley could do was nod.

Mrs Harte looked exactly as Stanley had pictured her. An attractive woman somewhere in the sunset of her forties. Her eyes held the surprised look of someone not unfamiliar with the knife of the local plastic surgeon. Well-cut, tasteful clothes. A woman who knew her way around a beauty salon. A woman who could dance, but hadn't done so in years.

'So,' Stanley said, setting down a photo album that featured a cruise in the Caribbean last autumn ('The last time he called me *dove*,' Mrs Harte had whimpered. 'That's his pet name for me. Or at least it used to be'). 'You're still convinced that your husband is, eh . . .'

'Being unfaithful?' Mrs Harte offered, taking a linen hanky out of a leopardskin handbag. Stanley hoped it was fake, but feared otherwise. 'Yes,' she said with an emphatic tone. 'No doubt about it. Take the other week, for example.'

'What happened?' Stanley hoped it was something more concrete than blocked pores after a supposed visit to Manly Makeovers. Turned out it was.

'He was in Zurich. On business. At least that's what he said.' She spat the words out, as if they had gone off. 'BUT,' she went on, and Stanley shifted in his seat, waiting for the punchline, 'he told me his flight got in at 11 p.m., which justified his arrival into the house shortly before midnight. BUT . . .' another dramatic pause, 'his flight didn't get in at eleven o'clock. It got in at seven. I found a copy of his itinerary in the inside pocket of his briefcase that he thinks I don't know about.'

Mrs Harte flung herself against the back of the armchair that Stanley's mother had bought him, 'as an office-warming gift', she'd said, hugging him. When Mrs Harte's linen hanky was too saturated to be of any further use to her, Stanley handed her a tissue from the box he kept on his desk.

'And . . . where do you think he might have been? From seven till midnight?'

'With *her*, of course.' Mrs Harte blew her nose noisily.

Stanley waited until she had finished before asking, 'And do you know who this woman is?'

'Someone younger than me!' she cried. 'And prettier. And thinner. No defects. That's one of Ian's pet hates. Defective products. And that's just what I am now. A defective product. I might as well be . . . ,' she flailed around for an appropriate comparison, 'a . . . a saw with no teeth. *That's* pretty defective, wouldn't you say?'

Stanley could do nothing but nod. A saw with no teeth *was* fairly useless, he couldn't deny it.

'So, Mrs Harte . . . Irene. What would you like me to do?'

Mrs Harte blew her nose one last time, wiped her eyes and sat up as straight as a die in the chair, all business.

'Most Saturday nights for the past three months he's been going out. To play *poker with his golf buddies*.' She put the *poker with his golf buddies* bit in inverted commas with her fingers. 'I mean, the man doesn't even know how many cards are in a deck.'

She leaned towards him. 'I want you to follow him, Stanley. Next Saturday night. Shadow him. Isn't that what you call it?'

'Oh, I can't. Not next Saturday.'

'But you have to. I simply can't wait another week not knowing. I would rather let Jacinta Macintosh take first place in the Gorgeous Gardens Awards.' When Stanley looked confused, she added, 'She's my next-door neighbour. *Very* competitive. Suffice to say, she's not a very good loser and her herbaceous border has seen better days.'

'Well, I . . .' Stanley began.

'I don't care how much it costs. Charge me anything you like. *Over*charge me, I won't mind.'

'It's not that, it's just I have to go to a party. An engagement party.'

'My goodness, you're a smooth operator, aren't you?' The last time I spoke to you, your heart was clean torn in two.'

'No, no, it's not *my* engagement party, it's . . .'

'Oh my goodness, it's *theirs,* isn't it? That cad of a brother of yours. And that floozy.'

'Well . . .'

'You poor, poor lamb.' Mrs Harte reached across the desk and patted Stanley's shoulder. 'How are you coping?'

'Eh, fine . . .'

'Stoic, aren't you? That's good. That'll stand you in good stead.'

'Yes, well, the thing is . . .'

'Don't worry. Ian always leaves the house at around half six on a Saturday evening. You should be able to,' she lowered her voice here, '*shadow* him and still arrive at the party on time.'

Stanley said nothing. Mrs Harte swept on. 'I understand, Stanley.' And she looked at him as if she did. 'You want to be at the party. Looking great, but maybe not *too* great. You don't want her to think you've gone to trouble. You don't want that.' Stanley couldn't help nodding. He had to stop himself asking Mrs Harte what she thought he should wear. She looked like a good source of that type of information.

'What time does the party start?' she asked.

'Eight o'clock,' Stanley told her.

'You'll be finished with Ian by then. And so will I, most

likely.' Her head dropped, as if it the weight of it were suddenly too heavy for the narrowness of her neck.

'You don't know that,' he told her, all the while thinking about her face crumpling, when he confirmed to her what she thought she knew. He wasn't looking forward to it.

She shook her head and tried to smile.

'Are you sure about this?' he asked. 'Have you really thought about it?'

'I've thought of nothing else,' Mrs Harte assured him, and Stanley saw the truth of it in the lines of worry etched across her forehead, that he knew she must hate.

The office smelled of Mrs Harte's strong perfume for a long time after she left. Stanley had just picked up a photograph of Mr and Mrs Harte wrapped around each other at the top of the Eiffel Tower – 'He called me *cherie* for months after that trip,' Mrs Harte had whispered – when the phone rang. He smiled when he saw Dara's name on the screen. 'Dara, how are you?'

'Hello, Stanley, it's Dara. Dara Flood.'

'Eh, right, it's lovely to hear from you.' He pictured her small white face and her careful navy eyes. It was true. It *was* lovely to hear from her. 'How are you?' he asked. Her voice sounded more worried than usual and Stanley dropped the photographs and picked up a pen.

'Well, the thing is . . .'

'Go on,' said Stanley during the pause that followed.

'It's just . . . it's hard to know where to begin really . . . but I was wondering . . . if you're not too busy, that is . . .'

'Yes?'

'Well, it's a long story, but I suppose the bottom line is . . . what I mean is . . . it's a question really . . . that's all it is . . .'

'What's the question?' Stanley asked, intrigued now. All kinds of possible questions occurred to him, none of which turned out to be the one that Dara eventually managed to ask him. 'Will you come to Paris with me? Next Thursday?'

Stanley dropped the pen.

He opened his mouth to say something, although he couldn't be sure what that something was, and ended up saying the first thing that came into his head, which was 'Why?'

Later, when he told Sissy how he'd responded to Dara's request, she ran to her bedroom, picked up two pillows, charged back down the stairs and used them to clip him over the head. She used both pillows. Several times. 'You. Total. Useless. Looking. Eejit.' She panted each word after each blow. 'A lovely woman asks you to go to Paris and all you can say is *why?*'

'I wasn't expecting her to ask me that. She took me by surprise, that's all,' Stanley said, warding off the pillow blows – still coming – with both hands.

'That's the best way to be taken. Don't you know anything?' Sissy – as strong as a gale-force wind – continued to administer the blows with both pillows. It wasn't sore as such, just difficult to conduct a conversation.

Dara Flood took his enquiry much better than Sissy. In fact, she was unsurprised by it, and Stanley felt that if *he* had been the one to invite *her* to Paris next Thursday, Dara would have responded in exactly the same way.

Instead of verbally beating him about the head with a pair of pillows, Dara Flood told him about Miss Pettigrew's premature booking of tickets and a hotel. 'Two rooms,' she hurried to add.

When Sissy ran out of steam and lowered herself onto a chair, tucking the pillows behind her head, Stanley told her – standing behind the couch for safety – that he had then suggested to Dara that it might be best to make contact with Isabelle Dupoint. By phone or letter. At least initially. He could ask his contact in Paris to perhaps call in to her. See what she had to say. See if Mr Flood was there. Or if she knew where he was. Save Miss Pettigrew the expense of a trip for two to Paris.

'Daft berk,' was Sissy's response.

Dara's reaction was not quite as vehement.

'The thing is, Stanley,' she said in her halting voice, 'I know what you're saying makes perfect sense and in normal circumstances, yes, I would agree, but . . .'

'You want to surprise her,' Stanley said.

'Well, yes,' said Dara. 'I mean, it's not like Eugene Flood is a man who wants to be found. Do you agree?'

Stanley nodded his head before he remembered that Dara couldn't see him. 'Yes,' he said. 'I agree.' There was no point beating around the bush about it. Dara – and Angel – didn't have time for that.

'I just think that if he *is* there . . . in Paris, I mean . . . and if he *is* married to this lady . . . Isabelle Dupoint . . . well . . .'

'You don't want them to know you're coming,' Stanley finished for her.

'We . . . ell, I suppose what I'm trying to say is . . .' Stanley knew what Dara was trying to say, but he waited anyway, even though it was a little excruciating, like watching a baby learning to walk. 'I just don't want him to get wind of us before I have a chance to speak with him. I'm afraid if he does, he'll just make another run for it.'

Stanley felt glad when Dara got the words out. Mr Flood wasn't going to win a Father of the Year award any time soon, but it was good that Dara accepted this about him. That she knew what she was dealing with. It made his job a lot easier.

'So . . . what do you think? I know it's a lot to ask. I mean, I'll pay you for your time. Obviously. Which reminds me, you still haven't sent me your bill.'

'Well, I didn't think it was necessary really. I mean, you cured Clouseau.'

'No, I did nothing. Hardly anything. I can't let you do any more work if you're not going to charge me. It wouldn't be right.' Stanley imagined Dara's face, set with worry.

'All right,' he said. 'I'll send you a bill. But it'll take Clouseau's rehabilitation into account. That's what we agreed, remember?'

The worry in Dara's voice slipped, but only a little. 'Even so, going to Paris, it's a big commitment,' she said.

Stanley opened the drawer of his desk where the invitation – the pink one with the melted red wax – lay. 'The thing is . . .'

'Don't worry, Stanley. I totally understand if you can't come.'

'We . . . ell, it's just that there's this thing on Saturday night . . .'

'A thing?'

'A party, I mean. An engagement party, actually.'

'Oh. I didn't realise you'd got engaged. Congratulations.'

For a moment, he didn't correct her. Instead, he allowed her good wishes to seep into the soil of his brain, like water after a long, dry spell.

'Stanley?'

'No, no, it's not me.' Stanley realised that this may have come out a little louder than he'd intended. He struggled for a more even tone. 'I mean, no, it's not *my* engagement party. It's my brother. Cormac. And Cora. His girlfriend. I mean, fiancée. That's what I should call her, isn't it? His fiancée, right?'

'Eh, yes, I suppose so. If your brother's engaged to her.'

'He is. Engaged, I mean. To her.'

Stanley picked up the book Sissy had bought him for his last birthday (*The Pocket Detective*) and beat himself about the head with it, not realising that Sissy would later pick up where he left off, albeit with two pillows instead of a book. He held the phone away from him when he did it, so that Dara Flood would not hear him.

'Good,' Sissy said when he told her about it later. 'I hope it hurt.'

'It did,' Stanley told her, and she nodded, delighted.

He brought the receiver back to his ear. Dara was speaking.

'Anyway,' she went on, 'we'll be back from Paris on Friday evening, so you'll have plenty of time to get ready for your engagement party. Or I could even try to book an earlier flight home. Friday morning or even Thursday night. I don't know why Miss Pettigrew has arranged for us to stay. I can't see the need, really.'

'No, no, Friday afternoon is fine. It's just . . . it's important that I'm there, you know? At the party, I mean.' He didn't say that his absence – and the absence of the two Newbridge silver candlestick holders he'd eventually settled on as a gift – might be viewed as an ominous development by members of his family.

'Of course, I understand,' said Dara, even though he knew that she didn't understand. How could she?

'OK then.'

'OK what?'

'I'll come with you,' he said. 'To Paris. I mean, I don't know how much help I'm going to be. My French is pretty elementary.'

'I actually speak a bit,' Dara told him. In fact, Dara had displayed what her teachers called a *surprising* aptitude for language in school. Surprising, they said, because they didn't expect a lot from Dara Flood. She wasn't great at the written form of the language. But she had an ear for it. That's what her French teacher told her, once she got over the surprise of it all.

'Thank you,' Dara said. The words were nearly a whisper, and in them, Stanley heard her relief. He shouldn't have kept her waiting with his ridiculous, pointless beating around the thorny bush of the bloody engagement party.

'Have you been to Paris before?' he asked.

'No. Have you?'

'Once.' Why did all roads lead back to Cora? The anniversary of their first year together. Not that they'd been together all that time, of course, what with Cora's beauty course in London that year. But still. They'd kept in touch. They'd been exclusive. Well, he had at any rate. He couldn't say the same about Cora. Not any more.

They never got to the top of the Eiffel Tower. The lift didn't go all the way and he couldn't persuade Cora to tackle the stairs.

'My feet are killing me. We've been walking all day.' It wasn't even lunchtime.

'But we're nearly there. Don't you want to get a picture of us at the top?'

'Let's get a picture of us here. We're nearly at the top, aren't we? Isn't this far enough?'

'There is one other thing that you should know.' Dara's worried voice pushed through his thoughts, like a breeze that picks up and warns of rain.

'What's that?'

'Well, it's just that Miss Pettigrew, she can be a little eccentric, and . . .'

'I know. She asked me to become a fan of "Ronald Reagan Rocks" on Facebook.'

'Yeah, she's very fond of him. She calls him Ronnie. She has this theory about him faking his own death and being alive and well and living on a farm in Montana, for some reason. But the thing is, she's ordered me a dress, and . . .'

'A dress?'

'Well, yes, I know, it's ridiculous, I agree. But she's insisting I wear it in Paris. In fact, she's insisting on a photograph of me at the top of the Eiffel Tower in the dress. Just to prove to her that I've actually worn it.'

'I see,' said Stanley, even though he didn't.

'It's just . . . well, it's a long story and it doesn't make that much sense, but . . . well, she was supposed to go to Paris. To the Eiffel Tower. In a red dress. Years ago. But she never did, and . . .'

An image of Dara Flood in a dress floated into Stanley's head. A navy one. Baggy. Falling to just above the the rims of her mucky Doc Martens. He thought red might suit her, but the navy persisted. His English teacher – Miss Smithers – had been right after all. His imagination *was* pretty measly.

'I . . . I just thought you should know . . .' Dara's voice trailed off into an embarrassed silence.

Stanley cleared his throat. 'Don't worry, Dara. I will meet you and your dress at Dublin airport next Thursday. We could go to the Eiffel Tower first. Get it out of the way. I'll take a photograph of the pair of you at the top and e-mail it to Miss Pettigrew, and you could even change back into your ordinary clothes for the rest of the trip. How about that?'

Dara laughed. It was a low, sweet sound. Like how he imagined molasses might taste. 'You must think me pretty peculiar,' she said.

'Compared to some of my other clients, you're reassuringly normal,' Stanley told her.

'What do you think my chances are? Of finding Mr Flood in Paris?' Stanley could tell she was holding her breath, waiting for him to answer.

'Slim,' he told her, not wanting to promote hope. Hope was one of the main ingredients of disappointment. He knew that better than most. 'But this Isabelle Dupoint, I suppose she might be able to tell us something. It's a long shot, but . . .'

'I'll e-mail you the flight and hotel details, OK?'

'I'll see you next Thursday, then.'

'See you then.' They both hung up at the same time, and Stanley leaned back in his chair, forgetting that he was, in fact, sitting on a stool. He landed on his back on the floor, clipping his knee against the hard wood of the desk. Even though there was no one else in the room and the blinds on the window were not fully drawn but drawn *enough*, he jumped up and brushed himself down and said, 'Well, that was pretty stupid,' the way people do when there *is* someone else in the room and the blinds are *not* drawn enough. This behaviour further embarrassed him and now he blushed like a schoolboy, his face so hot that he had to remove his jacket and roll up the sleeves of his shirt. He lowered himself once again onto the seat of the stool and picked up a photograph of Ian Harte. But it was Dara Flood he saw instead, this time in a red dress. A soft red, the material gathered against the gentle curve of her hip in a way that surprised him. Not least because he had no idea if Dara had curvy hips, gentle or otherwise. He just imagined she might.

Instead of berating himself for the frankly unprofessional nature of these thoughts, Stanley found himself thinking about Miss Smithers. Maybe she'd been wrong. Maybe his imagination wasn't as bad as she'd led him to believe.

*   *   *

It must be Saturday. Jelly and ice cream for dessert. And Nora in the afternoon. Just for an hour. Sometimes not even that long, depending on her mood.

'Pull the curtains around the bed and get in here beside me,' I tell her when she arrives in the ward and doles out six bingo cards and six sets of counters.

'Behave yourself, you!' she roars at me with her Dublin accent as thick as a loaf of brown, despite the years in this city.

It seems like every second person I've ever met in Manchester is Irish in some way or another.

I push myself up into a sitting position in the bed. My elbows creak with the weight of me, even though Fidelma can lift me out of the bed and into the wheelchair without breaking a sweat.

'You show me yours and I'll show you mine.' I know she won't agree to this. Thank God. There was a time when I would have stood buck naked in the bedroom of any willing woman in the country without hesitation. Sure of myself. That's what I was. I miss that.

The funny thing is, I win. I win the bingo. Every bloody Saturday. After a lifetime of losing, I win. I always knew I'd win. I just never thought it would take this long.

When Nora leaves, the ward is quiet. It's always quiet when she leaves, like the quiet after a storm. We gather ourselves. Pat ourselves down. Wait for her to blow some life into us next week. If we're still here.

If I was a betting man – and let's face it, that's what I am – I'd say my odds are not great. Not even I would put a flutter on myself, and I've been known to back a few howlers in my time, God knows.

That's the worst thing about the waiting. You have time. To think, I mean. There's no point in regrets, but here, there's room for them. And time. Lots of time. And so they come, the regrets, like uninvited guests at a party.

But I suppose the question you have to ask to deflect the regrets is, would I have done anything differently? If I could go back? If I could change things? And the answer might be no. Would be no. I had a chance, once, to take the road less travelled. To change, perhaps. I had it there, in my hands. I could feel it. The warmth of it. The possibilities. But then things happened. They were my fault, the things that happened. And I left them behind. Those possibilities. It was for the best. I never had the knack. Of staying. Some people don't.

I look out the window.

The dull black of a telegraph wire cuts through the winter white of the sky. Although I think it might be spring now. I caught the rough smell of lilac through the window the other day. It reminded me of the little garden at the back of the pub. My mother cut swathes of it from the tree there each year. Every April. She sang, 'We'll gather lilacs in the spring again' in that sweet, tuneless way she had. I don't know the name of the song. She sang it every spring. I remember the scent in the vases around the house. A strong, sweet smell. The smell of spring.

38

Dara Flood and Ian Harte were not the kind of couple who phoned each other, which suited Dara Flood just fine, given her tendency to worry each time the phone rang. They texted instead.

Dara had put a shepherd's pie into the oven – with a touch a cayenne pepper sprinkled through the mash to give it a gentle kick – when she got the text from Ian Harte.

'*Trip to Lyon cut short. Meet you Thursday evening after work. In The Back Door. Need to see your sweet face, cherie. Ian xxxx*'

Dara set the phone carefully on the windowsill and began loading the dishwasher. Could she pretend she hadn't seen the text? No, Ian often complained about how carefully she monitored her mobile phone during their dates.

Perhaps she could just text back, with a brief '*Sorry, can't make it. Hope to see you Saturday instead?*'.

But no, she couldn't do that. It would be the first time she'd ever said no to him, and he would want details.

Dara made coffee and sat at the kitchen table, with both hands wrapped around the mug. The meaty smell of the pie in the oven was comforting, but not comforting enough to forget about the mobile phone, which sat like a sulk on the sill.

It wasn't that she had deliberately set out to keep the trip to Paris a secret from Ian Harte. Nothing like that. After all, there was no sign of her passport yet. There was every chance she wouldn't get it before Thursday. It certainly wouldn't be the first time Miss Pettigrew had overstated her influence with 'The Administration', as she called it.

And Angel could get the call from the hospital between now and the trip. Any day now. Couldn't she? There would be no need to go to Paris at all if that happened. And what was the point of telling Ian about something that might never happen?

Except now it seemed she would have to. And even though Ian Harte was a well-travelled man and never tired of telling her about the places he'd been ('Venice: *riddled* with pickpockets. Smelly too') and the things he'd seen ('The Leaning Tower of Pisa. Let's face it, it's a defective piece of architecture'), Dara felt that the news about her own possible trip to Paris would not be well received. Perhaps because of the short notice. She wasn't the kind of person to go haring off to European cities at the drop of a hat. Or, in recent years, at all. Or perhaps it was the subject of Stanley Flinter. Accompanying her. She was unsure how Ian Harte would feel about this liaison, professional though it was. He could be a little sensitive about younger men. 'What age do you think I look?' was one of his favourite questions. 'No, really, go on, tell me the truth, I won't be offended in the least.' Dara never saw the point of this game. For a start, she already knew what age he was. And Ian knew that she knew. Hadn't he told her himself? But still, it was a game he never seemed to tire of. Possibly because Dara Flood always told him that he looked forty, tops, even though, with the hair fast receding from the top of his head, the beginnings of a Guinness paunch that forced him to adjust his belt after anything bigger than a two-course meal and the shy tips of some nostril hair pushing their way out of his otherwise handsome nose, he could pass for a man closer to his own age. She never told him that, not wanting to be the bearer of news that Ian would consider *diabolical* rather than just plain old bad. Some people might think him vain, but Dara saw the vulnerability beneath the vanity. The fear of middle age. She supposed she might feel that too. When her time came.

She stood up and moved towards the windowsill. She picked up the mobile phone and set her cup on the counter. She would go for *breezy*. A breezy tone. Nothing covert about breezy.

'*Sory Ian. Cant make Thursday. Going to Paris – for one nite. A last-minut thing. But luve to see you on Satrday. U still free?*'

That sounded outlandish, Dara felt, for a woman like her. But nothing else occurred, so she pressed Send and waited.

An immediate response.

'*GOOD LORD!!! Sounds lovely. Paris in the springtime. Who r u going with?*'

Dara bitterly regretted not telling Ian Harte about Anya's crazy ruse to find Mr Flood, the hiring of Stanley Flinter, and the persuasive plans of the reclusive Miss Pettigrew, who always got what she wanted, if you didn't count Manus Mac-Bride, whom she had wanted most of all. Now, any of her subsequent explanations – especially by text – were going to sound even more fanciful than they already were.

She bit her lip and punched his number into her phone, even though it was already stored in her contacts. It was a pattern of the number of clients Mrs Flood had, the last three digits of the house alarm in reverse order, and the number of times George used to jump through a hula hoop before he flopped, dizzy, on the grass in the back garden.

The phone rang three times before it moved on to voice-mail, which was odd, considering that he'd just had the phone in his hand, texting her. She began by apologising. 'Ian, I'm terribly sorry, I should have told you all this before now. Not that there's anything to tell really, but, well, it's complicated. Well, not really complicated, but complicated enough not to go into now, on your voicemail. I could meet you tonight? If you're free, that is. I know it's short notice, but, well, I just feel bad about Thursday night and not telling you. Not that there's all that much to tell. Sorry, I think I've said that before. Did I? Sorry. Anyway, ring me back. Or text me. What about The Back Door tonight at eight? Or somewhere else? A bit closer to home, maybe? Anyway, let me know and sorry again. I'll explain everything when I see you. OK, OK, goodbye then. It's Dara by the way. Dara Flood. I can't remember if I said that already. I'll . . . I'll talk to you later. Or see you. Maybe. Bye then.'

A curt text, two minutes later: *OK*.

OK? What did that mean? OK about The Back Door? Or OK about not telling him of her impending trip to Paris? Whichever one it was, the tone – Dara felt – was not the best. She decided to ignore it.

'*Gr8! See you at 8!*'

Dara wished for Angel then. The old Angel. The one with the faith. And the hope. Angel would know how to deal with Ian. What to say. Dara knew she wasn't great at dealing with people. Dogs, she could handle. Take Lucky. He had smiled at her yesterday when she fed him her dog flapjacks, which were mostly the same as ordinary flapjacks, but with less syrup and sugar and more oats. Of course, Tintin said it was more like a grimace. But it was a smile, Dara was nearly sure of it.

People were trickier. Angel would have made tea and opened a packet of coconut Snowballs. She would have smiled and said, 'Don't mind him', when Dara told her about the peevish tone of Ian's texts.

But Angel was at dialysis. And even if she wasn't, she'd be in her room, busy being someone else. Someone Dara was finding harder and harder to recognise. Dara pushed the thought away. Up to now, she had always presumed that Angel would come back to her. That this was a temporary arrangement. Now she wasn't so sure.

She phoned Tintin instead.

At first he was merely annoyed, as he often was at what he described at Ian's careless pillaging of Dara Flood's territory whenever it suited him.

Dara waited until Tintin blew some steam off before she interrupted with a timely 'Yes, but what am I going to *say*?'

'Say?' Tintin sounded confused.

'Yes,' Dara said. 'About all the stuff that's been going on, none of which I've told him about. He's going to think that's very strange, isn't he?'

'Well, it *is* very strange,' Tintin said. 'Isn't it?'

'Well, yes, but I mean, no, not really. It's just that we never really discuss things like that, you know?'

'What? Things like family and relationships?' Tintin asked in a seemingly innocuous voice.

'Well, yes, I mean, OK, sometimes he talks about his mother and how poorly she is and how difficult it can be for him to . . .'

'But does he ever ask about *you*? About *your* life? How difficult things sometimes are for *you*?'

'Who wants to talk about that kind of stuff on a date?' Dara asked, not unreasonably, she felt.

'I've heard tell of people discussing all sorts,' replied Tintin, 'when they are in a *relationship*.' He paused, allowing his emphasis on the word '*relationship*' to sink in, like mud.

'Look, Tintin, this isn't helping. I rang you to get some advice.'

'You want my advice?'

'Yes, I do,' said Dara, although she wasn't so sure about that any more.

'Fuck him.'

'Fuck him?' repeated Dara. 'That's your advice?'

'I mean, if you guys don't talk to each other, why should he be surprised that you haven't told him about Mr Flood? Or Paris? Or Stanley Flinter, for that matter?'

There it was again. That strange mix of chocolate sauce being poured over ratatouille. Stanley Flinter. In Paris. With her. Ian wouldn't think it was strange. He would view it as highly suspect.

'We *do* talk,' Dara said, wishing she had rung Anya instead, who might have been cynical but at least would have been more succinct about it. 'We talk about books. We go to the cinema. We talk about the films we've seen, stuff like that.'

'Don't forget Venice and how smelly it is,' Tintin added.

'He said other stuff about Venice too, you know,' Dara told him, although she wouldn't swear on Angel's life that that was strictly true. 'Besides, it *is* smelly. Everyone says so.'

'Only in the summertime,' Tintin corrected her.

'Are you going to help me or not?'

'Fine,' said Tintin, sighing a long, put-upon sigh.

'Go on,' said Dara.

'Tell him all about it. About Mr Flood, the found-and-lost kidney, everything. Give him the full monty. But . . .' Here Tintin paused.

'Yes?'

'DON'T apologise for any of it. For not telling him or anything. If he wanted to know, he would have asked, wouldn't he?'

'Well . . .'

'DON'T apologise,' Tintin said again. 'For anything. Got that?'

'I suppose I could—'

'HAVE. YOU. GOT. THAT?' Tintin said again, with a ferocious full stop after each word.

'Yes,' said Dara, who felt sure that she'd apologised – and more than once – in her voicemail.

★   ★   ★

Two hours later, Dara struggled along the road on her bicycle, the wind whipping her face like a lash and the rain driving against her like traffic. Of course, she should have asked Angel if she could borrow her car. But she was nervous of driving in these conditions. Yes, she was nervous about cycling too, but not *as* nervous.

There had been no response from Ian Harte to her chirpy, exclamation-ravaged text.

The Back Door was not a pub Dara would choose to go to. For a start, it was off her beaten track, wedged between a betting shop and a launderette down a narrow side street off the main drag at Fairview. It was a dark affair, full of passageways that led nowhere in particular, with a vague smell of men's toilets puncturing the gloom. Dara hated arriving first and tried to avoid it without actually being late. Ian was particular about timekeeping. The pub was full of old men who seemed to spend as much time there as they did in the bookie's next door, and no time at all at the launderette, judging by the shiny grime across the shoulders of their ancient jackets. The female population of the pub doubled when Dara walked in. The only other woman in the pub was a permanent fixture in the place. At least, she was always there whenever Dara was, leaning across the bar in a low-cut top that allowed her breasts to spill like a drink onto the counter in front of her and possibly explained why the barman often got confused with Dara's order and gave her a glass of Miller from the tap, when she'd ordered a bottle with an empty glass on the side.

The woman began to sing, as she often did. A slow lament of a song, about some handsome soldier who went to war and the woman who stayed at home and waited for him. She sang low down in her throat, an unlit cigarette dangling from the corner of her fire-engine-red mouth. Ian did not arrive until the song eventually drew to its macabre and miserable conclusion. The soldier eventually returns home only to discover that his lady love has thrown herself from the loft of her father's barn on hearing that he has been killed in battle when in fact he has *not* been killed at all, merely grievously wounded.

'Sorry I'm late, Dara,' Ian said when he reached their usual table. That's how Dara knew he was annoyed. The more good-humoured he was, the more flamboyant the language he employed when he spoke to her. If he was in a good mood – and he generally was – and arrived late, he might begin with 'My sincere apologies for my tardiness, my darling Dara. Can you forgive a foolish man?' Dara smiled when he spoke in this way, but Ian never seemed to get the joke.

He had come straight from work, it seemed, dressed as he was in a stiff, dark, doubled-breasted three-piece suit with heart-shaped silver cufflinks edging past the end of his jacket sleeves. Perhaps his mother had bought them for him, Dara thought. They did not seem like the kind of cufflinks a man would purchase for himself. He lowered himself into the chair – not his usual seat beside Dara, but opposite her – with the jaded sigh of a man who had gotten up two hours before he went to bed.

'Ian, the thing is, I . . .'

'You didn't get me a drink, did you, darling?' Ian looked pointedly at the table between them, where Dara's bottle of beer sat, the label torn off and already shredded.

'Eh, no, I . . .' Ian drank a complicated game of gin and tonic. The gin had to be distilled, preferably London dry. Gordon's was one of the few that would bring a smile to his face. Then there was the tonic: it had to be slimline. On this point there was no compromise. Two ice cubes: no more, no less. A wedge of lime – not lemon – rubbed around the rim of the glass before being placed astride both cubes. The gin should marinate awhile in the ice and lime before the tonic was added, spitting with fizz, in a slow trickle and – this was the important bit, according to Ian – at an angle. He never liked anyone to order the drink for him until he was there, so he could make sure that all his criteria were met.

'No matter. I'll go and get it myself,' he said with a smile that stretched across his face like a single sheet on a double bed.

He was gone quite a while. Dara could hear some minor disagreement about lemon and lime being essentially the same fruit, only a different colour: the usual barman was not on duty. She steeled herself and remembered what Tintin had said.

Ian eventually returned to the table with his drink and an air of disappointment wafting around him like a bad smell. Dara looked at the glass. Three ice cubes and not a lime in sight. She leaned forward and smiled.

'The thing is, Ian . . .' she began.

Ian tested the stability of the table with one hand and, finding it lacking, went in search of beer mats to slip under the offending leg. 'That's better,' he said, when he finally came up from under the table.

Dara tried again. 'I probably should have mentioned something before . . .'

But Ian was busy undoing the buttons of his jacket. He shook himself out of it, folded it in a way that Mrs Flood would have approved of and set it carefully on the stool beside his.

'I mean, I probably won't even end up going to Paris, but . . .' Her words were drowned out by the scraping of the legs of Ian's stool across the uneven stone floor as he sat down.

Dara stopped talking and took a long draught of her beer instead.

When Ian had finally settled himself, he looked at her, a sad sort of a smile arranged across his face. 'So you were going to go to Paris in the springtime without telling me, my little

Dara.' He shrugged his shoulders as if he'd always known Dara was going to do this. It was just a question of when.

Dara struggled with the apology that was already on the tip of her tongue, her lips forming the shape of it. 'No, I mean, it's more of a business trip really. And only for a night. There didn't seem any point in mentioning it. Not that it's a secret or anything. Of course not. And I don't even have my passport yet. Miss Pettigrew is trying to rush it through, but I'm not sure . . .'

'Miss Pettigrew?'

'My next-door neighbour,' Dara explained.

'Oh,' said Ian, sliding a finger around the rim of the glass with studied concentration.

'You see, I'm looking for my father,' Dara began. 'He left a long time ago. Before I was born actually. And my sister, Angel – well, it's Angela really, but we've always called her Angel because she's . . . sorry, I'm getting off the point. The actual point is that Angel needs a kidney. She's on dialysis, you see and, well, she got the call from the hospital recently. For a kidney transplant, that is. But, well, the thing is, it didn't work out and Angel hasn't been very well since and I had the idea that . . . well, it was Anya's idea, to be fair. Anyway, I . . . I've been looking for Mr Flood . . . my father, I mean . . . ever since, and . . . and there's a slight chance he may be in Paris. Or if he's not, there's someone – a woman – who might have some information. So that's why I'm going. To Paris. Just for one night. I'll be back in time for our date on Saturday.'

She stopped as abruptly as she'd begun. She was a little out of breath. She picked up her glass and drained it, trying not to think about a cigarette. She really wanted one.

For a while, Ian said nothing. Just traced the rim of his glass with his finger. When he looked at her, his expression was one of wry amusement.

'That's quite an episode of *EastEnders* you've got going on there, young Dara Flood,' he said to her with half a smile.

Dara flushed. Ian hated *EastEnders*. In fact, he hated all soaps. He would never have gotten along with Tintin.

'It's not ideal,' she acknowledged, 'but that's the way it is, I'm afraid.' Despite herself, she could feel her chin inching up. She surprised herself by thinking that Tintin was right. She had nothing to apologise for and she wasn't going to either.

Ian's expression softened and he reached for her hand across the tiny table and squeezed it. 'I just wish you'd told me all this, darling. Before now. I hate to hear that you're jetting off to Paris. In the springtime. Without me. *We* should be going places in the springtime. But with Mother so ill and my career . . .' His voice trailed off and he gazed into the middle distance.

The grip Ian had on Dara's hand was tight, but she concentrated on not pulling away. She was seized with a fierce mixture of relief – she had told him – and gratitude – he seemed to have forgiven her. But something else as well. Could it be uncertainty? Doubt even? *Why* hadn't she told him before? Weren't these the kinds of things normal couples discussed? But they weren't a normal couple. The relationship was going nowhere and that was just the way Dara Flood liked it. Wasn't it? No expectations to lead her towards the road she made such an effort to avoid. The road to *disappointment, uncertainty* and, of course, eventual, inevitable *decline*.

But the 'no expectations' that Dara insisted on had led her here. To this place. The Back Door. Summarising her life in a paragraph. Making it sound like an episode of *EastEnders* and, even though Tintin declared *EastEnders* the Queen Bee of soap operas, the situation left Dara with a niggle of uncertainty. Doubt even. It itched at her like a stray hair brushing against her face.

Perhaps Ian felt some of Dara's disquiet. 'We *will* go to Paris,' he announced suddenly. 'I mean, not now, obviously. You've got a lot going on with this . . . this quest of yours.' He smiled when he said *quest,* as if it were some childish game. She supposed she couldn't expect him to understand. 'But sometime soon. Maybe in the autumn. I could perhaps try and get some respite care for Mother, if she'd agree, of course. She can get a little sensitive if she thinks I'm abandoning her. I could show you the underbelly of Paris. The *real* Paris. None of that Louvres and Champs-Elysées nonsense that they try to distract the tourists with.'

Dara couldn't think of a suitable response to this suggestion.

'Stay right there,' Ian ordered her, standing up and rubbing at the seat of his trousers as he always did after sitting on one of the stools at The Back Door. 'I'm going to get you another drink and then tell you about this marvellous little bistro I found on the Left Bank the last time I was in Paris. You wouldn't *believe* the escargots. They are To Die For.' Ian beamed when he said this, and normally Dara would have smiled back and been interested in the escargots and how they were presented and what they came with, perhaps with a view to trying to cook them herself. Instead, she could feel the long, cold hand of something that could have been disappointment reaching for her. She'd never felt it before. Not with Ian. She'd never had any expectations before, she supposed. But she must have been expecting something after her revelations. Whatever it was, it hadn't arrived, because now all she felt was disappointment. Disappointment was like dry rot. Once it settled, it was nearly impossible to remove.

Ian left a cloud of aftershave behind him and Dara did her best not to cough. She usually liked the way Ian smelled. Like the cosmetics counter in Boots. Never the same smell. But now, with the dry rot of disappointment making itself comfortable in the foundations of whatever it was she and Ian were doing – the word 'relationship' mocked her when she attempted it – the smell was overwhelming. Offensive, almost. She tried to shrug the thought away but it clung to her like the smell.

Outside the pub, the rain had stopped. She declined Ian's offer of a lift home. 'I have my bicycle,' she explained. 'And I've a lot to do. Packing and all that.'

'I thought you said you were just going for one night?' The perfection of Ian's eyebrows arched high on his forehead.

'I am. It's just . . . well, I still need to pack a bag. Print out my boarding pass. Stuff like that.' Dara shoved her high-vis jacket over her head. Suddenly, she couldn't wait to get away.

'Don't forget to visit that little square I told you about. The bust of Louis XIV is a magnificent example of neoclassical art.' He'd given her a list of places to visit. Places that Dara was unfamiliar with, containing busts of people she'd never heard of. He seemed to think she would have plenty of time for sightseeing. In fact, after her rapid synopsis of her circumstances, he had not alluded to them again, other than a vague comment about her father's *skulduggery*, and how he hoped that that brand of deceit and carelessness was not somehow skulking around Dara's gene pool, waiting for an opportunity to reveal itself.

He had been very interested, on the other hand, in the subject of Stanley Flinter.

'A private detective? It seems such a *seedy* way of making a living.'

'He's been very helpful,' Dara couldn't help saying, even though it made Ian's eyes bulge in a way that reminded her of a toad. She thought of Stanley's eyes then, the dark brown of them, almost black. The way they caught the light when he smiled his slow, cautious smile.

'Helpful?' Ian said, like the trait was akin to an infectious disease. His attitude towards Stanley Flinter – she should never have told Ian his age, but he *had* asked – coupled with Dara's lingering sense of disappointment combined to provide her with an overall sense of irritation.

'Yes, helpful,' she said again, a little louder than necessary, as if Ian wore a hearing aid that was not turned up high enough. 'And kind and considerate and non-judgemental, which, when you consider the situation – an episode of *EastEnders* I think you called it – is commendable, wouldn't you say?'

Kind? Considerate? Non-judgemental? This was not what she'd planned to say to Ian Harte about Stanley Flinter. But those things were true. There was no getting around it.

Ian's nostrils flared and narrowed several times. 'I was only joking about *EastEnders*, Dara. I thought you had a sense of humour.'

'I do,' Dara said. 'I just don't happen to think the situation is a very humorous one.'

'No, I suppose it's not,' Ian said, taking his mobile out of his pocket and glancing at the screen. 'But it's only normal that I should worry about my girl cavorting off to Paris with another man. Isn't it?'

'This is about Angel, remember? I'm doing this for her. It's important, Ian. She's not well, I'm worried about her. I'm worried that she might . . .'

'OK, OK,' said Ian, pressing a finger against Dara's mouth. 'Christ, you're shaking. Are you cold?'

Dara shook her head and looked away from his face. She steadied herself with a breath. 'It's a business trip,' she said. 'You're always away on business and I never mind, do I?' The truth of this statement hit Dara like a bus. She didn't mind. She never minded. She never even thought about him when he was away. That couldn't be right. Could it?

'Yes, well, I know the minds of men,' Ian said, looking up as the door of the pub opened. 'I am one, after all.'

'Not all men are like that,' said Dara. 'Stanley is not like that.' And as she said it, she knew it was true.

Ian kissed her for a long time outside the pub. He usually waited until they were safely ensconced behind the tinted windows of his jeep before he bore down on her. Dara had the sensation that he was putting his stamp on her, before her trip to Paris. Marking his territory. His tongue pushed into her mouth, but now, with the dry rot of disappointment, it felt fleshy and cold. His mouth had the sour taste of lemons.

She pulled away. 'I have to go,' she said.

'I'll see you on Saturday, my darling,' Ian called after her.

Dara kept pedalling.

39

'I knew it,' said Tintin, rubbing his hands together and smacking his lips.

'What?' Anya looked up.

'She's got tits. No offence, Dara,' he added, leaning over to catch Dara's eye.

'None taken,' said Dara, cheerful. She was enjoying all the attention, truth be told.

'Of course she's got tits.' Anya was not for letting go. 'She is woman, for Godt's sake.' She stopped pinning the hem of the dress that Miss Pettigrew had ordered for Dara and sat back on her haunches, her ample bottom spilling across the floor in a manner that wasn't far from splendid, Dara thought. Today, Anya wore the dress that Tintin called her *midweek dress*, only because it was fractionally less fancy than her other ones. No feathers or sequins or bows, and although the pink of it fell under the description of 'shocking', it was not as shocking as it might have been.

'Besides, you cannot say stuff like dat,' Anya said through the cluster of pins poking from between her lips.

'Why not?' asked Tintin, distracted now by a surprise party brochure he had left on the table earlier for Anya and Dara to flick through, which neither of them had.

'Because dat is sexual harassment,' Anya explained in a slow, deliberate voice, as though she were addressing a six-year-old.

'It's only sexual harassment if you want to have sex with the person,' declared Tintin, like he was quoting from a manual.

'Is it?' Anya's brow creased, considering this possibility.

'Yes,' said Tintin, nodding his head for emphasis.

'I vill Google dis later,' Anya warned him.

'Google away,' Tintin told her in a way that made Anya consider believing him.

'Why don't you want to have sex with me, anyway?' Dara piped up, pushing her recently excavated chest up and out.

Tintin looked at her, as if he were trying to place her.

'Because I . . . I just . . . What are you on about?'

Dara stood up. The soft fabric of the dress slipping against the bare skin of her legs felt good. She looked down. Tintin was right. She *did* have tits. Small ones, yes. But tits all the same. There was no denying it.

'Why don't you want to have sex with me?' she repeated, running her tongue along her top lip. Slutty, she knew. But fantastic.

Tintin withered into a man two sizes smaller. 'Because . . . I . . . I just . . .' he said, backing up against the wall of the Portakabin. It took him a moment to come to. 'Wait,' he said, holding up both hands as if Dara was an overexcited bullock. 'Do *you* want to have sex with *me*?'

'No,' said Dara.

'Well then,' said Tintin, relieved but also a tiny bit affronted at the certainty of Dara's reply.

'You were the one who said I had tits. I just asked, is all.'

'I only mentioned it because I'm only after noticing them. Aw, feckit, I'm going,' said Tintin, moving towards the door, determined not to listen to Anya explaining to Dara how to lean forward and scoop her breasts, one at a time, into her hands before dropping them – fuller now – back into the cups of her bra.

'I don't look like myself,' said Dara, staring at the reflection of her not-too-bad-considering cleavage in the potbelly of the kettle.

'You're right,' Anya said, looking her up and down. 'You look better than yourself.'

As promised, the dress was red. 'But not a harlot-red, mind,' Miss Pettigrew had insisted, even though Dara had no idea what a harlot-red looked like.

Dara felt that it was a dress that fell, rather than sat. Everything about it was soft. The material, the lines of it, the colour. A soft red. She surprised herself by loving it.

'I love it,' she'd told Miss Pettigrew.

'I knew you would,' said Miss Pettigrew, and in fairness, her voice displayed not a single shred of surprise.

'How did you know my size?'

'Your bosom was always going to be the tricky bit. Seeing as I wasn't sure whether or not you actually had one.'

'Why didn't you just ask me the size of my, eh, bosom?'

'I wanted to surprise you,' the old lady told her, smiling at her. Dara had smiled back. She *was* surprised.

Anya stepped away from Dara, studying her handiwork. Dara felt the hem didn't need to be taken up, but Anya had insisted. 'Your calves actually quite nice-shapely,' she said, as if she'd uncovered something rare and unusual, like a real diamond ring in a Christmas cracker.

Dara looked at her legs. They were as white as icing. And of course shorter than she'd like.

'Lift arms up like gut girl,' Anya ordered.

'This doesn't feel right,' said Dara, obediently raising her arms, her voice muffled as Anya pulled the dress over her head.

'Is too tight?' Anya stopped pulling and peered at Dara's face through an armhole.

'No, it's fine. It's just . . . it feels a bit . . . frivolous, I suppose.'

'Frivolous?' The word sounded strange in Anya's mouth. In fairness, it was not a word she had much cause to use.

'You know, trying on dresses and going to Paris. I've always wanted to go to Paris. You know that.'

Anya released Dara from the dress, folded it and laid it gently on the layers of tissue paper in its box. She sighed, shaking her head. 'Life has handed you lemons and you are making lemonade, Dara. Dat is all.'

Dara's phone beeped and she jumped and ran to pick it out of the pocket of her duffel coat.

'News?' Anya asked, in her carefully offhand way, and Dara felt a rush of gratitude for her Polish friend, who would never admit to her worry about Angel.

But it was only a text from Ian Harte, making arrangements for their date on Saturday night.

'Meet you at the usual place on Saturday. 7 p.m. Can you wear the white lace all-in-one? And NO tracksuits! Am taking you somewhere special. Ixx'

The white lace all-in-one? Dara's buttocks twitched just thinking about the way the material rode up into the crack of her bum and bit into her skin like teeth. And what did he mean, somewhere special? The dry rot of disappointment she had felt during their last meeting shifted and spread. She found herself unable to dredge up any enthusiasm for going any place special with Ian. She put it down to nerves about her impending visit to Paris. It was not a convincing argument.

She deleted the text.

'I'm going to feed Lucky.'

Anya looked up. 'Dara, ve need to discuss Lucky's . . . situation.'

'I know, I know, he's going to have to get used to other people feeding him. But I think he's getting better. He let Tintin give him the leftover bolognese I brought in yesterday. He loves it spread on Ryvita.'

'No, Dara, dat is not what I wish to discuss,' said Anya, not quite looking at Dara.

Dara knew what Anya wanted to discuss. Of course she did. Since his arrival at the pound, no prospective owner had so much as sniffed in Lucky's direction. While the welts on his body were healing, his pelt remained bald in places, and that, coupled with his huge body, tiny head, long ears, short tail, squat legs and enormous paws, left him poorly equipped to attract so much as a sidelong glance from any of the visitors to the pound. He continued to throw himself against the bars of his cage when Tintin or Anya approached, but when he saw Dara, he stopped and pushed his nose through the bars of his cage, like a hand.

'There's a rescue centre in Stockholm that might take him,' Dara had told Anya after days of phoning and e-mailing.

'I wonder if the dogs bark in Swedish?' Tintin wanted to know.

'Is a long way to go for such an olt dog,' Anya said, not unreasonably.

'The kindest thing,' the vet declared in the cheerful voice he reserved for such conversations, 'would be to put him down.'

But there was something about Lucky that pulled at the strings of Dara's heart. The way he looked at her with his mismatched eyes. As if he knew. That he was in the last-chance saloon and Dara was the only one serving the drinks behind the bar.

She pulled the sleeve of her jumper down over her wrist. The bite mark had faded to a line of pale pink. It was a one-off. Dara knew that. A natural reaction to fear of the unknown. But it was there. In his record. As indelible as ink. Dara knew she couldn't save him forever. But she was going to save him for as long as she could.

'Could we discuss Lucky's situation tomorrow?' she asked, heading for the door of the Portakabin.

'You vill be in Paris tomorrow,' Anya reminded her, even though there was no need.

'I mightn't be, you know. My passport hasn't arrived yet.'

'It vill come. Miss Pettigrew vill make sure of dat.'

Dara, who couldn't help feeling that Anya was right, shivered.

'The day after, then?' Dara backed towards the door, before turning around and taking the steps with a jump.

'You vill still be in Paris!' Anya shouted after her.

'I'll be here on Saturday.' Dara kept walking, not looking back.

'Saturday is my day off. I vill be day-tripping with debt collector. You know dis.'

It was true. Dara *did* know this. She turned and smiled at Anya. 'Monday, so,' she said. 'Monday is good for me.'

Anya sighed and shook her head before turning back into the Portakabin. Dara knelt down at Lucky's cage and rubbed the nose he pushed between the bars. 'I've bought us the weekend,' she told him in a whisper. 'So for God's sake, watch a few Lassie DVDs while I'm gone and see how it's done, all right?' Lucky's gaze was thick with trust. As if he knew he could depend on her.

40

When she arrived home, the house was cold and murky in the dull grey of the evening light. Mrs Flood's clear-out had ascended to the attic. Dara could hear the rustle of her mother's black bag and her footsteps, heavy and slow, moving methodically through the cramped space in the roof. Angel was in her room, picking her way through a photo album. She had stopped at a photograph taken last Christmas. One of her and Joe and Mrs Flood and Dara in Miss Pettigrew's house on Christmas Day. In a line on the couch, with paper hats from Christmas crackers sitting at precarious angles on their heads. Angel in her usual position, between Mrs Flood and Dara. Everyone is looking straight at Miss Pettigrew – tipsy after three glasses of her sweet sherry – who manages to take the picture. Everyone except for Joe, who looks at Angel as if he is committing her to memory. As if he knows.

When Angel saw Dara at the door of her bedroom, she closed the book with a snap.

'Any calls?' Dara asked, as she always did, even though the answer was now always the same, since Joe had finally stopped ringing. The house seemed much quieter now he'd stopped. In the quietness, the realisation that finally dawned on Dara sounded like a door banging shut. Three times. Joe had finally given up on Angel.

'No,' said Angel. 'No calls.'

Something happened then. Something awful. For the first time in her life, Dara found herself groping around for something to say to Angel. Nothing occurred to her. When the doorbell rang, she ran to get it, guilt and relief jostling for position in her head.

The thin outline of the figure through the mottled glass of the front door seemed familiar to Dara. She shook her head. It couldn't be. Even when she opened the door and saw her there, clutching an umbrella that smelled of mothballs and mildew, she still didn't believe it.

'Miss Pettigrew. What . . . what are you doing here?'

'Well? Aren't you going to ask me in? Ask if I have a mouth on me?'

'Of course, it's just . . . I'm surprised . . . to see you out, I mean . . .'

'How else do you expect me to get here?'

Miss Pettigrew stepped into the hall as if she'd been here many times before. She closed the door quickly and leaned against it.

'Are you all right?' Dara asked, unwinding a scarf – a very long, itchy one that Mrs Flood had knitted her some winters before – from around the old lady's narrow neck.

'Of course I'm all right. Why wouldn't I be?'

'Let me take your coat. And your gloves. And your, eh, are those *gaiters* over your boots?'

'Certainly. It's raining, my dear girl. Hadn't you noticed?'

For someone who hadn't braved the elements in years, Miss Pettigrew was very well equipped for them. Under the raincoat, Edward hung in a sling that was more suited to a newborn baby. His tail stuck out of a leghole and he appeared to be taking Miss Pettigrew's reunion with the outside world a lot better than Dara was.

'Come through to the sitting room. Please, take a seat. I was just making some tea . . .' Miss Pettigrew looked pointedly at her watch. It was just gone seven. 'Or a sherry, if you'd prefer. I think there might be a bottle somewhere . . .'

Miss Pettigrew nodded and lowered herself onto the couch. Dara tried not to hear the snapping of her bones with every stiff move.

Dara struck a match and held it to the fire pack in the grate. Even though it was the spring side of March, the evening was damp and chill.

'Miss Pettigrew! Is everything all right?' Mrs Flood stopped at the door, blinking the way people do when their brain calls their eyes a stinking liar. The black bag slumped on the ground behind her.

'Of course everything is all right. Why wouldn't it be?' Miss Pettigrew's tone was peevish, and Dara could tell that her mother decided not to allude to the fact that her next-door neighbour hadn't been seen outside her front door since the alleged demise of Ronald Reagan.

'Your house seems more spacious than mine,' Miss Pettigrew said, looking around. 'Isn't that odd?'

Dara nodded. Mrs Flood's clear-out had given the house a curiously bare look, stripped as it was of its usual bric-a-brac. Even the footstool that Mr Flood had loved to prop his stockinged feet on in the evenings had been dumped into a black bag.

'I've been doing a bit of a . . . spring clean,' Mrs Flood admitted.

'Good for the soul,' Miss Pettigrew said, leaning forward to grasp Mrs Flood's hot, fleshy hand in her cold, bony one. The gesture was oddly intimate, and for a moment, Dara felt she should look away.

Mrs Flood sat on the couch beside her neighbour. She opened her mouth to speak, but no words came. Instead, she nodded, and Dara thought for a moment that she could see a glint of something that might be the threat of tears in her eyes.

'Go and get us two glasses of sherry, like a good girl,' Miss Pettigrew said, looking at Dara. 'In fact, just bring the bottle in. That'll save us a trip.'

When Dara returned to the sitting room – with the only bottle of sherry she could find, which turned out to be cooking sherry, two glasses and a plate of brownies she'd made the day before – she was relieved to find her mother restored to her usual self. Mrs Flood looked at Dara and shook her head. In her hands sat a passport. Dara's new passport. It had arrived on time after all.

Miss Pettigrew's smile was a beam. 'You see why I had to come? Mark in the passport office came good after all. Although there's no doubt that he owes me a few favours.'

Dara couldn't think what favours Mark in the passport office might or might not owe Miss Pettigrew. Her face grew hot under her mother's scrutiny.

'Well?' Mrs Flood finally said, leaning forward to set the passport down on the footstool before remembering that it was no longer there. 'When were you going to tell me about this?' She folded her arms across her chest and waited.

Miss Pettigrew poured herself a second glass of sherry – a large one – and threw it back with a defiantly slick flick of her arthritic wrist. 'Well, I'd better go. I'm having a *Sex and the City* night in. Myself and Edward are going to watch the entire last series, back-to-back, and drink Cosmos. Wednesday night is our girls' night in, isn't it, poppet?' She deposited a kiss on one of Edwards's ears. 'Don't forget to give my regards to Henri, won't you?' she said, a little out of breath.

'Henri?'

'The concierge at the Louis XIV. Darling man. A little lecherous, of course, but show me a Frenchman who isn't. Am I right, Mrs Flood?'

Mrs Flood raised her eyes to heaven and nodded as if lecherous Frenchmen were a common scourge in her life, up there with *poor Mrs Butcher*'s frizzy hair and Sandra-the-Skinflint Shanahan, who didn't believe in tipping.

'I won't tell you to enjoy Paris,' Miss Pettigrew added, 'because really, there's nothing else to be done with it.'

'Who's going to Paris?' Angel walked down the stairs, pulling Mrs Flood's ancient dressing gown around her. She stopped when she saw Miss Pettigrew. 'You're out!' she said, as if Miss Pettigrew was on day release from a maximum-security prison rather than simply out of her house that happened to be just next door.

'Angel! Darling girl! It's so lovely to see you.' Miss Pettigrew's bright blue eyes got brighter, her face lit with affection. Dara realised that Miss Pettigrew hadn't seen Angel since the found-and-lost kidney affair. Angel must have realised the same thing, because on her face Dara saw something that looked like shame. Miss Pettigrew was an old lady. Their next-door neighbour. Part of their family. Before, Angel had been a regular visitor to her home. A regular sampler of Miss Pettigrew's sweet sherry. Except she wasn't any more. Instead, Miss Pettigrew had walked to her front door – with her raincoat, her umbrella, her gaiters and her dog in a sling. She had opened that door. She had stepped out of that door. Stepped out into the world. Into the great adventure that was life. She had made it. Here. To their home. After five years of going nowhere. She had done that for Angel.

For the first time in a long time, Angel seemed to be present in the room. No longer an impression of herself, but solid. Full. Clear.

Miss Pettigrew began a slow climb out of the sofa. Angel held out her hand. Miss Pettigrew took it, and Angel pulled her until she was standing upright, in her support tights and her soft wool skirt and her twinset.

'Come here to me,' Miss Pettigrew said, and even though Angel didn't move, she didn't move away when the old lady gathered her in her paper-thin arms and held her there.

Angel said something, but Dara couldn't make out what it was. Miss Pettigrew shook her head. 'Don't worry, Angel. Everything is going to be all right. I know it is.' It was a platitude. Wasn't it? But the way Miss Pettigrew said it, lifted Dara's hope.

Miss Pettigrew released Angel from her embrace and winked at her, as if they knew something no one else did. Angel smiled. There was nothing vague about the smile. It was there. Faint, but real. Dara realised she was holding her breath.

'I just popped in to give Dara her passport,' Miss Pettigrew told Angel, as if popping in was something she did on a regular basis.

'Dara's passport?' Angel looked at Dara, her eyebrows raised in a question.

'Dara will tell you all about it, I'm sure. We'd best be getting on, if we're going to manage the whole series before bedtime. Come along, Edward, darling.'

'I'll walk you home,' Dara said, reaching for her anorak.

'No,' said Miss Pettigrew, and there was an edge to her voice. 'We can manage.' Dara could see her fear in the slight shake of her hands and the high breathiness of her voice. But she also saw the old woman's resolve, in the firm set of her jaw and the steely blue of her eyes.

When she opened the front door to let Miss Pettigrew out, she closed it immediately, knowing that her neighbour would not appreciate an audience as she negotiated the short length of the driveway with careful steps.

'When will you be back?' was the first question that Mrs Flood asked.

'Friday.'

'What time?'

'In the afternoon. I'm not exactly sure.' Dara knew precisely what time her fight was due back to Dublin. But if it was delayed, Mrs Flood would worry.

Dara tried to catch her sister's eye. But Angel was gone again, her expression obscured by her hair, which hung in greasy lines around the perimeter of her face, like a dirty fence.

'And this private detective person?' Mrs Flood said. 'I mean, what do you really know about him, Dara? How do you know you can trust him? He could be a serial killer, for all you know. Or a womaniser.' She said the word as if the idea of Stanley Flinter being a *womaniser* was even worse than the idea of him being a serial killer. Dara didn't think Stanley was a womaniser. Or a serial killer. It was his eyes, she thought. The way the light got inside them when he smiled and cleared all traces of sadness from his face, like sun breaking through cloud. Womanisers don't have eyes like that, she felt sure. She couldn't say the same of serial killers, but she doubted it.

She shook her head. 'You've met him,' she reminded her mother. She turned to her sister. 'So have you, Angel. Remember?' She willed Angel to say something positive. Anything.

'He seems . . .' Angel began, and Dara waited. 'Good,' Angel finally said. 'He seems like a good person.' Still Dara waited. She knew there was more. 'But,' Angel went on, 'I don't think it will do any good. Going to Paris, I mean. You won't find Mr Flood, and even if you do, he won't help. Why should he? He's never helped in his life. I'm sorry, Dara. I know you're only trying to help.' She looked at Dara then, willing her to understand.

Dara concentrated on the positives. She turned to her mother. 'You see? Angel knows that Stanley Flinter is a good person. She said so.'

Mrs Flood allowed herself to smile at her eldest daughter before she remembered herself. 'Yes, but *I* don't know anything about him, do I? And really, neither do you.'

'I trust him,' was all Dara said.

Mrs Flood shook her head and tutted a little before splashing sherry into a glass and bending her head to it.

'I have to go. It's the first definite lead we've had. Mr Flood was there. He lived there. Maybe he still does. Maybe this Isabelle Dupoint knows where we can find him. By this time tomorrow I could have had a conversation with him. He could have agreed to have himself tested. To see if he's a match.' Dara knew she shouldn't say such things. Make such promises. Not with Angel in the room. But the glimpse of her sister, the old Angel, during Miss Pettigrew's visit spurred her on. Made her reckless.

Mrs Flood made a sound, low down in her throat, that smacked of cynicism.

'It's a long shot,' Dara warned her sister before her mother could shape her cynicism into words. 'But there's a possibility. A slim one.' She looked at Angel, but she was already moving away from her, heading for the door.

The phone rang, and the three of them jumped, like old times. Dara reached it on the second ring. But it was only Miss Pettigrew.

'Just ringing to let you know I got back safe and sound,' she said, in the cheerful voice of a waning recluse. 'Sorry for ringing on the landline. I couldn't get a signal on your mobile.'

As Miss Pettigrew spoke, Dara turned and shook her head at her mother and sister. Even though she'd seen it many times before, she never got used to the sight of the hope draining from their faces. Angel left the room.

'I'd better go and pack,' Dara told her mother.

'What if the hospital rings while you're gone?' Mrs Flood said in a low voice, not looking at her.

'Ring me. I'll come home. Straight away.'

'You mightn't be able to get a flight in time.'

'There's lots of flights. I'll make it home. I promise.'

Neither of them commented on the likelihood or otherwise of the hospital ringing during Dara's brief absence. With Angel's meagre levels of hope at the moment, it seemed important that they guard their stock jealously.

'It's a waste of time and money. Going to Paris,' Mrs Flood said, shaking her head.

'It mightn't be.'

'You won't find him.'

'I might.'

'Even if you do, he won't agree to help Angel.'

'If we don't ask, we'll never know.'

Mrs Flood opened her mouth to throw out another argument, then seemed to think better of it and closed it again. She sighed instead, a long-drawn-out sigh that rattled through her like a train. She looked tired.

Dara sat beside her. 'What have we got to lose?' she said.

Mrs Flood shook her head. 'You just seem so . . .' she struggled to find the word, '. . . determined,' she finished. 'It's almost like you think you *will* find him and that he *will* be a match for Angel and of course agree to donate one of his kidneys to her. It's so . . . unlike you.'

'I know,' said Dara, surprised at herself.

'So, why?' Mrs Flood looked at Dara like she really wanted to know.

'I just want things to be better,' said Dara.

'Better than what?' Mrs Flood asked, picking at a loose thread on her cardigan.

'Better than this,' Dara said simply.

Mrs Flood just nodded. There didn't seem to be anything else to say.

41

Stanley had a busy week, what with doing background research on Ian Harte, taking photographs of Teresa Trinkets Traynor (he got a lovely one of her swinging a golf stick in a very professional manner with arms that were not up to their elbows in plaster of Paris, as they were supposed to be, according to her statement of claim), making sure Isabelle Dupoint was still registered at the address printed on the bail form, and celebrating with Sissy, who declared her period of heartbreak over 'the cad who must not be named, aka Duncan' to be officially *at an end*. It had been exactly a year and a day since Duncan told Sissy that the relationship had 'run its course'. Exactly a year and a day since Sissy's dreams of acquiring a genuine Dolce and Gabbana watch were scuppered. And a year and a day since she had had any *nookie*, as she liked to call it.

'Christ, I'm as horny as a dog with two dicks,' she told Stanley, leaning against the dishwasher, which had a tendency to thrash about in rather a frantic manner during the final stages of its cycle, before reaching a shuddering climax and falling suddenly silent, leaving the kitchen as quiet as several mice. 'I need to get the ride, and double-quick,' she added, in a way that might have been suggestive if she'd been speaking to anyone other than Stanley Flinter.

Stanley offered his brother Lorcan's services in this regard. Sissy considered the notion briefly before dismissing it out of hand. 'Men who talk about sex are, in my opinion, usually substandard bedfellows, am I right?' Before Stanley got a chance to respond to that bald statement, Sissy swept on. 'It's the quiet ones you have to watch out for.' She looked Stanley up and down as if she hadn't eaten in days and he were a plate of bangers and mash (her favourite dinner).

Stanley backed away from the hungriness of her gaze.

'Don't worry, Stanley,' she told him, reaching for a banana and peeling it slowly before wrapping her mouth around the tip of it. 'Your virtue is safe with me. Besides, I'd say you could classify yourself as a virgin again, with all the action your lad has had over the past fifteen months, wha?' She nodded towards Stanley's crotch as she spoke, and he covered the area with the tea towel he was drying the dishes with. 'Not even *I* would take advantage of you in your current state. You'd be rusty as a nail.'

By Wednesday night, Sissy's celebrations had slowed from raucous to what was, for her, low-key. She was making cocktails in the kitchen (Sex On the Beach and Slippery Nipples), in one of Stanley's shirts. The longest one she could find, which still barely covered the cheeks of her bottom. Due to the excessive nature of her celebrations over the past week, she had neglected her laundry, and all her clothes were in either the washing machine, the laundry basket, the tumble dryer or a dirty heap on her bedroom floor.

So Stanley arrived home that Wednesday night with quite a bit to do, given that he had allowed his paperwork to slide and hadn't thought much about the Paris trip, other than a persistent image of Dara Flood in a red dress at the top of the Eiffel Tower.

'I was going to bring that to Paris,' he said to Sissy, nodding at his shirt, which, frankly, looked better on Sissy than it did on him.

'No, you weren't,' she told him bluntly. 'I've packed your bag for you and I've locked the case. I'll give you the key just before you leave in the morning.'

'But . . .'

'And I've set out what you're wearing tomorrow on your bed. I've even ironed the shirt, and you know how much I hate ironing.'

Stanley nodded. He did know. Sissy went to great lengths to avoid ironing, including putting her clothes under the mattress of her bed at night in the hope that the weight of the mattress, added to the weight of her own heavy-boned body, would be enough to encourage the creases out of them.

Sissy handed Stanley a cocktail and took hers into the sitting room, where she lay across the breadth of the couch and began to manicure her toenails. Because her feet were so big – she bought size 8s, but really, there would have been fewer blisters if she plumped for 9s – it was essential that her toenails were filed, polished and painted at all times to lend her feet (planks, her mother called them) an acceptable level of femininity.

'You look tired, Stanley,' she told him, looking up. 'Here, sit on the couch and blow on my toes. That'll relax you.'

Stanley *did* need something to relax him, worried now as he was about what Sissy might have packed for him. It would not be wrong to describe her taste in clothes as *eclectic*. He sat down as Sissy lay back on the couch, both feet hovering under his chin, and began to blow.

'And I've put six albums on your iPod that I just know Dara will love. In case she wants to listen to some music on the flight. People can tell a lot about you from your taste in music, you know,' said Sissy.

'If that's true, you have a lot of questions to answer,' Stanley told her. 'I cannot *believe* that Air Supply made so many albums.'

'Twenty-one in total,' Sissy said, as proud as if she had produced each one of them herself. 'But Dara Flood is not an Air Supply kind of a woman,' she added.

'How do you know?'

'I just know.'

'But how can you be so sure?' This was a question Stanley often asked Sissy.

'I just know,' said Sissy.

Stanley envied Sissy her certainty. In a world full of questions and doubts, there was something about her conviction that felt, to Stanley, somehow reassuring.

'I'm a girl, amn't I?' she said. 'I might have shovels for hands and planks for feet, but I'm still a girl.'

'Anyway, it really doesn't matter. This is a business trip,' he reminded her, and not for the first time either.

'It's Paris in the springtime,' said Sissy, with bored conviction.

'It's work,' said Stanley.

'It's time,' said Sissy.

Stanley gave up. There was nothing else to do in the face of Sissy's persistent omniscience.

Stanley gave Sissy back her feet, all ten nails dry as a bone and the exact same jade green as her hairband. She had been aiming for 'cute', but Stanley didn't find it cute. He found it endearing.

'I'm going to make your favourite dinner,' he told her, scanning the room for Clouseau before rising from the couch. In spite of the dog's new-found ability to 'stay', he had developed the sneaky habit of ambushing Stanley from behind, leaping up on him and manhandling him to the ground, feeling perfectly within his rights to do so, as Stanley never had the wherewithal – or the time – to tell him to 'stay' before he pounced.

'Bangers and mash?' Sissy asked making sure Stanley remembered, even though he never forgot.

'Of course,' he said.

'Shop-bought sausages or those other yokes?' Sissy wasn't fond of Stanley's home-made sausages. There were a lot of *bits* in them (herbs and garlic). They made her feel *uneasy*, she said.

'Shop-bought,' he assured her.

'Why?'

Stanley shrugged. 'Because we're supposed to be celebrating your mended heart and because you're my best friend, and maybe even because your toes look like they've got some kind of fungal infection.'

Sissy wriggled her toes as she studied them. 'They do a bit, don't they?'

'This is a better colour,' said Stanley, handing her a bottle of Petal Pink. 'And it has the added advantage of matching your new sandals, see?'

Sissy nodded and reached for the nail polish remover, the cotton balls and her foam toe-separator.

'You'll make someone a lovely wife someday,' she told him.

'So will you,' he said, padding barefoot into the kitchen.

'Ha!' roared Sissy, arranging herself along the full length of the couch. 'Sure, who'd be man enough for the likes of me?'

Luckily Stanley didn't have to answer that question, because (a) he guessed that it was rhetorical, and (b) the doorbell rang.

'I'll get it!' Sissy called.

Stanley reached for a bag of new potatoes and began washing the muck off them. Sissy wasn't a great fan of vegetables, but he'd bought sugar snaps, which he decided to sweat in a pan with a knob of real butter and fresh mint. He thought she might like them. And the fact that they were a vegetable with the word 'sugar' in it might help too.

From the kitchen, he could hear Sissy talking. And then another voice. A female voice. High. Breathy. Carefree. It was Cora.

'Oh, I thought you had your kickboxing class tonight,' he heard Cora say, making no effort to disguise the disappointment in her voice.

'I gave that up. It was giving me terrible bulgy muscles in my calves, so it was.' There was silence for a moment, and Stanley suspected that Cora was inspecting Sissy's calves, which, he had to admit, had become a little overdeveloped since the kick-boxing classes began.

'So, how are the plans for the happily-ever-afters coming along?' Sissy enquired.

'Oh, you know, fine, the usual headaches . . . Is, eh, Stanley around?'

In the kitchen, Stanley scrubbed his hands with washing-up liquid in a vain attempt to eliminate the smell of potato skin. He dried them quickly and sniffed at them. Still a vague trace of potato, but it was too late to do anything about it. Cora stepped into the kitchen. She looked tired. Still beautiful, of course, but tired. And wearing a lot more make-up than usual, he felt.

'Cora, hello,' he said, dropping the fork that was in his hand as he stepped forward to . . . what? Shake her hand? Briefly kiss her on the cheek? Or perhaps pat her shoulder in a robust brotherly fashion? He still hadn't learned the protocol for such greetings with ex-girlfriends-cum-brother's-fiancées. Except now it didn't matter, because all he could think about was the searing pain in the sole of his right foot. He looked down. The fork's prongs were embedded in the fleshy softness of the skin at the base of his big toe. He managed not to cry out, but couldn't avoid a strangled yelp as he pulled the prongs out of his foot. Four bright red drops of blood rose from his skin in a perfect line, equidistant from each other. If it hadn't been for the agony, he might have admired the perfection of the wound. Still, it got him over the hump of the most appropriate way of greeting Cora, so he supposed it was worth it.

'Stanley! Are you all right?' She crouched over his foot, examining it from a position that was sufficiently far – Stanley hoped – to be out of range of any foot odours that could be forgiven for lingering there, after a day spent in socks and trainers shadowing Teresa Trickets Traynor around various beauty salons, restaurants and boutiques until he finally hit his target when she headed for the driving range. Still, he pulled his foot back from Cora's inspection and backed up until he bumped against the door of the fridge, leaving little pinpricks of blood across the whiteness of the ceramic tiles and doing his best to ignore the screaming indignation of his foot.

'I'm grand, not a bother, how are you?' Stanley often found that the best way of deflecting attention from himself was to ask people about themselves. People, he found, liked talking about themselves. And to this rule, Cora was no exception. In fact, she *was* the rule.

'Oh, me? Well, I suppose I'm hanging in there, in spite of the fact that Cormac has left all the engagement party organisation to me, which I'm supposed to do while minding a baby and tending to Cormac's every bloody need.'

'Where is Baby Cora then?' asked Sissy, who had followed Cora into the kitchen. Stanley shot her a warning look, which Sissy chose to ignore. She folded her arms and waited for Cora to answer.

'She's at Brenda's house. Brenda insisted on minding her while I did a few errands.'

'And what errand can we help you with?' Sissy pressed on.

'I . . . I think I left my scarf here. The other night. I was wondering if you found it?'

Sissy shot Stanley a rather triumphant I-told-you-so look before marching to the storage cupboard under the stairs.

'It's in the bottom drawer of the tallboy, actually,' Stanley told her.

'Oh,' said Sissy, opening the drawer. 'You folded it.' She shot Stanley a disappointed look before she handed the scarf to Cora. 'There you go,' she said. 'I'm not surprised you came back for it. You must be frozen in that get-up.'

Cora looked down at herself and shrugged. It was only then that Stanley noticed her 'get-up', as Sissy put it. A short skirt. A very short one that showcased the tautness of her thighs and the lengthy slenderness of her legs. A low-cut top, the bottom of it riding up to reveal a flat tanned stomach that told no tales of pregnancy. The material strained against the detail of her ribcage, gathered against the narrowness of her waist and sloped off her shoulders revealing the perfectly straight line of her collar bone, which jutted against the softness of her skin with a terrible kind of beauty.

Stanley distracted himself by dabbing at the spots of blood on the floor with some kitchen paper.

'Anything else we can help you with?' Sissy asked.

Stanley stood up and placed himself firmly between the two women in his kitchen. He knew Sissy was just being his friend, but despite what Sissy thought, Cora was no match for her protectiveness when it was at full throttle. He couldn't bear Cora's discomfort as she shifted from one foot to the other in the kitchen, fingering the tassels on her scarf. She had a way of looking vulnerable that made him feel somehow to blame for everything that had gone before.

'Why don't you join us for dinner?' Stanley said. 'There's more than enough for three.'

Cora turned the full beam of her smile on him, making him blink in its glare. 'What are you having?' she asked.

'Bangers and mash,' Stanley told her. 'And some sugar snaps.'

'Sugar snaps?' Sissy said, disappointed.

'You'll like them, Sissy.'

'Do you promise?'

'Yes,' said Stanley.

'No,' said Cora.

Sissy turned to her. 'Do you mean no, I won't like sugar snaps? Or no, you can't stay for dinner?' she asked.

'I'm sorry, Stanley, I'd love to stay, but I really should be getting back to the baby,' said Cora, ignoring Sissy completely. 'I just wondered . . . if I might have a word with you?'

'Of course,' Stanley said, concentrating on pouring boiling water into a pot and seasoning it rather too much. He hated an audience when he was cooking. He liked to do it alone. It relaxed him.

'No, I mean . . . in private,' Cora muttered, sliding a glance towards Sissy.

No one spoke for a moment. Then Stanley looked at Sissy, who nodded and moved towards the door. 'Call me if you need me,' she told Stanley, although the words were really directed at Cora. A warning shot across her bow. No funny business. Cora responded by closing the kitchen door.

'Drink?' Stanley asked, opening the fridge door and extracting two cold bottles of Corona.

'You remembered.'

'What?'

'Corona. My favourite beer. Do you have a piece of . . . ?'

But Stanley had already quartered a lime and wedged a piece down the narrow neck of the bottle. He hated himself for being the type of person who remembered details like these. Or being the type of person who didn't pretend to forget them.

'What did you want to talk to me about?' he asked, sitting down.

'Well, it's a little . . . delicate.' Cora began peeling the label off the bottle of beer. It was her habit, Stanley remembered, when she needed time to choose her words.

'Go on.'

'It's just . . . well . . . I'm having doubts, I suppose. Second thoughts, even.' Cora, who had lowered her head during this sentence, now peered up at him through a gap in her fringe. Her green eyes gleamed like a cat's in the dark.

Stanley reached for a neutral tone. 'Why are you telling me this?'

'What?' He could tell from her expression that this was not the reaction she'd expected.

'This is something you should talk to Cormac about,' he went on, before his resolve faltered. 'He's the father of your baby. Your . . . fiancé. You should be speaking to him.'

The bitterness of Cora's laugh took Stanley by surprise. 'Talk to Cormac? You know what that fella is like. Too busy shooting bad guys and shooting pool with the good guys to notice that I might need him.'

Stanley forced himself to stand up. There was a good distance between them. He could do this. 'This is not appropriate, Cora. Cormac is my brother, and—'

'He didn't put too much stock by that when you and I were together.'

And there it was. The truth. It smarted, like a crusty scab picked to reveal the cut underneath. The weeping wound. Cormac's carelessness. That's what hurt. That's what he couldn't let go of.

Stanley forced himself back into the conversation. Of course, he could have said 'Neither did you, as I recall', but he didn't. He didn't have it in him.

'That's in the past now,' he said, quietly.

'Don't you ever wonder?' Cora asked.

'What?'

'What it would have been like if we'd stayed together. Had a baby together. Moved in together. Got married even.'

Stanley shook his head and moved towards the door, his hand reaching for the handle, nearly there. He was so close.

But then Cora began to cry. Quietly at first. Turning quickly into a crescendo of sobs that drowned out even the angry roar of the extractor fan.

Stanley stood there, unsure of what to do next. Cora, on the other hand, did not hesitate. She stood up and sort of threw herself towards him, her long arms wrapped around his neck and her tears soaking into the hot skin of his neck. It was an uncomfortable sensation – itchy and gooey – and he struggled against the temptation to pull her off him and see to his neck with a towel.

Cora continued to cry, clinging to him like a limpet on a rock. All Stanley could do was stand there, his arms hanging by his sides. Through the fine mesh of Cora's hair, he saw the pot of potatoes, the water splashing over the sides like waves and extinguishing the gas flame underneath. His eyes moved to the clock. He'd promised Sissy he'd have her fed and watered in time for her date with Raymond – a sports journalist with a sideline in obituaries – at eight o'clock.

'It's *not* a date,' she'd insisted. 'I don't go on *dates* with men called *Raymond*. It's . . . unseemly.'

But it *was* a date. Her first date in a year and a day. Stanley wanted to make sure she didn't go on an empty stomach. Sissy had a tendency to get contrary when she was hungry. And a little more forthright than usual. Neither of these attributes were suitable first-date components, Stanley felt. He decided to count to ten. Slowly. Maybe Cora would have stopped crying by then?

And what if she hasn't, his inner voice – also contrary and forthright, regardless of food intake – asked.

Five . . . six . . . seven . . . Stanley would think about that when he got to ten.

Eight . . . nine . . .

Just as he reached *ten*, Cora did three things:

1. She stopped crying.
2. She released her rugby-tackle hold on his neck to accommodate a rummage about her person for a tissue – Stanley handed her one from a box of Kleenex on the counter – and she wiped the mascara tracks off her cheeks. Stanley

could tell that it was supposed to be waterproof mascara, by the disgusted way she looked at the black smudges on the tissue.

And then . . .

3. She kissed him.

Not like before. Not like that barely-there kiss at the corner of his mouth. The soft one. The one that blurred the lines between platonic and inappropriate. There was nothing blurred – or platonic – about this kiss. It *reeked* of inappropriate. It was hard. Insistent. Full-on. A tongue-and-gum kiss. An in-your-face kiss. There was nothing barely-there about this kiss. It was just . . . there, and for a moment, Stanley did nothing. Just stood, arms hanging down his sides, the box of tissues clamped in one hand. Later, when he thought back on it, he wondered why he didn't react immediately. What had he been thinking of? He couldn't remember. It was like, for a moment, someone had flicked a switch in his brain and turned everything off.

A power failure.

A system meltdown.

It was only when Cora's hand snaked down his body and reached for the zipper on his jeans that he came to.

He dropped the box of tissues and placed his hands firmly on Cora's shoulders, applying pressure until she came away from him with a wet sucking sound. He looked at her. Her cheeks were flushed and her eyes were filled with the kind of light that was hard to look at without squinting. All traces of her earlier crying jag were gone. In fact, she was smiling. At him. She *smiled* at him.

'Cora, I think you'd better . . .'

'I'm going to go now, Stanley,' she told him, still smiling. A knowing smile. 'I'll see you on Saturday.'

'But . . .'

'I can't cancel it now. Not at this late stage. It's all been arranged. There's a lot of people coming. I can't let them down.'

The way Cora said it, it sounded perfectly plausible. Practical, even.

The door opened, and Sissy walked in. 'Sorry, I was just wondering about dinner. I think I can smell something burning in here?'

She was right. The sausages. Stanley had forgotten about them, and now they sat under the grill, blackened and useless for anything other than the bin. Even Clouseau would refuse to consider them.

'I was just leaving,' said Cora, winking at Stanley and giving Sissy the benefit of her full-strength all-American smile. Sissy had to step back from the force of it. 'We can continue our discussion some evening next week, if you're free,' called Cora, in the sitting room now.

'No, I mean, the thing is . . .'

But just like that, Cora was gone.

42

The last time Dara Flood had been at the airport was for a trip she made with Angel to a salsa-dancing show in London. It was before the streptococcal throat. Before the discovery of the one kidney. Before everything changed. Snippets of the trip came back to Dara, as she sat on a hard plastic seat in the airport and waited for Stanley Flinter.

Celebrity-spotting down the King's Road. Angel knew them all. 'Oh look, isn't that Nick Bateman?'

'Who?' Dara asked, squinting at the back of a tall man with short dark hair, carrying clusters of shopping bags – the nice kind – in both hands.

'Y'know yer man,' said Angel, taking out her phone to get a picture of him. 'He was evicted from the first *Big Brother* house. Remember?'

Dara shook her head.

'You *do* remember,' Angel insisted. 'Nasty Nick. That's what they called him.'

'Oh yeah,' said Dara, as a muffled bell rang in her head. The thing was, Angel never watched *Big Brother*. She hardly ever watched television, in fact. She never had time before, in the life that bulged with all the things she did. But she knew stuff like that anyway. She put it down to sublimation.

Their visit to Bountiful Brides in Knightsbridge. Angel had made the appointment six months before, and even though there was a two-year waiting list, they got in. 'Joan Collins cancelled,' she explained, as she dragged Dara by the hand up the marble staircase of the boutique.

'We're both getting married,' Angel explained to the tiny but ferocious woman at the reception desk, even though this wasn't true. Neither of them was getting married. Neither of them was even engaged. But they spent two hours in the shop, hoisting each other into huge, unwieldy dresses, taking pictures with Angel's camera and drinking the champagne that the tiny but ferocious woman proffered – albeit resentfully, as if she knew – on a silver tray. She was a professional, that woman. She didn't bat an eyelid when Angel practised her vows to her reflection in an ornate mirror that could have come from the props department of *Sleeping Beauty*. Dara had the best photograph framed. It was in her room. On her bedside locker. The pair of them wrapped around each other, veils down, matching tiaras clinking together like a toast at a reception. Through the veil, you can see the smiles. Huge. All teeth and no lips. Dara remembered her face and how it ached with all the laughing they did that day.

'We'll have to think about it,' Angel told the tiny but ferocious woman before the pair of them ran down the stairs, in their ordinary clothes again, out into the ordinary world that now looked like a promised land that Dara had been to once.

Getting attacked by the pigeons in Trafalgar Square, the pair of them running around like lunatics, screaming, 'The birds, the birds!'

Salsa-dancing with strangers in the dark throb of a club in Soho, Angel calling over the shoulder of her partner – a tall, dark, handsome affair of a man – to Dara, 'Is it yerself?'

Riding the Tube and getting out at places with ridiculous names, just to see what life might be like there. Places like Goodge Street and Dollis Hill, Blackfriars and Swiss Cottage.

Silly things, really.

*   *   *

'Dara?' Dara snapped her head up and focused on the face of Stanley Flinter. He bent towards her. 'Are you all right?' he asked.

'Yes, I'm fine,' she said, standing up.

Stanley's smile had the tight, tired aspect of someone who had not slept well.

'How are you?' Dara asked him. She had to incline her head – but only slightly – to see his face. He looked like he'd been assembled rather than dressed, and she realised it was only because everything matched. A navy cord jacket over a dark blue shirt and a pair of skinny jeans that made his legs look long. Well long-*er,* at any rate. Tintin was right about that.

For a moment, it looked like Stanley Flinter was going to tell her something. Dara saw it in his hesitation before he replied with a carefully offhand, 'Fine.'

He reached for Dara's bag, lifting it.

'I'll carry that,' Dara said.

'No, I've got it. It's no weight at all.'

'I printed out our boarding passes, so we can just go straight to the departure gate,' Dara told him, checking – and not for the first time – in her bag for her mobile, the boarding cards, her passport and her wallet. Despite the clamour of Dublin Airport all around them, she heard the loud rumble of Stanley's stomach.

'Are you hungry?' she asked him.

'All I need is a coffee,' Stanley told her. 'Clouseau broke the kettle this morning.' He dragged his hand down his face. Dara agreed with him. He looked like a man who needed a coffee.

She consulted her watch. 'If we get through security in less than forty minutes, we'll have time for a coffee. And a rasher butty, if you'd like. I'll treat you.'

'With brown sauce?'

'You can't have a rasher butty without it, can you?'

They managed to get through security in under forty minutes, although only just. The machine beeped every time Stanley walked through it, even after he'd cleared his pockets of keys (attached to a keyring with a photo of Clouseau on it, Dara noticed) two pens, both well chewed at the top; a memory stick; a voucher for a free Fairtrade coffee (out of date by two months, Dara saw); a bottle of nail varnish, with the greenish hue of gangrene ('It's my friend's,' he explained, even though no one had asked); a flattened coconut Snowball ('My dog loves them,' he apologised to the woman, who only nodded in the bored manner of a TV licence inspector who's heard it all before); and a dog leash, the leather of which had been worn to strings by, Dara assumed, Jacques Clouseau.

Even after he had divested himself of these effects, the machine continued to beep and Stanley was removed to a cubicle, flanked by the woman – whose bored expression was now replaced by one of attentive caution – and a huge bear of a man whose hand gripped the tip of a truncheon as if, at any moment, it might be required. This man disappeared into the cubicle with Stanley, and the woman yanked at the curtain, shielding them from Dara's view.

Dara set her bag on the ground, raised her hand to her mouth and began to worry at her fingernails with her teeth. The curtain at the cubicle twitched and jerked, and at one point Stanley's hand poked out around the edge of it before disappearing again. Eventually the curtain was pulled back and Stanley reappeared, his face like a sunset after a long, hot day.

This time, when he walked – gingerly now – through the machine, it made no sound. The woman – her bored expression once again covering her face – handed him a plastic bag and nodded towards the cubicle.

'I'll be back in a moment,' Stanley whispered to Dara, who took her fingers out of her mouth long enough to ask, 'Is everything all right?'

'Christ, I'm sorry about that, Dara,' Stanley finally managed when they sat down at a café with their coffees and rasher butties smothered in brown sauce.

Dara, who had decided not to question him about the cubicle, found that her curiosity got the better of her. 'What was in that plastic bag?' she couldn't help asking.

The sunset reappeared on Stanley's face, making Dara regret the question.

'Well, the thing is . . .' He bent his head to his coffee and made a great production of sweetening it, shaking the sachet of brown sugar several times, before opening it and pouring it in, then stirring and stirring. He'd still be there, stirring, Dara felt, had she not reached over and removed the spoon from his fingers.

'It's all right. We're here now. We got through,' she told him.

'It was my Y-fronts,' he said then, looking up for the first time.

'Y-fronts?' Dara wouldn't call her knowledge of men's underwear encyclopaedic, but she felt sure that a man of Stanley Flinter's vintage – she guessed he was about thirty – should not be wearing Y-fronts. Or at least should not *admit* to wearing them. She surprised herself by giggling, as she was not usually given to giggling. The sound was strange, for its rarity and its girlishness. She felt that Tintin – who was always at her to *get girlie* - would approve.

'Well, they're not actually called Y-fronts. They're called something fancier than that. I can't remember what. But that's in fact what they are. They're Y-fronts.'

Dara could see the person at the next table straining to overhear them. She leaned across towards Stanley. She knew she should let it go. She normally would. But she had to know. 'Why were they in a plastic bag?' she asked.

'Sissy bought me these new ones, and . . .'

'Sissy buys your underpants?' Dara decided to say underpants instead of Y-fronts. She thought it might sound less offensive. It didn't.

'She buys nearly all my clothes. She insists.'

'Well, that's . . . decent of her, I suppose.'

'I've asked her not to. She charges me for everything. Even the ones I don't like. Then gets offended if I don't wear them.' Stanley's brown eyes looked as serious as a car crash, but there was the beginning of a smile flickering about the corner of his mouth, which brought Dara's attention to bear on the dimple – just the one – that dented his cheek.

'Anyway,' Stanley continued, 'the security woman told me that they're designer. The Y-fronts, I mean. They've got this metal bit on them. With the brand. I don't remember which one. Anyway, that's what made the machine beep, apparently.'

'Designer underpants,' said Dara with a smile. 'At least you can hold your head high if you're ever rushed to hospital in an emergency-type situation.'

Stanley smiled back. 'I wondered why they were so bloody expensive,' he said. They both laughed, but in the pause that followed, Dara felt she should change the subject. A conversation about underpants – designer or otherwise – didn't seem appropriate, somehow.

Dara had never travelled first-class. Neither had Stanley, as it turned out. They both agreed that it would be difficult to return to economy after the experience. First, there were the seats. Wider. Softer. With lots of leg room, even though they felt that the extra space was wasted on them, being individuals with not much call for lots of leg room. Without mentioning it, Dara made sure she sat beside Stanley's good ear, which meant that he got the window seat. Which was good. Dara did not like to be reminded how far off the ground she was.

'Don't forget to switch it off,' Stanley told Dara, as she checked her mobile phone for any missed calls or messages.

Dara sighed and ran her thumb across the screen of her phone.

'Even if Angel or your mother rings during the flight, there's nothing you can do about it until you get to Paris, right?' Stanley said, reaching for the phone, his fingers hovering over the 'off' button. He smiled a coaxing sort of a smile at Dara. She nodded and he turned the phone off and returned it to her. There was a kind of relief in that. Like a red light at a busy intersection when you're late. Nothing to be done but sit and wait.

Then there was the breakfast.

'Would you and your boyfriend like some champagne?' The air hostess smiled at them.

Stanley – who was reading his free newspaper – didn't hear her.

'Oh . . . no . . . he's not my boyfriend,' Dara told her.

'Oh, right, sorry about that,' she said, looking towards Stanley. Her expression suggested that she was genuinely sorry he wasn't Dara's boyfriend. 'So does that mean you don't want any champagne?'

'Eh . . .' began Dara.

'It's free.' The air hostess leaned towards Dara and delivered this gem in a conspiratorial whisper, which caught Stanley's attention despite the timbre of her voice.

They both indulged. 'It would be a waste not to,' said Dara, coughing as the bubbles went up her nose.

'I wouldn't normally drink at breakfast,' admitted Stanley, taking a huge slug of bubbly. 'And especially not champagne. But this stuff isn't bad at all.'

'That's because it's free,' Dara told him. 'Free stuff always tastes better.'

With the fizz of the champagne and the distraction of the food and the talking they did, Dara forgot that she was a nervous flyer. She found herself telling Stanley about Lucky. How he seemed to think Dara was going to make things alright for him. Find him his home, against all evidence to the contrary. How optimistic the dog turned out to be, filled with generous dollops of hope and expectation, at odds with everything that must have happened to him before, given the condition he arrived in. Dara had taken him for a bowl-half-empty kind of a dog. She'd been wrong about that.

Stanley in turn volunteered information about Sissy and her heart that she now declared 'mended', and her date with a man called Raymond last night that turned out to be a disaster on account of her discovery of a tendency Raymond had of picking wax out of his ear with the tip of his front door key.

When the plane began to bank towards Charles de Gaulle, Dara sat forward in her seat, her back rigid and her hands gripping the armrests.

'What's happening?' she asked in a whisper, forgetting about Stanley's ear.

'Pardon?' Stanley turned towards her and Dara realised that he looked, not at her eyes when he spoke to her, as people usually did, but at her mouth. She clamped her lips together to stop them shaking.

'The plane,' she said. 'It feels . . . funny.'

'We're descending, that's all,' Stanley told her.

'Already?'

'Look.' He pointed at the window and Dara leaned across him and looked. And there it was. Paris in the springtime. She was able to pick out the monuments, and for a moment, it felt like someplace she had been before. Someplace familiar. From this height, the Eiffel Tower looked like a souvenir of it-self. Something you'd buy at one of those gaudy tourist shops. The Seine reached its way through the city, as wide and as slow as her memory of Angel's smile. And somewhere further out, towards the suburbs to the south, was the Rue de Ste

Jeanne d'Arc, where a woman called Isabelle Dupoint might be sitting in a kitchen, dipping a croissant into a bowl of coffee and smiling across a table at a man called Mr Flood.

A noise distracted Dara. A grinding noise, loud and dangerous.

'That's just the wheels coming down for landing,' Stanley told her before she had to ask.

Despite the time that had elapsed since Dara's last plane trip, she remembered – much too clearly – everthing about the landing. The worst bit of the journey. The awkward angle of it. The ground rushing up at her. The screech of the brakes, backpedalling against the rigid tarmac of the runway. The bumping of the wheels before they managed to gain purchase on the ground. The breakneck speed of the plane towards the terminal building. And then the sudden, glorious quiet as the plane slowed almost to a stop, then turned and strolled the rest of the way, Dara felt, as if trying to make up for the terror that had gone before. It was only when it got to this part that Dara realised she was holding Stanley Flinter's hand. Gripping it, in fact. When she let go, there were white patches on his hand where her fingers had been.

'Sorry about that,' she whispered. 'I'm . . . it's just I'm a bit of a nervous flyer.'

'Don't worry about it,' said Stanley. 'Cora used to do that. She wasn't a big fan of landing, either.'

'Cora? Your brother's fiancée?'

'Eh . . . yes.'

'I see,' said Dara, even though she didn't see at all.

'No . . . well, I suppose that sounds a bit weird, but . . . the thing is . . . is that Cora and I used to go out.'

'Oh,' said Dara.

'It was a long time ago now,' Stanley added. 'A lot of water under the bridge since then. You know, with the baby. Cora junior. She's a dote, so she is. And they're getting engaged. Did I tell you that?'

'You mentioned it. The party's on Saturday, isn't it?'

'Yes.'

Dara didn't ask any more questions, although she wanted to. She found herself suddenly curious about this man beside her. She found herself wondering why she'd never wondered about him before.

43

Stanley decided that Miss Pettigrew was right about the hotel. She'd Facebooked him, declaring it to be *swanky*. Just off the Place de la Concorde, it was a building that looked small from the street but felt huge inside, with marble surfaces and complicated chandeliers, and doormen and porters that looked like they were going to a fancy dress party, and chambermaids with long skinny legs and short frilly pinafores, and the distant din of the city that crept in, like smoke, whenever the front doors opened. From his room – which was next door to Dara's – Stanley could see the Champs-Elysées, the Arc de Triomphe towering over the western tip of it. He remembered Cora slouched against the monument, her arms crossed, waiting. He'd wanted to see the Tomb of the Unknown Soldier, underneath the arch. Take a picture maybe. Say something. Just in his head. Not a prayer exactly, just . . . something. He'd wanted to climb the 284 steps to the top. Take in the panoramic view of Paris that he'd read about in the guidebook.

'Come on, Stanley. The shops will be closed.'

'Don't worry. They're open till six,' he told her. He knew. He'd checked.

'That only gives me two hours.' She gripped his face with both hands. 'Please, Stanley? Will you come?' And he went. He'd been younger then. More optimistic. He thought it might make a difference, all this compromising. But in the end, it didn't make any difference. None whatsoever.

The knock on the door startled him and he turned from the window and the view it offered and the memory it threw up.

It took him a moment to recognise Dara Flood. He'd forgotten about the dress. The red dress. The one she'd promised Miss Pettigrew she'd wear at the top of the Eiffel Tower. His English teacher had been right after all. Because Dara Flood in a red dress was nothing like he'd imagined her. Without her usual layers of clothing, she looked slighter than he'd imagined, her arms and legs longer, her skin smooth and white, set against the black of her hair and the dark navy of her eyes, long rather than wide. The dress was a halterneck. Sissy had one with straps that wound around her neck and he was almost positive she'd called it a halterneck. The style was perfect for Dara, emphasising the slender length of her neck, and the, eh . . . In fairness to Stanley Flinter, he *did* try not to notice Dara's breasts, but it was difficult. They pushed against the soft fabric of the dress, high and firm and – quite frankly – a lot more ample than he would have thought, had he thought about such things before now, which, he felt sure, he had not. Even though the dress was not tight and fell, rather than clung, down her body to her knees, he could see that he'd been right about her hips. The curve of them *was* gentle. That much was obvious to even the most casual observer.

'Dara,' he said, and it came out like a question rather than a greeting.

Dara's head whipped up and down the corridor.

'I know I look ridiculous in this get-up. Especially at this hour of the day. But if I don't wear it, I'll have to bring it with me and then find someplace to change and . . .'

'No, no, you don't look a bit ridiculous,' Stanley managed. 'You look . . .' He struggled for the most appropriate thing to say. But in the end, all he came up with was, 'Very nice. You look very nice.' He couldn't even stop at saying it the once. No, he had to go ahead and repeat it. In his head, he could already hear Sissy taking the stairs two at a time, grabbing the pillows and beating him senseless with them.

'I'll probably freeze. The material is a little . . . flimsy.'

'Do you have a cardigan? You could wear that.' Stanley saved Sissy the bother this time and delivered two swift – albeit imaginary – kicks to his own head.

'I suppose I could wear my hoodie.'

And then Stanley remembered where they were. 'You won't need your hoodie. It's sunny out. It's 22 degrees.'

'That's pretty hot, isn't it?'

Stanley nodded. He pulled the collar of his shirt away from the clammy heat of his neck. It *was* pretty hot.

'I'll just grab my room key and I'll be right with you,' he said. Dara nodded at him. Was she wearing make-up? He didn't think so. As far as he remembered, her eyelashes had always been that long and dark.

Hadn't they?

With the distraction of the dress, it was hard to remember anything.

He supposed they could be false eyelashes. Although he didn't think so. They looked nothing like the ones Sissy sometimes wore, even though she said they made her look like a transvestite.

Out in the street, Stanley turned to Dara. 'Where do you want to go first?'

There was no hesitation in her reply. 'Isabelle Dupoint's,' she said in a voice that seemed surprised by the question.

Stanley Flinter nodded and consulted his map.

'We can get the Métro to Gare de Juvisy and then a train to Sainte-Geneviève-des-Bois. It looks like the apartment is only two blocks from there.'

Dara nodded and began walking, checking her phone as she went. For a woman who had never been to Paris before, she seemed more sure of herself here, Stanley felt. She looked like she knew exactly where she was going.

He hurried to catch up.

44

Ian Harte was wrong about Paris, Dara decided. It was not overrated. Everything felt exotic. Even the dark, hot smell of the Métro, the thin wheeze of the train through the endless network of black tunnels, the rhythm of languages breaking over her head like waves and the heat of bodies, hundreds of them, like an electrical current, coming up from her feet. She clung on to a rubber grip with one hand and curled the other around the phone in her bag, so she could feel it ring, even if she couldn't hear it. Not that there was any signal way down here. But still. Just in case. In the dense heat of the carriage, home seemed a long way away. She tried not to think about Mrs Flood, waiting for her to return. Or about Angel, who was done with waiting.

Dara bit her lip and concentrated on the Métro map on the wall in front of her. The red dress was like wearing one of Angel's pairs of shoes. It wasn't uncomfortable. It just seemed to present her to the world in a way that she was unused to. A man in a shiny white suit blew in her ear, and when she turned towards him, he ran his tongue along his teeth in a gesture that he must have considered sexy but was most definitely not, not least because of the piece of meat – cured ham, she thought – caught between his premolars. She turned her head from his leer and backed away, stepping on Stanley Flinter's foot.

'Christ, Stanley, I'm really sorry, it's just that . . .' There was a hand on her leg, moving north. Because of the space constraints, she couldn't see who it belonged to. She twitched her leg instead and the hand stopped in its tracks, squeezed her thigh, lifted and was gone.

'Stanley, can you talk to me? Please?'

'What about?' Stanley looked worried, as if she was about to ask him to talk to her about something embarrassing. His Y-fronts, maybe.

'Anything. It's just . . . people are licking their teeth at me and touching my leg.'

'Who?' Stanley pushed his iPhone into the front pocket of his jeans and scanned the crowd.

'I don't know.'

'It's the dress,' Stanley told her.

'Is it slutty? I didn't *think* it was slutty. Oh God, it's slutty, isn't it?'

'It's *not* slutty,' Stanley said, loud enough for a few people to turn in their direction and stare. 'It's . . . nice,' he went on. 'It's a nice dress.'

'You're sure it's not slutty?'

'I'm positive.'

'Thank you.'

'You're welcome.' The formality of their conversation made them both smile.

'So,' Dara went on, 'could you just talk to me? About anything at all? I don't think people will lick their teeth at me and grope my leg if you're talking to me.'

Stanley looked dubious, but nodded and moved as close as he could to Dara without actually touching her, which in fact touched Dara very much. He thought for a moment. 'I could tell you about my brothers, I suppose.'

'Why?' Dara asked.

'Because I have so many of them. That conversation will take us all the way to Gare de Juvisy, at the very least.'

Dara nodded and smiled as Stanley told her about his

brothers. He went through them in age order, from the youngest – Adrian, followed by Neal, Lorcan, Declan and Cormac. Although he never got to tell her anything about Cormac, she noticed. They pulled into the station at the end of a story about Declan, who had bought his wife Cathy a course of laser hair-removal treatment for their first wedding anniversary and spent the next two-and-a-half weeks sleeping in the shed: a listing, leaking excuse of a garden shed with no insulation or electricity but plenty of garden equipment – shears, mower, rakes – covered in thick clouds of spiders' webs, Declan not being the keenest of gardeners. Cathy allowed him to take two things from the house during his exile. He chose a sleeping bag left over from his boy-scouting days and a copy of a book called *The Great Outdoors For Dummies*, left behind by one of Cathy's sisters on a brief visit to their house in between a tour of the African plains and a trek through the Himalayas.

'I was only trying to help,' Declan had pleaded with her after the first week.

In the end, it took a one-carat diamond pendant, a box set of *Grey's Anatomy*, a tin of chocolate Kimberleys (almost impossible to come by at that time of the year), a voucher for a complete makeover at Brown Sugar ('Not that you need it!' he had yelled through the letter box, in a blind panic of second thoughts), a promise of a shopping trip to Kildare Village, during which he would not complain about sore feet or hunger or queueing outside changing rooms or the scorch-marks on his credit card, and a weekend away in a luxury spa hotel with *at least* two treatments per day, neither of which involved anything to do with hair removal.

The experience left Declan broke, bleary-eyed and itchy (turned out that the shed was in fact a haven for most of the local mosquitoes). 'But,' Stanley finished, 'he never reoffended.'

'That sounds pretty harsh,' Dara said, trying not to laugh.

'To be honest, it needed to be done,' said Stanley, who had already alluded to Declan's form when it came to gifts.

The train lurched to a stop, pitching Dara forwards, towards Stanley. She threw her arms wide, her hands reaching for something to hold on to. They landed on Stanley's shoulders, and his hands in turn cupped the gentle curve of her hips in an effort to prevent her falling any further. For a moment they moved together, like dancers. Dara was surprised by how warm Stanley felt. How solid. She recognised his scent, although she couldn't place it. She didn't think it came out of a bottle. A sweet smell, like freshly cut-grass.

'Sorry about that,' Dara said, trying to right herself. It proved difficult, as a knot of people pushed past them, spilling on to the platform like an overturned bottle of fizzy drink.

'We're here,' said Stanley, even though there was no need.

The train to Sainte-Geneviève-des-Bois was a much quieter affair. It hummed along, with its handful of passengers in dark business suits and stiff morning papers. You'd still know you were in Paris, though, Dara felt. A man tore chunks off the top of a baguette clamped under his arm. A woman in a straw hat laughed down a phone and said '*ooh là là*' in a breathy giggle. A schoolboy slouched across a seat, plugged into an iPod. He could have been a teenager anywhere, apart from the beret – part of his school uniform, Dara supposed – perched at an angle on top of his head.

This time, Dara and Stanley got seats.

Stanley didn't tell her about Cormac. His eldest brother. There was no need, Dara supposed. No one in the carriage licked their teeth at her. Or moved their hands northwards up her leg. But even if they had, she felt sure that Stanley would have spoken to her about something else.

The journey was not long. Dara wished it were longer. As

they pulled into the station, she felt a chill, as if someone had touched her neck with cold hands. Stanley packed his map and notes and pen into his backpack and stood up.

'Are you ready?' he asked.

Dara wanted to shake her head, but instead she nodded. She wanted to stay on the train, but she stood up. She wanted to break into a run, in the opposite direction from Rue de Ste Jeanne d'Arc, but she walked, in tandem with Stanley Flinter, towards her destination. It only took five minutes to get to the top of the road.

Dara slowed first, before she stopped completely.

'What's wrong?' asked Stanley. 'Are your shoes hurting you?'

Dara nodded, even though her shoes were not hurting her. They were flat pumps. Miss Pettigrew had advised her to wear heels, but Dara didn't want to and Miss Pettigrew didn't push it, perhaps thinking that she had gone far enough with the dress.

'Could we sit in that park for a while?' Dara asked, pointing to a sliver of green between two towering apartment blocks.

Despite the diminutive size of the park, it boasted a giant chessboard with pieces that came up to Dara's – and Stanley's – knees. Ancient, splintering picnic tables with elderly people crammed down each side, sheltering from the bright glare of the sun and playing cards, betting with old centimes. Tiny dogs panted in the shade of tall, thin trees and summed each other up with studied indifference.

Beside the boules court, there was an empty bench, and Dara sat on it. Stanley sat beside her. They watched an old couple – perhaps a husband and wife – throw boules. They played in silence, but it seemed to Dara like a companionable silence. A silence that spoke of years and years of familiarity. A silence that was like a conversation between them.

'Dara?' Stanley finally said.

'Would you like a coffee?' Dara asked in a rush, nodding towards a café through the trees.

'Well ... I mean, sure, we could have a coffee, but ... wouldn't you prefer to ... keep going? We're nearly there.'

'Tiny ones. Espressos. We'd have them finished before we'd even started, wouldn't we?' Dara was already moving away, not waiting for an answer. The café was more of a kiosk with an awning. She was delighted to find a slow-moving queue that wound its way around the few plastic tables and chairs scattered about, huddling under limp umbrellas, their colours worn down by the sun.

When she got back, one of the tiny dogs had abandoned its patch of shade and was now preoccupied with the task of humping Stanley's shin. The sight made Dara – who was no stranger to the sexual partiality of dogs to human limbs – smile, because Stanley wouldn't shake his leg in an attempt to dislodge the dog, for fear of hurting him, given the dog's size. Instead, he was trying to talk the dog down.

Dara set the espressos on the ground and crouched beside Stanley's shin. She reached for the dog's front paws and gently encouraged them away from their vice-like grip on Stanley's leg, with promises of sticks and bones – in French – and a low clucking sound, deep in her throat. The dog released Stanley with much reluctance and, barking at him, limped away with a lollypop-pink erection that was, at the very least, out of proportion to its tiny body.

'I'm irresistible to all canines,' Stanley said in an effort to deflect his embarrassment.

Dara pretended to study his legs. 'What do you expect?' she asked. 'You *do* have shapely calves.'

'It's a curse,' agreed Stanley, picking up his coffee and arranging himself and his legs on the bench.

The espressos were finished much too quickly, so Dara

had a cigarette. And then another one. She took her time with them, smoking them right down to the quick, taking tiny pulls, so the paper wouldn't burn too quickly. But even with all the delaying, the cigarettes were finally smoked, the coffee gone and the daisy chain that Dara concentrated on finished.

'Dara?' Stanley asked again, only this time Dara couldn't think of anything to do or say to distract them from the task at hand.

'I know,' she said, although she still didn't move.

'We should go,' said Stanley, standing up.

'I know,' she said again. She glanced up. Stanley stood in front of her, looking down. He smiled at her. His slow, sad smile, as if he knew everything and there was no need to explain.

'It's just ...' Dara began, explaining anyway. 'I ... I don't know what to say. Where to start. What if he's there?'

'I doubt if he's there. But Isabelle Dupoint might know where he is, all right.'

'Yes, that's the thing. What if we find him?'

'That would be good, wouldn't it?' Stanley reminded her.

Dara shook her head and said, 'Yes,' at the same time. As an answer, it was a confusing one, but Stanley didn't comment on it. 'It's just ... I mean, he's a stranger to me. Yes, he's my father, but ... I've never met him. What will I say?'

'Something will occur,' was all Stanley said, but there was conviction in the quietness of his tone and Dara felt that he could be right. Something *might* occur. Mightn't it?

Stanley reached out his hand. She took it and he pulled her up.

'Ready?' he asked.

'Ready,' she replied.

45

The apartment block had seen better days. The front door of the building fell open with a long moan when they pushed it, revealing a narrow corridor of a hall with a payphone and several pigeonholes with junk mail sticking out of all of them. On the wall, a panel of buttons with handwritten names scrawled across the mean, narrow strip of paper allocated to each one. The button that Dara pressed made no sound, and after a while she looked at Stanley, who nodded, and they turned towards the lift.

Isabelle Dupoint lived on the tenth floor. Which wouldn't have been such a problem, had the lift been working. They both agreed that the lift probably hadn't worked in a long time. They began to climb.

Each flight of stairs had ten steps. Dara counted them. Ten flights of stairs. Ten steps per flight. One hundred steps in all. As she wound her way up through the body of the building, she concentrated on counting each step. Here and there, noises came at her. A baby crying. A door banging. The clatter of pots and pans. The muted tones of a radio, playing some old, sentimental song. A couple arguing. A man singing. The low throb of a washing machine. And, up near the top, the soft strain of a violin, the bow whispering against the strings in a low murmur of melody.

Eighty-seven.

Eight-eight.

Eighty-nine.

Dara kept going. Behind her she heard Stanley's breath, coming faster now. They climbed in step, their feet making little sound against the worn wood of the floor. At every second landing, a small square of sunlight, thrown by a window set high in the wall. Dara would have liked to stand in one of these little squares. To allow the heat to penetrate her body, warm her, let the light flow over her like water. But she kept going.

Ninety-one.

Ninety-two.

Ninety-three.

She saw the door as she made her way up the last flight of stairs. Like all the other doors. Heavy and dark, with its peephole buried in the wood, like a squinting glass eye. She stopped at the top of the stairs and Stanley bumped into the back of her.

'Sorry,' he whispered.

'That's alright,' she whispered back, edging forward to give him some room.

He nodded towards the door. 'We're here,' he whispered.

'Why are you whispering?' Dara asked him.

'I don't know,' he admitted. 'Why are you?'

'I don't know,' she admitted. And the pair of them laughed like people do when they are trying not to laugh.

It was Stanley who heard it first. 'Ssshh,' he hissed.

Dara looked towards the door. The sound was the clippety-clop of high narrow heels against ceramic tiles. Then keys being picked up, jangling against each other like chimes. More clipping and clopping, closer now. The slow, heavy slide of a bolt through a lock. The turn of a key and then, after all the noise, the door swung wide, making no sound at all. Framed in the doorway, a woman. Possibly the largest woman Dara had ever seen. Gigantic. Not just tall, but wide, too. She had to turn a little to accommodate her bulk through the doorway.

It was difficult to tell if she was a Frenchwoman. Even Tintin could not have called her a *typical* Frenchwoman. She wore her clothes in layers, draped over each other in shades of black and grey that made her look, if possible, even bigger. Even her hair was big; thick and black and bushy and running wild around her face and down her big: padded shoulders, like a garden neglected for years. Pale skin. Chipped red varnish covering long nails. Rings on every finger, the bands dulled and tight againt her skin. A gold locket lost in the deep well of her cleavage, glinting where the light caught it.

She stopped when she saw them.

For a moment nobody spoke.

It was Stanley who stepped forward. Dara's mouth was open as if she were about to speak, but so far no words had come out.

'Eh, bonj-your,' he said, in his halting way. He held his hand out and the woman looked at it, as if she wasn't quite sure what to do with it.

'Eh, noos sums . . . eh . . .' Stanley took a piece of paper out of his back pocket and consulted it, 'enchant-ay de voos . . . eh . . . ron-con-tray.'

Despite the atrocity of his French and the delivery of the sentence in his flat Dublin accent, Dara felt nothing but gratitude for Stanley Flinter. Going to the trouble of writing down something to say to Mme Dupoint. In case he'd been wrong about Dara. In case something did *not* occur.

The woman did not answer Stanley. Instead, she concentrated on Dara. Studied her, like she was a complicated recipe. Under this rapt attention, Dara shifted from one foot to the other and tried to think of something to say. Nothing occurred.

'You are ze daughter of Eugene Flood,' the woman said in a voice that surprised Dara. A small voice. Tender and sweet. It was not a question.

'I'm Dara Flood.' She held out her hand and Isabelle took it. Instead of shaking it, she studied it, running her fingers along the palm.

'You 'ave your father's hands, Dara,' she said, smiling.

Dara felt awkward, standing in a hallway, having her hand examined by a stranger. Isabelle Dupoint did not seem to sense her disquiet. It was like she knew Dara. Like she'd known her for a long time.

'Please,' said Isabelle Dupoint, eventually releasing Dara's hand. 'Come in.' She moved sideways, pressing her back against the door. Even then, Dara knew that there was no way either of them could squeeze past the vastnesss of her body. The width of the doorway simply wouldn't allow it. It took the woman a moment to realise this. She shuffled onto the landing and waved them inside.

The hallway was dark and narrow and would represent a serious challenge to Mme Dupoint, Dara worried, should she gain any more weight. The door at the end led into a bright, spacious living room, which surprised Dara with the delicacy of its furnishings and the softness of its fabrics. The walls were a seashell pink, hung with prints of French impressionists: Monet, Renoir, Manet. Tintin would have been glad about that, the image satisfying his theory about *typical* French people *only* appreciating French art. Dara scanned the room for photographs of Mme Dupoint and her family, but there were none.

Behind her, Dara heard the laboured steps of Mme Dupoint, negotiating the tight confines of the hallway. When she squeezed her way into the living room, she kept walking, motioning at Dara and Stanley to follow her. Out of a door, down another corridor, wider this time, Dara noted with gratitude, to a door that led into a bright, shiny kitchen where one cup, one plate, one spoon and one knife drained on the board beside the sink. Through the kitchen, another door.

Dara could not believe the size of the apartment, being used to Dublin apartments where cats – or even kittens – could not be swung.

Here, Mme Dupoint stopped and rummaged about her person, her layers of clothing jerking up and down with the movement. From a pocket – in either her skirt or one of her cardigans or jackets, Dara couldn't be sure – she pulled a single key. It slid into the keyhole and Mme Dupoint turned it with the ease of someone who had done this many times before. The door opened in one fluid motion and Dara felt her throat constrict, her mouth dry. For a moment, she expected to see Mr Flood, standing inside the room, perhaps smiling at her like he had smiled at her mother that day, the day he walked up the road and never came back. She could nearly hear him saying, *It's well you're lookin', Dara Flood.* But the room was in darkness and Dara could see nothing inside. Mme Dupoint leaned in and pressed a switch. Dara blinked in the sudden rush of light.

The room was tiny, with no furniture other than two hard-backed chairs and a fold-up table, on which sat a deck of cards, a bottle of wine and two crystal wine glasses, cloaked in a thick layer of dust.

'We used to play cards in zis room,' said Mme Dupoint, by way of explanation. Dara was just about to wonder why they had chosen this dark, poky little room to play cards in when Mme Dupoint added, 'Streep pok-air. 'Ave you 'erd of zees game?'

'Oh we have, of course,' Stanley said in the pause that followed. 'We play that all the time in Ireland.' Dara looked at him. 'Don't we, Dara?'

'Well . . .'

'I mean, not *us* exactly,' Stanley went on, pointing at himself and Dara. 'But my brother. Lorcan. *Lorcan* plays it. At least he says he does. It's his favourite card game, in fact.'

Mme Dupoint smiled at Stanley, as if noticing him for the first time.

'Are you Dara's lov-air?' she enquired in the matter-of-fact tone of someone enquiring about the weather.

'Eh, no, no, I'm not as it happens. Dara is my . . .'

Dara looked at Stanley. He had a way of using a lot more words than necessary when he was uncomfortable. She worried about what he was going to say.

'Dara is my friend,' Stanley said, looking at Dara with his thick, bushy eyebrows curved in a question.

Mme Dupoint turned to Dara. Dara knew that she was not a person who made friends easily. Anya informed her that it was because of *attachment* issues, due to her being *abandoned* by her father. Anya had a way of saying things like that and making them seem perfectly reasonable. Almost advantageous. Like having attachment issues was something that Dara had set out to achieve. Anya often nodded encouragement at her and patted her hand when she spoke about Dara's attachment issues.

'Yes,' said Dara, much louder than she intended. She lowered her voice. 'Stanley and I are friends.'

'He ees vairy 'andsome,' Mme Dupoint whispered at Dara. It was a stage whisper, so not only could Stanley hear her, but possibly the next-door neighbours as well. Although Dara had a feeling that the walls of a Parisian apartment might not be as paper-thin as those masquerading as walls in their Dublin counterparts.

'Eh . . . yes,' Dara finally said when it became clear that an answer was expected.

'Now, we shall entair ze womb,' Mme Dupoint told them, with a dramatic flourish of her hands. She led the way inside and sat on one of the hard-backed chairs. The seat of the chair was barely wide enough to accommodate even one of the cheeks of her bottom.

Dara and Stanley followed her.

Once inside, Dara noticed the walls. Every inch was covered in framed photographs. Black and white ones. Sepia-tinted ones. Blurred ones. Faded ones. Some out of focus. But most sharp in their clarity.

In each photograph, Mr Flood.

Mr Flood at the top of the Eiffel Tower.

Mr Flood sitting outside a café in Montmartre, smoking.

Mr Flood walking up the Champs-Elysées, his hands dug into the pockets of his jeans and a cigarette dangling precariously from the corner of his mouth.

Mr Flood in shorts, drinking wine.

Mr Flood sitting on the river bank, staring moodily across the wide expanse of the Seine.

Dara moved from one photograph to the next. The sensation was a compelling one. It was like being introduced to a stranger you're sure you've met someplace before. In each picture, Dara recognised herself. The navy eyes. Long rather than big. The sooty black of his hair, which he wore longer than Dara did, at least back then. The small face. The pale white of his skin. Even his fingers – always wrapped around a cigarette – were hers. He bit his nails, right down to the quick, just like she did.

In each photograph, a woman, long and thin. Elegant. Pale. Black hair in a complicated upstyle with stray wisps falling to frame a small, heart-shaped face. Carefully cut dresses in pale pinks and greens. Pashminas and wraps and stoles and . . .

Stanley turned to Mme Dupoint. 'That's you, isn't it?'

The woman nodded.

Dara looked at Mme Dupoint and then back to the photographs. The only thing the two women had in common was the gold locket.

'I was so bee-you-tee-ful zen,' Mme Dupoint said, looking

down at herself and shaking her head, as if her body belonged to someone else. Someone she was not fond of.

Dara looked at the photographs again. She nodded. It was true. Mme Dupoint *had* been beautiful then. Tintin would have been well within his rights to label her a *typical* French-woman, back then. In each photograph, her eyes rested on Mr Flood. *Gazed* at him, in fact. With a light that smacked of love and trust and faith and hope. Dara knew where a light like that led. She had seen that same light in her mother's eyes, in photographs taken long ago. It was like a candle blowing in the wind, that light. Easily extinguished.

'What happened?' Dara asked, crouching beside Mme Dupoint. She touched the woman's huge, fleshy arm with her hand. The intimacy of her gesture surprised Dara, but somehow it felt right. She felt some sense of kinship towards this woman. Some kind of solidarity, in their mutual experience of Mr Flood.

Isabelle Dupoint smiled at Dara. 'He spoke of you sometimes. Your family. The leetle house on ze Raheny road. He told me what happened, about the mess he had made. I told him to go back, even though I did not want him to.'

Dara's mind struggled to process this information. She had a thousand questions.

So did Isabelle Dupoint. ''Ow did you find me?' she asked, looking from one of them to the other.

'Your name was on the bail order. Back in 2001.'

Mme Dupoint's eyes closed. She pulled one of her wraps tight around her neck, as if she were cold. 'Zat was the last time I saw heem,' she said. 'I paid the bond, took him back here, made heem a croque monsieur and some nettle soup. Ee loved nettle soup. Said it reminded him of his moth-air, picking nettles in the springtime with her yellow rubber gloves on.' Mme Dupoint smiled at the memory, the way people smile when they hear a song they haven't heard in years and they sing along, surprised they remember all the words. She struggled out of the chair and moved to a photograph near the window. Nodded at it. 'Zen ee said ee was going to get a packet of Gauloises. I took a photograph of heem, from zis window. Walking up the road. I think I must 'ave known.'

'Known what?' asked Dara, looking at the photograph. It was of a man walking away, silky black hair tossing in the wind, a cigarette held between thumb and finger. It was Mr Flood.

'What must you have known?' she repeated.

Isabelle looked at Dara with a slow, sad smile. She shook her head. 'Zat ee would nevair come back,' she said. It sounded so simple, the way she said it. So inevitable.

'Do you know where he went?' Stanley asked.

'No. I waited for heem to come back. I waited for a long time. Much too long. I ate croissants and pain au chocolat and tarte tatin to pass ze time. Zat is why I am now like your mountains in Dubleen. How you say? Ze Shoo-gair Loaf?'

Even though the Sugar Loaf in Dublin was not *technically* a mountain, Dara nodded at Mme Dupoint and squeezed her hand.

'What was he like?' Dara was surprised at the depth of her curiosity.

Mme Dupoint smiled, and the change it made to her face was startling: like the sun coming out in the dead of night. Now Dara could see traces of the woman in the photograph across her face, faint but there.

'Ee was loving and kind and gentle and, oh so charming. My girlfriends seemply adored 'eem.'

No surprises there.

'Were you married?' Dara asked. 'Did you marry Mr Flood?'

Mme Dupoint shook her head. 'No,' she said. 'Ee was married to your moth-air. To Kathleen.'

'But on the bail bond. The form. You're down there as his . . .' Stanley began.

Isabelle Dupoint shook her head. 'No,' she said again. 'Zey let me take him home because I said I was his wife. And perhaps sometimes I thought . . . maybe one day . . .' She lowered herself again on to the chair. She seemed tired, as if she hadn't been wandering down memory lane, but racing. Sprinting.

'Did he have a job? While he was here?' Stanley asked.

Mme Dupoint shook her head, then reached her finger over to the wine bottle and drew a love heart in the dust there. 'He was a gambler. Zat was hees job, I suppose. Some days were better than others.' She shook her head and, for a moment, seemed lost in her own thoughts. Like she had forgotten about Dara and Stanley, standing on either side of her.

'Please, I am so rude,' she suddenly declared, rising again from the chair, using Dara's hand as a lever to pull herself up. 'We will 'ave tea now and you shall tell me every-sing, yes?'

Dara was glad to close the door behind her. It was like a shrine, that room. A shrine to Mr Flood. She turned the key in the lock and followed Stanley and Mme Dupoint to the kitchen. Mme Dupoint insisted they sit down, but it was hard to watch her slow, heavy movements through the kitchen, opening cupboards stacked high with food, and then another, bare apart from two cups, three plates and one chipped bowl.

'I do not get many visitors any more,' she offered by way of explanation or apology, as she set out the cups and plates on the table. 'My fault, of course. I was so busy waiting for Eugene to return, I forgot about my friends and my family.'

It was strange for Dara to hear her father being called anything other than Mr Flood. Eugene, she felt, didn't suit him.

Mme Dupoint poured tea into tiny china cups that she took from a cabinet in the sitting room. She put bread and cheese and salami on the table with a bowl of olives and capers. She insisted they eat something, and they did. Dara struggled to swallow the food. She was touched by Isabelle Dupoint's hospitality. It was more than she – or Mr Flood – deserved. She felt she had arrived at a dead end. Another one. And even though Isabelle Dupoint insisted that Mr Flood would give Angel his kidney if he knew the situation, Dara did not share this conviction.

'Did Mr . . . did Eugene leave anything behind?' Stanley asked.

'Apart from me, you mean?' Mme Dupoint said, but there was no bitterness in her words. She settled a cosy over the teapot and moved towards the door. 'Come,' she told them.

Her bedroom took Dara's breath away. Not because there was anything odd or strange about it. It was its familiarity that shocked her. Because, as it turned out, Mme Dupoint's bedroom was almost an exact replica of Mrs Flood's bedroom. The same exercise in lopsided symmetry. The same double bed dividing it down the middle, the left side unmade and tousled, the right side pristine with the bedclothes pulled taut as if Mr Flood – Eugene – had never slept there. A bedside locker on either side, the left one cluttered with empty sweet wrappers, half-eaten packets of biscuits, an empty bottle of wine, a cup, a glass, a plate with the remains of what might have been one of those tartes tatins Mme Dupoint had referred to earlier, a browning banana. The locker on the other side of the bed was empty, apart from a thick coating of dust and a set of cufflinks, tarnished now with the years. A wardrobe on either side of the room, the doors of one hanging open, revealing a row of dark layers Dara recognised as the ones favoured by Mme Dupoint. The Frenchwoman moved towards the other wardrobe and opened one door. Dara saw empty hangers, bumping softly against each other in an eerie sort of melody. When she opened the other door, Dara recognised the clothes. She would have thought they were the exact same ones that had hung in Mrs Flood's bedroom until very recently. One suit – just like the one Mr Flood had called his *funeral* suit – one pair of trousers, three shirts, a pair of runners (although these ones had laces), two odd shoes that sat together as if they were a pair – as if they *thought* they were a pair – and, at the end of the row, a jumper. A green jumper.

The bedroom – and everything in it and about it – filled Dara with a kind of resigned hopelessness. She imagined trailing Mr Flood along a line of bedrooms just like this one. Just like the one at home. What kind of a man would you find at the end of a line like that? It was not a question that needed much of an answer.

46

Stanley's phone call to Sissy on his return to the hotel was a measure of his desperation. For a start, Sissy was at work, and Stanley was under strict instructions never to ring her there. To this rule, she had added two exceptions. He could ring only if:

(a) a member of Stanley's family died. She generously included Chief Inspector Jacques Clouseau among family members; or

(b) Stanley won an amount of money no less than €1.5 million in the lottery or indeed, in any other capacity.

For all other reasons – like, for example, if Stanley won, say, €500,000, or if a member of his family was merely seriously injured as opposed to full-on dead – Stanley was ordered to text, e-mail, tweet or Facebook her. Or leave a message on her blog (*366 days of heartbreak* – although she might have changed the name of it now, given that she was now, officially at least, 'over' Duncan).

You could be forgiven for thinking that Sissy's job was one that commanded her full attention, but in fact she was a columnist for one of those magazines they call 'women's magazines', even though Stanley sometimes leafed through the pages and, more often than not, found an article that held his attention. Like the problem page, *Dear Angie*. Letters about betrayal. Lots of them. Stanley hated the fact that there was so much of it going around. But it was comforting to realise that he was not alone.

Sissy's column was full of Sissy. Stanley recognised her in

every line. Strong opinions on subjects such as liposuction: *eat till you're fit to burst and then get it all sucked out of you, as if you'd eaten nothing at all apart from a couple of limp lettuce leaves*; 27 ways to get rid of spots: *never squeeze unless it's an emergency, e.g. an hour before a first date with a man who boasts that rare combination of beauty and intelligence*, followed by a complicated methodology on exactly how spots should be squeezed in emergency situations, and things you should never leave home without – tweezers, bright red lipstick, a tube of concealer and one book, even if you'd never read a book in your life. They were handy things to have, on a DART say, if you saw someone you didn't want to speak to. Or you were in the hairdresser's and didn't feel like talking about your holiday plans. Just cover your face with the book. Something huge, she recommended. Vikram Seth's *A Suitable Boy*, perhaps. Nothing put people off quicker than a great slab of a book. Or a self-help book on anger management. Something discouraging.

Her column was called 'Sissy Clarke Ha Ha Ha', which served as a tribute to another of her favourite books, while also hinting at her self-deprecating nature, which her readers loved.

The thing was, Sissy could do this job anywhere, but her favourite place to write the column was on the couch in Stanley's house, wrapped in a duvet like a terribly long sausage roll with a significant supply of Pringles within arm's reach.

So there was no real reason why Stanley shouldn't phone her. Ten times a day if he felt like it. But she discouraged any contact, complaining that it interrupted her train of thought. Although as far as Stanley could tell, on the two occasions he rang her during work (once when his grandmother died, and that day in Cora's apartment when he walked up the stairs and heard those sounds but kept walking towards them, even though he knew that nothing good would come of it), the only thing he'd interrupted was Sissy's viewing of the romantic comedies she was fond of.

Today, she was watching *Four Weddings and a Funeral* ('I want to go to the wedding of someone I really LOVE for a change,' he could hear one of the characters saying).

'What's wrong?' was the first thing that Sissy said.

'Eh . . .'

'Who died?'

'No one, but . . .'

'OH! MY! GOD!' He heard her pull herself into a sitting position and struggle out of the duvet. Something fell. He guessed it was at least one tube of Pringles. The spicy ones. They were her favourites.

'I didn't win any money,' he hurried to tell her.

There was a pause, then some crunching, as Sissy walked the spilled Pringles into the floor on her way to the coffee pot in the kitchen.

'Then why the fuck are you ringing me?' she asked him. 'Aren't you in Paris?'

'Well, yes, but . . .'

'So that probably means *I'm* paying for this call. Nobody's croaked it, you haven't won a fecking penny *and* I have to foot the bill as well. This had better be good, Stanley.'

'It's Dara.'

'She hasn't won any money, has she?'

'No, it's . . .'

'Has someone belonging to her died? Her father, whatshis-face? Mr Flood?'

'No.'

'So? What are you ringing me for?'

'It's just . . . Mme Dupoint turned out to be a dead end. I mean, we found her, spoke to her. Mr Flood had been there. But he left. The same way he left Dara's mother.'

'So what? You knew it was a long shot, didn't you?' Stanley could hear the crinkling of paper. He guessed Sissy had found his stash of Reese's Peanut Butter Cups. She usually did.

'Yes, but she's taken it badly. She keeps talking about the bedroom.'

'What bedroom?'

'Mme Dupoint's bedroom.'

'Why were you in her bedroom? This sounds like one of those mental French films you force me to watch.' Stanley never forced Sissy to watch the French films he liked to watch. But she sometimes sat on the arm of the couch and monologued through them, commenting on the lack of plot and the slowness of pace in such a way that by the end, Stanley was as much in the dark about what the film was about as Sissy was.

'Dara said Mme Dupoint's bedroom was just like her mother's bedroom. It's really unsettled her.'

'What do you mean?'

'Nothing's been moved. Everything is just the way it was before he left. As if she's expecting him to come back any moment.'

'Where's Dara now?'

'She's holed up in her hotel room. She won't answer the door or her phone. I don't know what to do.'

'OK, OK, listen to me now,' said Sissy, her tone softer now, in spite of nobody being dead and no windfalls having been won.

'I'm listening,' said Stanley, who could only hear the steady sounds of crunching as Sissy popped the second of his pack-of-three Peanut Butter Cups into her mouth, whole, just the way she liked them. He hoped she might leave the last one alone, although not with any degree of expectation. They were too good to be left in a cupboard, once opened. He understood that.

'You need to man up,' Sissy told him when the crunching stopped.

'Man up?' Stanley was unfamiliar with the expression.

'Yes. Man up,' Sissy repeated. 'Don't just knock on her bedroom door. Bang on it. And say her name like you really mean it. Shout it if you have to. As many times as it takes.'

'What if she still doesn't open the door?'

'She will. If you stay there long enough.'

'But she probably just wants to be left alone. She hardly spoke on the way back from . . .'

'She doesn't. She wants to be distracted. You have to distract her.'

'How?'

'Christ, Stanley, the usual ways. Take her to a gallery. A park. A bloody monument. Paris is falling down with monuments. Feed her. Make her laugh. Drink wine. Don't you know *anything* about women?' Stanley felt there was a lot he didn't know about women, but he didn't like to mention it. Besides, even if he wanted to, he couldn't get a word in between the steady stream of Sissy's monologue. '. . . Compliment her, photograph her, walk the legs off her, take her to the movies, read to her, point out landmarks and tell her interesting little anecdotes. Keep them short, mind. You don't want to bore the stuffing out of her.' Sissy paused for breath and Stanley took his chance.

'Thanks, Sissy. That's . . . helpful. Enough to be getting on with.'

'So you'll do it?'

'Well . . . I might not do *all* of it. We're only here for today and a bit of tomorrow.'

'The most important thing on the list is to get her out of the room. Wallowing becomes dreadfully boring after a while.' This was true. Sissy had a short attention span for most things, and wallowing in particular. She couldn't do it for longer than twenty minutes at a time. She got Stanley to time her one day.

'I'll go,' said Stanley. 'I'm sorry to ring you at work.'

'No, no, I understand. It *is* a bit of an emergency. And I *like* Dara. Which is weird for me.'

Stanley nodded down the phone. Sissy was one of those people who took a long time to warm to people. When she finally did, she often wondered what had taken her so long.

A slow burner, Stanley called her.

A holy horror was the expression Sissy used.

Stanley hung up the phone and stood up before he had a chance to change his mind. He strode rather than walked to the bathroom. It was an ornate affair, with a bath that was big enough for two – or maybe even three: this *was* Paris, after all – set on tiny curved feet. He splashed cold water over his face and brushed his teeth until his gums bled. He used water from the tap to flatten the cowlick of his fringe and viewed his reflection in the mirror as a stranger might. He squared his shoulders and tried an expression of *determination* on for size. He looked like a character in one of those awful soaps Sissy liked to watch. *The Bold and the Beautiful*, or something like that. He drained *determination* from his face and went for something a little more neutral. He experimented with a smile. But the gap between his front teeth made him look boyish. Cora had told him that and it was true. The person in the mirror looked like nothing more than a short man with a boyish smile. He stopped smiling and practised *manning up*.

'Dara!' he said, and his voice sounded a little crazy, in the vast emptiness of the bathroom. 'We're going out and that's that.' He paused, as if waiting for her response. He shook his head and tried again. 'Dara, the thing is, well, we both knew this was a long shot and . . . well . . . now that we're here, why don't we make the best of it? I'd like to take you out.' No, that sounded very proprietorial altogether.

'Dara, we'd better go and take that photo for Miss Pettigrew before the light fades . . .' Yes. That was it. That sounded plausible.

The collar of his shirt chafed against his neck and he undid the top button. That felt better. So much better, in fact, that he went right ahead and undid another one. The cool air in the bathroom slipped down his chest. But now he looked a bit . . . well, relaxed. Blasé. Nonchalant. He refastened one button. He didn't want Dara to think he wasn't taking this seriously. Because he was. He had felt her frustration, her sadness, her loss, all the way back to the hotel.

'Do you mind if we don't talk?' she'd asked, not quite looking at him.

'Of course not,' he'd said. There was no need for her to say anything. He could see it all, in the careful set of her shoulders, the lonely length of her eyes, the usually white skin of her face stained pink with disappointment and maybe even anger, although he felt that anger was not a frequent caller to Dara Flood's life. Perhaps that was the problem. And not just for Dara.

He stopped looking at his reflection, stopped talking to himself in this stupid bathroom that threw everything he said back at him, in loud, empty echoes. He grabbed his room key and headed for the door.

47

Dara jumped when she heard the knock at the door. Although it was more of a thump than a knock. With the flats of both hands against the wood, rather than the delicacy of knuckles. She was lying on the bed, trying to work out what to say to her mother and Angel. Trying to pick up the phone to ring them. And yes, trying to cry. She thought crying might relieve the tightness in her chest. Might draw a line under the senseless journey she had embarked on. Put an end to the hope – withering now – she had felt on the flight this morning. The hope that she would find Mr Flood. That he would be a match. That he would agree to help.

But in spite of all her efforts, she couldn't cry. She forced herself to think of her mother and Angel. Of the disappointment on their faces when she told them of the cul-de-sac she'd arrived in. Again. Still she couldn't coax any tears out. Then she concentrated on Mme Dupoint. How she had cried when Dara turned to her in her bedroom and said, in a voice that was more like a whisper, 'It's just like my mother's room.' Mme Dupoint had cried so easily. Like there was nothing to it. No effort involved. Just lines of tears flowing down her cheeks and hanging off the end of her face like stalactites. Still Dara felt nothing. Numb. Worse than numb. A coldness dug into her, making it hard to feel anything at all. Not even the sting of tears. Not even that stretching at the back of her throat that she sometimes felt at the pound when a lovely family – a mother, a father and maybe two children, one of each, a boy

and a girl, a Hallmark family, a *perfect* family – came and went
without taking one of her charges home with them.

Still nothing. She had to content herself with lying on her
bed and ignoring Stanley's tentative knocks on the door and
the discreet beeps of his text messages. She knew this was not
a nice thing to do, but in the absence of tears, it was all she
had. She had accomplished nothing. She had dragged her un-
willing family down this path that had led nowhere. Promised
them some hope and faith where there was none to be found.
And while she felt she knew Mr Flood better now than when
she'd begun this journey, the knowledge served no purpose.
It left her cold.

The thumping, being impossible to ignore, roused her from
the bed and pushed her towards the sound. She opened the
door a crack.

'We should go out.'

It was a declaration rather than a question. It took Dara
by surprise. It seemed to take Stanley Flinter by surprise
too. She opened the door wider and gestured him inside.
He walked into the room and turned to her, pushing his fingers through his hair as was his habit and encouraging the
cowlick into a standing position. He waited for her to say
something.

'I can't go out. I need to ring my mother. And Angel. I need
to tell them.' Dara moved back towards the bed and sat down.

'Right, well, ring them now. I'll wait for you. We can go out
after that.'

'I can't ring them. I don't know what to say.'

'Just tell them what happened.'

'I can't. I want to have something good to tell them. Something positive. I can't give Angel any more bad news. She's
low enough as it is.'

Stanley moved towards Dara, hesitated, then sat on the bed
beside her.

'You're better off knowing the truth,' he finally said, nodding, as if he were persuading himself of this bald fact, as well as Dara. 'Angel mightn't like it, but she'll appreciate the truth. So will your mother. They're strong women, from what you've told me. You all are, all three of you.'

And just like that, Dara began to cry. Perhaps it was because Stanley Flinter had called her a strong woman and she wanted to show him how wrong he was. Perhaps it was because, after trying to cry for an hour-and-a-half, it felt almost like an achievement when her body finally relented and loosened its grip on her and allowed her to cry. Really cry. For the first time in a long time. It might have been the words themselves. Or the way he said them. With such kindness. Like he understood. Like he knew. Whatever it was, Dara cried and cried. She thought she would never stop.

At first, Stanley sat there beside her, saying nothing. Then he brought his hand up to her shoulder and patted her, like she was a dog who might bite. Finally he set his phone and his *Lonely Planet* on the bed, moved as close as he could to her without actually touching her and reached his arm around her back. She felt his hand hover before he brought it to rest on her shoulder and the patting continued.

'There there . . . Sssshhhh, it'll be all right . . . Don't cry.'

Dara couldn't be entirely sure, but she thought these were some of the things he said. It was hard to make out the words after she dropped her head, allowing it to lean against the warm fabric of his shirt. She knew she shouldn't, but the crook of his shoulder felt like someplace she had been before. Someplace safe. Stanley shifted when she did that, but he did not remove himself from her vicinity. The comfort of his hand against her shoulder was like a lullaby, sung over and over.

'I'm sorry, Stanley,' Dara finally managed, sitting up and looking around for a tissue.

'Don't worry about it,' said Stanley, handing her a handy pack of Kleenex from the breast pocket of his shirt. 'It's understandable.'

Dara stabbed at her face with a tissue and blew her nose. 'It's not, it's . . . I knew this was a long shot. I don't know why I'm so upset.'

Stanley looked at his watch. 'You're probably hungry,' he told her. 'It's past lunchtime in Ireland.'

Dara felt it was shallow to admit to feelings of hunger in the circumstances, but she nodded. It was true. She *was* hungry. 'But I'm not crying because I'm hungry,' she was at pains to let him know.

Stanley nodded. 'I know,' he said, 'but things always seem worse on an empty stomach, don't they?'

She nodded. She had a sudden urge for mashed potato. With butter and chives and salt and pepper. The thought was as comforting as the memory of George on her knee, the warm weight of him, smiling at her the way he used to do. Smiling with his tongue and his teeth and his gums and his ears and his whiskers. Smiling with his whole face. She stood up and the image faded.

Stanley handed Dara her phone. 'Call them,' he said, nodding encouragement at her. 'Call them and then we'll go out, OK?'

'I shouldn't have made you come to Paris with me,' she said. 'And now you're stuck here. It's such a waste of your time.'

'I've been stuck in worse places,' Stanley said, waving a hand towards the window, which framed the Arc de Triomphe like a painting.

Dara surprised herself by smiling. Stanley handed her another tissue. She blew her nose and wiped the tears off her face. She opened her mobile and pressed in her mother's number before she could change her mind. She felt guilty relief when the phone went straight on to message. She cleared her throat.

'Mam, it's Dara. I'm sorry . . . you were right. He's not here. Well, he was, but he left. Years ago. No one knows where he went. I . . . I'm sorry. I wish I had something else to say. To tell you. I'll ring Angel and tell her. Sorry. I'm sorry. Goodbye.'

Without pausing, she dialled Angel's number. The phone rang several times before it went on to voicemail. Dara hesitated before she left the message. It was not the kind of message she wanted her sister to hear. She stumbled through the words. At the end she said, 'I love you' before she could stop herself. They were not a family who said things like that. Angel would know how hopeless the situation was when she heard it. But it was too late. The words were out there and Dara couldn't take them back. She hung up.

'Do you feel a bit better?' Stanley asked, his voice tentative.

Dara shook her head. 'Sorry,' she managed.

'You don't have anything to apologise for,' Stanley told her. 'None of this is your fault. Aren't you doing everything you can?'

Dara said nothing. There was no need to tell Stanley that whatever she did wouldn't make any difference. He already knew that.

'Come on,' said Stanley, picking up Dara's bag. 'Let's go out.'

Dara opened her mouth to speak. Stanley rushed in first.

'We're here now. Let's get out of this hotel room. Go and have lunch. See a monument. There's no end to them. It would be a shame not to see a few before we leave. And the photograph. For Miss Pettigrew. We should get that done before the light fades . . .'

'You're right,' Dara said suddenly, standing up.

'Which bit?' Stanley asked, and Dara smiled at his confusion and at his eyes that were nearly black now, with all the dilation his pupils were doing. She guessed that Stanley was not

used to telling people what to do. She liked that about him.
And the fact that he was here, doing his best to be forceful.

'We should go out,' she said.

'We should?'

'Yes.'

'Where?'

'Everywhere.'

48

A strange feeling niggled at Stanley all that afternoon and persisted well into the evening as he wandered with Dara Flood around the Latin Quarter, looking for someplace to have dinner. He struggled to put his finger on it. He'd been feeling it since the Eiffel Tower, he supposed.

Dara, in her red dress, standing at the top of the tower, just as Miss Pettigrew had requested. 'Smile,' he had told her, even though he himself hated being told to smile.

'I am smiling,' said Dara.

'Well, smile a bit more then,' said Stanley. For some reason that made her smile and he got the shot. Dara, in her soft red dress, smiling at the top of the Eiffel Tower with Paris set out like a painting behind her.

'Is it OK?' Dara asked, and Stanley dragged his eyes from the image. 'It's . . . fine,' he told her.

That's when he noticed the woman. Standing beside him, quiet as a tomb.

'Get in ze photograph,' she told him in a grave voice. He looked behind him, the way people do when they think a person must be addressing someone else. But there was no one behind him.

The woman was somewhere in her fifties, dressed entirely in black. Her hands were encased in black leather gloves, as if she were mindful of fingerprints. Her eyes were covered by a pair of wraparound black sunglasses.

'Eh, no, that's OK. But thanks,' said Stanley, smiling at her.

She did not smile back. Instead she stood her ground and repeated her order. 'Get in ze photograph.'

'No, you see, the thing is . . .' Stanley began, before the woman reached across and grabbed his iPhone. At first he thought she was going to make a run for it, although he didn't think she'd get very far, in her high-heeled black leather boots. But she stayed where she was and withered him with a look. 'Bee-you-tee-ful women should not stand alone in photographs,' she told him, and something in her voice suggested to Stanley that perhaps she had once stood alone in a photograph and it hadn't agreed with her. 'Not in Paris,' she added, shaking her head. 'I will not permit it.'

Stanley took a different tack. 'You're very kind,' he began, 'but it's not like—'

'GET IN ZE PHOTOGRAPH!' Officially it wasn't a shout. But it was in the vicinity of one. 'Please?' she added, to temper it.

Later, when he told Sissy about it, he found it difficult to convey the menace in the woman's voice. He half-walked, half-ran over to Dara and stood beside her, nodding at the woman to take the shot. He hoped she might be able to do it without Dara noticing.

'What are you doing?' Dara asked, when the woman gestured to him and he obliged by shuffling closer.

'That woman over there. She's insisting on taking a photo of us.' Stanley kept smiling in the woman's direction, talking to Dara through gritted teeth.

'But . . .' Dara began.

'I know, I know, but could you just smile? Just one more time? For two seconds. Maybe five?'

'I just . . .' Dara began.

'I know, Dara, but . . . can you just let her? She seems a bit unhinged and I'm worried about my phone. I only just got it. I can delete the photograph afterwards. When she's gone.'

But Stanley didn't delete the photograph afterwards. The strange woman turned out to be a good photographer. She waited until Stanley's facial muscles relaxed. She waited until Dara said something and Stanley, who didn't quite hear it, moved his head towards her. She waited until Dara looked at Stanley, repeating whatever it was she had said, her eyes trained on Stanley's, as if he might hear her with his eyes as well as his one good ear. The sky behind them is a duck-egg blue. It stretches, gossamer-thin, over Paris, fragile as a shell, like it might crack into a thousand pieces if it ever fell down to earth.

'How about here?' Dara asked. She stopped outside a place called *Danseur*. An unusual name for a restaurant, Stanley felt. But nice, all the same. *Dancer*.

He peered inside. The restaurant was an exercise in gingham. Gingham curtains framed the window, pinched at the waist with gingham bands. Gingham tablecloths covered the tables, all of them set for two. The waitresses – two of them, identical, twins perhaps, definitely sisters – wore gingham aprons over short black dresses, their long dark hair pulled back from their small pale faces with gingham ribbons. The restaurant was dark, lit only by long-stemmed candles poking out of wine bottles, long empty, with crusts of wax running down their necks, like the ghosts of great nights past. It looked like a place where anything could happen, perhaps because of the clock that hung crooked on the wall, reaching both hands towards twelve. The writing on the face declared: *Service à toute heure*, as if it didn't really matter that the clock didn't tell the right time. A parrot, big and bright, perched on the bar, singing 'Chanson d'Amour' quietly to himself, like he was practising for later. The specials were chalked on a blackboard, in curly lettering, too tiny to make out. Stanley smelled coffee and garlic and something sweet. Vanilla, perhaps.

'It looks perfect,' he told Dara, holding the door open for her.

It wasn't until later, when he chanced a glance at Dara sitting opposite him, worrying at the menu, that he realised what the feeling was. Niggling at him.

It was happiness. Or something close to happiness. It startled him. He bent his head to study the menu, but the feeling persisted. In fact, it spread all the way through him, like butter on toast, melting into his pores until he felt warm and full with it. He cleared his throat. 'So, have you decided what you're having?' he asked, not looking up. He had an idea he was smiling and it left him feeling a little foolish.

'No.' Dara's fingers reached for her mouth. She began to bite her nails.

'How about the fish?' Stanley suggested. 'The sea bass sounds good.'

'Yes, it *sounds* good,' Dara agreed.

'But you're worried it might not taste as good as it sounds and you could be disappointed. Is that it?'

Dara put her menu on the table and looked at him with her serious face. 'I know it's stupid. I've never been good in restaurants. I usually go to the same one in Dublin and order the same thing. Pathetic, I know.'

'No, not at all. It's healthy caution is what it is,' Stanley told her, and felt such a rush of reward when she smiled at him that he became fixated on making sure that she ordered something that she would really, really like. Love, even. And then perhaps she would smile at him again. Dara Flood's smile might be small and careful, but it was undiluted. It was real. And because she used it so sparingly, it made him feel like a hero when he did or said something to encourage its appearance, however brief, across the small heart-shape of her face. He wanted to see it again.

He leaned towards her. 'I'll tell you what. I'll order the fish and you can try it, and if you like it, you can have it, OK?'

'But what about if I order something that you don't like?' A crease appeared at the top of her nose. Her worry crease. He was beginning to recognise it.

'I like everything,' Stanley declared in a voice that didn't sound like his own, it was that confident.

'We . . . ll, I was thinking about a garden salad.'

'It's hard to go wrong with a garden salad,' he told her.

'And maybe some of those sauté potatoes.'

'I've never had a sauté potato that I didn't enjoy,' Stanley said. 'Now, what about meat? My mother always says dinner's not dinner without a slab of flesh on your plate. She even says it to Lorcan, who's a vegetarian. Although only because he says it makes him more attractive to women.'

'And does it?'

'What?'

'Make him more attractive to women?'

'Eh, no, I haven't seen any evidence of that, to be honest.'

This time Dara laughed and Stanley felt like an American baseball player who'd just scored a . . . what did you call them? A home run. That's what it was. The waitress appeared at their table just then, with a jug of red wine, and it took everything that Stanley had to stop himself high-fiving the living daylights out of her. Of course, he knew he never would. Of course not. But the compulsion was there, all the same. He concentrated on filling both their wine glasses to the brim.

'Maybe a steak?' he suggested.

'The French aren't fond of cooking their steaks for very long. They like them pretty bloody, don't they?' The crease was back. Stanley could have kicked himself and very nearly did, only that he was afraid he might kick Dara as well, the space beneath their table being quite small.

'You could ask for it . . .' he unfolded a piece of paper he removed from his pocket and squinted at it, '*bee-yan quit*,' he

read from the page. For a moment, Dara continued to look
worried. And then her face cleared. 'Oh, yes, well cooked. Yes,
I suppose I could ask.'

'Wait.' Stanley looked at his page again. 'Ask for it *tray, tray
bee-yan quit*. Christ, my French is pure mule. What I'm trying
to say is, ask for it very, very well done. Then they'll have to
make positively *certain* that the beast is dead before they slap
it on your plate. Am I right?'

Dara laughed again. Her laugh was not like anyone else's
laugh that Stanley had ever heard. It was a low rumble of a
laugh, soft, her mouth tightly closed against it, as if she were
trying to contain it.

By the time their starters arrived – garlic bread for Dara
because, Stanley assured her, what could possibly go wrong
with garlic bread? – they had drunk all the wine in the carafe.

'I'm still thirsty,' said Stanley.

'Me too.'

'Should we order another?'

'I don't know . . .'

'We could get some water as well.'

'Do we have to drink it?'

'Christ, no. Just for appearances.'

'OK then.'

Stanley found himself delighted with the evening's progress.
For a day that had begun with such embarrassment – he still
coloured when he thought about the beeping designer underpants – and then sagged so badly in the middle with Dara's
upset in the hotel and his subsequent emergency call to Sissy,
it was turning out to the best day he could remember having. In ages. He didn't think about Cora. Or the Newbridge
silver candlestick holders he'd bought as an engagement gift.
Or about the engagement party. Or about the kiss. Well, he
did think about the kiss, to be honest. But only once, when he
excused himself to go to the bathroom. Standing at the urinal,

it crept into his mind like a hissing cat, demanding attention. *She* kissed *me*, he remembered.

A weird thing happened then. Anger happened. It arrived, flustered and out of breath, apologising for being late and promising to make it up to him. He stood at the urinal for much longer than was considered appropriate in these places. What was Cora – a mother, his brother's fiancée, for fuck's sake – doing with her tongue in *his* mouth? Just before the bloody engagement party that he didn't even want to go to? And not just kissing him, but reaching for his zipper. Like it was nothing. Like the past fifteen months hadn't happened. Hadn't *meant* anything. In *his* kitchen. *His* refuge. He had burnt Sissy's dinner because of Cora's presumptions. Her carelessness. Her casual disregard. And not just for him, but for Cormac and Baby Cora as well.

It was only when the man who had come to the urinal after Stanley zipped up his trousers, washed and dried his hands, inspected his teeth in the mirror and left the bathroom that Stanley realised he was still standing there, alone now. He pulled himself together and flattened his cowlick with water from the cold tap. The anger was gone but its brief appearance had left him invigorated, somehow. Like a cold shower after a long, hot, demanding day.

'Are you all right?' Dara asked when he sat down.

'Yes. I'm fine. Why?'

'It's just, you seem a little . . . you look a little flustered. Is everything OK?'

'Actually, yes,' he said, tucking into Dara's steak.

'Are you sure you don't mind eating my steak? It looks a little . . . rare.'

In fact, the steak was leaking a trail of blood through his garden salad and sauté potatoes. He loaded his fork with the pink meat and steered it towards his mouth. 'No, not at all,' he managed to say. He was suddenly starving. Everything – even the bloody meat – tasted fresh and new and exciting. 'What about your fish?' he asked.

'Actually . . .' Dara began, her face bright with surprise, 'it's really good.'

Stanley smiled at her. Her surprise tickled him like fingers at the back of his knees – his weak point. For a while, they concentrated on eating.

'Did you hear back from Miss Pettigrew?' Dara asked, when the coffee arrived. Stanley liked the way she bent her face to the steam curling from her cup, smelling it before she allowed herself to taste it. 'After you sent her the photograph, I mean.'

'I'll check my phone,' he said, his fingers already a blur across the keypad. He smiled. 'She says she knew you didn't have knobbly knees.'

'I didn't say I had knobbly knees,' Dara told him. 'I said I had a knobbly knee.'

'Which one?'

'The left one.'

'I never noticed,' said Stanley.

'In fairness, it's only slightly knobbly. But knobbly all the same.'

Miss Pettigrew had also enquired about their progress. In relation to Mr Flood. But Stanley didn't mention that bit. There was something a little, well, almost precious about the atmosphere at the dinner table. He couldn't remember the last time he'd felt this good. He didn't want to spoil it with talk of the elusive Mr Flood. Anyway, as it turned out, there was no time to tell her about Miss Pettigrew's question, even if he'd wanted to.

Something was happening. He looked up. All the diners were on their feet, draining the last of their wine and their coffee. The waitresses busied themselves clearing the tables, setting what remained of the candles on the bar counter beside the parrot, who had stopped singing 'Chanson d'Amour' and was now busy grooming his feathers with the tip of his long, wide beak. The clock with both hands raised to twelve began to chime.

Once the tables were cleared, the customers carried them to the sides of the room, hoisting their chairs, upside down, on top of them. The door opened with a tinkle of a bell and Stanley turned his head to look. Three swarthy men, short and stocky, with long, complicated moustaches, entered the restaurant, each carrying a musical instrument under his arm. A double bass, Stanley thought. A guitar, a set of bongo drums. They walked in a line, one after the other, until they reached the top of the room, where they bent with their backs to the diners and busied themselves with their instruments.

Stanley looked at Dara. 'What's going . . . ?'

But there was no time to finish the question, because the table between them, cleared now of all signs of their meal, was carried away by the waitresses without a word. The pair of them were left, in the middle of the room, sitting on the only remaining chairs in the place, with an empty space between them where their table used to be.

They stood up, not knowing quite what else to do, and immediately their chairs were carried off and stacked with the others.

And then the music began.

49

Dara recognised the music immediately. A low, earthy beat, impossible to ignore. Already she could feel her body straining to the irresistible rhythm of it. Sticky concoctions in tiny shot glasses were passed around, and in one fluid movement, their fellow diners downed the drinks, slammed the glasses down on the counter and roared, 'SALSA!' at the tops of their voices. Then, arranging themselves in pairs around the floor, they reached for each other with eager hands and began to dance.

Dara and Stanley owned a little pocket of space in the middle of the floor. They looked at each other, not moving. The room was hotter than before. Louder, too, with the slap of the dancers' feet against the worn wooden floor beating like a drum, and their breath coming faster now with each twist and turn they made. The dancers moved around Dara and Stanley like a carousel. As Dara stood there, trying to work out what to do or say, Stanley moved towards her, reaching for her hip with one hand and her fingers with the other. And just like that, they were dancing.

They moved like they'd been dancing together for ever. Stepping towards each other, moving apart, reaching for each other with their fingertips. They moved to the beat of the music, in and out, back and forth, side to side, their eyes locked together like a safe that would never open. He spun her around, drawing her towards him, and she pressed her back into the solid heat of his body, their hips swinging in time, his arm curled around her waist, their hands connected only by the very tips of their fingers. And then, with a brief touch on her waist, he spun her away again. The separation was like a respite until they melded together, again and again, leaving Dara breathless in a way that had nothing to do with the movement of the dance.

Maybe it was the wine, maybe it was the heat of the restaurant, the excited screech of the parrot, the clock yearning for midnight. Maybe it was just Paris. The bald fact of being there. Whatever it was, Dara sold her soul to the dance. She danced like she was not Dara Flood at all, but a collection of moves and sensations and sounds.

She stepped around Stanley Flinter, trailing her fingers along his chest, across his shoulders, down his back. Facing him again, leaning away from him, his hand against the small of her back as she bent backwards, almost reaching the floor before she felt the tug of his hand against her body, lifting her back to him, closer now, his thigh moving between her legs, the pressure of it hot and tense and exciting. They danced that way for a moment, their hands not touching, their hips locked together, their eyes beating a path into each other's faces. They were so close now, she could feel his breath against her mouth, the hot push of it, the dark passion-fruit pink of it. If she lifted her head an inch, they would be kissing. Almost an accident. His fingers glanced against hers and she felt the bright fizz of electricity through her body. She lifted her head an inch.

As suddenly as it had begun, the music stopped, and Dara found herself in the middle of the floor, back where she'd started, with her eyes closed, her breath rising and falling in her chest and her face reaching towards Stanley's mouth in a way that would have been difficult to explain had Stanley enquired about it, which, thankfully, he did not. Dara stepped away from him, trying not to think about the pleasure of his thigh as he eased it gently from the grip of her legs that seemed, to Dara, much too tight now.

'I'm out of breath,' she told him, even though there was no need. It was very apparent that Dara Flood was out of breath. 'It's hot. Isn't it? Aren't you hot?'

Stanley nodded slowly. He didn't look hot. Nor did he seem out of breath. In fact, he looked just the same as he always did.

The music started up again, slower this time, softer now. The dancers moved around them, past them, like ghosts. Dara didn't move. She tried to think of something to say, but nothing occurred. It was Stanley who reached across the tiny space between them and slipped his hands into the small of her back. They fitted perfectly. He pulled her against him, but instead of reaching for her mouth, he pushed his lips into the damp skin of her neck, just below her ear, and kissed her there. It was quite possibly the most delicious kiss she'd ever had. There was something so intimate about it, the gentle brush of his tongue against her skin, his mouth closing over the lobe of her ear, his hands against her back as she willed them to move; past the curve of her hips, over the swell of her bottom, down the track of her thighs. Dara's mouth watered. Her breath came in rags. She forgot everything. She waited. Stanley looked at her before he kissed her mouth. His eyes were dark. Almost black. Worry skulked at the edges of his face.

'You . . . you don't have a boyfriend, do you?' he asked in a whisper, biting his bottom lip with his teeth in a way that made Dara's legs nearly buckle with desire.

She didn't tell the lie lightly. Even though her response came within a second of his question, she thought about it. About telling him the truth. About Ian Harte. But she knew then that the kiss would never happen. She recognised that about Stanley Flinter. His integrity was not something that would allow him to kiss a woman who had a boyfriend, no matter how casual that boyfriend was. No matter how much she could insist that the relationship was going nowhere and that was just the way she liked it. She loved that about Stanley, that integrity. But she knew what it would mean, once she told him about Ian Harte. And she cursed herself for putting herself in this position, for not putting her limping liaison with Ian Harte out of its misery, as John the vet would have done, had it been a dog, months ago.

So, in that second of hesitation between Stanley's question and Dara's answer, she decided that she *would* put her limping liaison with Ian Harte out of its misery. Immediately. Well, as soon as she got back to Dublin. Saturday night. She was meeting him then. She'd do it then. And it was this assurance, to herself, that allowed Dara Flood to shake her head and whisper *no* to Stanley Flinter's question. It settled on her like a fog, this lie, damp and cold, and she shivered against the weight of it.

'Are you OK?' Stanley whispered, and his mouth was so close she could taste his words forming along the line of his lips.

'Yes,' she said, and when he kissed her, she closed her eyes and breathed him in to the very heart of her and wondered how she had lived for so long without ever feeling this feeling before.

50

There was a bit of a morning-after-the-night-before atmosphere between them when they left the restaurant, sometime after one o'clock in the morning. They had spent the last three hours alternately dancing, kissing and knocking back sticky concoctions in tiny shot glasses and shouting 'SALSA!' at the tops of their voices.

Now, out on the street, the world seemed strangely quiet. Dara could feel the lining of her red dress sticking like glue to the skin at the small of her back, the curve of her waist, the hollow between her breasts. She sucked at the cool night air and crouched on the pavement, rummaging in her bag for her cigarettes. Beside her she could see Stanley's legs, shifting their weight from one to the other. She kept on rummaging in the bag even though the cigarettes were in her hand now. It was Stanley who spoke first.

'You're a really great dancer,' he told her.

She smiled and stood up. 'Thanks,' she said, pulling a cigarette out of the pack. 'It's something we started – me, Mam and Angel, I mean – a few years ago. It was Angel's idea. She was the one who really wanted to do it. She wanted to do everything back then.'

Angel's appearance in the conversation was not a good idea. Dara could feel the day limping away from her, like a dog with a thorn in its paw. Her mother hadn't called back. Nor had Angel. Dara knew she should have tried to phone them again. She kept promising herself that she would do it later, later,

later. Now it was later and here she was, on some dark Parisian street in the middle of the night in a red dress with a man she barely knew but suddenly couldn't stop thinking about. She felt, for perhaps the first time in her life, some brand of reck-lessness. She felt like Tintin, reaching into his bag of Revels, expecting the best and spitting out the worst. She felt like she was dipping her toe into *the great adventure that is life*. The one Miss Pettigrew was always recommending. The water wasn't as cold as she'd imagined. She wanted to wade in. She wanted to get wet. And, best of all, not worry about the fact that she had no towel, no dry clothes, no change of underwear. There would be plenty of time to worry about all of that tomorrow. Wouldn't there? And the next day. And all the days after that.

She turned to Stanley and smiled. 'I didn't know you could salsa dance.'

'I never dance,' said Stanley, shaking his head as if he couldn't quite get over himself.

'Well, you *were*. You were dancing. I was there, remember?' Stanley looked at her in a curious kind of a way and Dara realised that she was flirting with him. In her head, she could hear Tintin roaring encouragement at her ('You saucy little madam, GO FOR IT!'). Dara smothered Tintin's voice with a fire blanket and concentrated on Stanley. 'And you're good at it. You've got a good sense of . . . rhythm.'

Stanley took this compliment on board, like it was a case of particularly good wine. He accepted it carefully. 'Well, I *did* go to a few salsa lessons. But only because Lorcan wanted someone to go with.'

'Lorcan?'

'He said it would make him more attractive to women.'

'And did it?'

'What?'

'Make him more attractive to women?'

'Eh . . . no, not as far as I could tell anyway.'

They both laughed. When Stanley laughed, his shoulders shook. Dara hadn't noticed that before. Perhaps because he hadn't laughed all that much before. Neither of them had. Now, here, in Paris, in the middle of the night, there was something of a carnival atmosphere between them.

'Shall we walk?' Stanley asked. Dara nodded. It seemed like the most natural thing in the world when he draped his arm across her shoulders. Dara reached her hand up to his, and his fingers closed over it, and she tucked her head into the crook of his neck and they began to walk. They walked like they'd been walking this way for years.

'Where are we going?' Dara asked.

'I have no idea,' Stanley replied, as if it didn't matter. And perhaps it didn't. They kept walking.

When they reached the hotel, they stopped outside the door of Stanley's room. He fumbled for his key, found it and then dropped it back into his pocket. 'I had a lovely time tonight,' he said, slowly and quietly, as if they were inside a bubble that might burst.

'So did I,' Dara said, and they smiled at each other in the corridor, like old friends do when they meet unexpectedly.

Dara reached inside her bag for her key. 'Well, I suppose I'd better . . .'

'I'd like to kiss you again,' Stanley said, almost to himself.

'I'd like that too,' Dara whispered.

And they leaned towards each other and kissed, there in the corridor, standing in the light of a full Paris moon hanging low in the sky, as if tired out at the night's end. They kissed like they were tasting each other for the first time. Like something neither of them had tried before, but liked. A lot. Dara thought Stanley tasted of dessert, something warm and sweet: sticky toffee pudding perhaps. She felt full with the pleasure of it.

'Dara?' Stanley pulled away and looked at her. Dara opened

her eyes and smiled. The cowlick at the front of his hair was up and about, in a way she was becoming familiar with. 'I was wondering . . . if you're not doing anything, that is . . . if you'd like to come with me . . . on Saturday night . . . to this engagement party I was telling you about. My brother's . . .'

'I'd love to,' Dara said, surprising herself with the certainty of her response. Then she remembered. 'Wait, hang on, what time is it at?'

'Eight.'

'Stanley, I . . .' She had a sudden urge to tell him about Ian Harte. She closed her mouth on the words. She didn't want to see Stanley's cautious expression come down on his face, like shutters. 'There's something I've got to do first,' she said instead. Angel was right. It was time Dara stopped waiting. She didn't think Ian would mind all that much. In fact, she felt he would take it very well.

'Don't worry about it, it was just an idea . . .'

'No, I'd . . . I'd love to come. Could I meet you there?'

'You're sure?'

'Positive.'

'Fantastic,' he said, and he suddenly looked tall. No, not tall, exactly. But tall-*er*.

'So . . . good night, then. I'll see you in the morning. For breakfast.' She made a stab at moving up the corridor.

'Or you could . . .' Stanley paused. Dara stopped.

'Yes?' She waited.

'You could . . . come inside?'

'For a nightcap?'

'Or a cup of tea? It's practically morning.'

'A cup of tea would be nice.'

Stanley lifted the key out of his pocket again and looked at it. Then he looked at Dara. 'To be honest with you, Dara, I don't want tea. Or a nightcap. Or anything really. I was just saying that to get you inside.'

'I know,' Dara told him, grinning.

'Oh.' He looked confused. 'Are you sure?'

'You can never be sure,' Dara told him. 'About anything.' Stanley nodded, like she was talking a rare language that they both happened to be fluent in. 'But I'm pretty sure,' she went on. 'About this, I mean. In fact, I'm almost positive. I know I shouldn't feel like this. Not today. Not after everything that's happened. But the thing is . . . I do. The thing is . . . I feel . . . happy.'

There was a moment when she felt sure that Stanley wasn't going to say anything. There seemed to be a fistfight going on in his head. Some kind of a struggle.

Then he lifted his head and looked at her. 'So do I,' he said.

And that seemed to be enough, for both of them.

The bedroom door opened, then closed, and remained closed until checkout time had been and gone and the maid – after knocking and knocking – finally let herself in and didn't seem at all put out by the antics she witnessed in the shower.

This was Paris, after all.

51

It was like they'd always been together, Dara felt.

'I'm starving. I could eat a . . .' Stanley consulted the dictionary he had brought, 'a *cheval*,' he declared. He sat on the pillows at the top of the bed, the sheets tangled around his legs. In the hot light of the Paris sun streaming in at the window they'd left open, his skin was paler than the sheets. At times like these, his eyes seemed black rather than brown beneath the fringe of his softly curling lashes and thick eyebrows. The cowlick at the front of his hair was in its usual position: upstanding, like the most devout member of a congregation. When he looked at her, he smiled, his one dimple punching a well in his cheek, and Dara felt a fresh wave of desire charge down her body like an electrical current. She shivered.

'Are you all right?' Stanley asked.

'Just hungry,' she told him, looking at him like he was a bowl of carbonara – her favourite dinner – and she hadn't eaten in days. She thought briefly about wrapping a sheet carefully around her body before getting out of bed, and then threw caution – and the sheet – to the wind. 'Do I have time for a shower?' she asked, casually, as if she were not strolling around a hotel room in Paris with a man she barely knew and not a stitch on.

'We've loads of time,' said Stanley, not bothering to check his watch. Instead, he looked at Dara. She could feel his eyes sliding down her body.

'Turn around,' Stanley said. 'If you don't mind,' he added quickly.

And just like that, she did. She didn't even suck her belly in or push her chest out. In a rare rush of confidence, she felt there was no need. In fact, she didn't even *think* about doing any of that. She just stood there, naked, looking at Stanley Flinter, who looked back at her. Although she couldn't be sure, she felt there was a smile somewhere around the corner of her mouth that might be described as *wanton*, were she a character in a Jilly Cooper novel. She almost put her hands on her hips. She'd never done this before. Displayed herself. Like a piece of art in a gallery. Never even thought about it. But here, in Paris, with Stanley Flinter, it was like she just couldn't help herself. She wondered what Stanley would say.

'You're beautiful, Dara Flood,' he said, looking right at her. He bit at the corner of his mouth when he said it, in a way that let Dara know two things at the same time. It was not something he said very often. And he meant it. He really thought she was beautiful. She concentrated on not covering herself with her arms. She stood there.

'So are you,' she said.

'Come back here to me,' said Stanley, leaning towards her.

'What about breakfast?'

'What about it?'

Dara couldn't think of any answer to that question, so she didn't bother. Instead, she got back into bed.

Stanley could not have been more different than Ian Harte in bed. For a start, he said nothing. Not a single word. There was no talk of clouds or marshmallows or any kind of smorgasbord. There was just this quiet concentration on her body. There was something undiluted about the way he touched her. It was focused. Studied. He touched her like he'd been doing it for years. He knew, as if by instinct, just where she liked to be touched. The back of her neck. The tips of her fingers. The soft skin along the inside of her thighs. Stanley took his time, examining every inch of her body, with his eyes, his mouth, his fingers. Because he was so quiet, Dara tried to be quiet too. But it wasn't easy. She sighed – without meaning to – when he ran his fingers up the curve of her breast. When he bent his head and fastened his mouth around her nipples, hard as football studs, she couldn't help moaning. When his fingers slipped down her belly and disappeared between her legs, she moaned again, louder now. And when he kissed his way down her body and lapped at the soft wetness of her with his tongue, she went all out and groaned. She just couldn't help it. In fact, in the end, as he moved inside her, she became a collection of sounds: moans, sighs, groans, even a cry – just the one – at the end when she came. And came again. And again. She'd had orgasms before. Of course she had. But never like this. The orgasm, when it came, felt like a collection of all the orgasms she'd had before. A symphony of orgasms. International, compared to the local ones that had gone before. A grand parade. She was breathless afterwards. Slick with sweat. She could feel her heart hammering, the sound huge in the narrow cavity of her chest. All the while, Stanley never said a word, although afterwards, when he bent his head to kiss her mouth, his breath was strained and ragged and hot against her skin.

They missed the hotel breakfast by a good hour; a first for both of them. In a small café nearby, they both ordered coffee and French toast, which they ripped into pieces and ate with their hands.

They liked their coffee the same way: strong and black with half a spoon of brown sugar.

'I'm still hungry,' Stanley declared, and Dara nodded. She couldn't remember the last time she'd felt this hungry. They ordered eggs and mushrooms and thin strips of bacon and more coffee and a basket of warm, sweet bread.

'How about a pastry?' enquired Stanley, when they had mopped up the sticky mushroom juice from their plates with chunks of bread.

'Apple and cinnamon,' Dara said, nodding.

'Perfect,' said Stanley, but when Dara looked at him, he wasn't looking at the menu at all. He was looking right at her. She smiled. She couldn't help it.

At the airport, no beep-beep-beep of the metal detector. Stanley wasn't wearing his designer underpants today. Dara knew. She'd glanced as he pulled an average-Joe pair of boxers up over the taut twin moons of his buttocks, pale and smooth.

Nothing average about that, Dara found herself thinking in a sleazy kind of a way that bore no relation to the person that she was.

'What are you thinking about?' Stanley asked, his smile a little triumphant as he ran the gauntlet of the metal detector machine without incident.

'Eh . . . your buttocks actually.' Dara had presumed she would lie and make some innocuous comment about the time of their flight or their gate number or perhaps the weather in Dublin.

'My buttocks?' Stanley repeated, slowly.

'Yes, your buttocks.' Christ, she wasn't even going to deny it. Or say that she meant someone else's buttocks. Or change it to *bullocks*. I was thinking about *bullocks*. People think about bullocks, don't they? Sometimes?

'What were you thinking about them?' Stanley looked worried, as if Dara might be thinking something awful about his buttocks.

'Just how lovely they are,' Dara told him, in the most matter-of-fact tone she could summon.

'Why . . . exactly?' Stanley looked confused, like a man with no previous reason to consider the attributes or otherwise of his buttocks.

'Well, they're a lovely shape. And they're firm. And, of course, smooth.'

Stanley took a moment to digest this news about his buttocks.

'Well, your buttocks are lovely too,' he told her.

'You don't have to say that just because I happened to be thinking about your buttocks and, well, admiring them, I suppose.'

'I'm not.' Stanley looked appalled at the suggestion.

'Why are mine lovely, then?' Dara challenged him.

'Because of their height,' Stanley said immediately, in a way that almost suggested to Dara that he *had* thought about her buttocks. And in a positive way too.

'They're too big,' Dara told him. Stanley ignored her.

'And, of course, their softness. I think they're the softest buttocks I've ever come across,' he said, stopping to set his bag on the ground. He wrapped his arms around her then, setting his hands on her buttocks and squeezing gently, as if testing their softness again, in case he had been mistaken before. From the smile on his face, it appeared he had not. 'See?' he said.

'And have you come across many buttocks?' Dara asked him.

'Not as many as I've bragged about,' Stanley told her.

Dara laughed. She might not know much about this man, but she knew for a fact that he was not a man to brag about buttocks that he may or may not have come across in his time. She reached up to kiss him but not before setting *her* bag down, wrapping her arms around him and placing her hands on *his* buttocks. There, at the safe end of Security, they kissed for the longest time, even though neither of them had yet checked the gate they were supposed to be at or what time boarding began. Because it was Paris, nobody took a blind bit of notice.

On the flight, they talked, as if they'd been talking for years. Although not about what was happening between them. Dara was glad about that. She didn't want to inspect the development too carefully, as was her habit. Or put a label on it. It was much too early for that. While she was unsure as to just what it was, this ... situation between herself and Stanley Flinter, she held out a hope – albeit a slim one – that it might be something. Something important. Something good. She wanted to nurture it like a seed that you grow in warm soil in a tiny pot on the windowsill of your bedroom, before you plant it into the precarious earth of the garden and subject it to the careless elements.

Instead, she talked about Angel. About the found-and-lost kidney affair. Of course, she'd alluded to it before, but now she really told him about it. The change it had wrought in her sister. How close they had been. How empty Angel seemed now, without her faith and her hope. About Mrs Flood and her fear and her worry and her resignation – not about Angel, never about that – but about the shoddiness of life in general and how she never let it disappoint her because her expectations were, in fact, so low as to be non-existent.

Dara found it easy to talk to Stanley about her family. It should have been a sorry tale, with much slow shaking of heads and anguished expressions. But it wasn't like that, she felt. He nodded like he understood. He didn't interrupt. He didn't say awful stuff about things happening for a reason, or that it would all work out in the end, he was sure, or that Mr Flood would turn up, eventually, like the bad penny that he was. Instead, he listened. Really listened in a way that Ian Harte never did, she realised. Ian Harte listened in a way that always made Dara feel he was waiting for her to finish whatever it was she was saying so he could speak again. In fact, when she thought about it, she realised that she always spoke quickly when she spoke to Ian Harte. As though she sensed his impatience.

'Tell me about Cora,' Dara asked, taking a sip of her champage – 'We might as well, it's free' – and slipped her hands under the cover of the table top, crossing her fingers, a habit that had persisted from childhood whenever she felt that something awful was about to happen.

Stanley shook his head. 'That was never going to work out,' he said, and he looked surprised, as if he hadn't meant to say that, but now that it was out there, a proper sentence, out in the world, he realised how true it was. He shook his head and grinned. 'We had nothing in common really,' he told Dara. 'Apart from Cormac, of course.'

'Did she and Cormac . . . ?' began Dara, not quite sure how to phrase the question. 'I mean . . . while you and Cora were still together . . . ?'

'They're a good match,' said Stanley, and Dara felt, had Stanley been a different kind of person, he might have said instead, 'They're welcome to each other' or perhaps even, 'They deserve each other.' But he didn't say anything like that, and Dara nodded and left the subject behind where it belonged, in the history museum of Stanley's mind, where it would gather dust and smell, eventually, of damp and mildew.

She reached across the space between them and kissed him. She wasn't a woman given to making the first move, but with Stanley Flinter it felt right. It felt perfect. She could feel the smile on his mouth as he kissed her back. It was Stanley who pulled away first, leaving Dara straining towards him, her eyes closed.

'Why did you stop?' she asked him, in a worried whisper.

'Because we've landed,' Stanley said, smiling his mono-dimple smile and reaching a hand across to unbuckle Dara's seat belt in a way that made her want to be back in their hotel room in Paris once again.

'We've landed?' Dara couldn't believe it.

But it was true.

They had landed.

52

Stanley wanted to nurse his thoughts of Dara Flood in the ICU of his head for a while before he transferred her to the general ward where everyone could visit. He wanted to marinate his thoughts in her, steep them until they were swollen with her. Until they tasted of nothing but her. He wanted to do all this in private, but, of course, with Sissy Clarke on the case, that was never going to happen.

He let himself in his front door, yelling 'Honey, I'm home' at the top of his voice, and Sissy knew. Immediately. He cursed himself for letting his guard slip with his cheery greeting, but he couldn't help it. If he had to describe how he felt, he might have to use the word *elated*. He didn't think he'd ever felt *elated* before but, really, there was no other word for it.

'What happened?' Sissy tore down the stairs wearing a pair of his boxer shorts – plain old Dunnes Stores ones with no embarrassing metal tag of designer status – and one of his T-shirts, albeit one that Sissy had bought him. It was pink, with a picture of two enormous hands cupping a pair of breasts on the front of it and a caption that said: *I'm in touch with my feminine side*. Sissy said it suited him. Stanley never wore it.

'Nothing happened. What do you mean?'

'Don't toy with me, Stanley Flinter. I'm going to make us some dinner-ding and you're going to tell me *everything*.'

Stanley was ready for her, knowing that she'd try to ply him with dinner-ding the minute he got home.

'No need,' he told her, his voice as bright as a summer's day. 'I stopped at the fishmonger's and got us some tuna steaks.' He held the bag up, the tuna straining purple against the plastic.

Sissy looked put out. 'Nobody says fishmonger's any more,' she told him. 'It's so 1954. Besides, they'll take ages to cook and I'm going out.'

'By the time you get dressed and put your face on, they'll be cooked,' Stanley promised her. 'You go upstairs and I'll get busy in the kitchen.'

'I'll put my make-up on here. That way, you can tell me everything while I'm getting ready.'

'There's nothing to tell.'

'Stanley, don't make me come over there and . . .' She stopped talking and moved cautiously towards him. 'Oh my God,' she said in a whisper.

'What?'

'Your top button's undone, you haven't tried to flatten your cowlick since you walked in and . . .' her eyes widened, 'you're *grinning*. You're actually grinning.'

It was true, however hard Stanley tried to peel it off his face. It was stuck fast like a plaster over a wound, long healed.

Sissy walked right up to him, her eyes sweeping across his face like a brush.

'You've had sex,' she told him. 'More than once, by the looks of you. And is that a . . . ?' She leaned towards his neck. 'You've got a hickey. It's *huge* so it is, you dirty scut.'

Stanley stopped fighting with his grin. He didn't even bother to hide the purple bruise on his neck in the shape of Dara Flood's mouth. There was no point. Not with Sissy at full tilt. Instead he widened his grin and pulled at the collar of his shirt, revealing the other side of his neck.

Sissy inhaled sharply. 'You've got *two*,' she said, her voice so high that Stanley felt only dogs could hear it. In fact, it brought Clouseau pounding down the stairs from where he'd been lying on Stanley's bed, pining since Stanley's departure, Sissy told him later. The huge hound forgot all about his Dara Flood training, gathered himself on his back legs and lunged at Stanley, who had the wherewithal to throw the bag of fish towards the table so he had the use of both hands to defend himself against the meaty might of the canine. Even so, the momentum of Clouseau's body at full throttle threw Stanley backwards and the pair of them landed on the couch, tangled like lovers in the duvet that Sissy called her *workstation*.

Sissy took her chance, picking up the tuna steaks, hiding them in the freezer and throwing two dinner-dings into the microwave. She opened a bag of salad, tossed it in a bowl, threw cutlery and plates on the table, filled two enormous glasses with a sturdy Merlot and sat at the table in Stanley's boxers and T-shirt, waiting for Clouseau to stop licking him as if he were a Wibbly Wobbly Wonder.

Her reflexes were lightning fast, Stanley had to give her that. He settled Clouseau with the box set of *Mad Men* (the dog's favourite TV programme: Stanley thought it might have something to do with the cigarette smoking, as June Robinson had been a vigorous smoker) and a gigantic lamb bone he'd been gifted by the fishmonger, who also sold meat and had a soft spot for Chief Inspector Jacques Clouseau.

'Tell. Me. Everything,' Sissy ordered after taking a huge slug of wine and a gigantic bite of her dinner-ding. Stanley poked at his with a fork. He thought it might be trying to be chicken chasseur but he couldn't be sure.

He shook his head. 'It's early days, I don't want to jinx it,' he told her, already knowing that this argument was about as effective as a broken umbrella in a hurricane.

'*I* don't count. You know I won't tell anyone.'

Stanley knew that but he wanted to nurse his thoughts of Dara Flood in the quiet of the ICU in his head. Still, he had to tell her something.

'I did what you told me to do,' he said.

'I only told you to bring her to a park or a monument or someplace. I didn't tell you to *sleep* with her.' Sissy looked at him, as proud as a duck with a particulary fluffy yellow chick.

'It wasn't intentional,' Stanley admitted.

'It never is,' said Sissy darkly, probably thinking of all the times men had *unintentionally* slept with her.

'But I'm . . . glad about it,' Stanley supplied, without even being coaxed. 'It was . . . lovely.'

'Lovely?' Sissy was unimpressed by the description, but Stanley was adamant. He nodded.

'Yes, it was, it was lovely.'

'Gories?'

'No.'

'Why not?'

'Because it's private.'

Sissy sighed but nodded. Stanley could not believe she was backing down so easily. Then she stoped sighing and nodding and looked at him. 'Just tell me how many times?' she asked.

'Sissy, I . . .'

'I wouldn't ask unless it was important,' she told him, fixing him with a look that he knew she felt was earnest.

He relented. 'OK, four times, if you must—'

But Sissy was on her feet, her glass raised in her hand. 'FOUR TIMES!' she shouted. 'By God, your born-again-virgin status is well and truly shattered.'

'Sissy, please, I wish I hadn't told you. Promise me you won't say a word? To anyone? I don't know what this is or where it's going. It's all so new and I haven't had time to properly think about it yet.' But his grin was back. In fact, it had never really left.

'What did Cora want the other night?' Sissy asked, as if she could read his mind.

'Nothing important,' Stanley said.

'Are you still going to the engagement party?'

'Of course. Dara is coming with me.'

Sissy didn't say anything to that. Instead, she whooped and clapped her hands like a seal, which said it all, really.

For a while, they bent their heads and concentrated on dinner. Stanley surprised himself by eating every bit of his dinner-ding which, when washed down with a good dollop of red, didn't taste all that bad.

'I think we should drink a toast to love,' Sissy declared, holding her glass towards Stanley.

'I never said anything about love,' Stanley said quickly, as his grin was elbowed roughly off his face by his customary caution.

'You didn't have to,' Sissy told him smugly.

Because there was no point arguing with her, Stanley didn't bother. Besides, he couldn't come up with one single argument that sounded legitimate.

'Will you do my eye make-up for me?' Sissy asked, finally accepting that no salacious details would be forthcoming from Stanley Flinter.

'Of course,' Stanley said, dragging his mind away from Dara Flood's face. 'Dramatic or subtle?' he asked.

Sissy was unimpressed by the question.

'Dramatic it is,' Stanley told her, reaching for her make-up sack – it was too immense to be called a bag – and digging around until he picked out the most dramatic eyeshadow he could find. It was St Patrick's Day green and went by the name of Sham-Rock!, which Stanley felt was dramatic enough even for Sissy.

'You're still smiling,' Sissy told him, as he concentrated on colouring in her eyelids, carefully, with his tongue trapped between his lips as it always was when he was concentrating.

'I know,' he said, shaking his head as worry crept into the corners of his eyes. 'I can't seem to help it.'

'Don't worry,' said Sissy, patting his arm. 'It'll just take a while to get used to it.'

'To what?' Stanley asked. 'Smiling?'

'Being happy,' she told him, setting her lips into a pout so that Stanley could paint her lips with her most dramatic lipstick yet: Rollercoaster Red.

53

Of course, when Dara thought about it later, she realised that she should have been on her guard. In Paris, for a moment, it was almost as if she had been a different person. An optimistic person. She had allowed hope to slide in through a crack in the walls she had built around her life. That's where she'd gone wrong, she realised. Later. She had forgotten about hope. How it tugs at expectations. Raises them. And how expectations, once raised, lead down the path towards *disappointment*. *Uncertainty.* Eventual, inevitable *decline*.

But that was later.

For now, everything was the same when Dara Flood arrived home to the house on the Raheny road. In fact, things were better than usual, which only encouraged more hope and raised yet more expectations.

Dara set her bag on the floor of the hall and stood there for a moment, allowing her thoughts – and yes, her hopes and expectations – to settle before she slotted herself back into her life.

'You're home,' Mrs Flood told her, coming into the hall.

'Yes,' Dara said, looking at her mother. Her hair was shiny today. Bouncy as a ball. It looked like it had benefited from some hot rollers and perhaps a few highlights. 'Your hair is nice,' Dara said.

'Yours could do with a brush,' Mrs Flood told her.

'Where's Angel?'

'In her room.'

Dara picked up her bag. 'I'll just go up and . . .'

'Well? That was a waste of time, wasn't it? Your trip to Paris.'

'I know. And I'm sorry. But I had to go. I had to see her. Just in case.'

Mrs Flood walked down the hall and opened the kitchen door, shaking her head as she went. From the kitchen, Dara could smell something. Something fruity. Sweet. She followed her mother.

'I told you it was a fool's errand, Dara,' said Mrs Flood, sitting at the kitchen table now. 'That man is gone and no amount of fancy trips is going to change that.'

On the counter, in a line, stood jars of what looked like strawberry jam. Home-made strawberry jam. Dara's favourite kind. She lifted one of the jars and turned to look at her mother.

'Angel made it,' Mrs Flood said before she could ask. A smile threatened the corners of her mouth.

'But strawberries aren't even in season,' Dara couldn't help saying. She was a great believer in using fresh local ingredients, which was one of the many reasons why her food tasted so good.

'I know. She got me to go and buy the frozen ones,' Mrs Flood said.

'Frozen strawberries?'

'Well, she thawed them out, but yes, they were frozen to begin with.' Mrs Flood liked to be clear about things.

'Why?'

'Because it's your favourite, I suppose,' said Mrs Flood, shrugging her shoulders.

'I know that, but . . .' Dara wasn't sure if Mrs Flood had noticed the somewhat strained relationship between the sisters in recent times.

Mrs Flood nodded. 'I think she missed you.'

'But why?' Dara was genuinely confused.

Mrs Flood didn't answer. Instead, she rose stiffly from the chair and moved towards the kettle. She paused on her way to glance somewhat curiously at Dara. 'You look a little . . . flushed, Dara. I hope you're not coming down with something. Angel can't afford to get an infection, you know that.'

Dara fought a sudden impulse to tell her mother that she *was* coming down with something. She was coming down with Stanley Flinter. She was smothered in him, wrapped up in him, surrounded by him on all sides. She couldn't stop thinking about him, and every time she did, she smiled, even when there was no valid reason for it. Like earlier, in the taxi.

'You're delighted with yerself, aren't you?' the taxi driver had told her, pulling up in front of her house.

Dara nodded. There was no denying it.

Even when he told her he didn't have change of a twenty, and she had to leave him with one of her last fivers before payday, she still smiled. In fact, the muscles in her face ached in this unfamiliar position.

'I'm just a little hot,' Dara told her mother. 'So, Angel? Is she feeling a bit better, then? Making jam and all.' Hope surged through her like electricity.

'Go up and ask her yourself,' said Mrs Flood. When Dara looked at the reflection of her mother's face in the shiny surface of the kettle, Mrs Flood was smiling. A proper smile with teeth and even a hint of pink gum. Dara took the stairs two at a time.

In her bedroom, Angel was sitting on the floor, playing patience with a dog-eared pack of cards. She was wearing clothes. Proper clothes. Of Mrs Flood's demented dressing gown, there was no sign. Nor was there any music. No Joy Division. No Leonard Cohen. No Morrissey, Radiohead or The Smiths. Without these usual diversions, in the soft glow from the lamp on Angel's bedside table, the room seemed curiously upbeat. It reminded Dara of Angel. Of her sister. Of the way she used to be.

'Dara! You're home.' Angel looked up as the door swung open, plunging her card game into an arc of shadow. Her face was paler than Dara remembered and she seemed thinner, perhaps because of the unfamiliar clothes. But her smile was her old one: wide and warm.

'Yes, I . . .'

'I am so glad to see you.'

'Me too.'

'I missed you.'

'You did?'

Instead of answering, Angel put the cards down and struggled to her feet, leaning on the edge of the bed. She looked at Dara and her mouth opened but she did not speak. Instead, she took a step forward and bent towards Dara, gathering her close. And even though they were not sisters given to random acts of gratuitous affection, they held each other then. Dara felt Angel's arms around her like the strings of a parachute, protecting her, as she always had done, from the hard crust of the world. For a moment, she felt like nothing bad could happen.

Angel's hair had the untended demeanour of hair that had been left to dry without product or implement. But it had been *washed*. This was a marked improvement.

'I'm sorry I didn't find Mr Flood,' Dara whispered into Angel's hair.

'I'm sorry too,' said Angel.

'I should never have gone to Paris. It was a stupid idea, getting your hopes up and . . .'

'No, I'm not sorry about you not finding Mr Flood. I'm just . . . sorry.'

'What for?' Dara stepped back and looked up.

'For everything. The way I've been. The things I said to you. They were unforgivable.'

'They were true,' Dara reminded her.

'I shouldn't have said them.'

Dara noticed that her sister did not comment on the accuracy or otherwise of the things she had said, and it was the very absence of this contradiction that strengthened Dara's resolve. There had been too much waiting. Worrying. Inching along the footpath of her life, as far from the kerb as she could get. Keeping well away from the traffic of the world, in case it ran her down. She had thought risk was something to be avoided, like potholes. She hadn't considered the other side of risk, the good side. How it rushed at you, bowling you over with its precarious thrill, leaving you light-headed and breathless. Swaying with the force of it.

Angel studied her. 'You look great,' she said. 'Have you done something different to yourself?'

Dara nodded. 'I've taken a leaf out of your book,' she told Angel. 'About life, I mean. I'm going to stop worrying about it. Well, I'm going to try, anyway.'

It took a moment for Angel to digest this revelation. She looked at Dara a little fearfully, and in her cautious expression, Dara recognised herself. 'You're not going to do anything rash?' Angel said, worried now that perhaps she had gone too far.

'What? You mean like bungee jumping or eating sushi?' Dara had a deep-seated fear of sushi. It was the raw fish. Raw carrots she could understand. But uncooked *fish*. It was too much.

'Well, yes, I suppose . . .' Angel said, in a way that suggested she hadn't considered either of these options.

'Christ, no,' Dara assured her. 'Nothing like that. I'm just going to live my life like a normal person. Like you. As if nothing bad is going to happen. That's what I mean.'

'Bad stuff might still happen, though.' Angel wasn't quite ready to let go of her worrywart of a sister.

'Yes, but it'll happen anyway, won't it?' Dara said. 'No matter what I do.'

Angel studied her sister's face and smiled. 'Look at you, all out and about,' she said, proud as a flag.

Dara smiled back. She *did* feel as if she had come out. The world was bright and clear after the close stuffiness of the closet. She couldn't even remember why she had spent so long in that dark, tight space that smelled of old runners.

'Anyway,' said Angel, sitting on the bed and pulling Dara down beside her. 'Tell me all about Paris.'

'Well, there's not much to tell really,' said Dara. She wasn't quite ready to share Stanley Flinter with the rest of the world. Even Angel. It was too soon. She didn't want to jinx it.

'Ah come on, Dara, give me something. I've had nothing but Leonard fecking Cohen for company recently, and I know it's my fault, but *Christ*, he's a maudlin git. It's been a terrible waste of time, all this feeling sorry for myself. I don't want to waste any more time.'

'You've been down,' Dara corrected her. 'It's completely natural. You've had a hard time. A setback.'

'I've been wallowing.'

'You haven't.'

'I have.'

Dara took a different tack. 'I'd wallow too, if it were me. I'd be brilliant at it.'

'But the truth is . . .' Angel began.

'What?' Dara was curious now.

Angel chewed at the end of a strand of hair. 'Well, I'm well and truly sick of it. To be honest, I'm bored out of my skull. Bored of wallowing. How shallow is that?'

'No, not at all,' Dara said. 'Even Anya can only do it for a weekend at a time.'

'Really?' Angel was surprised at this, having met Anya a number of times at The Doghouse.

'Well, she says she can do it for longer in Poland but she

finds it harder in Ireland. There's so much beauty here, she says. It really pisses her off.'

Angel laughed. Her laugh was like a favourite piece of music you hadn't heard in years. It made you want to sing along.

'I just wish my kidney wasn't so fucked,' she said.

'We'll get you another one,' Dara told her. She barely recognised her own voice. It sounded so certain.

54

The phone rang. The landline. It made them jump before they ran, taking the stairs two at a time.

But it was only Anya.

'Apologies, Dara, for ringing on landline. I cannot get through on your mobile phone,' Anya began. Dara took her phone out of her pocket and inspected the screen. No sodding coverage.

'That's OK,' said Dara, shaking her head at Angel, who nodded and moved away.

'You did not find Mr Flood?' In Anya's serious monotone, it came out as a statement rather than a question.

'No,' said Dara.

'I am sorry about it,' said Anya.

'I know,' said Dara. 'Thank you, Anya.' She waited, knowing that Anya had something to tell her. Something important enough to warrant a call to the landline. She was not wrong.

'I haf news to impart.' Anya did not mince words when she was on the phone. Or indeed ever. Dara waited. 'Is about Lucky,' Anya said, her voice as serious as a grave.

Dara steeled herself for the news, which she knew would not be good.

'He bit leetle girl this afternoon.'

'No!' said Dara.

'Yes,' said Anya. 'I am sorry, Dara but he vill haf to sit on the bench. There is no alternative.' Anya spoke about dogs sitting on the bench, as if they were substitute footballers waiting to be called up, rather than unfortunate dogs waiting to be put down.

'But . . . did you actually see what happened?'

'I saw the bite, Dara. Was bad. She needed sutures.'

In the background, Dara could hear Tintin, mumbling something.

'What's Tintin saying?' she asked. 'Put him on to me. Please.'

A rustling sound, which could have been Anya putting her hand over the mouthpiece of the phone. Dara could hear Anya hissing something at Tintin. 'You have to tell her,' she heard Tintin saying in his stage whisper that was louder than most people's shouts.

'No.' Dara could just about make out Anya's vehement response. 'We agreed, remember?'

A shuffling noise then, which might have been a tussle between the pair of them for control of the phone, the sound of something falling to the ground – Tintin perhaps: Anya was unusually strong – more whispers, urgent now, and then a deep sigh – Dara recognised it as Anya, who was given to sighing deeply – followed by the cross barks of Rocky, the tiniest dog in the pound. Tintin dubbed him *the tiny dog with the HUGE personality*, as if he were a tagline from a Disney film.

'Dara?' It was Anya again. Dara imagined her holding Tintin in a headlock with one arm and cradling Rocky gently in the crook of the other.

'What happened, Anya?' Dara asked. 'Lucky was doing so well. He wouldn't hurt anyone unless he was provoked. You know that.'

Another deep sigh. 'They arrived in SUV,' Anya began.

'Who?' Dara asked, confused.

'The family of leetle girl. She had Nintendo DS. So did her brother,' Anya spat. Dara nodded. In Anya's world, SUVs and Nintendos were up there with the devil's tools.

'Go on,' Dara said.

'Tell her about the stick.' Tintin's voice was muffled, as if Anya had her hand clamped over his mouth. Not beyond possible, Dara felt.

'Tell me about the stick,' she repeated.

'Leetle girl had stick,' Anya conceded.

'A big stick,' Tintin corrected.

'Perhaps twenty centimetres long,' said Anya, who liked to be precise about such details.

'Anya, would you mind if I speak to Tintin?' asked Dara. 'I think it might be easier.'

Another deep sigh. 'It vill not change outcome, Dara,' Anya warned.

Dara nodded. She knew that Anya would not make a decision like this without serious consideration. 'I understand,' she said.

A grunting sound as Tintin was released from whatever position Anya had him in, and then he was on the phone.

'She was a precocious little brat, Dara,' he said in a rush. 'Rattling all the cages with the stick, and Lucky's in particular.'

'Why didn't you stop her?'

'We were busy with her parents. They were interested in poor little Fleur. Yer woman was mad about Pilates and fancied the idea of a dog who could do it too. It was only later, when we watched it on the CCTV system, that we saw what the girl – Charlotte or Ruby or Iseult, one of those names – did. The witch.'

'Go on.'

'She pushed the stick through the bars at him. Hitting him. Then the stupid wagon dropped the stick and reached her hand in to grab it. And Lucky bit her.'

'But . . .'

'I know. She got what she deserved. But it's the second bite on his record. And we can't get anyone to take him. And John's saying there's no alternative . . .'

'John always says that,' said Dara, grasping at straws.

'I know, Dara,' said Tintin, 'but this time I—'

'He vill haf to sit on the bench.' Anya was back on the line, her voice clear as a bell. 'I am sorry for it, Dara.'

'I know,' said Dara. 'Thanks for letting me know.'

'Ve vill do it in morning. I vill come in. You vill take morning off.'

'No, it's OK, Anya, I can . . .'

'I insist,' said Anya, with her quiet gravitas.

'OK,' said Dara. 'I'll see you . . . afterwards then.'

'Goodbye, Dara,' said Anya, brisk now. She hung up.

55

It was Angel's idea. And of course, she talked Dara into it. She had always been good at that.

'We can't just . . . *charge in and take him*,' Dara argued with her sister. 'That would be like, I don't know, breaking and entering, not to mention stealing and God knows what else we'd be charged with.'

'It's not bloody breaking and entering. You have a fecking *key*,' Angel reminded her. 'And it can hardly be classified as *stealing* if the thing you steal is not even going to exist, come first light tomorrow.'

'It won't be at first light,' Dara said. 'It'll be after elevenses. John always brings buns on the days he's doing it. The fucker.'

'You know what I mean,' said Angel, leaning across Dara and opening the passenger door of the car. 'Come on,' she said. 'Time to go.'

'But we can't just rock up there and *take* him. I mean, what are we going to do with him then?'

Angel withered Dara with a look. 'We're going to bring him home, of course. Give him some of that canine stew you're always making. We'll get Ma to knit him dog coats with the days of the week on them. Why should we be the only ones scratching the living daylights out of ourselves?'

'Do you mean *keep* him?'

'Of course that's what I mean.'

'But . . . where would we put him?'

'In the back garden. He could have George's old kennel.'

'Mam threw it out, remember?' Dara said in a voice as taut as a tightrope. 'Last week.'

'Christ, she really is a thorough old biddy when she puts her mind to it,' Angel said, shaking her head in part admiration, part disbelief. 'Never mind, we'll ask Electric Eddie to build him a kennel. He's good at that kind of thing, isn't he?'

Neither of them spoke for a while. Just sat in Angel's car in the darkness of the car park at the back of The Doghouse. Dara's skin itched where her patch stuck to her, and her mouth watered with the need for a cigarette. She hadn't yet told Angel about her relapse. Although now seemed like a good time for an admission of this nature, given Angel's preoccupation with Lucky.

'Look,' Dara said, getting out of the car with indecent haste. She used one hand to grope around her pockets for a packet of cigarettes while the other reached for the patch. She reefed it off her skin, hard enough to smart. 'I'm telling you now. Two things in fact. We can't just rock up there – to my *place of work*, remember? – and steal Lucky. It's just . . . it's a crazy idea . . . I could get fired or struck off the register or . . .'

'What register?'

'I don't know. Maybe there's a register for animal minders. If there isn't, there bloody well should be. And I'll be struck off it.'

'What's the second thing?' Angel asked, in a bored kind of voice.

'What?'

'The second thing. You said there were two things, remember?'

'Oh, right,' said Dara as her fingers reached around the packet of cigarettes in the thigh pocket of her combats. She pulled them out and held them in front of Angel's face. 'I'm smoking again.'

'I know that,' said Angel, dismissive now as well as bored.

'How do you know?' Dara was genuinely curious, having spent the last few weeks taking inhuman measures to keep her return to smoking under wraps.

'Because your breath smells of mint all the time and you've been washing your hands so much, you've used up Mam's entire stock of Palmolive, and you know how many non-perishables she keeps in the house.'

It was true. Mrs Flood had converted her tiny utility room into a sort of larder where she stockpiled tins of food and household essentials, like washing powder, scouring pads and soap. 'Just in case,' she always said, when her daughters enquired about it. They didn't ask her to elaborate. They didn't need to. They knew what she had in mind. The outbreak of a nuclear war, perhaps. An epidemic, maybe. Or a pandemic even. That was worse, wasn't it? Or some unspecified environmental disaster. Something on that scale. The fact that none of them would be around to partake of the tinned peaches and tomatoes, not to mention blow their noses with any of the tissues in their industrial-sized boxes, was never mentioned by Mrs Flood. Because there was something cautiously optimistic in this omission, her daughters never brought it up either.

'But I can't have another dog,' said Dara, lighting up in the frantic way of smokers after a transatlantic flight. 'Not after George. You know that.'

George had been put down. The vet said it was the kindest thing to do, after the accident. Dara still remembered the trusting brown eyes of him, resting on her face as he lay on the bench, as Anya called it. She held his paw, the pads soft and warm against her hand. The sharp glint of the needle in the vet's hand. The tap-tap-tap of his fingernail against the tip.

'Will it hurt?' she'd asked.

'He won't feel a thing.'

Dara didn't believe him. They all said that.

'So what happened to getting out of the closet? Living your life? All that shite?'

'This is different,' Dara told her.

'No it's not,' Angel insisted, getting out of the car. 'Look, put this on.' From her bag she produced two of the woollen hats Mrs Flood had knitted for them over the years. Horrendous yokes that made you scratch at yourself like a dog with fleas.

'What do we need those for?' Dara found herself asking.

Angel stuck one on her head and pulled it right down to her chin. Because it was Mrs Flood who had knitted them, they were of course much too big for a normal-sized human head, so Angel could do this quite easily.

'You've cut holes in them,' Dara noticed.

'For the eyes. See? And one for the nose and mouth too. So we won't suffocate.' Sure enough, the holes in the wool fitted perfectly over Angel's blue eyes, bright with the things that Angel held dear. Things like faith. And hope.

Dara lowered her cigarette from her mouth. 'But why . . . ?'

'They'll do as balaclavas, you see?' Angel explained. 'So we won't be recognised on the CCTV.'

'They'd pick these out of any line-up,' Dara pointed out, nodding at the herd of reindeer that ran around the bottom of both hats. A limping line of mostly purple reindeer. Mrs Flood had found it difficult to source wool in the more traditional russet-red colour.

'Just turn them inside out, see?' Angel had an answer for everything. 'Christ, these things are even itchier on the other side. Try yours on.'

And Dara did. She studied her reflection in the side of the car, which was lit by a solitary guttering lantern at the back of the pub. Angel stood beside her and put her hat on again too, pulling it down to cover her chin and staring at Dara through the jagged peepholes she had cut through the wool.

The pair of them fell around with the laughing, taking care not to make any noise. Through the thick, itchy wool of their hats, the sound was pretty muffled anyway.

'Let's go,' said Angel.

'I don't know,' began Dara, picking strands of wool out of her mouth.

'Come on,' hissed Angel, already at the entrance of the car park.

'I'm not sure,' Dara whispered, moving towards her sister now as Angel nodded encouragement at her.

'Nobody's ever sure,' Angel told her, looking left and right, then left again before she crossed the deserted road. There were some traits she had inherited from her sister.

Now Dara and Angel stood on either side of the road, shadowy silhouettes lit only by an occasional impression of the moon, glancing between wide sheets of cloud.

'Well?' Angel hissed across the road at her.

'I'm worried,' said Dara.

'What have you got to lose?' Angel asked.

'Well, there's my job, for one thing. My *livelihood*, remember? And of course my professional reputation, for another. I wouldn't get a job shovelling elephant dung if this gets out.'

'Would you like a job shovelling elephant dung?' asked Angel.

'Well, no, but . . .'

'There you go then. Anything else?'

Dara paused before she sighed a sigh that Anya would have been impressed with. She squared her shoulders, pulled her hat down over her face, looked left, right, then left again before she crossed.

'If anything happens . . .' she began when she reached her sister on the other side of the road.

'It won't,' said Angel with her old sense of certainty, solid as a wall.

'Yes, but if it does, just run like fuck, OK?'

'But I can't run as fast as you,' Angel reminded her.

'Exactly,' said Dara with a grin.

They climbed the gate and crept up the laneway towards the pound. The hedgerows, thickening as spring swelled into early summer, shifted and stirred in the cool breeze. Dara heard a slow scratching noise. Claws against bark. A badger perhaps. The belligerent howls of cats, toying with each other in the tall rushes of the riverbank. The scuttling of mice, taking their chances through the long grasses in the field beyond, their tiny sqeaks audible now in the dense quiet of the night.

Outside the Portakabin that Tintin called Anya's *corner office*, Dara fiddled with the padlock, turning the combination lock until it opened. It was the same combination she used for everything: her bank cards, her mobile phone pin number, her password for her e-mail account – 0310. The third of October. The day Mr Flood walked up the road and never came back. Oddly, it had always been a good day in the Flood household. Mrs Flood made sure she marked it with some special activity, regardless of whether it was a school day or not: a visit to the zoo, tickets to a play, a trip to a bookshop to buy brand-new books that smelled nothing like the library books they usually borrowed. When they were younger, they accepted these gifts as children do, although they *did* wonder, given that it wasn't Christmas or their birthdays or even a holy day, when Mrs Flood sometimes treated them to hot chocolates and sticky buns at the local café after Mass. Later, Dara assumed it was Mrs Flood's version of flipping Mr Flood the bird. Two fingers up to a husband with no staying power. A shrug of indifference to the man's fecklessless. A *fuck you* in the face of his cold carelessness.

See? We don't need you. We're doing just fine on our own.

Mrs Flood paraded her girls about on that day every year, wearing their Sunday best, regardless of the day of the week.

As if they were on display. As if Mr Flood could see them, like they were a programme on the telly and he was lying on a couch somewhere, scratching his balls, watching them.

Dara turned her attention to the CCTV system, switched it off, reached for the key to Lucky's kennel

Out in the yard, the dogs began to stir, Jeffrey throwing himself against the bars of his cage in a rage of ecstasy at the unexpected nocturnal activity. Dara knelt down at his cage and pressed her face between the bars, allowing Jeffrey to lick her nose before buying his silence with the biscuits she'd made earlier. She moved through the pound in this way, Angel stepping in her wake, presenting her hands and her face to be licked before offering one of her biscuits in return for their complicity, which they gave without question. They loved Dara Flood's home-made biscuits almost as much as they loved Dara Flood. At the end of the enclosure, Lucky's cage. Dara stopped two feet from it and Angel bumped into the back of her.

'What?' Angel asked, rubbing her chin, which had banged against Dara's head.

'Sssshhh,' Dara whispered. From the cage, a low growl.

'Jesus,' said Angel.

'He's just confused,' Dara said.

'He doesn't sound confused. He sounds ferocious,' Angel said, her fear appearing like cracks through her voice.

'Don't worry,' Dara told her, kneeling down and shuffling towards the cage.

Lucky lay there, his paws covering his eyes, refusing to look at her. The growling continued. Dara stretched her face towards the cage and made soft kissing noises with her lips. Lucky's ears twitched. He slid his paws down his nose, his eyes reaching for Dara's face and settling there. 'Terrible business yesterday, Dara old chum,' he seemed to be saying. 'Fright-fly sorry about it. But what's a chap to do, eh? When his crown jewels are being fiddled with by a filly with a stick, um? *And* she called me ugly! Right to my face too. She said I was the ugliest hound she'd ever seen. *Quite* uncalled for, wouldn't you agree?'

Dara lifted her hand slowly towards Lucky's mouth. He sniffed it first before he allowed himself to lick it. A wet lick, from her fingertips right down to her wrist. Slowly. Thoroughly. He left no inch of skin untouched by the rough length of his tongue. It was an important lick, Dara felt. A lick that meant something. The sealing of some bond between them. She slid the key into the padlock on the cage and opened it. Lucky pushed himself up on all fours and glanced around the cage before stepping out, in the dainty way he had, despite looking like a dog that had been thrown together, what with his huge body, his tiny head, his long, floppy ears, his stump of a tail, his short legs, not to mention his enormous paws.

'Holy Mother of the Divine Lantern of Christ,' said Angel, in a convincing parody of Mrs Flood's voice and incantations. 'He's quite the . . . collection, isn't he?'

'There's a bit of everything there all right,' Dara agreed. 'He's an interesting-looking dog. Aren't you, Lucky?' she whispered at him, pulling her hands down the length of his ears, the way he liked. It took ages. There was no doubt about it. His ears were astonishingly long.

'Interesting,' repeated Angel. 'Well, that's certainly one word for him.'

'You're not regretting this, are you?' Dara turned to her sister, worried.

'Christ, no,' Angel said, bending down and offering her hand to Lucky, who sniffed at it in quite a desultory fashion before getting back to Dara. 'He looks like a dog who needs somewhere to call home.'

Dara nodded, reaching inside her jacket pocket for the lead. She clipped it onto Lucky's collar and stood up.

'Do you want to go home, Lucky?' Dara asked. The dog barked. It was the first time she had ever heard him bark, given his tendency to either growl ominously or stew in a menacing type of silence. The sound was unexpected. There was something joyful about it. It was more of a laugh than a bark. An infectious one. It was high-pitched. Girlish. A little camp, almost. It was like a fully-grown, huge, hairy man opening his mouth and speaking as if his voice had forgotten to break, back when he was a teenager.

Dara tugged lightly at the lead and Lucky fell into step beside her as if he'd been walking beside Dara Flood for ever.

His stump of a tail did its best to wag, all the way home.

56

It wasn't until the following day that Angel began to feel unwell. At first it was nothing serious. A cold perhaps. The beginnings of a headache. Some vague aches down her legs.

'It's nothing,' she insisted, blowing her nose and suppressing a cough that sounded chesty.

'I shouldn't have let you come with me last night,' Dara said, pulling the covers up around Angel's chin.

'I wanted to. It was my idea, remember?' She pushed the covers back and reached down to pet Lucky, who had taken a shine to Angel, like most people did. He settled himself at the end of her bed with his enormous head resting along the length of Angel's feet and refused to move.

She developed a temperature. Not a terribly high one, but high enough to stain her cheeks and dampen her forehead. High enough for Dara and Mrs Flood to worry more than usual.

'You should go to the hospital,' Mrs Flood said, examining the thermometer. Dara agreed.

Angel was adamant. 'No,' she said. 'I'm going on Monday for my dialysis. That's time enough.'

'But what if . . . ?' began Mrs Flood.

Angel compromised, in a low but firm voice. 'I'll have a rest now and see how I feel when I wake up. I'm just tired, that's all.'

'I'll remove that . . . creature from the room, so,' said Mrs Flood, making a move towards Lucky, whose hackles rose all over his body until he resembled a very large porcupine.

Mrs Flood had been out when the girls arrived home with Lucky. An emergency callout to Mrs Butcher, who had – against her better judgement – spent part of the afternoon in a steam room.

So her first sighting of Lucky was the following morning, in the back garden. He introduced himself to Mrs Flood by digging up her best rose bush and defecating neatly in the hanging basket she'd watered and left in the flower bed. But her reaction had not been as adamant as Dara had expected. Maybe because of the absence of Leonard Cohen about the house. Mrs Flood examined him thoroughly before looking at Dara and asking, 'What class of beast is that?'

'He won't be any trouble,' Dara said as Lucky did a maniacal loop of the downstairs of the house and skidded down the hall, knocking over the coat stand before settling down to chew holes in the arm of Mrs Flood's good winter coat. Dara tickled him under his chin, just the way he liked it, until he finally agreed to release the coat from the grip of his jaws. She hung it up and turned to her mother. 'He's had a bit of a hard time recently,' she explained, lifting the dog into her arms.

'Haven't we all?' Mrs Flood said, but she moved towards Lucky and pulled gently at his ears, without having to be told that this was something he was fond of. Dara felt hope – more of it – surge.

'Could he stay?' Angel asked her mother, nodding at Lucky at the end of the bed.

'He's probably riddled with fleas and the Lord knows what else,' Mrs Flood said.

'He is not,' Dara said, offended on Lucky's behalf. 'I dewormed and de-fleaed him myself. I also clipped his nails.'

'He smells like mackerel.' Mrs Flood hated fish, and mackerel in particular.

'He does *not* smell like mackerel,' said Dara, stung. 'I washed him. I used apple-scented shampoo on him. He smells like an orchard, so he does. Come here and smell him.'

'I can smell him from over here, thanks very much.'

For some reason, Mrs Flood's dry response struck them as funny, and the three of them laughed, Dara and Mrs Flood with their mouths closed, containing it, Angel with her head thrown back against the pillow, her eyes shut. Dara took her chance. 'In fact, the only thing he really needs is a good—'

'Don't even think it, Dara Flood,' warned Mrs Flood.

'A good haircut,' Dara swept on. 'And I know just the woman for the job.'

'No way,' said Mrs Flood, backing out of the room. 'That dog's pelt is as coarse as a rug. I'd never get my scissors through it.'

'I think a trim would take years off him,' Angel piped up, and Mrs Flood sighed and shook her head, which was how the sisters knew that she would do it.

Later, Angel declared herself well enough to take Lucky for a walk. Dara insisted on going with her and promised Mrs Flood that they would not go far.

'When will you be back?' asked Mrs Flood as she always did, the lines across her forehead deepening like furrows.

'We'll be half an hour, max,' Dara called to her mother before she closed the front door and struggled down the driveway with Lucky straining at a lead he was obviously unused to.

But they weren't back in half an hour. They were back much sooner than that.

'Sorry, Dara,' Angel said, out of breath despite the leisurely pace Dara had set. 'I'm out of puff. I'm fine, really. It'll just take some time to adjust to the outside world again, I suppose. Would you mind if we turn back?'

Angel waited until Mrs Flood had left for work before she went back to bed. 'I'm just going to lie down for forty minutes,' she said to Dara brightly, demonstrating her fitness by jogging up the stairs. But when Dara went to check on her half an hour later, Angel was fast asleep, the covers pulled tightly up to her chin, her clothes still on.

With Angel asleep and Mrs Flood out, the house seemed very quiet. Worry liked to visit when things were quiet. He crept up on Dara, stealthy as a thief, and she only realised he was there when he had already made himself at home, sitting at the hearth in her head, warming his toes at the fireplace of her thoughts. She worried about Angel. Her tiredness, her temperature. It might just be a cold. Flu perhaps. But it might be something else. Something worse. Even Worry didn't like to go too far down that road. He backtracked and concentrated on Anya. The phone call from her.

'Lucky has been abducted!'

'NO!' Dara did her best to inject her tone with credible amounts of shock and outrage.

'The police are looking for two women with lice.'

'Lice?'

'They kept scratching their hairs in CCTV footage.'

'Oh.'

From the landing came a long, mournful howl.

'Wat is dat?'

'Oh, it's just the telly. *I'm a Celebrity, Get Me Out of Here.* One of them is doing a Bush Tucker Trial.'

'*I'm a Celebrity* is not on at moment.' Anya said.

'It must be a repeat.'

'We will discuss dis further on Monday, yes?'

'Yes, Anya.'

Dara worried about the conversation she would have to have with Anya. She would have to tell her the truth.

Lying was a skill she was not particularly familiar with. Although she had done a good job of it with Stanley Flinter. Worry bore down on this thought, squeezing it like a spot. Dara got up from the couch and moved into the kitchen, dislodging it.

She worried about Mr Flood. Although her worry was edged with anger now. And frustration. Her mother was right. She'd never find him. But if she did, she'd cut him open herself and reach inside him and lift his kidney out, whether it was suitable or not. It was the least he deserved. The very least.

And Ian Harte. She worried about how to tell him. She hadn't had to break up with anyone since Melancholy Olly. 'Oliver Browne, I mean,' she corrected herself. And look what had happened there.

This redirected Worry neatly back towards the subject of Stanley Flinter. Worry thanked Dara for this new arrival, in that polite manner he had, stretching and shifting and draping his legs over the arm of her couch. 'Where were we?' he seemed to say. And then, 'Ah yes, Mr Flinter, wasn't it? Mr Stanley Flinter.'

Because Dara *felt* something when she thought about Stanley Flinter. Something that was dangerously close to anticipation, which was a first cousin of *expectation*. She'd never felt anything like it before. She didn't know what to do with it. Worry did, though. He rubbed his hands together and prepared to have a field day.

Lucky padded softly down the stairs and poked his head around the kitchen door. He settled himself in a puddle of sunshine on the floor next to Dara, resting his huge head on her small feet and closing his eyes. Dara reached down to pull gently on his ears and Lucky released a low moan of satisfaction.

Oddly, Lucky was the one thing in Dara's life that she didn't worry about. It was like he'd always been here, snoozing in the shade of the pear trees at the end of the garden, as George had loved to do. Already, he'd chased the neighbourhood cat (she belonged to Electric Eddie, but she granted everyone along the road a daily audience, whether they wanted one or not) dug a hole where Mrs Flood's rose bush had been and buried a bone he'd found (Dara suspected he'd nicked it from Edward's stash, accessible through a small hole in the hedge that separated the Flood garden from that of Miss Pettigrew), and agreed to do his business squatting behind the shed rather than fertilising Mrs Flood's hanging basket with his deposits.

She checked her mobile phone regularly. Nothing from Stanley Flinter in response to her earlier text: *Hi S. Just checking u still want me to go to party 2nite? D.* She had gone for offhand, but as soon as she pressed SEND, she began to worry. It was too proprietorial. Clingy. Needy. All those things the women's magazines were forever warning you against. At least, that's what Tintin maintained, and God knows, he read enough of them.

So she worried about that, along with everything else. She'd always been able to worry about more than one thing at a time. A multitasker, Tintin called her.

She checked her mobile phone again.

A text from Miss Pettigrew asking about Angel, who she had spied from her armchair in the front window where she liked to sit so she could *keep an eye on things*, walking down the road with Dara and a strange creature who had taken the eyes out of Edward's head.

And she enquired after Paris. And Stanley Flinter. Dara texted back, saying Angel was in better form and had gone for her first walk in ages today. She didn't mention the temperature. Perhaps Angel would be better when Dara next visited the old lady and there would be no need to worry her.

About Stanley Flinter, she made no comment. Nothing about their arrangement tonight, which might or might not be a date. If he ever texted her back. She knew that the absence of any news of Stanley Flinter would be analysed in minute detail by Miss Pettigrew, who had a lot of time on her hands and considered herself a bit of an expert on relationships. 'I've loved and lost, Dara,' she explained when Dara queried the source of her wisdom in this regard. 'But at least I played a hand, my dear,' she added, looking at Dara with her drawn-on eyebrows knitted together like one of Mrs Flood's scarves. 'At least I played a hand.'

Throughout this marathon of texting and worrying, Angel slept. Dara crept upstairs at half-hourly intervals to place her hand across her forehead. She was hot and clammy, but it was difficult to tell if she was hotter and clammier than before. Dara lifted a blanket off the bed, leaving the long imprint of Angel's body under one light sheet. She opened the window, enough to allow some air to circulate, but not enough to create a draught. Angel did not stir until after five, when she declared herself better. She accepted the bowl of fresh fruit Dara had prepared for her, but did not accept Dara's suggestion that she cancel her plans for the evening.

'You have a lover to let down gently and an engagement with a potential suitor to attend, my little socialite, remember?' Despite the lightweight delivery of the words, there was a steely undertone of drop-dead-serious in Angel's voice. Dara began to regret telling her of her plans. But Angel had just woken when Stanley's text finally came through (*Sorry Dara, Clouseau buried my phone in the back garden and I've only just uncovered it now. Yes, still on for tonite. Looking forward to it. Sx*) and had swept aside Dara's reluctance to tell her about him.

'I have end-stage renal failure,' Angel declared. 'You have to do whatever I want.'

'That's hardly fair,' Dara told her.

'Life's not fair, my lovely Dara,' Angel said, smiling. 'There has to be some bloody advantage to having a crappy kidney.'

'I stole Lucky from the pound for you,' Dara reminded her. 'Wasn't that enough?'

'No,' said Angel, settling herself on the couch. 'That was for your own good. This is for mine. I need some excitement.'

So Dara told her everything. Well, not quite everything. She left out the bit where she had stood in the hotel room, naked, and Stanley had told her she was beautiful. Some bits should be kept all to yourself, to be taken out and remembered at some future date when happiness might be scarce on the ground. A stockpile, like the tins of tomatoes and peaches in her mother's makeshift larder. It was important to have one, Dara felt. Even so, it seemed she had said too much.

'Oh my God!' Angel said, her hands cupping her mouth, when Dara eventually stopped talking. 'You really *like* this Stanley Flinter. And he likes you too. A kiss at the end of his text? That's not for the faint-hearted, you know.'

'Well, I . . .' Dara began to say before she stopped and closed her mouth. Instead, she nodded. She looked worried.

Angel was delighted about Dara's plans for Ian Harte. Putting the relationship out of its misery, she called it.

'I know, it's just . . .' Dara bit her lip.

'It was going nowhere anyway,' Angel reminded her.

'I *am* going to do it. I just don't have to do it . . . you know . . . today.'

'Today works for me,' Angel said, not budging.

'I don't know what to say.'

'Something will occur to you,' Angel told her firmly. 'You can ring me afterwards if you like. Before you go to meet Stanley. Make sure I'm still alive.'

'I wish you'd stop saying stuff like that.'

'It's black humour. I'm experimenting with it,' Angel said.

'I don't want to leave you in the house on your own,' said Dara.

'Mam will be home at seven. I'm sure I'll manage,' Angel told her cheerfully.

'But . . .'

'But nothing. It's time, Dara Flood.'

There was nothing Dara could do, other than regret her decision to take a leaf out of Angel's book and live her life as if nothing bad was going to happen. Just look at what had happened the minute she'd experimented with that idea. Bad things. Like Angel getting a temperature. And Lucky. Look at what had happened there when her guard was down. A death sentence, no less.

And had she been worrying about something bad happening? No. She'd been in a shower in Paris with Stanley Flinter, worrying about nothing at all.

It was a sign, surely, that this method of living was not for the faint-hearted and certainly not for the likes of Dara Flood.

But this was not the way Angel saw things. In fact, Angel seemed to be taking Dara's new modus operandi very seriously indeed.

In the time she had left, Dara took to the kitchen and baked the living daylights out of every ingredient she could find in the presses. When Mrs Flood arrived home, she would find herself unable to fit the milk and butter she'd bought into the fridge, on account of the bowl of beef stroganoff, the chocolate fudge cake, the ramekins of strawberry mousse, the cellophane-wrapped package of puff pastry and the sauce Dara had made for the vol-au-vents that she had finally – eventually – run out of time to make.

57

At exactly half past six, the front door of an imposing, meticulously maintained house on the Howth Road opened to reveal a tall, well-built man. For a moment, he stood in the doorway, his chin raised and his shoulders pulled back, as if posing for a photograph. He moved towards the Mercedes jeep parked in the driveway, flipping open his mobile phone with one hand and running his fingers through thinning hair with the other.

A voice floated out of the house after him and the man's mouth moved to form something like 'I love you too', without looking back. Once inside the jeep, the man adjusted the rear-view mirror and carried out a careful inspection of his face and his nose in particular, out of which he tweezed a few stray hairs. Music poured out of the jeep. 'I am a Rock', Stanley thought. The jeep roared out of the driveway and turned in the direction of the seafront.

Stanley followed a discreet distance behind in his van. In the seat beside him, his Nikon, a notebook and pen, and the Newbridge candlestick holders that he hadn't had time to wrap because of all the time he had spent sitting on his couch and thinking about Dara Flood.

At exactly half past six, a small woman hurried along the length of the Raheny road, scratching at the nicotine patches on her arm and upper leg. She wore white skinny jeans that her friend Tintin had assured her made her legs look long.

Well, long-*er*, at any rate. She wore a sheer top that covered a bottom she considered too wide. The top was a very dark blue and matched her eyes, which were long rather than big. The top was loose but hinted at a narrow waist and gently curving hips.

The woman did not know it, but in that moment, she looked exactly like her father – Eugene Flood – who had walked up the very same road for a packet of cigarettes twenty-seven years ago and never came back.

Ian Harte drove aggressively, as if the road was something to be defeated rather than navigated. He was fond of his horn: not just beeping it, but holding his hand against it in a long, loud moan of irritation. Even Cormac, who drove his Audi A8 much too fast and liked to call drivers of small cars like Nissan Micras and Opel Corsas *roadkill*, would not be as free as Ian Harte with the hand gestures, the leaning out of the window and the shouting. There was a moment when Stanley thought he'd lost his subject, as the jeep roared through a busy junction just as the light changed from amber to red. He watched the back of the vehicle scorch around a corner and disappear from view. Stanley was forced to stop and wait. He had time to wonder if Mrs Harte – Irene – would be more disappointed or relieved when he told her of his loss of her husband.

But around the corner, the jeep had been pulled over by a guard. A guard with long, thin legs and arms that seemed a little comical when you considered the short sturdiness of his body. It was Lorcan, clocking up another speeding fine to make up his monthly quota, before heading to the engagement party. Stanley pulled into a garage and shuffled down in his seat, until he could barely see over the dashboard.

Ian Harte attempted to charm his way out of a ticket. When he smiled, his face changed and Stanley conceded that Mrs Harte was right. Her husband *was* an attractive man. Clear blue eyes, one of those square lantern jaws and a set of teeth that would dazzle you with the sheen off them. In fact, Stanley thought he saw Lorcan blink a little in their glare.

Lorcan nodded as Ian explained, still hand-gesturing but not the lewd gestures of earlier. Now he placed one hand across his chest, the other one circling and circling as he tried to give Lorcan a valid reason for whatever misdemeanour Lorcan had pulled him over for.

But of course Lorcan was having none of it. Stanley could read him like a picture book. His shift was over in half an hour and he wanted to get the guy written up, so he could be home in plenty of time to put on his 'pulling' outfit: a pair of baggy jeans that hid the skinniness of his legs, a blindingly white shirt that he washed by hand with nothing but Daz, and an exact replica of the sunglasses Tom Cruise wore in *Top Gun*, which he said made him more attractive to women, although Stanley had seen no evidence of that to date. Cora had apparently told him there'd be loads of women at the party, and even though she hadn't specified their status, Lorcan, being an optimistic type of a fellow, took it that they were the available type who mightn't say no to a spot of casual, no-holds-barred, no-questions-asked, no-strings-attached, good old-fashioned sex.

Later, at the party, Lorcan would describe the bloke he gave the ticket to earlier as a 'pillock'. By then, Stanley would have no choice but to agree.

Dara Flood decided to walk all the way to the park. She had texted Ian and asked him to meet her there instead of their usual place. It was still bright, although the earlier heat of the day had waned and there was a coolness now that made Dara wish she had brought her hoodie. She tried to think of things to say to Ian Harte, but found herself thinking instead about Stanley Flinter. And even though she shouldn't be smiling when there was so much to worry about, she smiled. She couldn't help herself. She smiled all the way down the road.

Ian Harte didn't take a left where he should have, given that that was the direction of his pal Dickie's house, where the poker game was supposed to be taking place that evening. Stanley felt the familiar tug of disappointment he always felt when his subjects did not take such turns. In his experience, they rarely did, but this unpleasant truth did not make his job any easier when it came to divulging such details to his clients.

Ian drove slower now, with fewer emphatic hand gestures, perhaps chastened by his brief brush with the law. He turned into the car park at the edge of St Anne's and parked. From the road, Stanley could see him adjust the rearview mirror and begin the careful inspection of his face again, paying particular attention to his nostrils, which he parted with his fingers, gazing inside the hairless holes. Stanley drove past the entrance to the car park and pulled up by the kerb, a little further down the road. He reached for his jacket. It had been a warm day, but now that the sun was dipping, there was a coolness in the air that had not been there before.

He got out of the car with his Nikon. Mrs Harte wanted pictures. He would have to make his way into the park through the forest and climb a fecking tree. There was no other choice. He began to walk.

Dara Flood reached the Edenmore entrance to the park. This was the entrance Mr and Mrs Flood had used, on many Sunday afternoons after a roast beef dinner, taking turns to push Angel, asleep in her pram. Mr Flood would push the pram with one hand and hold his wife's hand with the other. 'Even over potholes and across roads,' Mrs Flood told them one Christmas Eve when she was low after a pot of mulled wine. 'He never let go of my hand.'

Dara never told her mother that he *had* let go of her hand. The day he'd walked up the road for a packet of cigarettes and never come back. He'd let it go pretty good that day.

Dara picked her way over the parts of the path where tree roots swelled under the tarmac. In the trees, wood pigeons cooed at each other like sweethearts. Dara looked left and right, then left again before she crossed the road into the rose garden. Still nothing occurred to say to Ian Harte. She picked up a twig and puffed at the tip of it, as if it were a cigarette. She continued to walk.

The tree was perfect. Smooth-barked, with branches low enough to the ground to allow Stanley swing himself into its leafy folds. Near enough the car park to grant his long lens access to Ian Harte, still sitting in his jeep, still examining himself in the rearview mirror.

The light was failing now. Stanley found a foothold and moved his hands along the smooth bark of the tree till he found a branch he could hold on to. He began to climb.

In the car park, Ian Harte stood at the closed door of his jeep, leaning against it on one leg while the other bent behind him, the sole of his cowboy boot flat against the metallic green of his car. In his mouth, a single blade of grass. His head was cocked to one side, his thumbs tucked into the front pockets of one of the pairs of stiff jeans he wore on their Saturday dates. He stared into the middle distance, even though Dara was positive he had already seen her. It was like he was on a film set, surrounded by cameramen and lighting people, waiting for them to shout ACTION.

She stopped walking and watched him for a moment. There was something a little . . . manufactured about Ian Harte. Why had she never noticed it before? Here he was, leaning against his car, pretending to be a cowboy or something, wearing skinny jeans that were so tight, they chafed against the skin of his inner thighs and left a roaring red rash in their wake. Dara knew. She'd seen it, no matter how hard Ian tried to hide it from her. But she'd hidden things from him too, hadn't she? In fact, she'd told Stanley Flinter more about her life in the last few days than she'd ever told Ian Harte. And it had felt good, this exposition of herself. Scary, yes. But good all the same. In fact, it felt great. She began to walk towards Ian, quicker now. It was time.

At first, Stanley didn't think much of anything when he saw Dara Flood. She appeared suddenly, at the edge of his long lens, and came into focus, piece by piece. Her black hair, cut close around her pale, heart-shaped face, and those amazing navy eyes – long, rather than big – staring at something in front of her that Stanley could not yet see. She was beautiful. That was Stanley's first thought. Later, he wondered why realisation took its time in coming. But it was only a matter of seconds. Less than that, really. It just felt longer, as Stanley trailed Dara across the car park with his viewfinder. It was only when she reached the car – the jeep – that it came to him, like something – a cement block, perhaps – landing on your head from a great height when you're walking down the street, minding your own business. Ian Harte strode into the viewfinder, took Dara's face in his hands, tilted it and bent low to kiss her.

As it turned out, Dara needn't have worried about the most appropriate way to end her limping liaison with Ian Harte. Stanley Flinter did that for her. She'd been right about him. He *was* a very helpful person. In fact, she never got an opportunity to say anything at all to Ian Harte. Because as soon as she was close enough to say something, Ian was already all over her, his grip tight on her head, twisting it at an awkward angle, his mouth clamping over hers while still managing to say, 'Oh Dara, Dara, Dara, wait till you see what I've got for you.' He grabbed her hand and manoeuvred it south, towards the tip of his zipper. Dara pulled her hand out of his grip and pushed at his chest. She had to push hard before she could release herself from his hold.

'What are you doing?' he asked, looking down at the front of his trousers straining against the tightness of the material.

Dara took a deep breath. 'Ian, I need to talk to you,' she managed to say before they heard the sound. They both turned in its direction, squinting into the forest. It was the sound of somebody trying not to make a sound. A muffled sort of a shout followed by the hard smack of something big landing on something hard. Turned out there was a bench under the tree that Stanley had climbed. A wooden bench, hard and unforgiving. The kind of bench that digs into the bones of your bum if you sit on it too long. After the smack, a low moan. Then a short silence. And then the sound of thrashing, like someone beating a path towards them through the dark green of the forest, thickening with spring. And there he was, standing in front of them. His chest heaving with exertion, the beginnings of what would be a spectacular shiner and a long bloody graze down one side of his face that might require stitches.

'Stanley?' Dara said, taking a step towards him. 'Jesus, you're hurt. What are you doing here? Why are you—'

'DON'T!' he roared at her, holding up one hand as if to shield himself from her. The other hand closed tightly around the strap of a complicated-looking camera.

Ian took two steps back, leaving Dara out front. 'What do you want?' he asked in a loud voice that shook. The type of voice that people use when they are *trying* to be brave, Dara would realise later.

'I don't want anything from you,' Stanley said, his voice unrecognisable to Dara with its unfamiliar seal of bitterness.

'It's Irene. She asked me to follow you.' He took a step to-wards Ian, who backed away until he could go no further, blocked as he was by the monstrosity of the jeep. Ian had the confused look of someone watching *Russian Ark* for the first time. When he finally managed to open his mouth and speak, his voice was a shaking whisper.

'Irene?' was all he managed to say.

Stanley's smile was mostly a sneer. His eyes were as cold and black as a November night. He did not look at Dara. He concentrated on Ian Harte. Dara couldn't take anything in. She stared at Stanley, who refused to look at her.

'Yes,' Stanley said. 'Irene. Your *wife*?'

'You have a wife?' All the things that had niggled at Dara about this relationship suddenly made sense now. Ian's mouth opened and closed, like a fish on a hook. He said nothing.

'And *you* have a boyfriend,' said Stanley. It was a statement rather than a question, and for the first time since he'd yelled *DON'T*, he looked at her. In that look, Dara saw his contempt. There was no doubt about that. But there was also resigna-tion, around the edges of it. That was worse, Dara felt. His resignation. She flinched from it and looked at Ian Harte in-stead, who stood there, shaking his head like he had water in his ear. He looked from one of them to the other.

'You two know each other?' he finally said.

'Well, yes,' Dara began. 'We—'

Stanley interrupted her. 'No we don't,' he said, before al-lowing his cold stare to settle on her confused face. 'I don't know you at all.'

58

Cormac was at the bar surrounded by his usual posse of admirers, when Stanley arrived at the party. Of Cora, there was no sign.

'Ah, there he is. Stan my little man. How's it going?' Cormac's voice roared through the crowd, catching Stanley as surely as if he'd reached out a hand and grabbed him.

Stanley's original plan had been to find a dark, quiet corner where he could sit and get drunk without anyone noticing. He stopped and looked at Cormac, his face already flushed from too many drinks, then strode over to his eldest brother.

'Jesus, what the hell happened to your face?' Cormac asked, his eyes wide as he took in Stanley's collection of cuts and bruises and the hole in the knee of his jeans where the denim had snagged on a branch during the fall from the tree to the bench.

Stanley ignored the question. Instead, he said, 'I've asked you not to call me that.' His hands, buried in the pockets of his jacket, tightened into fists.

Cormac smiled his indulgent smile. 'What?' Stan the little man? I always call you that.'

'I know you do. And I'm asking you nicely, for the last time, to stop it.' The anger Stanley felt was cold. White and cold. It rose through his body like flood water.

'All right, Stanley, keep your fucken hair on. Come on, have a drink. It's on me. What'll it be? A nice little wine spritzer perhaps?'

Usually Stanley paid no attention to the camp attitude Cormac adopted when he spoke to him. But not tonight.

'Fuck you,' he said.

'Jesus, Stanley, what's all this? Fightin' talk?'

'Fuck. You,' Stanley said again, moving closer to Cormac. Close enough to smell the slippery, hair gel smell of him. Close enough to spot the dark crust of Guinness at the corners of his mouth. To see the tiny red thread veins in the whites of his eyes.

'Is this about Cora?' Cormac leaned towards Stanley, unsteady, his voice as unconcerned as it always was.

'No,' said Stanley. 'It's about you. What you did. To me.'

'Ah, for fuck's sake, Stanners. Build a fucken bridge and mince your little way over it, will you?'

'I *am* over it, you ignoramus.'

Cormac placed one hand over his mouth. The other one he perched daintily on his hip. 'Ooh, Stanley. Ignoramus? You're getting the big guns out tonight, wha?'

Stanley reached out and filled a fist with the collar of Cormac's shirt.

'You're welcome to Cora. The pair of you deserve each other.'

'Get your hands off me, you little fucker.'

Cormac pulled at Stanley's hand, but Stanley never budged. He pulled his other hand out of his pocket and curled it into a fist.

The punch felt like slow motion to Stanley. The whip of his fist reaching through the air, towards Cormac's face. The solidness of it. The hard crack of it. The wet squelch of it. Cormac staggered against the force of it, his back banging into the counter. He doubled over, holding his face with his hands. 'You've broken my fucken nose, you wanker.' It was difficult to make out the words, but the tone was unmistakable. Disbelief. Cormac's words were smothered in it. He lowered his hands from his nose and examined them. 'I'm bleeding,' he said, to no one in particular. 'You've actually made me bleed.' He steered himself back on to the bar stool, shaking his head.

Stanley smiled. 'Good,' he said. Later, he would feel shame. He'd never broken anyone's nose before. Or made them bleed. But right now, he wanted more. 'Stand up, Cormac,' he told his brother in a voice that was rigid with resolve. 'I'm going to hit you again.'

'Stanley, what the fuck? What are you *doing*?' This from another of his brothers who had arrived at the sidelines. He couldn't tell which one. He concentrated on Cormac, reaching for him again, reefing him off the stool by his shirt.

Perhaps Cormac was distracted by the pain of his broken nose. Perhaps he never thought Stanley had a second punch in him. Let's face it, he hadn't thought his youngest brother had the first punch in him. Whatever the reason, Cormac stood there with a vacant expression on his face. His mouth began to form a word, but no one got to hear what it was, because Stanley swung his fist again. This time, he caught Cormac on one of the cheekbones he was very proud of, ever since an old girlfriend had admired his bone structure and his cheekbones in particular. 'Unusually high,' she'd assured him. 'You'll age well, so you will.'

The sound that Cormac made was as high as his cheekbones. A squeal more than a shout. He stumbled back and glanced against a high stool, which teetered before it fell, bringing Cormac down with it.

'I'd fucken leg it, if I were you, bro.' Stanley glanced up. It was Lorcan, looking at him with a mixture of pride and fear.

'I'm not going anywhere,' said Stanley, stepping over Cormac's writhing form and leaning against the bar. He was shaking. 'I'm getting a Jameson. Do you want one?'

'Ah sure, why not,' said Lorcan, never one to turn down a

free drink, even this one, which left him right in the eye of the storm.

Stanley had time to pay for the drinks and toss his one back before Cormac managed to scramble to his feet again. His face was a mess. Blood streamed out of his nose, there was a cut on his cheek and his left eye was already beginning to swell and close. He lunged at Stanley. 'You deaf little runt. Come here ta me.'

Stanley had to jump a little to reach Cormac's head, and when he did, he curled his arm around his brother's neck, holding him in a tight headlock. Cormac swung his fists as best he could in this awkward position but only managed to land some fairly lame slaps on the buttocks that Dara had admired only yesterday. It seemed like such a long time ago now.

'Aw for fuck's sake, would yiz ever take that outside,' the barman pleaded with them. 'I'm only after gettin' the place done up.' He shook his head with the bleak knowledge of a man who knows that ringing the Guards won't help. They were all fecking well here, in his pub. His newly refurbished pub.

Stanley shoved Cormac onto a chair, releasing his head and stepping out of harm's way. He raised his fists and waited, but there was no need. Cormac – who had begun the celebrations shortly after lunch – was no match for Stanley's anger. He realised that. His shoulders slumped, he shook his head and raised his hand, like a guard at a broken set of traffic lights.

'You look like shit,' Stanley told him, setting his glass on the counter and nodding at the barman for a refill.

'You broke my fucken nose,' Cormac said again, more surprised than angry now.

'Well you broke my fucken heart,' Stanley reminded him.

'I suppose you think we're quits now?' Cormac asked, leaning his face towards Stanley's.

'I suppose I do,' said Stanley. It was probably just as well. His hand – the one he'd used to break Cormac's nose – throbbed. He didn't think he could manage another punch. He reached the other hand into his pocket and found a packet of tissues. 'Mop yourself up,' he told Cormac. 'You're making a mess of the place.'

Cormac took a tissue and dabbed gently at his nose, inspecting the tissue after each dab for blood, shaking his head as it grew red and soggy.

'What'll you have?' Stanley asked.

For a moment, Cormac looked confused. More confused, that is. He looked at the barman, who had come as soon as Stanley summoned him, perhaps hoping that the evasion of any further . . . unpleasantness might be directly related to the swiftness of his service.

'I'll have whatever he's having,' Cormac told the barman, nodding towards Stanley's glass.

There was a sound of high heels trotting across the floor towards them, and suddenly there she was, between them, as she had always been. Beautiful, of course. Perhaps as beautiful as Stanley had ever seen her. Her forehead creased in concern as she examined Cormac's battered face. She looked from one of them to the other and back again. Stanley caught the glint of her eyes, a sea-green, cold and sharp.

'Were you two *fighting* over me?' Cora asked, as a smile spread across her face like a rash.

'Yes,' they said at the same time, before they clinked their glasses together, nodded at each other and tossed the whiskey down their throats.

'Well . . . who won?' asked Cora, confused.

'Cormac did,' Stanley told her, standing up.

'But . . .'

'Congratulations, Cormac, you get to keep the girl. Well done you.'

'But . . .' Cora's mouth opened and closed like a fish.

'I'm going now,' said Stanley.

'You can't go yet,' Cora told him. 'You've only just arrived.'

'I've had enough,' he told her, reaching for his jacket that had somehow become separated from him during the . . . melée.

Cormac accepted an ice pack from the barman and nursed his face with it. 'Probably just as well,' he told Stanley, his voice reverting to its usual gruffness. Only Stanley could hear the trace of affection straining at the tight leash Cormac kept on it. 'We don't want any more trouble.'

'I'll see you out, Stanley,' said Cora, winking at him in a way that only he could see it.

'No you won't,' Stanley said, looking up at her. He didn't even bother saying, 'But thanks all the same. For offering. To see me out', as he might once have done.

'But I . . .' Cora began.

'I'll see myself out,' Stanley told her, and he didn't even have to make an effort to get his voice to sound grim. It just did. All by itself. Cora's mouth opened and then closed. He nearly felt sorry for her but he steeled himself against it. He began to walk away. 'Oh, and there's one more thing,' he said, turning back.

'Yes?' she asked in the high, breathy tone that reminded him suddenly of Dara Flood, only because it could not have been more different. He ran at Dara's image and it faded, like hope.

'There's no need for you to call to my house again. To pick up a scarf or a hat or a pair of gloves or whatever item of clothing you happen to be missing. Not without ringing first. There's nothing of yours at my house any more.'

Cora had the grace to look away. In fact, she looked at Cormac, checking to see if he'd heard what Stanley said. He had. 'What's going on, Cora?' he mumbled through his fast-swelling nose. 'What have you done?'

Stanley never heard what she said. The inevitable lies she told. He didn't care. He'd had enough.

He turned and walked away, past his parents, who had only just found out what the wedding was going to cost from Cora's father, who said things like, 'It's only money, isn't it?' and, 'She's my princess. Princesses should have fairy-tale weddings, shouldn't they?' So wrapped up were they in the mathematics of the upcoming nuptials, they never noticed their youngest son punch their eldest son in the face. Twice. Stanley was glad about that. He kept walking.

Past Cormac's colleagues, who should have been Stanley's colleagues if things had been different. Instead, they were his clients. Suspicious men with too much time on their hands. Stanley resolved never again to take on their cases. No matter how much he needed the work. It was too depressing. Let some other eejit skulk behind thorny shrubberies in the thick of night taking photographs of betrayal and deception and treachery. He'd had enough of that. He kept walking.

Past Adrian and Neal and Declan and Lorcan. Lorcan's mouth was at full throttle and Stanley didn't need to hear what he was saying to know what he was talking about.

'That tub of Silcock's Base I gave Mam is supposed to be an excellent repair cream for damaged skin cells,' Declan said, when Lorcan took a brief breather for a slug of his drink.

Neal was too busy watching the door for Freda the barmaid, who last night had made a vague allusion to a remote possibility of her attendance at the party, which Neal had taken as a positive sign. Of Freda though, so far, there was no sign at all.

Stanley kept walking.

59

Dara saw it from the top of the Raheny road. The ambulance. Parked right outside the house, the lights on the roof pulsing a blood red. She pitched her cigarette on the ground and began to run. Even then, it took a long time to reach the house. Like she was running on a conveyor belt, making no progress as her feet pounded the pavement. She could see two people in the driveway. Miss Pettigrew, her long, bony fingers clamped against her mouth, Edward pining at her legs on the ground beside her. Electric Eddie holding what looked like a bearded dragon in his arms. Dara ran harder, her breath tight in her chest. She was almost there when she saw it. The stretcher, wheeled by two sturdy men in white coats. And between them, on the stretcher, lay Angel. With an oxygen mask tied around her face.

Dara was at the top of the driveway now. The men with the stretcher kept coming at her. Angel lay there with her eyes closed, the lids pale, almost translucent. She did not move. A strand of her hair lay limp across her face, like a shadow, and it was this one small thing that pushed Dara forward until she was close enough to reach for the damp strand and move it. The men stopped to accommodate her.

'I'm her sister!' Dara shouted. Her voice sounded strange, as if it were coming from someplace else. From someone else. Dara reached beneath the sheet covering her sister and squeezed her hand. 'Angel,' she whispered. Angel's hand was still and cold.

The men began to move again, quicker now. Dara could hear the rasp of the wheels against the ground, the grunt of the men as they lifted the stretcher into the dark cavity of the ambulance. The long drag of Electric Eddie's clogs against the ground as he approached her. Edward's whines, frantic now, as he tried to regain Miss Pettigrew's displaced attention. Even the wet dabbing of Miss Pettigrew's tissue against the corners of her eyes. All these sounds rushed at Dara, pushed at her like a crowd. She ran to the back of the ambulance.

'What happened?' she roared in at them.

'She's had a bit of a turn,' one of the men said, turning away from Angel and smiling at Dara.

'Will she . . . is she going to be all right?' Dara asked, gripping the handle of the ambulance door.

'We're taking her to Beaumont. They'll take good care of her there,' said the man, not meeting Dara's eyes. 'Could you tell your mother that we're ready to go now? She's coming with us.'

'I'll come too,' said Dara, one foot already on the step of the ambulance.

The man shook his head. 'I'm sorry, love, there's not enough room. Follow us in your car.'

'It's not my car. It's Angel's,' said Dara, and she began to cry then, a silent cry that pushed hot, salty tears between the fingers she held over her face.

'Go and see to your mother, love.' The ambulance man patted Dara's shoulder and steered her in the direction of the house. 'Angel is in good hands.'

Dara nodded and stumbled towards the front door, past Eddie and Miss Pettigrew and Edward, who watched her go with wide, unlikely smiles, as if they could will Angel better with such facial contortions.

In Angel's room, Mrs Flood flung clothes into a plastic bag. A jumper that Angel never wore, a pair of leggings with a hole in the knee. Two odd socks. One of a collection of huge, itchy hats.

'What happened? Why didn't you ring me?' Dara asked, and Mrs Flood jumped, startled. She turned towards Dara, and Dara saw what her mother would look like when she was an old lady. Her face thinner. The pale blue of her eyes faded, somehow smaller, the skin on her face looser. She moved towards her mother. 'Mam,' she said. 'I'm so sorry, I should have been here. I thought she was OK.'

Mrs Flood bent to pick up Angel's iPod that had fallen from the desk. 'She collapsed. In the bathroom. She got sick. I . . . I didn't have time to ring you. I have to go.' All through her words, she kept filling the bag. Her eyes had the glazed expression of someone who was lost. Someone who had no idea where they were or how they had got there.

Dara approached her mother, gently taking the bag from her.

'They're waiting for you,' she said. 'In the ambulance. You go. I'll pack her a bag, all right?'

Mrs Flood nodded, saying nothing. She turned and left the room.

'I'll follow you in the car. In Angel's car. OK?' Dara shouted after her.

Mrs Flood hesitated on the second step from the top. Dara heard it creak under her weight.

'Be careful in that car,' was all Mrs Flood managed, as she moved down the stairs and out the door.

★　　★　　★

'Is there anyone . . . ?' Fidelma stands at the foot of the bed, pausing like a comma. She looks different, somehow. Fuller perhaps, softer than before. The skin on top of her upper lip is stained a bright pink. Veet strips, I'd say. Those things are lethal. I don't know how many women I've warned against them yokes. I pull myself straighter in the bed.

'What?' I say, and this relaxes her. I am still a gruff old bastard. She can ask her question. She approaches the bed, straightening the covers, even though there's no need. They're as stiff and as starchy as the day I arrived. Like day-old porridge, these sheets. No comfort to be gained from them.

'Would you like me to call anyone?' Her neck is creased, but the skin there is still soft. If I reach out my hand, I could touch her. Her smile is hopeful, like the light thrown by a candle before it gutters and dies.

'No,' I tell her, and my voice is steady. Almost strong. Like the voice of the man that I used to be, whatever good that ever did anyone.

Now I can see it, coming down the track. The last stop on the line. I've been waiting a long time for it. Sometimes wishing for it, when the chemo got too close.

But now that it's here, looming in front of me, getting closer, I can see it with both eyes and I want to close them.

Delay this rude awakening.

Scatter some leaves on the line; a points failure; some driver who didn't turn up for his shift.

'Are you sure, Mr Waters?' and her voice is soft as feathers.

I nearly tell her. Tell her my name. Give her a number she can call. I still remember it. The number.

Instead, I shake my head. Close my eyes. I feel her breath when she sighs. Her footsteps fade as she walks away.

60

Somehow, the night moved into the early hours of the morning. Angel was wheeled around the hospital like she was a piece of lost luggage nobody came to claim. Blood was pulled out of her arm, tests carried out, X-rays taken. Eventually she was settled beside the dialysis machine and Dara sat with her there, taking comfort from its familiar hum. Angel lay on a bed. She did not move. Long, narrow rails ran down each side. Dara gripped a rail with both hands and willed Angel to wake up.

'She's just sleeping now,' the nurse said, curling her hand around Dara's shoulder, smiling. 'It's good. She needs to rest.'

Mrs Flood returned with two plastic cups of tea that smelled of washing-up liquid. Her smile was as watery and grey as the tea, which Dara could not drink.

'I'm sorry, Mam,' Dara whispered.

'It's all right. It'll be all right.' Mrs Flood concentrated on her tea.

'I shouldn't have left her.'

'She was only on her own for half an hour.'

'I should have been there.'

Mrs Flood said nothing. There was nothing to say.

A 'progression'. That was what the doctor called it when he finally arrived. 'The high blood pressure is not unusual in the circumstances,' he added quickly, as if this addendum might help. It did not.

Dara thought about Angel, slumped on the bathroom floor when Mrs Flood got home, half an hour after Dara left. Some people could sustain years of dialysis before they were faced with such a progression. Angel was not going to be one of those people, it seemed.

The walk from the renal ward to the canteen, to get more of the dreadful tea that Mrs Flood insisted on, required every muscle, every sinew, every ligament, every breath in Dara's body. She was breathless at the top of a set of stairs and had to stand for a moment, in the harsh light of the corridor, to gather herself. She did not have to steel herself against tears. There were none. It was the anger she had to secrete about her person. She seethed with it. The injustice of it. The careless malevolence of it. How benign it sounded. *A progression.* Like it was something good. Something to aim for. Progress towards something. She nearly laughed at the paradox. But she did not laugh. She steeled herself. She smothered the anger with the fire blanket of her resolve. She buried her fear deep in the soil of her mind. She ran at her guilt. She should have been with Angel. But this was not the time for guilt. There would be plenty of time for that later.

'When can she come home?' Mrs Flood asked the doctor, worrying at the relic of Padre Pio she kept in the pocket of her trousers.

'We'd like to keep her a while,' the doctor said instead of answering the question. 'Her blood pressure is still too high. We need to monitor that. Get it under control. Then we'll see where we are, all right?' He slid a pen into the breast pocket of an authoritative suit and smiled at Mrs Flood, who did her best to reciprocate.

'I understand,' she said, even though she didn't. Neither of them did. There was nothing to understand. This was something that went under the heading of *one of those things*. People might shake their heads when they heard about it and say things like, 'That's terrible news' or, 'I'm very sorry to hear that'. 'It's just one of those things,' Mrs Flood would be forced to say in the absence of any other explanation.

They sat on either side of Angel's bed and looked at her. Dara laid her hand on Angel's chest and took comfort from the rise and fall of it every time Angel breathed.

It took a while for Dara to realise that Mrs Flood was crying. She had thought she was saying a prayer maybe, her hands covering her face, her head bowed. But she wasn't praying. She was crying. She tried to bury the sound of it in her hands. Dara reached for the cubicle curtain and pulled it around them. She knew her mother would hate people to see her like this.

Mrs Flood looked at Angel before she spoke, checking to see that she was still asleep.

'We're never going to get the call,' she said in a fierce kind of whisper, her hands curled in fists now, bunched at her eyes as if she could stem the flow of her tears in this way. She could not. They squeezed through her fleshy fingers and ran down her wrists, dropping between her feet.

Dara moved around the bed until she was squatting beside Mrs Flood's chair.

'Don't say that.' She reached for her mother with both hands. Mrs Flood's fleshy bulk, usually so soft and warm, felt cold to Dara's touch. 'Of course we're going to get the call. You know that.'

But Mrs Flood only shook her head and cried, harder now. She leaned into Dara and cried. It felt strange. Her mother gathered in her arms like this. A part of her did not know what to do. It brought to mind an incident when she was ten and had tumbled into the sting of a bank of nettles. Vinegar. That's what Mrs Flood had rubbed on her arms and legs and neck and face. It stung nearly as bad as the nettles, Dara remembered. But before the vinegar, there had been shushing and rocking. Dara remembered, with a clarity that nearly blinded her, the feel of her ten-year-old self in her mother's arms, as she shushed and rocked her.

So Dara shushed and rocked Mrs Flood, just like her mother had done when Dara was ten.

Eventually Mrs Flood pushed herself away from Dara, blew her nose, wiped at her eyes and declared herself ready for yet another cup of the dreadful tea. Dara insisted on going to get it. She needed to be somewhere where her family was not. Just for a moment. Just to gather herself. Neither of them would ever mention the call again. The possibility of not getting it. It didn't matter anyway, because even though Dara had worried about that possibility – more than once, if she was honest – she'd never said it out loud. But Mrs Flood had. And now the words were out, like escaped convicts, and there was nothing either of them could do to take them back. It was like a thorn, lodged too deep in the sole of a foot. You couldn't see it. But it was there. It was real. The pain of it was sharp. It hurt to walk.

This was the very heart of the things Dara had struggled to avoid. Things like *disappointment*. And *loss*. And the long, slow road to eventual, inevitable *decline*.

PART THREE

61

Stanley Flinter kept himself busy. He worked late most nights, finishing even the jobs he usually left till last. The filing, the throwing out of yet another plant he had managed to butcher, tedious paperwork, rehanging the shelf that had collapsed that day. The day Dara Flood came.

He even made phone calls to the accounts departments of insurance companies who liked to keep him busy but weren't all that keen on paying him for it. *He* usually apologised to *them*. But not this week. This week he found the calls easier to make.

'I'm terribly sorry, Mr Flinter, but we don't appear to have received that particular invoice,' the accounts clerk told him.

'That's what you said the last time I rang,' Stanley said. 'And I sent it to you again. By e-mail, you might remember.'

'Oh, the system's been down . . .'

'And by fax.'

'I think Sonya forgot to put paper in the damn machine again . . .'

'And by post.'

'Snail mail? No wonder I haven't got it yet.'

'And I dropped a copy in on my way past last Wednesday. I handed it to you myself.'

'Oh.'

He rang Cormac's colleagues – the ones Cormac had recommended him to. *As a favour.* He told them he was no longer in a position to take on their cases. Some were angry, others resigned, some pleaded with him to reconsider, one man even cried as he begged. To all of them, Stanley was polite but firm. He rang Cormac to tell him – politely and firmly – not to send him any more customers *as a favour*.

'Are you going to Ma's on Sunday?' Cormac asked. 'It's her weddin' anniversary or Mother's Day or Easter or some shite.'

'It's her birthday,' Stanley told him.

'Yeah, that. Are you coming?'

'No,' said Stanley.

'You're not still fucken contrary, are ya?' No mention would ever be made of the punches – either of them – administered by Stanley Flinter to the eldest of his brothers last Saturday night.

'No.'

'Fair 'nuf,' said Cormac and hung up.

He cleaned his house, even though it was not Thursday, nor was it his turn to do so. Sissy did not object. Instead, she closed the freezer door, where her hand had tightened around her favourite dinner-ding – roast vegetable lasagne – and began to graze a carrot with a peeler.

'I'm making dinner for you,' she called up the stairs to him. When there was no answer – Stanley was pulling Sissy's long hairs out of the plughole in the bathroom and couldn't hear her over the extractor fan – she thundered up the stairs, taking them two at a time. 'I said, I'm making you dinner,' she repeated, standing at the bathroom door.

'Oh, right,' said Stanley, not looking up. 'Yeah, fine, thanks.'

'Aren't you going to tell me not to make dinner-ding?' she asked.

'No, it's fine. Whatever you're making is fine,' he said, flushing a thick tumbleweed of her hair down the toilet.

'Look,' said Sissy, holding the peeler in front of her. Stanley glanced up.

'What?'

'Look at me. I have a peeler. I'm peeling carrots. For you. For dinner.'

'Oh. Yeah, lovely, thanks,' said Stanley, returning to the bath to peer down the plughole.

'OK, that's it,' said Sissy, tossing the peeler towards the sink. It clattered against the porcelain before settling across the plughole. Stanley looked at it, confused, as if wondering how a peeler had managed to make its way into the bathroom.

'What?' he asked.

'Here I am, doing my best to cheer you up, and you can't even pretend to be impressed at my carrot-peeling capabilities.'

'Have you actually peeled any?' Stanley asked, ripping off a pair of yellow rubber gloves and washing his hands.

'Well, no, not a whole one. Not yet. But still, I was *going* to.'

'Come on,' said Stanley, picking up the peeler. 'I'll peel and you can chop.'

'How about if *you* peel and chop and I'll pour the wine and light some candles? It'll distract you from your heartbreak,' Sissy suggested, wrestling him into a link and frogmarching him down the stairs.

'I'm not heartbroken, just . . . well, just a bit disappointed, I suppose.'

'Same thing,' said Sissy. 'Close relatives, at any rate.'

'It's *not* the same thing,' Stanley said, sitting down on a kitchen chair, the bag of carrots on the table, unpeeled. 'I mean, it's not like we knew each other all that well, or for that long or anything. She didn't owe me anything. We were . . . I don't know what you'd call it. Acquaintances, I suppose. I'm just . . . disappointed.'

'It's probably just as well,' said Sissy in a studiously matter-of-fact voice, pouring wine into two glasses that she had placed side by side, so she could make sure the measures of wine in each were identical.

'What do you mean?' asked Stanley.

'Well, she sort of smelled funny,' Sissy said. 'Didn't she?'

'She did *not* smell funny. That's a really weird thing to say. Even for you.'

'A dog smell,' Sissy continued, as if Stanley had not spoken. 'She smelled of dogs.'

'She works in a *pound,* for God's sake. And anyway, she did *not* smell of dogs.' Stanley thought then of the way he had kissed her neck in the restaurant that turned out to be a salsa-dancing club. The way the smell of her rushed at him. A warm smell. Something spicy, like cinnamon.

Sissy was on a roll.

And wearing a high-vis jacket. I mean, come on, Stanley. It was fecking *daylight* outside.'

'You're supposed to wear some form of reflective clothing when you're cycling on the road,' Stanley said. 'It's the law. Besides, it's a sensible thing to do. Isn't it?'

'And her clothes. I mean, all those tracksuits and hoodies and runners. I mean, I know they're Nikes, but still. She looks like she's about to say "not guilty" in the fecking Four Courts.'

'She wore a dress in Paris,' said Stanley. 'A red dress.'

'Well, I hope it covered up that wide arse of hers.'

'There's nothing wide about Dara Flood's arse,' said Stanley, hardly aware that he had stood up.

'Jesus, Stanley, I was just trying to cheer you up,' Sissy said, stung. 'Stop pointing that bloody peeler at me. You're making me nervous.'

'Sorry,' said Stanley, sitting back down.

'I'm supposed to say stuff like this. That's what friends do for each other when one of them gets dumped.'

'I did not get dumped.'

'Whatever. I'm supposed to point up all Dara's faults. Her big arse, her desperate taste in clothes, the manky smell off her, the lumpy wart on her bloody nose . . .'

'She does not have a lumpy—' Stanley began.

'I KNOW!' Sissy roared. 'I'm just giving you examples. So you get the bloody gist. We're supposed to DISS her, see? Together. It's called purging.'

'Oh, right, well, I see, I didn't realise . . .'

'It's hopeless,' said Sissy, sitting down and hiding her hands in her hair.

'No, it's not. I get it now. I can do it. I could say, I don't know, something about her hair, maybe.'

'What about her hair?' Sissy looked at him, interested now.

'I don't know. I could say it's got split ends or something.'

'Does it have split ends?'

'No.'

'Hopeless,' Sissy said again.

'No, it's not. I'm just not used to it. I need a bit of practice.'

'Hopeless.'

'Will you stop saying that?'

'Just ring her back, why don't you.'

There had been one missed call from Dara Flood. One voice message. Left shortly after the incident in St Anne's Park. He thought Dara might have been walking home from the park, in fact. He heard her dragging on a cigarette between sentences.

'Hi Stanley, it's Dara. I just . . . I wanted to talk to you about . . . well, you know what I mean. I'm so sorry about everything. Could you call me back? Of course, I'll understand if you don't. But I'd really like it if you did. Well, goodbye. I'll . . . I'll talk to you later. Maybe. I mean, if you ring back. Sorry, I'm making a mess of this. It's Dara, by the way. Dara Flood. Did I say that already? Sorry. I'm sorry. Goodbye.'

Stanley listened to it four times before he deleted it. 'Why should I ring her back?' he asked Sissy.

'Because you want to, that's why. You should ring her. Or call round to her house. Give her a chance to explain.'

Ciara Geraghty

'There's nothing to explain. It was pretty self-explanatory in the park.'

'Well then, you could check her hair. See if there's any split ends in it.'

A small smile dawned across Stanley's face. 'I'm pretty sure she doesn't have split ends. Her mother's a hairdresser. She's always cutting Dara's hair.'

'Well then, you'll have to make do with her wide arse and her Salvation Army clothes, won't you?'

'I suppose it wouldn't do any harm to call her. Just ... I don't know, for some ... what do you call it in your column? It begins with a C, I think.'

'Closure,' Sissy told him with a bored sigh. 'Now, will I put on a couple of roasted vegetable lasagne dinner-dings to go with those carrots? I'm fading away to nothing here.'

62

The landline rang at five-thirty in the morning. Dara Flood was sleepwalking at the time. She never went far, mostly down the stairs, a slow lap of the ground floor that didn't take long, and back upstairs, careful to avoid the second step from the top that creaked on contact.

Oddly, Mrs Flood did not leap from her bed as she usually did.

Perhaps it was because she had finally convinced herself that they would never get the call.

Angel was in bed. She had been released from the hospital the day before with a strict prescription of bed rest. Her blood pressure was high but not as high as it had been that day. The ambulance day. Her face was flushed with it. She lay in bed, her hair spread like a fan around her head. She smiled. 'It'll be all right, Dara, don't worry.'

Dara nodded and patted the covers on Angel's bed. It was strange to have her Angel back. Appropriate somehow, now that everything seemed so hopeless. She tried to think of something to say. Something positive. But there was no need. When she looked back at her sister, Angel was asleep.

Back in the familiar comfort of her own bed, Dara found that sleep was elusive, like the pot of gold at the end of the rainbow. You think you're nearly there, it's just in the next field. But when you get there, it's moved to the next field. And the next, and the next.

'Just lie down, close your eyes and think of something nice,'

Mrs Flood advised, when she came upon Dara drinking Oval-
tine in the kitchen in the small, slow hours of morning. That
was always Mrs Flood's advice whenever Dara couldn't sleep.
Think of something nice. Dara tried, but nothing occurred.

When Dara jerked awake, she was unsurprised at her elevated position, standing as she was on a kitchen chair, no
doubt checking that the top window was securely closed and
locked against the world outside. Of course it always was,
but it never did any harm to double-check, did it? Her body
jerked, as it often did when she awoke mid-walk, and she half-
fell, half-jumped backwards, landing on the kitchen floor in a
squat, having hurt nothing more than her hand, where it had
glanced against the edge of the kitchen table. She ran for the
phone.

'Hello?'

'Eh, hello, would this be the home of young Dara Flood?'
roared an unsteady voice down the line. The voice was familiar, although it took Dara a moment to place it.

'Eh, yes, this is Dara Flood.'

A pause then, as the man indulged in a coughing fit. Then a
hacking in the back of his throat followed by a wet spit. Dara
held the phone away from her ear.

'This is Mr Slither Smith,' he announced, in a rather grand
manner.

'Oh.' Dara knew this was not an appropriate response
to such an announcement, but with the scarcity of sleep
the night before and the jolt into wakefulness, nothing else
occurred.

'Aye. Slither Smith. Of the Bailieborough Smiths. You and
yer wee man came down to have the céilidh with me a while
back. Remember?'

Of course Dara remembered. How could she forget? Slither
stretched out on the floor of the pub like a corpse. Although
when she thought about it, it was Stanley she saw, holding

Slither's head with such care, like it was a box of eggs, reaching for his jacket and slipping it under Slither's head.

'Hello . . . eh . . . Slither. You're up very early this morning.'

'Sure I haven't been to bed yet, young Dara Flood. I've been celebrating this lock o' days.'

'Celebrating?'

'Aye, my win. I knew I'd win eventually if I kept at it. Nobody believed me, o'course. But they believe me now, don't they? And me with the pockets of my Sunday best saggin' with shillin's.' He paused, and Dara could hear the steady gulp of liquid – she guessed Guinness – being poured down his throat.

'Eh . . . well . . . congratulations, Slither. That's . . . nice.'

'Nice is one word for it,' Slither agreed. 'But mighty is a better one, wouldn't you agree?'

Dara sat on the bottom step of the stairs. Her feet hurt and she wondered how long she'd been walking. 'Mighty,' she repeated. 'Yes, that certainly is mighty.'

'And it's all on account of yerself, Dara Flood,' Slither added with a wet cackle.

'What did I do?' she asked, curious in spite of herself.

'Sure wasn't it yerself who put the bet on for me. Lord Lucan Returns, no less. You put every last penny farthing I had left on him to win – even though I asked you to go each way, but we won't fight about it now – and didn't he thunder down the track in first and him with the odds of a horse whose mother was a donkey and his father no better? I didn't find out about it till the next day – I wasn't well that day, some bug or other – but bejaysus, there's been lepping and singin' here since then to beat the band, so there has.' Slither began to laugh, which quickly turned into a wheeze and then a cough followed by some more hacking and spitting. Dara waited, the receiver at arm's length.

'So, how much did you win?' she asked, when Slither had recovered himself. When he spoke, his voice was narrower than before. Cagey.

'Ah now, Dara Flood, I'm sure I wouldn't be at liberty to say. That's between meself and me financial advisers, so it is. But put it this way. I paid off the slate – Jamsie was able to duke off to Las Vegas for a week on account of the money I gave him – and I've enough left to keep me in porter and spuds for a lock o years. And maybe finally persuade Bridgie down at the barracks to step out with me of an evening, who knows?'

Even though Dara had never met Bridgie down at the barracks, she found herself pessimistic about Slither's prospects in this regard. She did not voice her concerns.

'Well,' she said instead, 'that's great. It's great news. I'm glad about it. I didn't know that I was lucky. With horses, I mean.'

'Well I meant to ring you sooner, but as I say, we've been busy up here with the singin' and the leppin' and the whatnot.'

'That's fine. There was no need to ring me,' said Dara, rubbing at her eyes with the heel of her hand. She was suddenly tired. 'How did you get my number anyway?'

'Jaysus, Dara, sure didn't I Google it?' said Slither, with the disdain he reserved for people who underestimated his close relationship with technology. 'There was every need to ring ya. Sure don't I have something to tell ya?'

Dara sighed, low enough so Slither wouldn't hear her. 'What is it?' she asked, making an effort to inject enthusiasm into her tone. Enthusiasm was something else that seemed to be avoiding her at the moment.

'Hould yer whisht, young Dara. I have to ask you something first.'

'Yes?' Dara said, more nervous than interested.

There was a pause. Then the rustling noise of paper, pages perhaps, being turned. 'Well,' said Slither, finally, 'I was wondering if you'd have an auld tip for me for the two-thirty at Listowel next week? You might be on a winning streak, so I should strike while your iron is hot, so to speak.'

'Oh, well I don't think my, eh, iron is as hot as you think it is, to be honest. I think Lord Lucan Returns was a one-off. A fluke. Besides, I don't even know what horses are racing in Listowel. Or anywhere else. I don't know anything about horse racing really.'

'Couldn't ya Google it, Dara?' said Slither with patience that sounded like it was worn to a frazzle, it was that thin. 'Aren't you hooked up to th'auld interweb up above in Dublin?'

'Well, yes, but I . . .'

'Take a look at it and send me an auld text later, like a good lassie.'

Dara argued no further. She felt there'd be no point. 'So what were you going to tell me?' she said, instead.

'First of all, I have to tell you why I didn't tell you before,' said Slither.

There was the sound of a match rasping against something coarse. Slither's thumbnail, perhaps. A pause, while Slither inhaled and then a long-drawn-out sigh of pure pleasure as he exhaled. Dara's mouth watered and she tugged at the patch behind her knee.

'The thing is, Dara Flood, he swore me to secrecy.'

'Who?'

'Your father, of course. Who else? Eugene Flood. Except that's not his name any more.'

'What do you mean?' For some reason, the first thing Dara thought of was that her father had had a sex change operation and changed his name to Emma or Penelope, maybe. A girlish name.

'After he left your mother, he travelled around the place. Around Ireland, mostly. Small, out-of-the way places. Kips, mostly. But then he took a notion and duked off to France. Paris, if you don't be minding. I think there might have been a lassie involved.'

'Yes, I know that.'

'What?'

'I said I . . . it doesn't matter. Go on.'

'He wandered around for a while after that, but it was in Belgium that he met his Waterloo, so to speak.'

Slither took some time out to snigger at his little joke. Dara waited.

'He fell foul of a man that people only ever fall foul of the once, if you know what I mean. Seanie-the-Shylock Shanahan. A nasty piece of work, by all accounts.'

'He owed him money?'

'You catch on quick, Dara Flood. Not like your father. That fella had silage for brains, so he did.'

'What happened?'

'The usual. He owed more money than he had. Than he'd ever have. But Shylock wasn't the kind of man to waste time on more than one beatin'. He knew a bad debt when he seen one.'

'Go on.'

'Well, Shylock gave Eugene the one beatin' he promised him and then he gave him a week to come up with the money. He never said what would happen after that one week, but Eugene knew well. He was thick, but he wasn't *that* thick.'

'So he changed his name?' Dara resisted the urge to shout at Slither. To tell him to get to the point. Slither was a story-teller. There was nothing to do but listen and hope for a conclusion.

'He took to his heels. I met up with him about a week later. Shylock had given him just about the best hidin' I'd ever seen. All but killed him. I barely recognised him, to be honest, what with the gummy mouth where his teeth shoulda been and his face swollen and painted all the colours of the rainbow with the collection of bruises he had. His ribs were shattered and his arm was in a cast. Oh, Shylock went up the town on him and no mistake.'

Dara Flood, who wouldn't even swat a fly but would catch him instead in cupped hands and release him out of a window, winced.

'That's when he changed his name,' Slither went on. 'He had to. After the beating, Shylock told him that if he didn't have the money in a week, there'd be no need for an ambulance after he was finished with him.'

'What did he change it to?' Dara asked.

There was a pause. She could nearly hear Slither deliberating down the phone.

'I won't tell anybody. I just want to talk to him, that's all.'

Slither released a long, slow breath. Dara was glad they weren't having this conversation face-to-face.

'Gene Waters. He said it had a nice ring to it and it wasn't a million miles from his own name, so he wouldn't have a problem remembering it.'

Gene Waters. Dara supposed it did have a certain ring to it. She opened her mouth to ask the next question, but Slither beat her to it.

'Manchester. That's where he went. There was a good bit of work there at the time if you had a shovel and a pick and knew what to do with them. I have his address, but I haven't heard from him in a while now. I got the card from him at Christmas all right.'

Slither paused then, to pull at his cigarette and take a sup from his glass. Dara couldn't decide how she felt. Or if she felt anything at all. She sat there in her men's pyjamas, on the bottom step of the stairs.

'Why are you telling me all this now?' she asked suddenly, and if there was suspicion in her voice, nobody could blame her.

'I should have told you in the pub o' course,' admitted Slither. 'But he made me swear never to tell anyone anything.

If anyone came lookin' for him, I wasn't to say a word. He said his life was in danger, and after seein' the state of him in Manchester, I believed him.'

'So, what changed?' Dara asked.

'You've been on my mind, young Dara Flood,' Slither said, like a man unused to having anything on his mind weightier than a pint and a fag and a copy of the *Racing Post*. 'Sure, aren't you the cut out of him? And then of course, Lord Lucan came in and didn't me conscience start playing up on me. It wouldn't let me go. Night 'n' day it was on at me to ring you and tell you.'

An embarrassed silence followed this admission. Dara rushed to fill it. 'You're very good to ring and let me know. Thank you, Slither. I appreciate that.'

'What's this your e-mail address is and I'll send you his address up above in Manchester,' said Slither, all business now. 'And the next time you come to Bailieborough, I'm going to treat you to a tin of Coke and a bag of chips from McGoverns. You've never tasted the like, Dara, I'll tell ya that for free.'

'Thanks,' Dara said again. She had the feeling that Slither rarely gave anything away for free.

'Now don't forget, willya?'

'Forget what?' asked Dara, who had already forgotten.

'About the two-thirty at Listowel,' said Slither with a touch of impatience. His good deed done, he was anxious to get back to the business of the day.

'Oh no, I won't forget,' said Dara, standing up. 'But I wouldn't hold out much hope. I . . .'

'You let Uncle Slither worry about that, all right?'

'OK then, if you're sure.'

'I am, to be sure,' Slither declared and hung up without another word.

63

'Eh, hello, Mrs Flood. I'm looking for Dara,' Stanley said when the door finally opened.

In her hand, Mrs Flood held a note covered in large, loopy writing that Stanley recognised as Dara's.

'She's gone,' she said, looking at the note and shaking her head.

Her clothes had the creased, tired appearance of clothes that had been slept in. Her hair had the neglected look of a bird's nest, long abandoned.

'Do you know where she went? I . . . I need to talk to her. It's important.' It was only when he said the words, out loud, that Stanley realised just how important it was. His resolve tightened.

'You'd better come in,' Mrs Flood said, turning and walking up the hall. Stanley followed her into the narrow little kitchen. It surprised him by being untidy. 'Please forgive the mess,' said Mrs Flood, as if she had read his mind. 'We've been . . . coming and going quite a bit recently. What with Angel and everything.'

'Angel?' he repeated slowly.

'Did Dara not tell you?'

'Eh, no. I haven't spoken to her recently.'

'She's been in the hospital. She just got home yesterday. She had a bit of a turn.'

'Is she . . . will she be all right?'

Mrs Flood swiped at crumbs on the table with her hand. Some of them fell on the floor but she didn't seem to notice.

'God willing, she will,' she said. She threw the crumbs into the sink before flicking a switch on the kettle and sitting down heavily on a kitchen chair. 'Her blood pressure was high. It's still high but not as bad, thank God.' Mrs Flood bit her lip as she said this.

The kettle hissed as it boiled and Stanley nodded at it. 'Would you like me to make you a cup of tea?' he asked.

'I should be making you one,' said Mrs Flood, although she did not move. She looked exhausted.

Stanley made two cups of tea. When he opened the fridge, he could hardly find the carton of milk, hidden as it was behind a huge bowl of beef stroganoff, a chocolate fudge cake, ramekins of what looked like strawberry mousse and a package of puff pastry wrapped in cellophane that made him think of vol-au-vents. He wrestled the milk out of the fridge, along with the chocolate fudge cake. Mrs Flood looked like she could do with something sweet.

'Did Dara make this?' he asked, setting the cake on the table in front of her.

'She did indeed. Sure, doesn't she make everything around here?' Mrs Flood accepted the slice of cake Stanley handed her, protesting that she would never eat all that but managing to just the same. 'I didn't realise I was hungry,' she admitted, licking Dara's delicious chocolate sauce off her fingers.

'So, do you know when Dara will be back?' asked Stanley.

Mrs Flood said nothing but picked up the note that lay crumpled on the table between them.

'Where did she go?'

'Manchester,' Mrs Flood said, shaking her head slowly. 'She got a call. This morning. From Slither Smith. I believe you've already had the pleasure of Slither's company?'

Stanley nodded.

'Well, he's given her an address in Manchester for her father. For Mr Flood.'

'Jesus,' Stanley said before he could help himself.

'Don't be taking the Lord's name in vain, like a good boy,' Mrs Flood told him gently.

'Sorry,' said Stanley. 'But are you sure . . . ? Did she go on her own?'

Mrs Flood nodded. 'As if I don't have enough to be worrying about,' she said, and there was a bitter edge to her voice. 'I've tried ringing her, but there's no answer. She didn't even say when she'd be back.' She picked up the note and handed it to Stanley.

Deer Mam, I didn't want too wake you. I got a call this morning from Slither Smith and he's given me an address in Manchestir for Mr Flood. He's prety sure I'll find him their. I'll be back as soon as I can. Please don't worry about me. And don't say anything to Angel. Not yet, anyway. I don't want to get her hopes up again.

Lots of love, Dara xxxx

Stanley folded the note and kept folding it until it was half the size of a matchbox. He thought about Dara, on her own, holding on to the arms of her seat, with her knuckles straining white against her already pale skin as the plane landed. He should have let her explain. That day in the park. He should have rung her back.

'How can I not worry?' Mrs Flood asked, cutting herself a second slice of chocolate fudge cake. Stanley could understand why. It was easily the best fudge cake he'd ever had. He made his decision.

'I'll go,' he said, standing up so suddenly, his chair fell backwards.

Mrs Flood jumped as it clattered against the floor. 'Sorry about that,' said Stanley, picking it up.

'It's not you,' Mrs Flood told him. 'It's me. I'm a bag of nerves. What with Angel. And now Dara. She's in no fit state to be going anywhere. She's up the walls about Angel. She hasn't been sleeping right. Well, she never did. Not really.' Mrs Flood shook her head, and for a moment, it was like Stanley was not there. Like she had forgotten he was there. She wiped her hands down her face. 'I've been hard on the girl. Too hard. And now she's gone to Manchester, all on her own. It should be me going. *I'm* the one he walked out on. I told them he left all of us, but really, he never left Dara. He never even saw her. Maybe if he had, things might have been different. She was cut out of him when she was born. Still is.' Mrs Flood did not look at Stanley as she spoke but he could see the bright glint of tears in her eyes.

He put his hand on her shoulder. Patted her once, then a second time. Mrs Flood looked at him. 'Dara was right about you,' she told him. 'You have kind eyes.'

'Dara said that?'

Mrs Flood nodded. 'And she said you were a man she could trust. I gave that notion short shrift, but I think she might have been right. About you, I mean.'

Hope floated somewhere inside Stanley. He fished his iPhone out of his pocket and began pushing buttons.

'What are you doing?' asked Mrs Flood, wiping her eyes with her sleeve.

'I'm booking myself on the next flight to Manchester,' he said.

'Will you ring me when you get there? When you see her? Tell me when she'll be back?'

Stanley promised, and checked his watch. 'OK, the next flight is in three hours, so I've time to . . .'

'Grand, you've time for a haircut, so.'

Mrs Flood got up and moved towards an enormous bag slumped against the wall. It bulged with tools Stanley recognised. Tools that Sissy left lying in wait around the place. Tongs and straighteners and hot rollers and a long pair of dangerous-looking scissors. Mrs Flood looked much more authoritative with the bag in hand. Stanley took a step back.

'A haircut?'

'Well, you can't go to Manchester like that, can you?' she said, looking at Stanley's hair with something approaching fascination. 'I've never seen the like of that fringe. No, you can't be let out in that condition. I've product that will see to that cowlick very nicely, thank you very much. It's a pity we don't have time for the twelve-week blow-dry. Never mind, we can think about a long-term strategy when you get back. Now, pull a chair over to the sink. That's it. Sit down and lean back, like a good lad. That's right. All the way. Don't look so worried. You're in good hands.'

64

'Are you sure this is the place?' asked Dara, when the taxi pulled up. She made no move to get out but peered out the window instead, trying to see through a dirty curtain of grey rain.

'Yeah, this is the place,' said the taxi man in the same monotone he had employed since Dara had first got into the cab, at Manchester airport. His tone of voice had one setting: bleak, and he used it to talk at Dara for the entire twenty-minute journey. In that time, he opined on a wide range of subjects, from immigration (nothing against immigrants per se, but . . .), single mothers (he was sure they weren't *all* welfare scabs), and the weather, the melancholy greyness of which he seemed to take as a personal affront.

Dara nodded in all the right places and punctuated his monologue with an occasional 'Oh really?', or 'Yes, I know' and once a 'But that's terrible', which followed a long-drawn-out tale of woe about a barking dog and a sleepless night and a report made to the council in the morning and the van that came to bring the dog away.

But mostly she stared out of the window as the roar of the city fell away to be replaced by grey suburban streets, sodden with rain, the people marching like ants down the pavements, their heads bent against the weather, wrestling with umbrellas.

The taxi man coughed. 'That'll be thirteen pounds and thirty-five.'

'Oh right, of course, sorry.' Dara reached for her wallet in the front pocket of her backpack.

'Better watch that around here,' the taximan offered, nodding towards her wallet. 'There's folks that'll take that off you for free.'

'Oh, right, thanks, keep the change,' Dara told him, reaching for the handle of the door. As soon as she was out, the taxi roared away, with the speed of a getaway car after a botched robbery. Only for the smell of burning rubber, you'd think it had never been here at all.

The street was one of those long, wide ones, flanked on both sides by trees whose swollen roots made speed bumps along the footpaths and the road. Dara picked her way along, careful to avoid cracks and litter, dripping cans and sodden bits of paper turning to mush underfoot. It was the kind of road that must have been impressive, once. Large redbrick period houses shielded from the road by gardens that were deep as well as wide. Now, the houses seemed to be divided up into various flats and bedsits, judging by the variety of sagging, faded net curtains hiding their inhabitants from the likes of Dara Flood, who studied them as she walked by. She stopped when she got to number 124. In one window, a man poked at something in a pot with resigned distaste. In another, clothes on the backs of chairs, trying to dry. A woman sat at a kitchen table and counted coins out of her purse, piling them in neat towers. The sound of a baby, crying, reached out of a window near the top of the house.

The garden in front of the house had grown wild, a riot of briars and nettles, thistles and stingers. Through the wilderness, threads of yellow, where dandelions danced on hairy stems. Weeds poked hardy heads through cracks in the path that led to the house.

Then, as Dara neared the front door, she noticed it. Around the side of the house. A kitchen garden. Beautifully tended. Or at least it had been until recently. Rows of lettuce and carrots and turnips and leeks. Running in long, neat lines. A herb garden to one side. Dara stepped towards it. Chives and rosemary and parsley and mint, bulbs of wild garlic and the soft leaves of basil. She picked one of these and rubbed it between her fingers, inhaling its familiar sweet smell.

Dara moved to the front door and scanned the list of names on the wall. No Gene Waters. Or Eugene Flood. She checked her page. Number 124. She took a few steps back until she could see the number of the house, painted over the fanlight above the door: 124. This was the place.

The door opened with a moan when she pushed it. It had once been painted red, but that was a long time ago. The paint had faded now, and was beginning to peel away from the door in long, thin strips. A smell of damp coats in the hall. In it were two bicycles, rusted and buckled, cloaked in web as thick as cotton wool. A table at the end of the hall was covered in flyers filled with capital letters and exclamation marks. Pizza parlours UNDER NEW MANAGEMENT!!!! Indian takeaways with BRAND NEW MENU!!! and FREE DELIVERY!! Taxi companies promising £1 OFF YOUR NEXT FARE!!! A launderette undertaking to TAKE THE PAIN OUT OF YOUR STAINS!!!

A wide staircase on the left creaked when Dara put her foot on the first step. The creak bounced against the bare walls and echoed around the hall, startling her. She went back outside. Even the light of the dull day seemed bright after the gloom of the hall. She sat on the step and reached for the patch on her arm before remembering that she hadn't stopped to stick one on that morning. She lit up.

65

Stanley's flight was delayed. He stood at Dublin airport with his brand-new hair and tried not to scratch his back where strands of it had settled. His hand reached for the tuft of his cowlick and came away, disappointed. Mrs Flood had been as good as her word. She had *seen* to his fringe. She'd left the length, mostly, but had cut away a huge amount of hair nonetheless. It had made quite a mound when he swept it off the kitchen floor afterwards.

'Jesus, Mary and Joseph, but you've a terrible amount of hair,' she told him as she moved around his head, tutting and sighing.

He'd had to really fight to dissuade her from shaving him as well.

'I suppose that's *designer* stubble, is it?' she asked, her tone sceptical at best.

Stanley said no. It was just your average, common-or-garden stubble, he assured her. But she wouldn't let him leave the house until he'd shaved his face clean. He had to use one of Dara's razors. 'She's only used it the once, as far as I know,' Mrs Flood told him, handing him the disposable. 'I'll run it under the hot tap, it'll be grand.'

Afterwards, Mrs Flood stepped away and looked at him, in a vigorously critical manner. Stanley stood there, between the kitchen table littered with cups and cartons and the leftovers of Dara's fudge cake, and the sink where the suds from the head-crushing shampoo Mrs Flood had given him gathered around the plughole. His head hurt from her spirited ablutions. Still, he had to admit she had done a good job. Even Sissy would approve, he felt. He looked older. As if he knew more things. Experienced. He looked like clever things might come out of his mouth if he opened it.

But he had nothing to do with his hands, now that his fringe had been dealt with. Instead, he shovelled them deep into his pockets. A copy of Slither's e-mail with Mr Flood's address was in his left hand. Mrs Flood had found it and printed it for him. He touched it with the tips of his fingers and thought about Dara Flood.

'You'll bring her straight back home when you find her, won't you, Stanley?' Mrs Flood asked as he made his way to the front door with his new hair.

'Well, I'll ring you. As soon as I meet her. Or I'll get her to ring you. I'm sure she will anyway. She probably has her phone switched off on the plane.'

Mrs Flood shook her head. 'I'm worried,' she confessed.

Stanley put his hand on her shoulder. Since Mrs Flood had kneaded his temples, Stanley felt a strange bond between them, unlike any feeling he'd had in the past for the barbers who had tried – and mostly failed – to face up to the challenge of his fringe.

'What are you worried about?' he asked gently.

Mrs Flood bit at the edge of her lip, just like Dara did.

'I'm worried that she'll find him.'

Stanley looked at the screen. Forty minutes' delay. He'd go into the men's and double-check he wasn't wearing the designer underpants with the metal tag, then he'd tackle Security.

66

After that first cigarette, Dara came up with a sort of a plan. She would stay here, at number 124, until something happened. Until someone told her something. Anything. About Mr Flood. Or Waters. She would not leave until she knew something. Something more than she knew now, which, she had to admit, was not a lot. Nothing useful anyway.

She smoked three cigarettes and finished the bottle of water she'd bought in the airport. Then she needed to go to the toilet. She fought it for as long as she could, standing up and pacing up and down the garden, sitting on the step with her legs tightly crossed, her body jiggling as if to the rhythm of a song that only she could hear. Up the road there was a line of shops: a pizzeria, an Indian takeaway, a taxi company and a launderette. Dara recognised their names from the flyers with the capital letters and the exclamation marks on the hall table of number 124.

Also a coffee shop. *Angel's* was the name written in a semi-circle across the front window. Dara – who didn't believe in such things – took this as a sign. A positive sign.

A bell tinkled when Dara opened the door and stepped inside. She didn't even order her coffee before she ran for the toilet. Although she made up for it when she came out by asking for a latte with an espresso on the side and two croissants. Plain ones.

'To go, please,' she added, pushing coins across the counter towards a plump woman in a white coat and netting around her hair, which she wore in a tight bun.

It was only when Dara smiled at the dog that came into the café through a door behind the counter – a golden retriever that the woman called Rosy-Lee – that a conversation ensued.

'I'd recognise that smile anywhere,' said the woman, smiling herself to reveal two long, thin front teeth that reminded Dara of Fluffy, Tintin's unfortunate rabbit. Dara concentrated on the woman's eyes instead. Kindly brown ones, the colour of the chocolate on an eclair. 'You have to be related to Gene Waters,' she told Dara.

Dara felt a jolt of energy, like electricity, roar through her. She was getting somewhere after all. 'Yes, I'm his daughter,' she told the woman, whose name turned out to be Deirdre, although she pronounced it 'Deer-dree' when she introduced herself.

'His daughter?' The woman's smile slipped off her face and was replaced by confusion. 'Oh. I didn't realise he had any family.'

'He does,' Dara told her, even though there was no need to repeat it. 'I've . . . I've come to visit him. A . . . surprise visit. But he doesn't seem to be in. You don't happen to know where I might find him, do you?'

The woman set both hands on her generous hips. She cocked her head to one side. 'Well, now that I think about it, I haven't seen that fella in some time. Weeks, I'd say. And he always used to come in here for his tea on the way home from work.'

'Work?' Dara asked, feeling she was inching ever closer to the elusive Mr Flood.

'Yes, a building site down at the docks. But there's no use going down there today. It'll be closed.'

Dara's face fell. 'Why?' she asked.

'Eh, because it's Sunday, my love,' said Deer-dree, in a louder voice than before, as if she thought that Dara was perhaps a little slow.

'Oh, yes, of course it's Sunday, I just . . . I forgot,' said Dara, picking up her coffees and her bag of croissants.

The woman bent across the counter and sat her big, floury hand over Dara's small, dry one. 'He's probably just found a new caff to have his tea in. Where the women are younger and prettier than me and old Rosy-Lee here.' She winked at Dara when she said that, as if they both knew something about Mr Flood. Dara might be able to guess what that something might be, but she didn't know for sure. She didn't know anything for sure.

67

On the flight, Stanley looked at the photograph Mrs Flood had given him.

A man with a shock of silky black hair framing a small, pale face and navy eyes that were long rather than big. He stands behind a woman whose smile is wide and careless, like nothing bad could ever happen. Her hands sit across her swollen belly. There is such intimacy in the gesture. Such gentleness. The woman has pale blue eyes and sallow skin. She looks like Angel who lies in the crook of her arm, asleep.

'I found it just the other day,' Mrs Flood told Stanley, handing him the photograph. 'I've been doing a bit of a . . . clear-out lately.'

'You're beautiful.' He said it without thinking. He looked quickly at Mrs Flood, but she was staring at the picture, lost in the world of it.

'I was,' she said. 'Back then. I was expecting Dara in that photograph. She was born about two months after it was taken.' Stanley tucked the photograph into his wallet.

'I'll give it to Dara,' he said. 'I think she would like to have it.'

The plane began to bank towards Manchester airport. Out the window, Stanley could see a damp grid of grey. He thought about Dara, somewhere down there, navigating the strange streets of a strange city, on her own, looking for Mr Flood. Finding Mr Flood. He knew she would find him. That much he knew. It was afterwards that he worried about. What would happen after she found him.

He closed his eyes and thought about Dara Flood. The smooth softness of her shoulders. The gentle curve of her hips. The birthmark in the shape of Italy hidden at the back of her knee.

'I've never been to Italy,' she'd said when he discovered it that morning. The morning he woke up beside her.

'We should go,' Stanley had replied, regretting the words immediately. Already, in his head, he could hear Sissy Clarke thundering down the stairs with the pillows at the ready. He shouldn't have said that. It was too soon. Too much. But Dara had smiled at him and said, 'That would be nice,' as if it wasn't too soon. Or too much.

Stanley fastened his seat belt and clipped his tray back. He didn't know what he was going to do once he found her. But there was one thing he was certain of. He was going to find her.

68

Back at the house with her coffees and croissants, Dara Flood decided to take some action and pressed every single bell at the front door of the house. Two people answered. One was a girl, perhaps seven or eight. 'Mummy says I'm not to answer the door when she's gone out to work,' the girl told Dara in a solemn, worried voice.

'No, she's right, you shouldn't,' Dara told her, appalled at the idea of a child, alone, in this falling-down wreck of a house. 'You shouldn't even answer the doorbell.'

'Why did you ring, then?'

'What?'

'If you didn't want me to answer the doorbell, why did you ring it?' It was not an unreasonable question. Dara struggled to answer it.

'Because . . . because I didn't know you were there,' she said, lamely.

The girl thought about this. 'Do you want to come in and play Snap with me?' she asked then. 'That's a card game. I'm really good at cards.'

'Eh, no,' Dara said. 'No thank you. And really, you shouldn't . . .'

'OK, I have to go now, *Hannah Montana* is coming on,' said the girl and hung up.

Dara hesitated before she began pressing on the bells again. The second person was at the top of the house. An elderly woman with a hearing problem. 'What?' she roared at Dara when she asked about Gene Waters. Dara repeated the question. 'Whatever you're selling, I'm not buying!' shouted the woman down the intercom.

'No . . . it's . . . I'm not selling anything!' Dara shouted back. 'I'm looking for a man called Gene Waters.'

'Well, why are you ringing on my door, then?'

'Because I . . . I just wondered if you might know him.'

'No,' the woman replied.

'I just . . . I think he lives in this house,' Dara said

'Well why don't you ring on his door, then?' the woman asked.

'Because I'm not sure which . . .' But the woman was gone.

Nobody came or went. Perhaps because it was Sunday. Although the building had the dilapidated, barren appearance of a house abandoned by its inhabitants long ago, Dara felt. Once she thought she saw a curtain twitching and the outline of a head behind it, cocked in her direction. When she stood up to get a better look, the silhouette disappeared and it was hard to know if it had been there at all.

Nothing happened till lunchtime. By then, Dara's bum was numb from the unforgiving concrete of the front step of number 124. Of Mr Flood – or Mr Waters – there was no sign, and the day, which had not improved with its passing, began to dwindle into a duller shade of afternoon. Apart from her earlier visit to the café, Dara had not moved from number 124. She had smoked nine cigarettes. She knew she couldn't sit here for ever, but with uncharacteristic optimism, possibly because of Slither's change of heart and subsequent telephone call, she felt that if she sat here long enough, something might happen. Not something good, necessarily. But something, all the same. Beside, she couldn't go home empty-handed. Not again. Not when Angel was so sick.

The woman arrived shortly after two. Dara had followed her progress down the street, each step punctuated by the sharp plink of her heels against concrete. At first, Dara presumed she was just another passer-by. She looked at Dara in the way that people glance at other people as they walk by. But then she came to such an abrupt stop at the gate, Dara thought for a moment she would fall over. Instead, she studied Dara's face, then nodded and hitched a long, slim handbag under her armpit, clamping it in place between her arm and her chest. She opened the gate and began to pick her way carefully up the garden path. She was a curious collection. Greying hair in rollers on her head. A full face of make-up with lipstick smudged across her long, yellowing front teeth. A pink skirt and twinset over which she had pulled a faded housecoat, a sticky bright yellow stain on the front of it that Dara recognised as egg yolk. The housecoat had grown too small for her and puckered against the buttons fastened across her ample chest.

Dara got to her feet, as pins and needles shot down her stiff legs. She stood in front of the little pile of cigarette butts on the step. She had forgotten her plastic container.

'Well, there can be no denying you and that's a fact,' the woman told Dara, stopping in front of her and reaching for her hand, which she pumped up and down several times. Her accent was one of an Irishwoman who had lived in Manchester for many years. 'You've got to be Gene's, haven't you?'

Dara nodded. She supposed it must be true, however unlikely it sounded.

'I'm his daughter,' she told the woman, her body still juddering from the enthusiasm of the handshake.

'And I,' said the woman, touching her rollers with her free hand, as if making sure they were still in place, 'am Doreen Hall.'

Dara felt as if something was expected of her after this announcement. Some kind of response. Recognition, perhaps. When nothing occurred, Doreen swept on.

'I am the proprietor of this establishment.' She nodded towards the house, smiling, and Dara turned to look at it again, perhaps thinking that she had missed something before. But no, the house still had the sunken appearance of age and neglect, the roof still green with moss and weeds and sagging with rain, as if spent.

'Does Mr Flood ... I mean, Mr Waters, my father ... does he still live here?' Dara arranged the question as casually as she could.

Doreen nodded towards the stairs. 'The basement flat, he had. I told him it was too damp and poky, but he said dampness and pokiness were things he could manage, so long as he could have a patch of garden to tend.

'The vegetable patch?'

Irene smiled towards it and nodded. 'That's him all right. I've never eaten as much salad as I have since Gene Waters arrived. Good with his hands, that fella,' she said, again touching the curlers with the tips of her fingers and smiling the smile of a woman whose garden had once been tended by Eugene Flood. Or Gene Waters. Either way, it was a smile that Dara was beginning to recognise.

'Have you come to collect his personal effects?' Doreen asked then, when she stopped patting her curlers.

'His personal effects?' Dara asked.

'Yes, his ... I just presumed ... I thought ... since you're here and ...' Doreen's voice limped away. She coughed and began again. 'He's been in the hospice for the past few weeks. I meant to visit him, of course, but I've been busy, what with the house and the tenants. They're a grasping lot, always wanting something for nothing, you know?'

'The hospice?' Dara knew what Doreen had said. And she

knew what hospices were for. But she had to ask again. She had to be sure.

This time, Doreen's hands clamped around her mouth. 'Oh my word, I'm so sorry, lovey. I thought you knew. I thought that's why you were here. To be honest, I've been expecting somebody. He always said he had no family, but everybody's got somebody, haven't they?'

Dara nodded mutely. 'So he's . . .'

'Yes, love, I'm so sorry. He's got . . . he's been unwell. He hasn't been well for a long time.'

Doreen set her bag on the step and pulled Dara into a tight embrace. Dara stood there and struggled for something to say. After a while, Doreen released her. Her eyes were bright with tears and she patted the pockets of her housecoat. Dara pulled a tissue from her backpack. 'Here,' she said, handing it to Doreen, who dabbed at the corners of both eyes and blew her nose noisily.

'Oh, you must think me a foolish woman,' she told Dara through the wad of soggy tissue. 'It's just, you're so like him. The way he used to be, anyway, when he first arrived. You caught me off guard, so you did.'

'Do you happen to know the name of the hospice?' Dara asked, almost hoping that Doreen would say no. This was not the way the story was supposed to end.

'It's St Jude's, I think,' said Doreen, picking up her bag and sliding it once again into the tight space between her arm and her chest. Dara thought this was a cruel name for a hospice. Hopeless cases. 'He's been getting letters from them. Bills most likely, God help him.' She crossed herself when she said this. 'I have the keys. We'll go in and have a look.'

Doreen was right about the basement flat. It was damp and poky. Dark too, even when she switched on the lights. In the corner, a two-bar electric heater. A shelf, nailed to the wall over the sink, held a mug, a plate, a saucepan with no lid or handle. On the kitchen table, a bundle of papers. Doreen moved towards them. Dara opened a door and found herself in a bedroom, with one single bed and a chest of drawers standing on three legs, a bundle of gardening magazines propping up the space where the fourth leg should have been. As she turned to leave, she saw them. On the floor, sitting in a patch of light thrown by a small window. Trees. Miniature trees. Five of them. Perfectly formed and mature, with thick bark and branches sprouting young green leaves, tiny and delicate, with fine veins threaded through them, as faint as a single line of a spider's web.

Dara bent down to touch one. Despite everything, she smiled at the warm, woody feel of it. She pressed her finger into the soil. It was hard and dry. On the floor beside them, a plastic measuring jug filled with water, long stagnant. She picked it up and refilled it with fresh water from a rust-stained sink in the bathroom. She poured a small amount of water into the soil around each of the trees. It seemed like the least she could do.

69

'This is the place,' said the taxi driver in the same monotone he had employed since Stanley had first got into the cab, at Manchester airport. His tone of voice had one setting: bleak, and he used it to talk at Stanley for the entire twenty-minute journey. In that time, he opined on a wide range of subjects, from immigration (nothing against immigrants per se but . . .), single mothers (he was sure they weren't *all* welfare scabs), and the weather, the melancholy greyness of which he seemed to take as a personal affront. Stanley sat in the back of the cab and didn't even pretend to listen. The taxi man droned on regardless. Instead, he thought about Dara Flood. Her slow, careful smile. The surprise of her laugh, low in her throat, her mouth closed against the sound, containing it.

Outside number 124, a woman stood at the edge of the kerb, waving to someone in the back of a taxi. The car moved away and disappeared around the curve of the road.

Stanley stepped out and nodded at the woman before opening the gate and walking up the pathway, choked with weeds and moss, towards the front door. Behind him, he felt the eyes of the woman on him as he progressed towards the house that had seen better days. Of Dara, there was no sign, although there was a mound of cigarette butts on the ground beside the step. Nine of them. Perhaps she hadn't had time to pack the plastic container? He scanned the names beside each of the doorbells. He took a step back and looked up at the number of the house, printed over the fanlight: 124. Yes, it was the right house. The right street.

'Can I help you, dearie?' Stanley turned. The woman stood at the bottom of the steps, looking at him like she was about to pick him out of a line-up.

'I'm looking for Mr Flo . . . I mean, Gene Waters. I believe he lives here?' Stanley nodded towards the house.

'A lot of people live here,' the woman said, examining the length and breadth of Stanley Flinter and almost smiling when her gaze reached his hair, as if she knew he'd had it cut this morning and approved of the style.

'I'm actually looking for his daughter. Dara Flood. I think she might have been here. Earlier, perhaps.'

'And who might you be?' the woman asked, walking slowly up the steps towards Stanley.

'I'm her . . . I'm a friend of hers,' Stanley told her, moving back as the woman reached the top step. She smelled of fry-up and hairspray, which was not the best combination.

'Are you her boyfriend?' The woman looked at him with a determined, patient air, as if she was not going to take a 'mind your own business' for an answer.

'No,' said Stanley. 'Not really.'

The woman immediately took to nodding her head, up and down, up and down, so fast that Stanley feared for the rollers that just managed to cling on. 'I understand,' she said, which Stanley felt was peculiar, since he did not understand it himself. Still, Stanley's status as not really Dara Flood's boyfriend seemed to put the woman's mind at ease. Stanley seized his chance. 'So,' he asked, 'does Mr Waters live here?'

'My word, but that fella's awful popular today. Not a visitor for months and months and suddenly everyone is beating a path to his door. Still, I suppose where there's a will, there's relatives, am I right?'

'A will?'

'Just my little joke,' the woman said, smiling to reveal long, yellow teeth with bright red lipstick smeared across the top ones. 'He's in St Jude's Hospice. I've put your young Dara into a taxi bound for there. She's just left. I knew who she was the minute I saw her. Cut out of him, she is. Or at least the way he used to be.'

Stanley began to run.

'Where are you going?'

'St Jude's!' he shouted, not stopping.

'Don't you want to know where it is?' the woman called after him.

'I'll get a cab,' Stanley said. 'Thanks,' he added, running up the road, keeping an eye on the traffic, ready to hail the first taxi he saw.

70

The taxi didn't take long to get to St Jude's. Looking back, Dara found she didn't remember much of the journey. It seemed to her like she had been on that journey for a long, long time.

The hospice was a long, low building made of sturdy red brick, dwarfed by a life-size cross that stood to the side with a bloodied and beaten statue of Jesus nailed to it, his head bowed with the weight of the crown of thorns wrapped around it. At the bottom of the cross knelt a statue of Mary, her face hidden by her hands as she wept for the loss of her only son to a God who must have seemed cruel and careless to her, on that day at least.

'Are you all right, love?' Dara pulled her eyes away from the cross. The taxi driver looked at her with a mix of pity and concern. He knew what this place was for.

'Sorry, I was just . . .' Dara reached for her bag. 'How much do I owe you?'

'Well, the meter says £10.75, but just for you, I'll make it an even tenner, how's that?' Beneath the rims of an enormous pair of bifocals, his eyes were kind. Dara smiled and handed over the money.

'Thank you,' she said, getting out of the cab.

'You take care of yourself, love, won't you?' It sounded like a formal request, and Dara found herself nodding, telling him that she would. She moved towards the building.

'I'm looking for Mr Floo . . . sorry, I mean Gene Waters,' she said to the young girl at reception.

The girl did not hesitate before she answered. She did not have to tap any keys on her computer or consult any book. She answered immediately. Confidently. As if there could be no doubt.

'He's in St Killian's Ward,' she said, smiling a perfect smile at Dara with her wide mouth and her white teeth and her glossy lips.

When Dara did not move, the girl went on, 'You just go straight down that corridor and it's the second turn on the right, then all the way to the end, through the double doors and you're there. He's in the bed beside the window. On your left-hand side.'

Dara stayed where she was. It seemed impossible. That Mr Flood was here. In this building. Dara realised now that she had been expecting something else when she arrived. A case of mistaken identity. Or that he'd checked out with no forwarding address. It seemed impossible that he was here, in this building, in St Killian's Ward. In the bed by the window on the left-hand side.

'Are you OK?' The girl's voice was kind. Concerned. Dara took a breath. She nodded before she moved away.

★   ★   ★

*I feel different today. Better, I think. Through the square of window,
the heavy-handed greyness that has persisted over days and weeks,
and perhaps months, has paled. There is a patch of blue in the sky
that hints of sunshine later. Maybe.*

*It's hard to focus. I can't be sure what day it is. There is a sense
of calm in this not knowing. Release. That's what it's like. I feel my
grip loosening, the road slippy underfoot.*

I hear a voice.

*Coming down the corridor. A girl's voice. She sounds like my
mother, God rest her. She sounds like my mother when she was a
young woman. Years ago. When I was a boy in short pants. The
voice is soft and low. A little hoarse. Gravelly. I turn my head and
look past the beds, to the door at the top of the ward. But the light
is fading and it is getting harder to see.*

The voice nears.

*I use my elbows to push myself up, but the effort is difficult and
I tire quickly. Still, I wait, my eyes trained on the door, for the
voice that sounds like my mother's voice, when she was a young
woman.*

*Of course, I know it is not her. I know it, and yet some part of
me – the boy in short pants part of me – believes it to be her. She
will come and she will fold me in her arms the way she used to do,
holding me on her lap in the rocking chair by the fire, even when
I had grown too big for such carry-on. She will hum the tune she
used to hum and rock me and I will push my nose into the soft skin
of her neck, the way I used to do, and catch the faint smell of her. A
sweet smell. The smell of warm cake crumbling along a knife.*

*I didn't climb into my mother's lap when my father was around.
Boys didn't back then. My father's affection was of a different variety. He taught me how to punch with a closed fist. Harder than
you'd think. I practised on a sandbag in the barn. We fished together, hours and hours spent on the Borora in a splintering rowboat
that had once been red. We said little, the pair of us, but I could feel*

the solid heat of his arm when the line jerked, and he'd roar, 'Get the net, boy, we'll not go hungry the night!'

I wait and I listen. My eyes hurt now, the light of the day suddenly too bright. It is a relief to close them, to allow the lids to flutter and drop. The sounds of the ward fall away and all I can hear is the voice. My mother's voice. She is nearly here. I want to wait for her. My body feels light. Weightless. Warmth wraps itself around me, like the soft blanket she'd tuck around my toes in my bed in the attic where the heat of the fire did not penetrate.

'Good night, my love,' she'd say, lowering her face to mine, kissing my forehead. Warm cake crumbling along a knife. The smell lingered when she left, like wisps of cloud trailing along the sky.

The voice gets closer still. I try to wait. To resist the tug I feel. It is like being pulled gently by a hand. A mother's hand. Pulled out of the decay of this body, pulled somewhere that is not here. I don't know where it is, but it is not here.

The warmth is inside me now. I am lit up with it. Alive with it. I think I might be laughing. Or crying. It's hard to know. There's one thing I do know. I am leaving. I've spent my life leaving, but this time, I think, this might be the last time. The final leave-taking. I close my eyes. I am glad about it.

By the time the nurse – Fidelma, I think – comes in to say, 'You've got a visitor, Mr Waters,' I am gone.

I am long gone.

71

Stanley threw a twenty at the taxi driver, shouted at him to keep the change, got out of the cab and began to run towards the building. He skidded to a halt just inside the door. He didn't have far to go. He didn't have to ask anyone anything.

Because there she was, Dara Flood, sitting on a tattered couch in the reception area, her two hands wrapped around a plastic cup. She was wearing a tracksuit. A navy one. With a white T-shirt underneath. And runners. White ones with navy stripes. Her duffel coat lay on the seat beside her and her backpack leaned against her legs, faithful as a hound. For a moment, he didn't say anything. Just looked at her. She seemed to sense the weight of his stare and glanced up. Her face was paler than usual, her navy eyes darker, with shadows below them like bruises. She looked tired, like she hadn't slept in the longest time. And cold. The kind of cold that is hard to shift.

He moved towards her. She stood up and looked at him, with that vulnerable look she had, as if awful things were about to happen. He reached her in three steps. Folded his arms around her and felt her lean against him. Felt the softness of her skin touch his neck in a way that was almost unbearable. She didn't ask him what he was doing there. How he'd known where to find her. What the hell had happened to his fringe. None of that. When she did speak, it was a whisper. He felt the breath of the words against his ear.

'I'm glad you're here.' That's what she said. And for the first time in a long time, Stanley felt a sense of possibility. That something could happen. Something good. He held her tight and buried his nose in the silky blackness of her hair.

Gently, he pushed Dara away and looked at her face. 'Did you find him?' he asked then. Dara bit at the edge of her lip, and Stanley thought perhaps that she had not heard his question. Then she nodded. Slowly. Carefully.

'Yes,' she said. 'I did. I found him. I found Mr Flood.'

72

It wasn't really a morgue, the room in the basement of the building. It just happened to be the room where they put them. It was cold as January down there.

It was dark, too, the room lit only by a small window, set high in the dull grey of the wall. The light it threw was feeble. Weak. Dara moved inside.

He was laid out on a table in the centre of the room, covered with a stiff white sheet. Dara and Stanley stood on either side of the table. Dara looked at Stanley, who raised his eyebrows at her, in a question. She nodded, and he reached for the sheet, hesitating only for a moment before he touched it, arranged his fingers around the edge of it.

'Wait,' said Dara, and Stanley stopped and looked at her. He waited.

Dara closed her eyes and counted backwards from ten. She concentrated on the task, breathing in on the even numbers, out on the odd ones. Then she opened her eyes. Stanley was there, still looking at her. Still waiting.

'Are you ready?' he asked.

She nodded.

He lifted the sheet back in one fluid movement, and suddenly there he was. Mr Flood. Her father. There could be no denying him.

He was in his pyjamas. White ones with a navy stripe. They looked brand new. They made her smile, those pyjamas. She didn't know much about him, but she felt sure he would have hated her to see him in them.

They ballooned around his chest, like they were two sizes too big. He looked like a man who used to be bigger. There was a shrunken quality to him. His skin was like the skin of an apple that is well past its best-before date. Withered. That's what it looked like. He looked all used up. Wasted. Gone was the silky black hair that Mrs Flood had loved to wash and cut on a Friday night. The chemotherapy had taken it, strand by strand. That's what Fidelma had told Dara. The chemotherapy had also taken away any chance of Mr Flood being able to donate any of his organs. To anyone. The cancer had started in his lungs but had spread through his body, as thorough as a fire in a forest where it never rains.

Without his hair, there was something vulnerable about his head. The whiteness of the skin there. Dara reached out her hand and touched him. On the white skin of his head. He was still warm. That's what made her cry in the end. The soft warmth of him. She had not expected that.

73

There were things to be taken care of. Things that neither of them expected.

'He wanted to be buried in Ireland,' Fidelma, the nurse, told them. Stanley noticed that she concentrated on him when she spoke, perhaps thinking that funeral arranging was a man's job, like taking out the bins or strimming or gluing things back together when they break.

He nodded. He hadn't the remotest idea how to repatriate a body. About funeral arrangements. But he nodded. Fidelma seemed to expect that from him.

He felt the slightness of Dara's hand in his. This was something he could do. He could hold Dara's hand. Let her know that he was here. That he was her friend.

Dara leaned forward. 'What was he like?' she asked Fidelma. 'What was Mr Flood like?'

Fidelma smiled at her, the way most people smiled at Dara Flood, Stanley noticed. A motherly sort of a smile.

'There's not a lot I can tell you, I'm afraid,' she said, picking up a file and flicking through it. 'He was a bricklayer by trade and he loved gardening. He told me one day about the trees he kept in his flat. You know those miniature trees. From Japan?' Again she looked at Stanley.

'Bonsai trees,' he said, and she nodded, remembering. 'He said they were the only things he ever got right, those trees.' She frowned then, as if she had said something she shouldn't have.

'I'm sorry,' she said, turning to Dara now. 'He was very ill by the time he came to us. He was dying, even then. And he knew it. It can turn people in on themselves, dying. He seemed quiet. He was a quiet man.' She shrugged, not in a careless kind of a way, not at all. It was more like an apology, that shrug. Like she was sorry she couldn't give Dara Flood any more.

'Did he have any visitors while he was here?' Dara asked.

Fidelma hesitated before she answered. 'No,' she said.

Dara stood up. Stanley followed suit.

'Well,' Dara said, picking up her backpack. 'Thank you. Thank you for everything.'

Fidelma looked at Dara for a moment. Then she stood up, came out from behind the desk and gathered Dara in her arms. Stanley let go of her hand and tried to blend into the wallpaper as the women embraced. He felt he was intruding on something. Something intimate. Something between women.

'I'm sorry, love,' Fidelma said, and there were tears in her eyes as she pulled away from Dara. 'I'm sorry you didn't get here in time. I'm sure you would have liked to speak to him before . . .' Her voice trailed away.

'I'm not sure,' said Dara. 'I feel like I've been looking for him for ages, but walking down the corridor towards the ward, I couldn't think of a single thing to say to him.'

'Something would have occurred, I'm sure,' said Fidelma, patting Dara's arm like she was someone she'd known for a long time.

'Now,' said Fidelma, a little brisker. 'There's a few bits in his bedside locker. Can you go through it and see what's what?'

When Dara said nothing, Stanley stepped in. 'Yes, yes, we will. And we'll fill out this form as best we can and get it back to you, all right?'

'Good,' said Fidelma. 'Good. Well, that's settled.' She returned to her side of the desk and sat down. Stanley took Dara's hand and led her out of the room.

Halfway down the corridor, Dara stopped.

'Stanley, I . . . I just want to say . . .'

'Don't,' he said. 'Don't say anything.' He touched her shoulder. The slender curve of it. 'We'll sort it out when we get home.' He believed it. He didn't think about Cora, or Cormac, or Ian Harte, or even Mr Flood, whom they had found and lost on the same day. He thought instead about Dara. About the slender curve of her shoulder. The slow carefulness of her smile. The world was a sad, strange place. But right here, in the corridor of this hopeless hospice, he felt something he hadn't felt in a long time. He felt hope. The kind of hope that could last.

74

Dara rang her mother from Manchester airport. There was no answer. She tried Angel. Several times. Her phone was switched off. The landline in the small house on the Raheny road rang and rang. She put her phone back in her pocket. Stanley had gone to get coffees. He had dealt with the details of their flight home. It was not leaving until 8 p.m.

There was time.

Dara reached inside the backpack and pulled out the tin container she had found in Mr Flood's bedside locker. In a drawer, right at the back. She placed it on her knees and studied it, not touching it. It might have been a tea caddy once, the container. It was old. Dented in places, the lettering worn away to faint shadows. A chequered pattern, like the tops of pots of home-made jam. Dara opened the lid.

The inside of the tin was stuffed with notes. Banknotes. Rolls and rolls of them. Tight rolls, bound with thin, stretched elastic. Dara stiffened in her seat before she scanned the area around her. Nobody paid her any attention. She returned to the tin. Wedged in among the notes were two envelopes, curling at the edges and dirty with fingerprints, as if they'd been taken out and put back many times. She picked one up. In large, loopy handwriting, not unlike her own, was the name Slither Smith, c/o The Market Bar, Bailieborough, Co. Cavan. It was a bulky affair, the envelope. She slid it back inside the tin and reached for the other envelope. The same large, loopy writing on the front: *The Flood family, Raheny Road, Dublin 5.*

Dara hesitated. She thought about her mother. About Angel. She should wait. Shouldn't she? The moment of hesitation was brief. She slid her thumb underneath the seal and pulled it across the top of the envelope, leaving the paper jagged and gaping. Inside, a single sheet of paper.

Dear Kathleen, Angel and Dara –

Dara paused. Mr Flood knew her name.

This is not an easy letter to write. If it was easy, it wouldn't matter. But it does matter. It matters a great deal. To me, at least.

Kathleen. You were the love of my life. There's no other way of saying it. Because that's the truth of it. I loved you. I love you still. I couldn't stay. I had done things. Foolish things.

I remember the day in Howth. The promises we made to each other. I meant them. I broke every one. You don't know you're having the best day of your life until you have time to look back. I remember everything about that day. The bag of chips we shared, the brown paper of the bag sodden with vinegar. Do you remember the boat we saw, sailing out past Ireland's Eye? The sturdy sail of it, curved with the wind. I remember the feel of your hand. The way you curled your fingers around mine. I watched the boat and felt the sun against my back and my belly full with the chips. That was it. That moment. Such a small thing. Not things you'd notice. But that is what I remember. Nothing ever topped it.

I hope the girls are doing well. I am sure they are a credit to you. I know you won't believe this but I have thought about them every day. Angel with her blond hair and her blue eyes, the image of her mother. And I'm glad you didn't call Dara Meryl. She looks like a Dara. I saw a photograph of her once. It was in the paper. The Evening Press. *I have it still. The three of you at the*

*St Patrick's Day Parade in Dublin. Slither cut it out and sent it
to me. She looks like my mother, God rest her, when my mother
was a girl. Beautiful, and sorry I was that I never saw her. Never
felt the weight of her in my arms.*

*I know everything was my fault. Everything. Some people just
aren't very good at things. I can't look back and say I did my
best, because that wouldn't be the truth. All I can do is write this
letter and hope that you might say a prayer for me the odd time.
I won't ask for forgiveness. But I am sorry. That much is true, for
what it's worth.*

*Nothing more to say but this. I finally won. I can hear you
laughing. God, I loved the way you laughed. The way you'd make
me laugh. But there it is. I finally won. The money is in the tin. It
should cover the funeral expenses. May be some left over for you
and the girls to take a trip. Italy, maybe. Remember we talked
about going to Rome some day? We'd meet the Pope and eat ice
cream to beat the band. The plans we had, Kathleen.*

All my love,
Eugene Flood

Dara returned the slip of paper to the envelope and pushed
it back inside the tin. The newspaper cutting was there too.
Yellow now. Stiff with age. Before today, Dara would have
said – had anyone asked her – that she had never been at the
parade. In the picture, she is sitting on her mother's shoulders,
her short thin legs dangling around her mother's neck. She is
wearing jeans with a patch on the knee. She remembers the
patch. Mickey and Minnie holding hands. An anorak, zipped
against the cold, the hood up. Her hands gripping tightly
across her mother's forehead. One of her mother's hands
holds Dara's leg, so skinny her mother can reach all the way
around it with her fingers. Mrs Flood's other hand rests on
top of Angel's head. The three of them are looking up, smiling. Not at the camera, but at something beyond the reach of

the picture. Looking at the picture, Dara suddenly remembers. It was a man walking on stilts. A clown, with a huge red smile painted across his face. Dara remembers wondering at his height. Marvelling at it. She had never seen such a tall man. Later, Angel explained about the stilts hidden beneath his baggy trousers. She remembers now.

The caption below the photograph reads: *Happy families: Kathleen Flood enjoys life with her daughters Angel and Dara.*

75

The little house on the Raheny road was deserted. Dara did a lap downstairs, calling her mother's name. On the kitchen table, a sliver of chocolate fudge cake sat on a plate, hardening around the edges. Empty cups and plates, surrounded by crumbs. A chair lying on its back across the floor. Dara picked it up. The bag Mrs Flood called her hair bag lay on its side on a chair, its contents spilling out the top.

'Mam,' Dara called, her voice louder now. She fished her mobile phone out of her pocket and scanned the screen. No missed calls. No messages. She rang Angel's number again. The phone was turned off. She punched in her mother's number and, from the hall, she heard it ring. The phone was lying on the floor of the hall, as if it had fallen from a pocket. Dara picked it up. Six missed calls. All from Dara.

'Mam!' she shouted again, and now she heard the panic at the fringes of her voice. She ran up the stairs, forgetting to avoid the second one from the top that creaked on contact.

The bedroom door was ajar. Dara could hear her breath in her chest, coming fast. She heard no other sound.

'Mam,' she called, softer now, pushing the door with her hand. The room was empty and dark, with the curtains still drawn as if they had never been opened. The bed was unmade and her mother's nightdress and dressing gown and slippers lay in a heap on the floor. In the bathroom, the bath was full. Dara dipped her fingers in. The water was cold.

Angel's bedroom door was shut. Dara hesitated outside it

before she opened it. 'Angel?' Her voice was a whisper now. A shaky whisper. But the room was empty, the bed unmade, although the imprint of Angel's body remained on the sheet.

Dara sat on the edge of her sister's bed and struggled to gather her thoughts. Her mother was not here. Angel was not here. They had left the house. In a hurry. A terrible, terrible hurry. There was only one place they could be.

76

The hospital reception area was a throng of people, rushing like shoppers on Christmas Eve. Dara forced her way through the crowd. There was a queue at the desk but she pushed her way to the front. The receptionist refused to look at her, in the way that receptionists do when customers do things they are not supposed to do. Dara gripped the desk for support. She had taken Angel's car. Driven to the hospital. About the journey, she could remember nothing. Except the fact that she had made it in just under six minutes. She'd parked right outside the front entrance, not stopping when the security guard shouted at her that she couldn't park there.

'It's set-down only!' he roared. Dara said nothing. She ran.

She gripped the reception desk.

'Angel,' she said, and it was hard to get the word out with the breath that heaved around her chest. 'My sister. Angel. Angela Flood. Please.'

'There's a queue,' the receptionist told her, nodding at the line of people frowning at Dara. Her voice was as thin and as sharp as a steak knife.

'Please.' Dara said. 'I think something might be wrong. Can you check? Can you just look on your computer. Please?'

A voice piped up from halfway down the queue. An elderly voice. 'Ah, would ya help the poor girl? She's in a state, so she is.'

Dara didn't look back to see where the kind words came from. She gripped the desk. The receptionist sighed but began to peck at the keys on her computer, in a grim kind of way.

'Angela Flood,' she said as she pecked. 'Angela Flood,' she said again, still pecking. Dara gripped the desk. It felt like the world had stopped turning and if she loosened her grip, she would come away from the earth, like a balloon on a string, while a little girl at a funfair cries as she watches it rising, getting smaller and smaller. Dara held on.

'Ah yes, Angela Flood, she's in ICU,' the receptionist said. The tone of her voice never changed. She might as well have been directing Dara to the cafeteria.

'ICU,' Dara repeated, her voice sounding stupid and dull in her ears.

'That's the Intensive Care Unit,' the woman said briskly. 'On the second floor. Take the lift and . . .'

Dara let go of the desk. She did not float away. Nor disappear. Instead, she turned and ran, weaving her way in and out of the glut of people. She wanted to shout at them. Tell them to get out of her way. She could barely believe that people were just wandering about, going about their ordinary business, when Angel was in intensive care. She kept running, not waiting for the lift but taking the stairs, two at a time, her breath coming in gasps, sore in her chest. Now she was in the corridor, the close, dense smell of the hospital all around. It reminded her of earlier. Of the corridor in the hospice. Hushed and dark. Leading to a place she did not want to go.

It was her mother she saw first. Outside the double doors that led into the ICU. She stopped walking. She looked at Mrs Flood. At her mother. She waited, her hands cupped around her mouth as if to contain a sound she had not yet made.

Mrs Flood saw her. 'Dara!' she cried, and she began to run. Dara tried to read her face, but her image was blurred and distorted. She realised she was crying.

Mrs Flood stopped just short of Dara, opened her mouth then changed her mind and reached for Dara with her arms. She shushed and rocked her, just as she had when Dara was ten.

'Hush now, alanna. Don't cry, my love. Everything will be all right.'

These were some of the things that her mother said as she shushed and rocked her. Dara didn't fight it. She did not struggle against her mother's arms that wrapped around her like heat thrown by a log fire. It was only when she felt the drops on her neck that she realised her mother was crying too. Still she did not move. She held on like she would never let go. As if she was ten again, her skin prickling with the sting of a hundred nettles.

'What happened?' she finally asked, her voice muffled against the soft cotton of her mother's jumper. She didn't look at her face. She couldn't.

Mrs Flood released Dara, held her at arm's length. She smiled.

'Angel's back from theatre,' her mother said.

Dara shook her head, not understanding.

Mrs Flood reached for Dara's hands. She smiled. 'We got the call,' she said.

EPILOGUE

I am close enough to hear the voices. Sometimes I get close enough.

'You can't wear orange. It's disrespectful,' Tintin says.

'It's not a funeral, it's a month's mind,' Anya tells him. 'Whad effer dat is.'

'It's means it's a month since the funeral and that people mind if you wear a bright orange dress with a purple feather boa. And those heels are never going to play. Graveyards are muddy affairs. There'll be sinking, if you wear those.'

'But they're Manolos,' Anya tells him, looking down to admire them.

'So?'

'What?'

'So what if they're Manolos?'

'They're special,' Anya tells him, sighing. 'You should wear something special to a month's mind.'

'I thought you said you bought them for my surprise 30th?' Tintin looks put out.

'But dat is not for another two years.'

'A year-and-a-half,' he reminds her with a scathing look.

'I need to break them in before party.' Anya comes back with a robust defence.

'But you don't even know what a month's mind is,' Tintin reminds her.

'You just told me, didn't you?'

'Yes, but . . . oh forget it.'

'Here comes Dara and Angel and . . . is that Mrs Flood?'

Tintin and Anya get out of Tintin's car, which is an ancient BMW that cost less than Anya's Manolos, even though she found them in a charity shop in Killiney.

Yes, it is Kathleen. She looks more beautiful than I remembered. Younger than I expected. Perhaps it is her smile. Smiles do that to people. She is flanked by her daughters. Angel. And Dara. Two women climb out of the back of the car. One of them has purple hair and purple nails and a purple twinset and purple high heels. Tintin is right about the heels. There is sinking, in the soft ground. Kathleen and her daughters reach for her with their hands. 'I'm fine,' she tells them, waving them away. They hesitate before they turn away. They force themselves not to look back. It is Miss Pettigrew. I'm nearly sure. She extracts a snow-white poodle from the back of the car. She holds him in her arms. She closes the car door. She takes a breath. She begins to walk, like she is learning how.

The other woman clamps both hands against the body of the car and uses them as levers to push herself out. She keeps coming and coming until finally there she is, tall as well as wide, adjusting layers and layers of black fabric about her person. Her hair is dark and wild. My mother would call it a wren's nest. It is only when I see the locket in the deep well of her cleavage, glinting gold in the sun, that I realise. I look at Kathleen, but she is smiling still. 'Ça va?' she asks, taking Isabelle's hand and squeezing it. Isabelle smiles and nods. 'Ça va, Kathleen,' she says, and the women hug each other then. Like sisters. Like people who have known each other for years and years. But they can't have. Can they?

Angel still looks pale, but it is a good kind of pale. A convalescent pale. It's been a month since the transplant. The successful transplant. She has returned to work. She plans to go to the hill-walking festival in Donegal next month. She will travel to Beijing next summer. Already she has bought a phrase book and can say 'Where is the Great Wall, please?' in halting Mandarin, even though Dara has told her that you can see the Great Wall from the moon, so there is probably no need to ask for directions. Still, she is getting ready.

Angel is holding somebody's hand. A man's hand. He could be a fireman, this man. He has the height. And the width. The reassuring good, sturdy features of a fireman. He bends and whispers something in Angel's ear. She looks at him and smiles and he kisses her. A soft kiss, like he is being careful with her.

'Oh, Joe, look, isn't that Sissy Clarke Ha Ha Ha?' *Angel asks, as a woman whose own mother calls her a 'grand hoult of a girl' climbs out of a white van. Her toenails are painted the exact same colour as her sandals – a bluebottle blue – and her eye make-up is rather more dramatic than might be considered appropriate at a graveyard.*

'The columnist? I think it is. I recognise her from the telly. She's sometimes on* The View*, isn't she?' *says Joe, looking only briefly before turning back to Angel.*

We are on a hill, in a graveyard in Bailieborough, Co. Cavan. This is where these people have gathered. There are a lot of them, considering. Nobody cries. In fact, they are a remarkably happy-looking bunch of people. There is something of a carnival atmosphere about the place, perhaps helped by the weather, which has veered towards summer, this past month.

I concentrate on Dara Flood. She looks around her as she moves towards the grave. She wears a skirt. A red one that stops just below her knees. I see a patch plastered to the back of her shin. Funny, she doesn't strike me as a smoker. She bites at the edge of her lip and her navy eyes – long rather than big – scan the cemetery. When she stops looking anxious – as she does now – beauty settles on her, like a gown. I follow her gaze to a man. A short man. Flanked by an enormous hound, who strains at his lead. I know this dog's name is Clouseau, but if you ask me how I know that, I couldn't tell you and that's the truth. The dog whimpers towards another dog, an unfortunate-looking creature with a head that is much too small for his body. Lucky. That's his name. Some people might call the title ironic, given the dog's eclectic appearance. Clouseau strains towards Lucky. He is not a dog who discriminates on the basis of aesthetics. He recognises good character. He always knew Lucky was not a bad dog. *Just* a dog to whom bad things had happened. He breaks free of the lead – his owner's grip on it has loosened, as if he has been distracted – and rushes to his fellow canine, sniffing in a mannerly way at his bottom before travelling around to the front for a quick lick. Lucky tells him about a hare he has seen in the long grasses at the top of the hill. Both dogs know they don't stand a chance, but they tear away anyway. They have this in common. Optimism.

Stanley Flinter looks like a man who has not noticed that his gigantic lurcher has slipped his lead and is plotting against the local hare population with his dear friend and companion. Today he is wearing a suit. A navy one with a silver pinstripe. He scrubs up nice, Stanley Flinter. Although the trousers could do with being taken up an inch or so. His hair is dark and looks like it's been cut, perhaps as recently as this morning. It will take some getting used to, seeing him without the tuft of his cowlick standing on end. Kathleen was right about the twelve-week blow dry. It really does work.

Instead of noticing the absence of Clouseau – surprising, given the sheer girth of the dog – Stanley Flinter allows his stare to settle on a young woman. A beautiful young woman. It settles on Dara Flood. And when it does, something happens to Stanley Flinter. It's in the way he moves his hand to his hair to flatten a cowlick that no longer needs flattening. It's in the darkening of his brown eyes to a colour that is nearly black. But mostly it's in his smile. The wide one that keeps getting wider He looks like a man who got more than he ever expected. A lot more. He moves towards Dara Flood and she moves towards him. They meet at the grave of Slither Smith, God rest his soul. Still, it was a nice way to go. Sitting in his favourite place, up on the high stool at The Market Bar, his pockets full of cash and a pen in his hand, poised over a yellow betting slip. They didn't notice till closing time. Thought he'd fallen asleep over a pint, as he was wont to do. I heard tell that Dr Mac cried when he heard, but that couldn't be true. Could it?

Dara and Stanley meet there, the gravestone between them. The one that says 'Here lies Slither Smith. A horse of a man.'

For a moment, they say nothing.

Dara worries a little at her lip with her teeth before she speaks. 'I'm glad you're here,' she says. She whispers it, but the words ring out anyway, like bells on Christmas morning. There was no need for her to say it at all. Isn't it written all over her face? 'I know it's too soon. You're not supposed to say stuff like that this early on. Tintin would kill me. But the thing is, I've wasted too much time already. And it's true, so . . .'

He touches her neck, and the gesture is so tender, I have to look away for a moment. When I turn back, they are kissing. The kind of kissing that might be deemed inappropriate by some, given the nature of the environment. Dara kisses him in the same way that she dances. Like no one is watching. Like she has forgotten herself.

'I'm glad too,' Stanley tells her.

When Dara smiles, everything changes. The world looks like a place where my horse comes in first every time. They reach for each other again, leaning over the gravestone as if it is not even there. They look like two people who have found something. Something they've been looking for, for a long, long time.

I move up. Higher now. I can't hear anything. I can just see them. Sometimes that happens. They are in a circle around the grave. Dara throws a handful of rose petals. Red ones. Some take to the air, borne by the gentle breeze of the day. Some float to the ground, at rest now in the warm, rich clay of the earth.

There is such beauty in them.

Such beauty in the world.

If you don't take the time to stop and look, you miss it.

You miss it.

ACKNOWLEDGEMENTS

A huge thank you to the staff at the Renal Unit in Beaumont Hospital who answered all my questions, and to the patients there, who shared their stories with me. At the time of writing, there are about 550 people in Ireland waiting for a kidney transplant. The donor cards are aptly named. Gift of Life cards. Because that's what they are. I urge all of us to carry a Gift of Life card. By the time we are in a position to donate our organs, I'm pretty sure we won't need them anymore. This is one, small thing that we can do. It will make a gigantic difference to someone's life.

Huge thanks to Ger Nichol, my agent who is always in my corner. Your support for the books and your faith in me are things that I appreciate more than you know.

Thank you, as always, to my editor, Ciara Doorley, and to the great team at Hachette Books Ireland and Hodder UK, who care about the books as much as I do and go to great lengths to make sure they are better than I can make them.

My thanks to David Ryan, who put paid to some of the theories I had about private detectives and who provided me with lots of information and some great stories too.

Thank you to the lovely staff at Annaghmakerrig in Co. Monaghan who provided peace and quiet and food which, other than a pen and paper, are the only things a writer really needs. Thanks also to the resident ghost, Miss Worby, who roams the house by night and sits on peoples' shins as they lie in their beds (according to Kevin Gildea, whose shins she chose to sit on that week, thank God). To ensure that she couldn't sit on mine, I remained upright during the night and wrote, to take my mind off the creak on the stairs, the shadows moving in the corners of my attic room and the rattle of the wind against my bedroom window. I got a lot of writing done that week.

Thanks as always to my family. My husband who came up with one of the subplots in this book and never lets me forget it. Unfortunately, my publishers wouldn't entertain your idea. They 'claim' that '*Finding Mr. Flood* by Ciara Geraghty and her husband, Frank MacLochlainn, aged forty-one-and-a-half', as you suggested, is just too long to print on the cover of the book.

Thank you to my sister Niamh, who looks after my youngest daughter with as much love and care as she looks after her own children. Thank you to my mother, Breda, who repositions my books in every bookshop she visits. And to my father, who waits for her as she does it. Thank you to my three children, Sadhbh, Neil and Grace (in age order as opposed to order of preference!). You fill my life with noise and mess and love and, while I could take or leave the noise and the mess, I couldn't do without the love: keep it coming.

Thanks to my brother-in-law, Brian, for his information on taking photographs of someone from a distant tree at night. Thanks to one of my oldest friends, Elly, for her information on wedges (the shoes, not the food). Thanks to my other brother-in-law, Neil, for his information on weight lifting. Thank you to my friend, Niamh Cronin, who takes the dilemmas of my characters as seriously as I do.

A big thank-you to my cousin, Neasa Jones, who was the link between my sepia-tinted memories of Bailieborough in the 'olden days' and the Bailieborough of recent times. Thanks also for being a great advocate of the books and for forcing all your friends to buy them.

Many thanks to all the readers of *Saving Grace* and *Becoming Scarlett*. Your feedback, your support, your interest and of course, your hard-earned cash, help to keep me at the kitchen table, keep me ignoring the crumbs and the mess, keep me writing.

Thank you to Mark Anderson, aka The Fuzz, who let me know that Stanley Flinter, standing at five feet five inches, was indeed a short man but not short enough to be refused entry into An Garda Síochána. And for helping me come up with A Better Plan.

I set a couple of chapters of this book in Bailieborough, Co. Cavan. This is where my mother is from. And her mother, my grandmother, to whom I have dedicated this book. Bailieborough is a place where I spent many summers, when I was a child. Things were different in my grandmother's house. She gave me my breakfast in bed every morning. She bought me jam tarts every Friday after she'd collected her pension. She fried burgers from John Ed's butcher shop in a pan because she knew how much I loved them. We ate them with huge, floury potatoes and a heap of buttery cabbage on the side. I can still taste it. Nothing ever tasted as good. She didn't insist on much, but she liked me to be home every day at one o'clock for my dinner, at five o'clock for my tea and at nine o'clock for my supper. She never asked if I'd brushed my teeth but she made me have a bath every Saturday night, whether I needed one or not. She sang 'We'll Gather Lilacs' every spring and she carried a hankie, sprayed with perfume, in her pocket and held it to her nose, when the slurry truck drove past. She loved walking, rashers, watching *Dallas* and eating Iced Caramels. She let me do things my mother never did. Like cycle to Virginia with my friends that I called 'the twins', and paint the room at the back of the house that everyone called The Chalet. She could make a cake of brown bread with her eyes closed and she recycled shopping bags long before anyone got around to thinking about the environment. My father called her The Big Woman. He cried when she died. We all did. But we laugh now. When we recall one of her tall tales. Or the expressions she had. Or the songs she used to sing. Or the tall tales she used to tell.

This tall tale is for her.

Ciara Geraghty

SAVING GRACE

It all started with a bottle of Baileys that was a year out of date but I drank it anyway . . .

One minute, well, Friday night, you're in a long-term if long-distance relationship with the perfect Shane. The next, Saturday morning, you're waking up in bed with the mother of all hangovers . . . and Bernard O'Malley, newest member of the I.T. department.

Another entry on the list of things you can't forgive herself for. The worst is Spain. What you did there. And what happened to your brother. Ever since then, your life has slowly spiralled out of control . . .

You dust yourself down, have a cigarette and pull on your stiletto boots. But you know that something's got to give. You just hope it's not the zip on your skinny jeans . . .

Out now in paperback

HODDER

Ciara Geraghty

BECOMING SCARLETT

Meet Scarlett O'Hara – wedding planner extraordinaire – who's famous for making dreams come true.

From scuba-diving ceremonies to flamingos at the reception, her colour-coded checklists make everything look simple.

Scarlett's personal life ran just as smoothly. Until now.

Her dependable boyfriend has moved to Brazil.

She's had to give up her Dublin flat and move back home.

And she's pregnant.

Worse still, she doesn't know who the father of the baby is . . . even though she's slept with *exactly* 4½ men in her entire 35 years.

How will Scarlett cope now all her best laid plans have gone with the wind?

Out now in paperback

HODDER